HEIDI HANLEY

THE
PROPHECY
KINGDOM *of* UISNEACH
✦ BOOK 1 ✦

Printed in the United States of America
First Printing, 2018

Sword and Arrow Publishing
P.O. Box 344
Charlestown, NH 03603
www.kingdomofuisneach.com

E-book ISBN: 13: 978-0-9982736-0-0
Paperback ISBN: 13:978-0-9982736-1-7
Editor: Jill Shultz
Cover Design: Damonza
Author Photo: Cecile Lackie
Uisneach Map: Donna Therrien

Lovingly dedicated to Charles Frost –
extraordinary poet and dear friend.

ACKNOWLEDGMENTS

Marsha Downs (a.k.a. Magdrael) – for your patience and dedication as a reader and for becoming something so much more than a colleague. Love you, soul sister.

Jill Shultz – there are not enough words to express my gratitude for your editorial guidance, support and friendship. I thank Maker for leading me to your doorstep.

Katherine Burgess – wherever you are. Thank you for introducing me to the muse and to a deep part of my own soul.

To my family, for your patience in the process. I hope I didn't make your ears bleed too much!

Word Weavers, for encouraging me, even though my genre was so different. Your perspective was more useful than you know!

To Charles and Bruce Frost. It was not the book I set out to write, but it was the book the Great Author gave me to write, and I would never have done it without your early encouragement to "Write!"

To the musicians who inspired me to great flights of fancy, fanned the flames of passion and kept me company on the journey. Special thanks to Adrian von Ziegler, Keith Harkin, Celtic Thunder, Ray Boudreaux, Brian Crain, James Bay and BrunuhVille

To Sue Church – welcomed to the journey last, but not least. Thank you for the validation.

Cindy Brandner – Your early support, encouragement, and advice to "take it one step at a time," meant so much.

To the Muse. In a split-second, everything changed and this book became possible. I am eternally grateful.

Kingdom of Uisneach

PROLOGUE

ONCE UPON A TIME

atrina became increasingly aware of the woman sitting in the corner of the hospital room as the dull yellow light of the bedside lamp changed to a shimmering green. Without fear or surprise, she took in the woman's long salt-and-pepper hair, thickly braided and decorated with feathers and dried flowers, her storm-gray eyes and berry-colored lips. A face shaped by mist and mystery, like an ancient stone wall with all its shadowy tones and character. While everyone here in the hospital wore either a standard-issue johnny or shapeless green scrubs, this creature was clothed in the living earth, her bodice and skirt a portrait of nature, of lichen and oak and maple leaves in autumn, with ruby, amethyst and emerald woven into the garments. Far from being formless, the woolen dress draped over her bosom and cascaded down to mid-calf in uneven layers and lines. Her waist was belted by pheasant feathers and her feet clad in soft leather boots. Around her neck hung an amulet of crystal, wood and wren feathers. She smelled of balsam and sage with a hint of ginger and cinnamon.

Forest woman, Katrina thought. Beautiful and vibrant. *But what is she doing here?* On her shoulder perched a great black crow, perfectly still. His gaze jumped sharply from the crone to the new mother in the bed. Katrina looked again at the black bird, stunned by the gold chain around his neck that held a black medallion, rimmed in gold. Carved into the medallion was a golden tree, its roots spreading across the bottom of the disc, its full canopy of leafy branches fanning out across the top.

The woman spoke, breaking her reverie. "You have a daughter."

"Yes," Katrina replied, not sure if that was a statement or a question.

"She's a bonny lass. Hair like a wee dormouse." The crone's gentle laugh was warm and inviting, as were those deep, old eyes that seemed to wrap Katrina in their gaze. "What will you name her?"

Katrina didn't answer. Something made her uneasy. Though she intuited this was not an evil woman, that she had no intent to harm her or her baby, Katrina was sure nothing good would come of this visitation.

"No matter," the woman responded, not the least perturbed by Katrina's silence, "she'll be called Mouse, in any case."

"Mouse?" Katrina finally said, surprised. "Why would I call her that?"

"She'll seem as timid, but she isn't. She has the heart of a stag, this one. Time will prove it." The crone had not moved, yet now Katrina could barely breathe for feeling so closed-in by her presence.

"Katrina…"

Katrina shivered. *Oh, no, she knows my name. Who is this woman?*

"I've come to prepare you, to tell you that you'll raise the lassie, but you'll not keep her." The words were delivered as gently and compassionately as possible, but Katrina's hands automatically clasped her belly as though to hang on to the child who had only separated from her body an hour ago.

"No," Katrina whispered, hearing the uncertainty in her voice. Even as she resisted what this woman was telling her, she remembered a dream from early in her pregnancy, of a girl-child wandering in a forest. The girl, strong and beautiful – a warrior – led others on a journey whose destination was not revealed. She'd tried to force the dream's foreboding essence from her mind upon waking, but now it came flooding back and she understood its connection to this woman's calling. "Who are you?"

"I am called Cailleach." She pronounced it *Kyle-yock*, the word rolling with Gaelic grace off her lips. "I know this may be hard for you to hear, but in time, you'll support your daughter as she meets her destiny. When she's ready, you'll let her go, and I will watch over her as she begins a new life in a different place. She is meant for a grand adventure and holy purpose, this girl, one that will save a world from destruction."

Katrina almost refused, but realized it would be pointless. This whole visit was surreal and out of her control. The woman smiled softly. "It will be all right," she promised. "You'll know what to do when the time comes. For now, I would suggest you begin to use your own special gifts. That will help her more than anything else."

"What gifts?" Katrina asked.

"You've the Sight and the healing. Learn the craft, Katrina. This is your time as well as your daughter's."

A nurse walked into the room with her baby girl, who was swaddled tightly in a pink receiving blanket. Katrina's attention turned momentarily to the infant. When she looked back, Cailleach and the crow were gone, as was the peculiar light; the lamp once again quietly glowing against the night.

The nurse handed Katrina her baby. With a bittersweet smile, Katrina pulled the infant close to her. Drawing back the edge of the blanket, she was struck by two things. First, the baby was already squirming and wiggling as if she had someplace to go. Second, she had a full head of lush hair, ash-blonde mixed with browns. *Like a mouse. How had the woman known that? I will not call her Mouse. I will name her something bold and heroic. Briana*, she decided with conviction, *"noble one."* Whatever the future held, and she prayed it had nothing to do with anything the crone said, she could at least give her daughter the gift of a strong name. With a sigh that did not so much accept destiny as soften a little toward it, she rewrapped her daughter, settled her against her breast for her first meal, and murmured, "Hello, Briana. Welcome to your life and whatever adventures it may bring."

A Sound in the Woods

ray mist rolled across a bloody field. Air redolent of fear, vomit and putrid flesh choked her. Men lay dead or dying in unthinkable positions in front of her. Crouched and partially hidden behind a tree, she watched through hanging branches as an auburn-haired man came toward her, holding a bloody sword in one hand and a crown in the other. Her heart raced and her stomach rolled violently. Good guy or bad? Desperately, she felt around for something to protect herself. Her fingers made contact with cold steel. She rose up slowly, lifting the weapon in front of her. The man spoke soothingly, holding out the crown to her. She couldn't make out his words, but let her sword drop slightly. A flash of blonde hair caught her eye. She turned to see the back of another man as he slung a quiver behind him and walked away. Faceless but familiar. Who are you? She was about to follow him when a fierce battle cry forced her attention back to the auburn-haired man as he rushed toward her, now looking angry and afraid. Too late, she realized, as cold metal cut across the skin of her thigh, followed by burning and a river of red that flowed down her leg. She turned to face the source of the attack and saw a different, gray-uniformed man preparing to stab her again. Pain and rage overwhelmed her. She screamed.

Briana sat bolt upright in bed, drenched in sweat, her heart pounding. Reaching across the tangle of sheet and quilt, she found a pillow and clutched it to her chest. The dream again. Third night in a row she'd confronted the grisly scene, felt the giant's icy blade slice into her body and felt compelled to follow the faceless blonde-haired man. Closing her eyes, she willed him to appear, but he would not. She sighed, cast the pillow aside and sat up, pulling her hair off her sweat-dampened neck.

A hint of pre-dawn light cast shadows around the nest Briana called her bedroom. Beyond the colorful heap of throws and pillows on the floor were clutters of tiny treasures she'd collected from the outdoors, stones, shells, lichen and bark, stashed everywhere, on shelves, in cupboards and on windowsills, collecting dust. She scanned the bookcase of fairy tales, fantasies and mythic adventures underneath the picture of an old Irish abbey. On the bookcase's top shelf, medieval figures defended a king and queen who stood atop a castle she'd built herself from tiny stone fragments. Briana kept looking until she found him – the archer, dressed in red, with bow nocked. His helmet of long blonde hair reminded her of the faceless man. Longing rushed through her, not new, but more intense during this past week of the dream. *Who are you?* He wouldn't answer. He never did.

Sighing, she glanced at the clock beside her bed. Red digital numbers flashed 6:00. *Sweet mother of God, Debbie and Samira will be here in an hour*, she thought, as she touched the lamp beside her bed.

"Once a month at least, we'll do something together, without Rob or any other guys," Debbie had promised the night before her wedding.

True to her word, they were off for a day of shopping, eating and a bottle or two of wine. Briana threw a change of clothes in a small bag, knowing they would spend the night at a hotel.

Showered and ready to go, she dashed into the kitchen for a glass of juice and slice of cold pizza. She was chewing the first bite when her mother came in from the deck, cup of coffee in hand.

"I'd say good morning, but it doesn't look like you slept well," she said, lightly touching a dark smudge under her daughter's eye. "Again," she added, arching one eyebrow.

Briana put the juice bottle back into the refrigerator, saying nothing about the dream. "I'm fine." She didn't want her to worry and definitely didn't want her analyzing it, which she would surely do. "Debbie and Samira will be here in a few. I've got to get my stuff." She took another bite of the spicy pepperoni pie and chewed as she went to her room for her bag.

When she returned her mother was leaning against the counter, looking speculatively at her. "Mouse, we need to talk. Really soon." At Briana's glare, she corrected herself. "Briana. Sorry. After calling you Mouse for twenty-five years, it's a hard habit to break."

Briana shook her head. "Seems I am doomed to be called a mouse my whole life. Why on earth did you give me such a nickname?"

"You looked like a wee little dormouse when you were born," her mother said, retelling the family legend as she reached out to caress a length of her hair. "It just sort of stuck."

"Well, I wish it would un-stick. I'm…"

"Halloo," Samira interrupted.

"Hello, Samira," Katrina said. "Where's the other musketeer?" The three friends had dubbed themselves the three musketeers in high school, the moniker still a part of their collective identity.

"She's out talking with Rob on the phone. Like they only separated thirty minutes ago. How she is going to get through the next twenty-four hours is beyond me. OMG, they are like oozing 'I miss you's' all over the place. This is going to be a long day."

Briana laughed. "Never fear, we'll repatriate her." She turned to her mother, who wasn't laughing. "Mom, are you okay?"

Oblivious, Samira grabbed Briana's bag and headed back out to the waiting car.

"I'm fine, but I do want to talk to you tomorrow, please. It's important."

"Sure. Will you be okay alone tonight?" It was the first time her mother would be alone in the house since her father's recent death. *Maybe it was too soon to leave her overnight.*

"I'm really fine. You go and have fun."

"Call my cell if you need anything." At Katrina's smile and hand flutter, shooing her out, she nodded. "Well then, I better get out there because OMG, I've got a rebooting to do on Debbie's love-soaked brain."

They both laughed. Briana kissed her mother before grabbing her purse and heading out the door.

⌁

After a full day of shopping, the three musketeers were settled at a tall table in a wood and brick tavern in Portland, Maine's historic port district, half-empty glasses of wine and a nearly empty tray of nachos evidence of some serious girl time. Above the bar, framed pictures of local fishing boats surrounded a well-sculpted mermaid lounging in a chair, providing a relaxed atmosphere, the key component needed for their conversation and laughter. Then Samira brought up one of her favorite topics – men, and more specifically, the lack of one in Briana's life.

"You're twenty-five and as far as I know, still a virgin."

"So? Is that a crime?" Briana asked, lifting the glass of chardonnay to her lips.

"No, but it's ridiculous in this day and age, given that you could have any guy you wanted. You can't wait for your King Arthur forever."

Briana swallowed and set the glass down. *In this day and age* – the words reverberated in her head like an ancient omen. *That's the problem, isn't it? I don't really belong in this day and age.* She shook her head at the odd thought.

"Maybe you should be a little less picky, Mouse," Samira continued, with an intentional emphasis on the nickname that put Briana over the edge.

"Maybe, Samira, you should be a little pickier."

"What's that supposed to mean?" Samira asked, flicking back a long strand of ebony hair.

"All right, ladies," Debbie intervened. "This is supposed to be fun, so let's stop with the sniping. Besides, Samira, when Briana finds her Arthur or Lancelot, or whomever, we're going to be so jealous we'll wish we'd waited."

The door of the tavern blew open and a group of men sailed in, laughing, their heavy knitted sweaters, Carhartt pants and ball caps giving them away as local fisherman. Samira's head swiveled and a smile spread across her face. She waited long enough for the men to settle onto barstools before cruising to the bar herself.

Briana rolled her eyes. "I rest my case."

"She is who she is, Briana. She's got a heavy flirt archetype."

Briana almost spit out the wine in her mouth. "You think?" she said, laughing.

"But she does have a point. You might want to be a little more open to some of the attention you attract. You've got looks and a figure to die for, but it seems like you have this wall built up around you. Men get just so close, feel the steel and get intimidated."

"That's hardly fair," Briana said, glancing at the mermaid above the bar for help. The ocean goddess only stared back with a moody eye.

"I know it is, but unfortunately, perception is everything and that is the energy you give off, sweetie. Is it your plan to spend the rest of your life just gardening and reading? Don't you *want* to find someone to share your life with? And don't you even think of crying."

Briana stared at Debbie with moist eyes. Tears, whether of sorrow or joy, came easily to Briana, a trait she tried often, and failed often, to control. How could she tell her best friend that she thought she was waiting for, longing for, someone who likely didn't exist? That she sometimes talked to a medieval action figure and hoped he would come to life? That she was aware of her rapidly ticking biological clock, but couldn't settle for less?

"I need to go to the bathroom," she said, quietly.

Alone in the bathroom, Briana stared into the mirror searching for the ice princess that her friends apparently saw. A woman with small features stared back, with the gray eyes her mother said were as "gentle as a summer drizzle when you're happy or as fierce as an evening thunderstorm when you're pissed." Nothing remarkable to either attract or repel a man. She was too short and rather skinny, with humble breasts.

The bathroom door swung open, interrupting her reverie. Offering a polite greeting to the other woman, Briana finished drying her hands and returned to her friends in time to be introduced to one of Samira's new friends.

"Briana, this is Dave. Dave, Briana. Dave's a lobsterman, owns his own boat and likes locally crafted beer. He also reads fantasy novels. Seems like you have a lot in common."

Briana glared at Samira. *Could she be any more obvious?*

"Hey, Briana. Mind if I pull up a chair?" Dave asked, already doing so.

"Well, my friend found out quite a lot about you in five minutes. That must have been awkward," Briana said, picking up her wineglass and taking a hefty sip.

"Truth be told, I asked about you first, so I know you're a gardener, read fairy tales and just lost your dad. I'm sorry about that."

"Thanks. Actually, I'm a landscape designer."

He stared at her, clueless. They spent the next two hours chatting amiably but not deeply about their work, music and books they liked.

He wasn't horrible, but Briana was grateful when he announced, "Well, a lobsterman's day starts pretty early, so I'll say good night. Nice meeting you ladies."

Samira and her new friend were exchanging emails and cell phone numbers and Briana held her breath, hoping Dave wouldn't ask for hers. He didn't. After the men left, Samira turned to her with a disappointed look on her face.

"Another one bites the dust?"

"He was nice enough."

"But not Mr. Right?"

"Hardly," Briana replied, picking up a menu that had been ignored for some time. "Time to eat again?" she asked brightly.

❧

The next day was unseasonably warm for Camden, a true April Fool's Day. Briana welcomed the heat of the afternoon sun on her back as she worked quietly in her garden, alone, her mother in town running errands. The birds sang and she hummed the tune of "Follow the Yellow Brick Road" as she plucked early weeds out of the iris and tulip beds. It may have been a bit soon to begin an assault on the flower beds, but Briana craved the grounding she received from connecting with the earth.

Yesterday's escape with her friends had been a welcome change from the sadness that cloaked the home where she and her mother now lived without the larger-than-life presence of her father. Two months ago, during a deep-sea fishing trip, her father had suffered a massive heart attack while reeling in a huge blue tuna. The crew reported that the last thing Edwin Brennan saw was the fish of a lifetime on the end of his line. They tried to comfort Katrina and Briana with clichés like "he died doing what he loved most," but little relief those well-intended sentiments really provide. Briana asked herself repeatedly why he had to die at all? *The man had just turned fifty, for God's sake.* Absolutely no one, including his physician, realized that underneath the facade of vitality, a cardiac event was brewing. The shock of it protected her and her mother for a few weeks, but once Katrina's parents went back to Ireland, the cards were put away and the casseroles stopped coming, the grief set in. Winter made it easy for Briana to put projects on hold. Her mother handed over the care of a few expectant mothers to another certified midwife. They managed the internet orders for their small herbal business, but that was about all they could manage. They had no salves, elixirs, or candles for what troubled them.

Once in a while Briana would catch her mother watching her with an odd, fearful expression.

"Why do you keep looking at me like that? Are you worried I'm going to die, too?" she asked once, while they were working in the greenhouse.

"Of course not," her mother replied, forcing a smile.

"I'm not going to leave you, Mom."

"All children leave their parents, Briana. When you fall in love, you'll move away, as you should." Her words were reassuring enough, but Briana did not miss the shudder as her mom turned back to cutting herbs.

She now remembered her mom's request to talk and promised herself that when her mother returned, she would give that her full attention.

Briana was startled by a sound in the woods, the crunching of leaves and branches. She left her weeding to cross the road and enter the forest. What compelled her to pursue a possibly dangerous sound, rather than pick up her tools and go inside, was anyone's guess. Whether man or beast awaited her in the darkness of the trees, she went just the same.

The steady crunch drew her closer to the stone wall that separated the safety of the road from the mystery of the dark woods She crossed through a gap between the stones. The moment her foot passed the stones, a wavelike sensation washed over her. Her skin tingled and she shivered. *Something is afoot.*

The sound led her deeper into the woods. Fear should've been sending off warning bells in her head, but it did not. She only felt… curious. It seemed she was being beckoned. Briana saw no footprints, tracks or other signs to indicate what she was following. Leaves lay still on the ground, ferns stood unbroken. There was no sign of animals.

Up a slight rise and then down around a fallen and decaying birch tree she went, the crunching noise always about the same distance ahead. Coming around a stand of pines, she noticed a very large oak tree in a clearing, its ridged gray-brown bark aged with swirls of moss-green lichen. The branches above, heavily laden with acorns, seemed miles away. A marvelous specimen, to be sure, but size was not the most remarkable thing about this oak. What brought her up short was the green door, carved with ancient-looking symbols. Its silver handle glowed faintly, almost inviting her to take it in her hand. She realized as well that the noise had stopped. Briana looked around, turned and scanned the woods a second time, but found nothing. Heard nothing. Whatever, or whoever, she'd been following seemed to have disappeared! *Curiouser... and curiouser...*

Acting on instinct, she took hold of the silver door handle. Warmth filled her palm as she pushed effortlessly to reveal an entryway into the tree. Peering into the darkness, she could see the edge of a staircase leading down. She didn't know how it was possible, but without hesitation she walked inside, with no more difficulty than walking through the front door of her home.

Briana stood at the top of the stairs and let her eyes adjust to the darkness. When she could see enough to find the step below, she stepped down. As she did so, a candle flared beside her, its soft flame illuminating the next step. She stepped once more and another candle lit up, followed by another, as she took step after step. Holographic images of her life floated in front of the wall, pictures of her father, mother and herself at different ages and stages of life, followed by images of her friends, her landscaping work and college graduation. Memories inspired fleeting and labile emotions within her. *What is this? A life review? Am I dying?* Before panic could set in, she came to a landing with a small table upon which a book lay open to a page showing an acorn-laden tree that reminded her of the spiritual Tree of Life. She tried to touch it. Her hand passed right through, reminding her of the hologram of Princess Leia in *Star Wars*. *Spooky.* On the other side of the landing was a staircase that went up, candles lighting each step. She followed. Floating in front of this wall were holographic scenes of tall-masted sailing ships and rocky coastlines, upon whose cliffs perched ancient castles and homey little cottages with wildly colorful gardens. Tiny people tended quaint farms dotted with abundant apple trees. She saw a woman with salt-and-pepper hair in an earthy-looking dress and a necklace of feathers and stone. She looked ancient, but beautiful, and Briana stopped for a moment to gaze at her in wonder. Images of waterfalls and fighting men followed, and then a man with long blonde hair and deep blue eyes.

He took her breath away. *An old soul*, she thought. His eyes seemed to be looking directly at her, making her heart race. She felt instantly connected to this man, whoever he was. This image disappeared, unfortunately, to be replaced by a fearsome dark-haired man and another who wore a crown. A huge, gray dog appeared, and she smiled. "Hey boy," she called, and laughed, because certainly he couldn't hear her.

Finally, she came to another wooden door. The pictures on the wall disappeared completely from her vision and her memory. Pausing for only the briefest of seconds, she opened the door.

Light poured in as Briana stepped into a world that was nothing like the one she had come from.

Chapter Two

Leaving Kansas

All manner of civilization was gone. No houses, no telephone, no pavement or power lines. No sound of cars or planes or people talking. She tried to process what she was seeing, but there simply was nothing to put it into context. *I am not*, she told herself with the only shred of certainty she had, *in Kansas anymore*. Her heart thumped so hard she put her hand on her chest. Someone once told her that in a crisis, if you feel like you're going to lose it, take some slow, deep breaths and remember that when you can't control a situation, you can control your response to it. *I will not panic*. She slowed her breathing until her heart began to beat normally again. Reassured that she didn't seem to be in any danger, she took inventory.

She stood on a grassy bank next to the oak she'd come through. Behind her stood an old forest of oak, yew, birch, pine, rowan, hawthorn, blackthorn and cherry trees, some bent gracefully, others gnarly and darkened with age. The forest floor was carpeted with moss, wood violets, trillium and scattered patches of Jack in the pulpit. Before her, a wide, querulous river provided a dramatic soundtrack to the otherworldly scene. Beyond that, a meadow, home to one single tree, broken and bent, pretty much dead, but still standing, with a few eggplant-colored leaves and little bell-shaped things scattered on the ground. *How tragic*, she thought, *that this lovely tree is dead*. Not only dead, but possibly murdered, given the saw lines all up and down its trunk, with chunks hacked out here and there. It was an otherwise beautiful, pristine place. The air seemed sharper, the colors and textures more vibrant. Like the difference between the first part of the *Wizard of Oz* in black-and-white and the second part, after the house landed on the witch in Munchkin land, when everything went Technicolor.

She stood in place, looking at this wonderland for what seemed like hours but was perhaps only seconds, when the sound of giggling hit her ear. *Is that the munchkins?* Turning this way and that, she finally saw a stone bench under a graceful willow. It took her another moment to register the fact that sitting on the bench was a plump, older woman who looked much like a garden gnome. Beside the lady gnome, a much thinner, male gnome danced around in merry circles, doing back flips. Both of them offered happy grins, their cheeks flushed with excitement, their brilliant blue eyes dancing with merriment. They were dressed in loose hip-length tunics, his mauve, hers a deep teal. He wore light-brown leather leggings underneath the tunic and she an ankle-length wool skirt. Soft leather boots with brass buckles protected their oversized feet. Perched atop their heads of curly gray hair sat conical, bright red caps. A giggle bubbled up within her. The gnomes giggled back but still not a word from either party until Briana declared authoritatively, "Well, Toto, we most certainly are not in Kansas!"

"Who's Toto?" asked the small woman at the same time the old man stopped flipping and asked, "What's Kansas?"

"It's a dog and a place," Briana answered, with relative calm. "More importantly though, who are you and where am I?"

With a deep bow, the male gnome said, "Name's Jack Wells and this gentle lady is me wife, Genevieve." At this, Genevieve rose and then squatted in a gnomish-style curtsy.

"Pleased to meet you, Your Ladyship," she said, with an almost reverent attitude.

"Your Ladyship sounds a bit pretentious, don't you think?" Briana replied. "People call me Mouse." Squinting, she added, "Or you might just call me by my real name, Briana."

The two turned toward each other, clapping their hands together in joy. With broad, silly smiles, they clasped her hand in theirs and said, "So you *are* the Mouse. Of course you are. You are exactly who we expected."

"Expected? You were expecting me?"

"Of course, milady," said Jack. "The whole kingdom is expecting you. The prophecy said the Mouse would be coming and Cailleach told us that it would happen anytime now. We've taken turns coming here to see if you'd arrived."

"Kyle-yock? Who on earth is that, and really," she was fast growing impatient, "would you mind telling me just what is going on?"

"Cailleach," Jack repeated, and she noted the subtle difference in how he pronounced the name. His accent sounded Celtic, neither Irish nor Scottish but something in-between, charming and comforting to the ear. With a little hop and bow, he spread his arms expansively and announced in a most formal tone, "Welcome to Uisneach, milady."

"Uisneach…" She repeated the gentle, swishing sound of *oosh-nay* softly a couple of times. The name sounded oddly familiar, yet she was unable to place it.

"Well, milady, there's much to tell you, to be sure, but most of it can wait till we get you home."

"Home? I can't stay here. I have to get back to my…" She turned back to the oak only to discover that its door was gone. A plain oak stood in its place, nothing magical. How would she return home? She moved closer to the tree and touched the bark where the door had been, searching for a crack that might open the door again. No chink or fissure, nothing to indicate that a door had ever been there. "I think I had better sit down," she said, feeling faint.

The gnomes looked concerned. Each took an elbow to guide her to a seat on a nearby rock wall. She felt a shiver race over her that had nothing to do with being cold. It was suddenly clear that whatever had brought her here meant for her to stay. Her stomach began to roll objectionably. She lowered her head to her hands, taking in deep breaths to shed the nausea. When it passed, she looked again at the gnome couple, but could find no words. They exchanged looks of sympathy, and Mrs. Wells patted her hand.

"'Twill be all right, milady. It may seem strange at the moment, but you are right where you are destined to be, and that is the truth. Things will all make sense soon enough."

Really? she thought, because everything seems a bit odd to me at the moment. No. Try bizarre, whacko, incredible, terrifying, unbelievable and… well, kind of cool, actually. Soft squeaks drew her attention. Two small red squirrels sitting on the branch of an oak stared at her curiously. A flash of orange drew her attention to a stone, upon which curled a small salamander, carrot-colored with black spots. The amphibian slowly turned its head upward and gave her a slight smile. *A smiling salamander. What next?*

"Next" turned out to be a deer, poking a cautious glance through a stand of pines before gently entering the space, where the party seemed all but begun. Mrs. Wells used some hand gestures that seemed to welcome a whole woodland community, and in short order, a fox mother sat with two tumbling kits, and next to them, a pure white weasel. Delight turned to fear as something large lumbered through the woods.

Seeing her concern, Jack placed a clubby hand on her arm. "Not to worry, Miss. 'Tis only a bear, and they are harmless on this side of the river."

She watched, one hand holding on to the wall, ready to push off and run if need be. She held her breath as the brown bear came within ten feet of her, sat down on his massive haunches, and stared at her.

"What do they want?" she asked, but before either of the Wellses could respond, an enormous crow flew in between two large black cherry trees, aiming straight for her. His ebony wings spanned the length of a man's arm, but with the grace of a prima ballerina, he flew right past her and perched delicately on one of the oak branches. The most unusual thing about the corvid was not his size but the shiny black medallion, ringed in gold, hanging around his neck. In the center of the medallion, etched in gold, was an image of the Tree of Life, with a spreading canopy of leaves above and an unruly network of roots below. The dazzling piece of jewelry was perfect for a crow, if one were to imagine a bird wearing jewelry, which she supposed she now must.

"Caawww," the crow announced, in a loud, sharp voice. Briana responded with a tentative hello. He turned his attention from her to the gnomes, which was almost insulting, but she watched with fascination as the black bird cawed to the Wellses.

Jack Wells said some words in a low tone in a language Briana had never heard. Then he nodded and turned to Briana. "Well, milady, 'tis truly time to be going."

Genevieve picked up the small knapsack sitting beside her before reaching out to take Briana's hand. Together, they headed deeper into the forest.

"Wait a minute." She stopped, pointing to the dead tree across the river. "What happened to that?"

Jack Wells shook his head sadly. "That is one of our problems, and part of the reason that the prophecy must be fulfilled, and not a moment too soon. You see, even though faeries have been hiding themselves for many centuries, the trees remained, and occasionally a faerie could be found practicing magic. But Lord Shamwa has been in evil devil since he cursed the king. He's been sending his Gray Military around the kingdom, killing the faerie trees. Once they're gone, and the faeries with them, there will be no more magic in Uisneach. Part of your charge will be to help restore the forests."

What could she possibly do to make it right? "You said one of your problems. Is there another, and am I meant to fix that, too?"

Jack and Genevieve smiled in tandem. "Oh, aye," said Genevieve, with a twinkle in her eye. "It's your first task. You've just got to save our king, who's been locked away in a castle on the far side of Uisneach for ten years, cursed by Lord Shamwa, his own prime minister. Once the king is released, he'll make everything right, and that's the truth!"

Briana sighed. Magic trees, hidden doors, giant jewelry-wearing crows, kings, and political upheaval. It was too much! Best to just follow the gnomes along this yellow brick road. She positioned herself in between them and turned to meet the forest and what might just be her "Grand Adventure." The yellow brick road turned out to be a dirt path that headed underneath a natural arch formed by several white birches on either side of the trail, like some kind of portal.

They walked for what seemed like hours. Considering that Jack said someone came daily to see if she'd arrived, she realized this must be very important to them, if they were making this trek every day. The trail twisted and turned through ancient woods over large, gnarly roots, at times requiring a scramble over boulders or downed trees. The forest wasn't much different from those she hiked through at home, except maybe a little more primordial. Everything – the trees, the stones, the rippling brooks and even the air – was pure and crisp. Here and there she'd see an unfamiliar plant or flower, or a faerie tree, tall and slender with silver bark that glittered when a sunbeam found its way through the dense canopy to bounce off its trunk or branches. The purple leaves swayed in a rhythmic dance even though there was no breeze. Tiny mauve and pearly bells dangled in bunches and tinkled mellifluously, the sound reminding her wistfully of the wind chimes in her garden at home. The Wellses stopped and began whispering something that sounded like a prayer or blessing. They started to move again. Briana turned back to the tree with a sudden thought. "Did any of the destroyed trees have faeries still in them?"

"Yes, milady," Jack answered mournfully, his head bowed down in grief. Tears welled in Genevieve's eyes.

Briana raged at the disregard this Lord Shamwa had for the life of the forest. As they walked, Briana saw no sign of humans, no trash, artificial bridges or clear-cuts. It was as though she and the Wellses were the first to ever walk through here. They didn't say much as they walked but the chatter in her mind more than made up for the lack of conversation. *Okay*, she told herself, *the stress of everything going on in my life caused me to have some kind of mental breakdown while I was out gardening. In an effort to avoid the reality of Dad's death, my mind just decided to go on some kind of shamanic journey. Yeah, that's it. Pretty soon, I'm going to snap out of it and have a fabulous story to tell. So, if that's the case, I may as well relax and enjoy it.* This idea calmed her. She paid attention to the vibrant flowers above three-lobed leaves and the feathery fronds that carpeted the forest floor. Her ears tuned in to the individual sounds of forest life; in the distance, she heard a waterfall. As they continued, the sound of falling water grew louder. The gnomes walked around the side of a gargantuan boulder and pushed aside some small trees to reveal a white ribbon of water dropping a hundred feet or more into a pool of clarion water. Sunlight streamed down through the leafy treetops, blessing the open space created by the enchanting falls and its pool.

"Like a rest, milady?" asked Genevieve. "You'll never drink water more fresh or cold than right here at Faerie Falls."

"Faerie Falls," she repeated, delighted by its mystical beauty. "Are there real faeries here?" she asked, half teasing.

"Aye, there might be, but they aren't likely to let you see them – at least, not yet. Faeries are rather shy around newcomers," Jack said. In a stage whisper, he added, "Even when the newcomer is the Mouse of the Prophecy." He leaned nearer to Briana and really did whisper, "That might draw one or two out, but I doubt it. They'll be takin' their dear time about meeting you."

Briana shook her head in amazement and leaned down to get a drink from the pool. She cupped the water and smiled at the mini-world beneath the surface. Dazzling colored fish darted among colorful rocks in a now-you–see-them-now-you-don't kind of way. Cold, sweet water satisfied a thirst she hadn't been aware of until the first drop touched her lips. Birdsong echoed against the granite face behind the falls.

The missus wandered nearby, collecting something from the base of a few trees and around some fern patches and putting it in her pocket. When Briana asked what she was picking, the woman responded with a merry wink. "Oh, just some wee mushrooms. 'Tis a special kind that grows near the falls. Pickle them with a few herbs and they're a lovely addition to a meal. We'll have some for supper, we will."

Interested, Briana joined her and found a few herself, adding to the harvest. They stopped when Genevieve advised her to never pick all of anything, but to leave a few for the wee folk. She produced a couple of shiny red apples from her knapsack and they enjoyed the juicy fruit as the forest sang to them. Although Briana had a gazillion questions whirling in her head, she found it impossible to ask them. She wanted to enjoy this peaceful, refreshing moment as long as she could.

Jack said, "Milady, we must be going. I very much want to get you to our home before dark, so you can see our little community."

Rising from her mossy seat, she signaled them ahead. "After you."

They wandered over hills, down into shadowed, hidden valleys and around frog ponds full of orange lilies until they came to a steep part of the trail. Jack turned to her with a wink and a smile.

"Almost there," he said, cheerfully. "We go up this way, across a wee bit of ridgeline, and then we shall be home. Ready?"

Mouse nodded. "Does your village have a name?"

Genevieve replied with a proud smile. "Baigsith. It means 'Village of Harmony.' It's always been a peaceful place, and with your help and the king's, we hope to have it remain so."

Briana didn't respond but let the tranquil name linger in her mind as they moved forward, hanging onto tree limbs and scrambling up steep rocks to the top of the ridge, where the path flattened out. From the spine of the hill she saw a valley of old oak forest below on one side, and on the other, a good part of the trail they'd travelled, including the head of the waterfall some distance away. She marveled again at how far these gnomes had walked each day. After another quarter of an hour, the trail ended in front of two huge boulders sitting side by side. On closer inspection, she saw that the path went between the slabs. Her eyes widened as she considered that she was a good bit bigger than the gnomes, and might not fit. As though reading her mind, Jack, already in front of the narrow opening, said to her, "Don't think about it, milady. Just walk through. You'll fit, I guarantee it!"

She started to argue, but a feeling of trust came over her and she did as instructed. Before she could even wonder if it had worked, she realized the rocks were behind her. "Huh."

Jack and Genevieve smiled happily, as if to say, *I told you so.*

Finally, they reached a quaint hamlet, with plumes of chimney smoke rising from numerous small homes nestled serenely in the gently sloping hills of the valley. "Hobbit houses!"

Jack cocked his head at her comment. "What's a hobbit?"

"They're little... never mind," she stopped herself, knowing the reference would be lost on them. Splashes of color dotted the glen from the brightly painted doors and shutters on the miniature thatched cottages, vibrant against whitewashed walls and golden straw roofs. Gardens overran every home and doorway, with bright red geraniums, petunias, sweet William, lobelia, fern, vinca and ivy spilling from the gay flower boxes. Blue morning glory, purple clematis and pink and orange honeysuckle grew up trellises beside the doorways. She noticed several varieties of plant life that were unfamiliar, though equally lovely. Old stone walls meandered through the town. Every so many feet there was a pot of something

– pansies, begonia, petunias and assorted plants unknown to her, trailing down the sides of the container. Worn wooden gates provided a measure of privacy for each home, but were at the same time inviting, with welcome signs hung near posts or doors. A meandering stream bordered by ferns, trillium, primrose and hosta ran through the middle of Baigsith, just wide enough to require a bridge. Tiny cascades eddied and pooled along its length. In the middle of town grew a spreading chestnut tree, its limbs and leaves creating an umbrella that could, in all likelihood, shelter the whole village. Her hands itched to play in this botanical wonderland.

Surrounding the homes were patchwork plots of farmland and larger gardens, worked by a small army of gnomes. Deer meandered unconcerned between the postage-stamp parcels of land, as did ducks, chickens, sheep and other livestock. Small children scampered about everywhere, laughing in the midst of their games. The sound of their chatter and singing rose up, a happy hallelujah.

Genevieve clasped Briana's hand. "What do you think of our wee village?"

"Oh, Mrs. Wells." She smiled, utterly enchanted. "It's darling. I can't believe it."

"Oh, 'tis real, milady, and we will do anything we must to keep it this way." It seemed the threat of Lord Shamwa was never far away. Somewhere in the recesses of her mind, Briana was beginning to think she would also do anything possible to help them keep it this way.

Raucous, joyful voices spun her attention to the center of town, where gnomes were gathering in a large circle. There was an awful lot of cartwheels, backflips, hand-clasping and general merrymaking going on. The closer Briana and her companions got to the group, the quieter everyone became, until suddenly there was an expectant hush. Jack Wells drew himself to his full stature, as much as that was, and said, "It is with great joy that I present to the good citizens of Baigsith, the prophesied one, the Mouse, the hero of Uisneach, milady Briana!" Briana nearly jumped out of her skin at the cheer that went up from the people. A mass of jolly bodies pressed in, patting her and shaking her hand, giving her happy hugs whenever and however they could.

There was no denying the honor that came with their belief that she was here to liberate the king and their wonderful kingdom. With the honor, though, came a tremendous amount of uncertainty and a heavy responsibility. And truth be told, she was still not one hundred percent sure any of it was real.

Rolling with the celebration, she allowed herself to be guided to a building that was quite a lot larger than the others. In fact, it was exactly the size needed for someone her height.

"Not everyone in Uisneach is a gnome," said Jack. "There are others who are tall as you, and some even taller. While different clans tend to stay together, sometimes folks come and stay for a time. So we have built a bigger house for their comfort. Though you're always welcome in our cottages, it might be a tight squeeze for you. This is your home, whenever you're here with us."

Touched by his thoughtfulness, she smiled and thanked him as she opened the door to her new home.

Wood and stone welcomed her, along with the gloriously earthy incense of peat burning in a corner fireplace. Had she imagined a magical cottage for herself, it wouldn't have come close to the charm of this home. Chairs cluttered the room, each with a gnome in residence; the space was large enough for half the town to gather. A natural wood-and-fiber couch graced one end and a long, sturdy oak dining table the other. A second fireplace, big enough for cooking, with some small built-in ovens, stood opposite the corner hearth, and a smaller table, presumably for food preparation, stood nearby. Windows on three walls offered breathtaking views of Baigsith, the forest behind the village and the mountains beyond. Above the cooking area was a sleeping loft accessed by a set of ornately carved stairs, which she ascended to discover an armoire, mirror and full-sized bed covered with a pile of handmade quilts. They had thought of everything to make her comfortable, including a private space and copper tub for bathing. She made her way back downstairs, eyes glittering with excitement.

"Do you like it, milady?" asked a gentleman who resembled Jack Wells.

"Very much," she replied. "You've gone to a lot of work to make me feel welcome."

"My name is John Wells, milady." He bowed low. "I built this cottage."

"And a master at building you most assuredly are." She smiled and then cocked her head. "Are you related to Jack?"

A giggle rippled through the group. "Well, I supposed you could say we're kin."

"Oh? How are you related? Brother, father, uncle, what?"

"No, milady, nothing like that. We all have the last name of Wells here. Why, there's Bubby Wells, Moira Wells, Caitlin Wells, Ralph Wells. Oh, for sure you'll get to know everyone soon enough. No need to introduce everyone right this minute."

She thought this communal last name very odd indeed, but declined to say so. *After all*, she thought, *it isn't the first oddity of the day!*

Out of the throng emerged a plump woman followed by a gaggle of younger gnomes. The matron's arms were loaded down with baskets of food, which she placed on the long dining table. The children quickly disseminated plates and cups all around. "You must be starved, poor girl. Come on, everyone, let's sit down to eat while we hear the whole story of how Jack and Genevieve found the Mouse."

The gnomes obeyed without delay and soon the table overflowed with food and drink. Briana thought there was nothing in the world like the aroma and taste of fresh hearth-baked bread, warm and slathered in butter, the ultimate comfort food. Add a tankard of strong ale... well, clearly, heaven did exist. Besides bread and beer, there were big bowls of boiled vegetables and platters of roasted meat and stewed apples, all smelling delicious and eliciting guttural appreciation. Apparently no storytelling would happen until bellies were filled. For some time, quiet chatter and "pass me the butter" were the only sounds of this gathering.

Briana ate with as much gusto as everyone else. It occurred to her she hadn't paid much attention to her physical needs. They'd eaten on the trail, but she hadn't wondered about where the food had come from, or what might be the usual cuisine for gnomes. Neither had she considered any future needs, such as clothing. Dressed for gardening, she had on a pair of old jeans, a tee shirt that ironically displayed the bold statement, "Proud to be a Tree Hugger," and a ratty pair of sneakers that should've been thrown in the trash. *Quite the savior*, she thought. *What will I do tomorrow, assuming I don't just wake up in my own bed at home?*

Ebenezer Wells, a portly gentleman by anyone's standards, rose from his place at the head of the table and looked directly at Briana. Clearing his throat, he began to speak with great pomp and circumstance, his hands waving wildly about and chest puffing out further and further with every word. "All across the kingdom of Uisneach, good people have hoped for and anticipated the arrival of the prophesied Mouse who would release our beloved king from his captivity and save and unite the five blessed realms. The great prophecy has been given to us, and we believed whole-heartedly, since Lord Shamwa's traitorous acts upon our beloved king, that the time was imminent for the prophecy to be fulfilled. We began our vigil several months ago, and made preparations to receive the liberator. That glorious day has arrived, and it is with heartfelt gratitude and humility that we welcome you, Milady Mouse. You honor us with your presence. We…" A gnome standing next to him coughed loudly. Ebenezer stopped, and with a flourishing bow, took his seat.

Jack Wells followed. She listened as the events of the day were told to the assemblage, which may have been the entire borough, if sheer numbers were any indication. She was astounded at just how many gnomes could fit inside the cottage. Some sat at the table while others found space elsewhere. Every so often a gnome would throw another peat brick on the fire, the smell and crackle keeping the room cozy. Hours passed, nighttime fell, and the Wellses reached the end of the narrative. As the story wound down, so did Briana; it wasn't long before her yawns and drooping eyelids reminded the residents of Baigsith that their savior had endured a long and emotional day. Genevieve led her toward the loft stairs. Kindly good nights and blessings followed her as she was assisted upstairs.

A white linen nightgown lay atop her bed. It seemed the gnomes had thought of everything. Only half aware of how it happened, she soon found herself tucked into the cloud of her bed, so comfortable and peaceful that sleep took her before she had time to say, thank you.

AN AWFULLY BIG ADVENTURE

atrina was trimming herbs in her garden, while she, a small child, played in her own miniature herb garden, learning the names of things – thyme, rosemary, lavender and sage. Mother was instructing her to pay attention because the knowledge of these little plants would be useful someday, but she just enjoyed their textures and scents and tastes. She liked to watch things grow.

Rising up out of the dream, Briana feared opening her eyes. Would she see the apple tree outside her bedroom window and her digital clock telling her it was 7:10 in the morning? Would the cozy warmth blanketing her be her own familiar comforter? Or would she awaken to a magical world in which all the people had the odd notion that she was their savior? She didn't move, until a youthful voice spoke in her ear.

"Milady? Miss Mouse? Are you to get up at all today? Why, the sun is full up and first breakfast is waiting on you."

She groaned. *Resistance is futile*, she thought, opening her eyes to see the sweet, eager face of a young female gnome staring curiously at her.

"Ah, so there you are, Miss Mouse. I thought you'd never wake up."

As the little helper bustled around the room gathering clothing, Briana took a deep breath. *So*, she thought, *I didn't dream this. I am in a place called Uisneach with a bunch of gnomes.* Under the covers she tapped her feet together three times. Nothing. It had worked for Dorothy but apparently wouldn't help her return home. The gnome still stood in front of her, stubby arms holding out a pile of clothing, nothing like the jeans and tee shirt she was accustomed to wearing. As she received the outfit into her own hands, she asked the girl her name.

"Esmerelda… "

"…Wells," Briana finished for her, with a kind smile.

Esmerelda returned the smile, bobbing her head up and down. "Yes, milady."

Would they never stop calling her milady? She took a closer look at the clothes. Simple and well made, they were, unbelievably, exactly the right size. She opened her mouth to ask how they knew, but closed it again, deciding it didn't really matter. She'd been taught that one should never look a gift horse in the mouth. She dressed quickly, washed her face and pulled a wooden comb through her rumpled hair. Esmerelda's smile told her she looked fit for company. As she turned to make her way toward the stairs, she caught sight of herself in a full-length mirror with runic carvings all around the cherrywood frame. The beige woven tunic and lace-up vest over brown leather leggings weren't exactly a staple of her wardrobe, though they worked well with the brown leather boots that were laced up knee-high. She reached down to adjust the boots' wide cuffs, then stomped to test them out. They seemed good and sturdy. A narrow belt was slung around her waist, with an empty sheath attached. *Middle Earth me*, she mused.

"Take a good look, milady. 'Tis important."

Briana looked again. This time she saw past the outfit to a self virtually vibrating with passionate possibility. Her eyes widened. *Not a gentle woman of the shire, but a woman of the woods – more like one of Robin Hood's… well, "hood." Not a shy bookworm, but… a gorgeous and self-assured warrior.*

Where did that idea come from?

"That is who you truly are," said Esmerelda. "This is the Mirror of Truth."

Strong, beautiful, and fearless? Really? Briana could hardly believe it, though she liked the idea. Unfamiliar energy surged through her, sparking something into life that had lain dormant until this moment. Mouse no more – she was Briana, woman of the deep forest, savior of trees and all things under four feet tall.

Genevieve joined Esmerelda behind her, holding a long, hooded cloak, beaming with satisfaction.

"The garments suit you," Genevieve remarked.

"You… are… so… beautiful," Esmerelda said, shyly.

"Beauty is as beauty does," Genevieve countered, with a slightly raised eyebrow and a tiny smile. "Come along milady, breakfast won't wait forever."

Briana smiled, grateful for the older woman's dose of humility. It would be easy for her head to outgrow itself if she dwelled too long on the woman in the mirror. Pride and vanity had no place in her current circumstances, but she found herself standing a bit taller, anyway. There was no telling what this day would bring. She resolved to meet it without fear and perhaps even with open curiosity. After all, there was a kingdom to save. On a whim, she thrust her fist into the air and proclaimed, *Carpe Diem!*"

Esmerelda and Genevieve looked mystified. They shrugged and followed her down the stairs. Scrumptious smells wafted up to meet them: bread, bacon, and hints of orange and maple. *Scones? Yum.* The wooden table once again overflowed with food.

Breakfast was a busy, loud event. Chatter stopped abruptly when her new friends noticed her arrival, replaced by ooh's and ahh's as she took her place at the head of the table.

"May I have a scone, please?" she asked. Eager to please, they kept passing her plates and asking if she wouldn't like this or that, all at the same time. She laughingly held up a hand for them to slow down.

"I can't possibly eat all of this," she protested, as things inexplicably appeared on her plate. Yet she grinned as she accepted a warm raspberry-walnut scone, which smelled heavenly and tasted even better. *Pure decadence*, she thought, as its buttery flakiness melted on her tongue. Hot herbal tea had been poured three times when the clanging of a bell set everyone in motion.

"What's that?" she asked.

"Governor Wells is calling a meeting at the tree. We best go, milady. He doesn't like to be kept waiting."

She swallowed the last of her tea and followed her new friends outside to the center of town, where the gnomes were gathering under a gigantic spreading chestnut tree. Governor Ebenezer Wells continued to sound the bell with an air of solemnity as the gnomes congregated. Briana thought she'd never seen anyone take a job quite as seriously as this little man. She squashed a desire to giggle and adopted a similar air of seriousness.

"To-day," he drew out the syllables portentously, "we begin a new chapter in the history of Uisneach. Before we send Milady Mouse on her way," he announced, startling her, "She must be given a clear understanding of the prophecy and exactly what she is undertaking."

Maybe he said more, but her brain stopped at "on her way." *They're sending me off? Why, I've barely gotten settled in. Surely they won't make me go so soon.* On the other hand, she certainly couldn't save a king and kingdom by sitting beside a cozy peat hearth in a gentle village. She muttered, "I would've liked a couple of days to get, I don't know, used to things."

Briana refocused in time to hear the beginnings of what sounded like a reading of the prophecy, which began with a poem.

"When the wheel of the seasons forgets to turn,

The trees are nearly gone.

From ancient oak a Mouse appears,

A queen is met with cheers.

She'll journey far to save a king,

In castle strong under gloomy spell he rests.

Five keys will lift the curse.

Help arrives from king's right hand,

Rare magic and a map.

Crow and crone lead and teach the future
ordained queen of Uisneach.

From evil one, gray ghosts race from west to east,

A war they want to wage.

True queen and faithful rise up strong

Message from the ages.

Power wielding from dryad's gift,

Faeries sing and place a ring upon their own,

Granddaughter of a king.

But heart is turned toward druid love,

A choice she'll have to make.

Sacrifice is sure reward for children of the mist.

King and queen pledge fealty, royal banns proclaimed.

Wedding day breaks the cat,

When joy and sorrow blend as one.

Holly crown, faerie tree,

Throne and council, a queen's surprise,

From hill to hill an ancient symbol taken.

Two worlds collide in time,

Treasure lost the cat must find.

Dark and light now must meet,

River battle ends one part, brown king protects to death.

Briana frowned. It seemed a rough and unhappy ending.

Genevieve whispered, "There's more to the prophecy, but the pages were stolen, so we don't know how it ends."

"Who stole them?" Briana whispered back.

The gnome shrugged. "A true mystery."

For the next quarter of an hour she listened to the story of the five ancient kingdoms that made up the island of Uisneach, kingdoms with Gaelic names that each plucked at a separate heartstring. Appleduir was the southernmost kingdom, what most of the gnomes referred to as Wellsland. Cedarmara was on the western shore, a land of legendary towering cedar trees that grew from the high mountains of the northeast all the way down to the sandy shoreline, with a beautiful natural harbor that protected the only ocean-faring fleet in Uisneach.

To the north lay Evalon, the land of ten thousand faerie trees. At the heart of Uisneach was Tynan Ibor, and here, deep in the forest under protective magic, stood the sacred Uisneach Tree. The Dromdara mountain range, with Poet's Gap in the middle and Art Aron, or Bear Mountain, near the southern coast, separated Tynan Ibor from the Dromdara lands, which contained both Lord Shamwa's abode near Long River and the king's castle to the north, along the coast.

The most important kingdom at the moment, the goal of Briana's journey, was Dromdara and the king's castle of Ard Darach, where the king, indeed the whole castle, was imprisoned by Lord Shamwa's curse.

No one had heard from King Brath for a decade.

❧

KING BRATH'S FATHER, the beloved King Barclay III of the Five Kingdoms, reigned for half a century and maintained a unified and prosperous league of nations. The last war had been generations before his reign; the men in his guard spent most of their time improving the land and the lives of the people, more ambassadors than soldiers. He died at a good old age, peaceful in the certainty that all was well in Uisneach. His wife, Queen Eleanor, died a year later, of a broken heart, it is said, forcing their son, Brath, to take up the crown.

King Brath, young in age but advanced in wisdom, carried on his father's example. A kind monarch, he was just as well loved. The kingdom flourished under his dynasty, due in part to his modernization of agriculture and building methods.

All that changed one evening while he sat with Lord Shamwa, his prime minister, at dinner in the great hall, discussing plans to build a canal between two lakes to better transport produce. The druid, Artanin, co-conspirator with Shamwa, slipped a single drop of a poisonous herb into King Brath's cup of wine. Within a few seconds Brath was confused and weak. Less than a minute later, he was unconscious. Other members of his cabinet attempted to revive him, but Lord Shamwa took control; no one questioned their prime minister's loyalty. Without so much as a raised sword or blocked doorway, Lord Shamwa had his aides carry King Brath to his room. Minutes later he announced the king's death, and most everyone believed him. He convinced the knights that the poisoning was the work of the wicked Artanin.

All but one of the knights rode out into the night, intent on raiding the Druid Grove and taking the perpetrator into custody. While they rode out, Shamwa brought Artanin out of hiding, and the druid cast a spell over the castle so that no one could enter or leave Ard Darach. King Brath did not die, thanks be to Maker, but was now captive in his own castle, frozen in time, as were the few people who remained at his side at the time of the curse.

Shock paralyzed the kingdom. Lord Shamwa used the opportunity to further train his Gray Military. It seemed their only two directives were to prevent anyone from gaining access to Ard Darach and to destroy all of the faerie trees in Uisneach. All trade and travel was effectively stopped by troops positioned across the island. Markets and whole villages were burned. The good people of the kingdom, having endured every imaginable suffering under Shamwa, became oppressed, entirely incapable of fighting back. Shamwa preyed on the weak and the poor, forcing them to join his army. The few who, for whatever reason, wished evil on the kingdom, were also welcomed.

It was no ordinary murder of crows that blackened the sky and spread the word to the five kingdoms that King Brath was not dead, but a prisoner in his own castle; rather, it was a clan famous for their ability to change shape from avian to human. Their shapeshifting abilities made it difficult for Shamwa's troops to find them, never mind stop them. Thus they were able to spread the news of the curse and bring to each kingdom a copy of a prophecy which had until then been unknown to all but the mysterious witch, Cailleach, who lived somewhere deep in Tynan Ibor.

From that day to this, ten years later, they had done more than guard their lands against invasion; they had watched and prepared for the advent of a Mouse to save them.

✍

A collective sigh wafted over the gnomes, some of whom glanced surreptitiously at Mouse. The Governor punched his stubby fist to the sky and declared with great drama, "Today, my friends and compatriots, we can take comfort in knowing that the reign of the evildoer is almost over, for the Mouse has emerged, and it is with renewed hope and promise that our king will soon sit upon his throne and our lands, the faerie trees and freedom will be restored." He scarcely got the last word out before the cheering of the crowd drowned him out.

"Three cheers for Mouse," someone called out.

"Hip, hip, hooray! Hip, hip, hooray! Hip, hip, hooray!"

Cheering went on for several minutes, interrupted only when Governor Wells began ringing the bell again. When all was quiet, he continued. "While celebration is certainly in order, we must also remember that there is much to be done to prepare Mouse." Another pause and clearing of his throat. "And I might add, our future queen, for her mission. We prepare her to cross the abyss and undertake the journey to Ard Darach."

The sensation of being sucked down in quicksand overwhelmed her. In a span of hours she had turned from being plain old Mouse to woodland warrior Briana to future Queen Briana. Talk about shapeshifting. She sought out the comforting smile of Genevieve, who immediately sat down on the bench beside her.

"I'm not queen of anything," Briana whispered to her. "I can't be."

Taking Briana's hands in her own, Genevieve smiled and said gently, "You are our queen, Briana. I knew it from the moment I laid eyes on you." Her blue eyes began to twinkle. "However, a real queen does more than just sit on a throne, issue orders and lop off heads, you know. She is courageous, patient, and kind. She knows everything about the people she rules. Before you can truly be queen, you must take the journey that will build those qualities and give you opportunities to know your people. And of course, your king needs you."

Briana used the certainty and strength in the other woman's face to fortify her own resolve. But there were a few unanswered questions.

"So, is Shamwa the king now?"

Genevieve shrugged. "I suppose so, but king of what? He raised taxes, but having also ended all trade, no one has much of anything to give. And with everyone trying to stay hidden, who exactly is he ruling? He's the king of nothing, really, but he is keeping the kingdom under a state of terror, so that we're barely living."

"This trip I'm supposed to take, this mission, will Lord Shamwa know about it? Will he be coming after me?"

"Aye, likely he will, but we'll do everything we can to help you. There's some of Brath's faithful ones who'll be looking for you, too, to see you safely across. You'll not have to do this all by yourself."

Briana shook her head. "I'm no hero, Genevieve. Much as I'd like to help, I've nothing to offer on such a quest."

The little woman wrapped her arms around Briana's hips and smiled widely. "Oh, lass, you have so much more than you know. You have magic."

Briana started. "Magic? I don't know any magic."

Genevieve's head was pumping up and down excitedly. "But you do. Maybe you don't know it yet, but 'tis certain that the Mouse of Prophecy has powerful magic. Most everyone in Uisneach has some kind of magic, even though it's been weakened." A look of disappointment crossed her face. "Sadly, we gnomes don't have much, but we'll do what we can to help."

The strong part of her thought if they had so much faith in her, she ought to be able to rise to this challenge. On the other hand, the somewhat muddled and unbelieving part of her argued, *Maybe it's just a crazy dream.*

"Genevieve, I think I need some time by myself, to take this all in."

"Of course, milady. I'm sure you're feeling a bit gobsmacked right about now. We'll go prepare the celebration feast and let you be." She pointed down a cobbled path that led to the edge of the village. "I suggest you follow that road out through the village gates. There's a lovely meadow beside the river where you can sit quietly for a while." She squeezed Briana's arm and left her.

Under different circumstances, Briana might have appreciated the rough beauty of the earth-hued stones that she walked upon. She might also have smiled at the brightly colored pots of flowers on fence posts, the wee bird houses and tinkling fountains in the yards of many of the village homes. Normally she would've taken pleasure in breathing deeply of the clean, crisp air. All of it barely registered, however, as she wandered through the skillfully crafted wrought-iron gate that led her out of the village and into a quiet field.

A sturdy wooden bench overlooked a serene section of the river. She settled herself, hoping the quiet flow of the water would smooth out her tangled thoughts. Overcome with foreboding at the thought of saving the king, she dropped her face into her hands. *Brath and Briana, King and Queen of Uisneach.* A bolt of lightning shot up through her spine. *Marry a man I don't even know? Insane.* She decided to run as fast as she could back to the oak tree that brought her here. Just then, a loud caw and flapping wings halted her.

The same crow she'd seen in the oak forest landed with effortless grace on the arm of the bench beside her. She didn't flinch. In his mouth swung a medallion, a replica of the one that circled his neck. He bobbed his head and pushed the medallion toward her with his beak. She reached out tentatively. The medallion lay in her palm, inky dark and warm, beautifully crafted with the symbol of the tree etched in gold. No jewelry she'd ever seen had been so flawlessly made. The crow bobbed his head insistently, directing her to turn the medallion over. On its back was a shield featuring two thrones made of carved ash trees whose branches reached across to each other, and a symbol of a white weasel and braided crowns. Breathless, Briana looked up at the crow with sudden understanding. They stared at one another for what seemed an eternity, neither making a sound, yet communicating perfectly.

"Is there some purpose to this medallion?" she asked, turning it over again. No answer, though she sensed there was. "It's frightening to think I'll go out on some journey through a country I don't know all by myself," she murmured.

Crow hopped from the arm of the bench onto her lap and looked up at her.

She smiled. "Well, perhaps not so alone after all."

She looped the medallion's silken cord over her neck and allowed the disc to fall neatly at the soft hollow in her throat. Pleasant warmth spread from her throat to the rest of her body. Power flowed through her, and whatever doubts and fears she had vanished. "I am braver than I believe," she reminded herself. Crow made a soothing little sound Briana wouldn't have associated with a crow, and flew up to a nearby limb.

They sat together in companionable silence a little longer and then, as suddenly as he arrived, he left. Centered once more, she returned along the path into the village and back to her cottage, ready to accept whatever would come next.

CHAPTER FOUR

ACROSS THE VOID

From head to toe, Briana was a mass of aching muscles. She appreciated the magic that reduced years of training to two days, but her body didn't. It had been a brutal boot camp. *Why*, she thought, *don't they have some magical cure for sore muscles?*

Jack was determined to make her as ready for this journey as possible. "We don't have much time, milady, but we'll do what we can, and trust that help will show up quickly. Mostly, you need to know how to feed, shelter and protect yourself until the king's men arrive to escort you to Ard Darach. And they will, that's the truth. If the crow has done his part, then they are on their way even as we speak."

Some of her skills were already sharp and hadn't required much magically-enhanced instruction, such as her ability to start a campfire. She was a whiz at assessing the dryness of wood. Briana always kept some birch bark tucked into her backpack because it was such a fine fire-starter. They used flint here, not matches, a technique she picked up quickly enough. Jack Wells, her campfire mentor, beamed as she built her teepee of twigs, adding larger branches once the fire took.

Back home, her knowledge of herbal remedies was considered advanced; here, she was told she would "get by" until Cailleach could teach her more. Of course, she had to learn how to identify the local mushrooms, nuts and berries – and to remind herself to not pick something that looked just like a safe item from her world.

One skill she rather surprisingly wouldn't have to use was her ability to make a lean-to out of pine boughs. The gnomes provided her with the most remarkable sleeping gadget, part pup tent, part invisibility cloak. Its lightweight fabric provided great insulation and camouflage for any surroundings. She could pop it out in the middle of a clearing, climb inside, and no one would see her.

"This is fabulous," she exclaimed to Jack, jumping in and out of visibility with delight.

"You'll still need to be careful where you pitch it. You'll not remain hidden if someone tumbles into you."

Some skills proved much more difficult and more of a strain on her body, such as weaponry and rock climbing. She was taught to use a variety of blades, from a dirk to a broadsword to a Scottish-style claymore. Due to their size and weight, it took a fair amount of time to learn how to use the weapons effectively, but once mastered, she was surprised at how the practice seemed to increase her flexibility and coordination and overall grace. They practiced until her arm could wield no more.

"I think you'll do," Jack judged as she slid the smaller dirk, the one she would carry with her, back into its scabbard at her belt.

"Don't warriors usually name their weapons? Should I choose a boy's name or a girl's name?" she mused.

"Don't bother. This is not your forever knife, lass. There's another that will be yours to name as you wish. This one's temporary."

She waited, anticipating more information. The gnome led her away from the village and down a narrow path without another word.

The next and most challenging drill involved climbing the steep face of a rock cliff. She stood before the massive stone face then turned, grimacing. "No can do, Jack. I'm terrified of heights."

"Well, milady, you'd best shake it off in a hurry. You'll have to excel at these skills if you are to rescue our king. You might even need them to save yourself, sometimes. Let's get on with it. Up you go."

Briana's first attempt was nothing short of pathetic. She managed about ten feet and froze.

"Well, you can't bloody well stay where you are!" Jack hollered.

"I... can't... do... this," she choked, out of breath and paralyzed with fear.

"Come on, milady. I'm only four feet tall and I can do it! You've got the strength and the reach. If a gnome can do it, surely a full-size woman can."

She reached up to the next handhold. "Anything for my king," she sputtered, anger trumping fear.

She made it up fifteen feet when the screech and flutter of a small hawk distracted her. She missed the next protrusion and her foot slipped. "No!" she yelled, dropping into a free fall. Halfway down, something slowed her, and she landed neatly in a spongy patch of moss.

Looking up into the face of a grinning Jack, she gasped, "What... was... that?"

He winked. "Perhaps you have a wee bit of magic in you, after all."

"Not possible," she said, though her mind began to work out the possibility that she did. "Even if I do, is this really necessary?"

"Yes, milady. 'Tis a matter of life and death – yours and King Brath's. Can you give it another go?"

Gingerly pushing herself back to a standing position, she faced the stone wall, took a deep breath, and grabbed for the first handhold.

"That a girl," he said, his voice soft, but proud. "Now, focus, lass. Focus."

Taking deep, intentional breaths she inched her way to the top of the fifty-foot cliff, grinning as she dragged her body over the edge. She sat quietly, catching her breath and basking in a sense of accomplishment. When her legs stopped trembling and her breathing returned to normal, she peered impishly over the edge to see Jack grinning below.

"Now," she shouted, "just how do I get down from here?"

The next day, Briana stretched the six hundred and forty aching muscles of her body – a new and rather miserable part of her morning ritual. She dressed and went downstairs, which was pleasantly quiet for the first time since her arrival. No one else was up, not even the sun, and after reviving the fire in the hearth, she sat alone with her thoughts.

I should pray or something, she thought, *but to who? Is God still here in this world?* The gnomes referred to the Maker, which she assumed was their version of God.

She closed her eyes, allowing the warmth and earthiness of the peat fire to find its way deep within her heart. *Hello?* She paused a moment. *Whoever you are, whatever you are, if you can help me, I invoke you now.* Nothing happened. *Maker,* she tried again, and found resonance.

Maker, are they right that I'm destined to rescue this king? I'm scared, but the gnomes believe in this prophecy and you, and I'm willing to try. Will you help me? Is there a sign or something I should be looking for? The second she asked the question, her mind's eye saw the medallioned crow. The bird had something to do with all of this, she was certain.

Sensing a presence, she turned as Genevieve sat in the chair beside her, pulling a woven shawl tighter around her shoulders.

"Genevieve, what is this for?" she asked, stroking the polished black surface of the medallion.

The woman shook her head. "No one knows exactly. I understand that several people have one, but last I knew, even Cailleach didn't know what they were for. It's believed to be a key of some sort that will help remove the curse, but how is a mystery."

Briana sighed. *Layers upon layers of mystery.*

Genevieve smiled comfortingly at her and let the peace of the crackling fire wrap around them. They sat together until the house woke up and the gnomes filled the table once more with a breakfast fit for a queen. Briana tucked in with gusto, wondering when her next meal might be and what it might look like.

There was nothing left to do but go. She had the clothes on her back, a cloak, the tent, a knife, a leather water flask and a knapsack with dried meat and bread to last a few days. Thanks to the their training, she'd also be able to find some food on her own.

"And there will be people to help you along the way," Jack assured her.

A battalion of Wellses escorted her down the path through the village, out the gates, past the bench where the crow brought her the medallion, over a sturdy stone bridge that crossed the river and through a narrower trail into the woods. She remembered Hansel and Gretel and wondered a couple of times if she ought to use a little of the bread to leave a trail, in case she changed her mind and wanted to come back.

The trees thinned out as they came to an opening. The lead gnomes stopped. Briana joined them and suddenly realized they were standing on the edge of a canyon that was perhaps forty feet across. Its walls of ancient gray stones plunged down into a torrential river several hundred feet below. Briana jumped back with a choked sound that never quite made it out of her throat. She looked back to see them all staring expectantly at her.

"What? You can't possibly... I can't possibly!"

Jack and Genevieve stepped forward on either side of her. "Yes you can, Briana," Genevieve said, patiently. "We've not steered you wrong yet, have we?"

"But it's impossible! If I walk off that edge, I'm a goner."

"Can you not just walk across the rainbow?" Jack asked, sounding truly perplexed.

"What rainbow?" Puzzled, she turned again to face the abyss and nearly fainted in surprise. Indeed, a bridge of ethereal, shimmering color spanned the gorge. "How on earth..." she started, and then shut her mouth and stared. Although the rainbow was now plainly there, it still didn't seem solid and she couldn't imagine it would hold her weight in order to cross.

She shook her head. Jack nodded back, with a "come on already" look. "You first."

"We can't," Jack responded. "We don't have the magic, but you do. You must trust me, Briana. You can walk across that bridge as easily as you walked the path to get here. Oh, one other thing. Do you see those two birch trees?" He pointed across the canyon to a white-barked tree that split into two trunks at about mid-height. She nodded. "In the notch of those trees you'll find a box that holds a map. 'Tis a special map, so don't be surprised when you open it."

She extended her head skyward and closed her eyes. "Sure thing, Jack. I'll just whip across this transparent bridge, get the magic map and be on my way."

"That's my girl!"

"I was only kidding. This is ridiculous. I cannot walk across that chasm – it will kill me. There has to be another way."

"Please, milady," a small girl pleaded. Briana looked down to find her with tears in her eyes, looking up imploringly at her. "If ye don't go, King Brath won't be saved and the faerie trees will die and we'll all die. Ye must go, ye just must."

Briana looked at her masses of wild black curls and big eyes, then back at the expectant and encouraging faces surrounding her, then back again at the abyss. *They were depending on her. Could she do it?* She heard Judy Garland's voice singing in her head about birds flying over the rainbow.

Come on, Briana, she thought, *you can do this. Take the first step. You are who they believe you are. The step you take will lead you into a new world, a new life. What if the rainbow is the beginning of a road that will take you home?*

She lifted a foot and put it onto the bridge. She did not lose her balance, nor did she fall helplessly to her death. Closing her eyes just in case, she moved the other foot beside the first and stopped, invoking the words of the song in her head. Opening her eyes, she saw underneath her only the wide band of color, not the abyss or raging river. *Is this magic?* She took another step, and then another, and a few more. And then she was on the other side and the bridge was gone. She breathed a sigh of relief. "I did it Jack, I really did it!"

"Well done, milady!" Jack yelled across to her. All the gnomes were jumping and flipping and dancing in joy.

Her heart swelled with tenderness for the gnomes of Wellsland, who had welcomed her, trained her and made her a part of their family. *I will not let them down,* she thought, before turning her attention to the birches.

The box sat in the notch where the two trunks met, perfectly camouflaged by its birch bark covering. A grapevine and amethyst clasp secured it. She worked it open. Inside she found a soft and leathery white cloth, rolled up and tied with a strip of leather. "Wonders never cease," she muttered, as a beautiful map of Uisneach came magically alive before her. The compass and legend in the lower corner glowed red. Tiny boats bobbed in the harbor at Cedarmara. Light snow fell on Mt. Aron, while the dark woods were lit in a pre-dawn glow. Long River, which dissected the land, surged across the map. She found her current location and sure enough, there was a rainbow where she'd crossed the river.

"Have you found it?" Jack yelled.

"Got it!" she called back. "It's beautiful. Why didn't you tell me?"

He shrugged, grinning. "Didn't know, milady. Gnomes can't see the map." Another confirmation of her prophesied role. "Go on now, Mouse – you've got a king to save!"

Looking once more at the parchment, she determined that there really was only one way to go at this point: forward. A sob, held in check until now, found its way out, but she smiled bravely. She rolled the map and tucked it safely into a long pocket in the side of her leggings and took her first decisive step forward.

CHAPTER FIVE

FARMER IN THE DELL

The forest proved a much different sort of companion than the gnomes had been. Their frenetic, jolly energy and the constant training, teaching, eating and storytelling was replaced by silence, occasionally broken by bird trills or the rattling of leaves and branches. She felt a little lonely. Maybe a little nervous. Her usual strategy of reciting lines from stories that fit her circumstance failed miserably. Her current situation only reminded her of "Red Riding Hood"… and the wolf. Or "Hansel and Gretel"… and the witch's oven. "The Old Woman in the Wood"… and the robbers. Silence seemed preferable. Briana concentrated on the wildwood, identifying the plants and animals she saw. Many of the trees were familiar: maples unfurled their green spring leaves and catkins dripped from aspen and birch. Oaks rose up majestically on old, thick trunks. No faerie trees, unfortunately. She still couldn't fathom the vicious destruction of the faerie trees, nor could she believe she would somehow be able to protect them, and yet, a strong desire to do so rose up in her. What an amazing thing it would be to save a faerie and its tree. "When I am the queen, I will protect you, I promise." A shiver ran through her at the prophetic sound of her words.

The sun blazed nearly straight-up noon when she came to the first crossroads. Well-worn paths were wider here, crossing in completely opposite directions. Missing was any sort of sign or marker to indicate where the trails led. It took her a second to remember the map. She unrolled it.

To her astonishment, everything she'd seen the first time was gone. Now the map showed only the road behind her and the juncture she stood at. Everything else was blank; even the compass was gone. *How odd. Where did everything go?* She closed her eyes and took some deep breaths and tried again. Nothing there. Anxiety snaked through her as she wondered what to do. *Without the map, I am well and truly lost.* She considered turning back, but instead, took a step forward and scanned as far as she could down each of the roads. They looked about the same. It would be up to destiny to lead her right. She allowed herself to be still for a minute and then, without faltering, walked straight ahead. After a few feet she opened the map and burst out laughing. Snow fell again on Mt. Aron, the river thundered across the land and the sun shone brightly through the trees at Tynan Ibor. Gone now was everything behind her – those routes were no longer an option. Instead, new paths and new directions appeared. So, at each crossroads, her decision would dictate the course of her journey. *Was it possible to make a mistake? Would she arrive at Ard Darach, no matter what choice she made? Or could she wander in circles and end up back in Baigsith?*

"The gnomes were pretty clear that I would find my way. They also said someone would show up to help me. I guess for now, I need to keep going and hope I don't run into Lord Shamwa before that help arrives." She rolled up the map, tucked it into her knapsack and went on, following the path in front of her.

Later, with sweat trickling down the back of her neck and her armpits growing damp, Briana did a little happy dance when she spied a clearing where a stream twisted down from the upper slope of a forested hill into a small, clear pond. After cooling her skin with a wet bandana, she filled her water bag. Her stomach grumbled, reminding her she'd had nothing to eat since early morning. About to reach into the pack for a bit of lunch, she caught sight of an apple tree heavily laden with fruit that didn't look wormy. She pulled a couple of those instead, deciding it was wiser to save her food. She found a downed trunk next to the water and sat down to enjoy the apple, but stopped a split second before taking a bite. Apples in springtime? Rotating the fruit, she considered its potential threat.

"It won't hurt youz," said a boy, his voice straight out of *Oliver Twist*. He startled her so badly she threw the apple up with enough force that it landed in the middle of the pond with an emphatic plop. She jumped to her feet and felt around for her dirk. He giggled. Finally jerking her weapon out of the scabbard, she pointed it in the general direction of his voice. She saw nothing. Another giggle spun her around to a large boulder half out of the water at the pond's edge. Midway down the stone, the boy peered from beneath a ragged mop of black hair. Freckles bridged his nose, connecting both cheeks. Her stared at her in pure merriment, with the roundest, brightest blue eyes she'd ever seen. Smudges of dirt streaked his face.

"Yer a funny one," the ragamuffin declared, bringing the rest of his slight body out from behind the rock. "Afraid of an apple?"

He was not a gnome nor anything apparently magical, only a little boy fishing this water hole, if the pole and bait box told the story.

"Of course not," she said, sheathing her weapon. "I was just wondering how apples could be ripe this time of year."

He regarded her quizzically. "Apples grow year-round, now that the seasons don't change. Youz can eat it if you like."

She stared at him for a moment. "Who are you?"

"I'm Rippa, short for Ripparivendar. Who are youz?"

She had to think. *Mouse? Briana? Something else? What was the safest?*

Rippa's huge eyes narrowed, regarding her suspiciously. "Youz ain't one of Lord Shamwa's tricks, are ye?"

A quick shake of her head. If this little urchin was asking that question, she could, in all likelihood, trust him. "My name is Briana. I am certainly not connected to Shamwa."

He looked sideways at her. "How do I know youz tellin' the truth?"

"Do I look like one of Shamwa's minions?" she replied, with a raised eyebrow.

He watched her struggle to get the dirk back into its sheath and giggled. "Prob'ly not."

"What do you mean about apples growing year-round *now*?"

"Since the curse, there's no winter, so things grow all the time."

Of course, she thought. The gnomes mentioned the seasons had stopped changing when the curse was put on Ard Darach. They had no idea why, but believed that once the curse was lifted, seasonal cycles would resume.

"Do you live around here?" she asked, eager to learn a little more about the child and any other people in the vicinity.

"Course I do. Just over that hill is our farm. Ye want to come and meet my folks? It's been ages since we had a visitor. Ye'd be welcome and Ma would give youz a proper dinner, not some old apple."

Briana quickly considered her options. Genevieve's remark about her needing to get to know the people surfaced and made the choice clear. "I'd love to meet your family, Rippa. Is it far?"

"Naw. I'm not allowed to go too far from home on 'count of maybe the Gray Military be around." He disappeared briefly behind the boulder, but popped out again holding his pole, fishing creel and two respectably sized fish, which he held up proudly. "Hope youz likes wee fishies!"

She nodded, smiling. They headed up the hillside, following the stream. She made a point of mentally mapping their route in case she had to find her way back alone. Rippa chattered nonstop about his pa and ma, Rodnner and Gertrude Tollemy, and baby sister, Penelope, describing a simple, wonderful way of life on their farm. There was no village nearby. If they needed anything they couldn't provide for themselves, they took a horse and wagon on a two-day journey north to Cedarmara, but that was rare. He kept a brisk pace for such a small boy, and it wasn' t long before they crested the hill and were heading down into a sunny valley, the farm spread out neatly before them.

The main house was a thatched-roof cottage with a chimney at each end. A large byre, fenced paddocks and another outbuilding completed the compound. Crops ripened in squared sections around the farm. Rippa's father stood in one of them, furrowing with horse and plow. In front of the cottage, a plump woman with a baby swaddled on her back worked in a smaller garden, a basket overflowing with freshly harvested vegetables beside her. A few feet away, chickens pecked at the ground near their coop. A cock and hen warred in an age-old fight; when they got too close to the woman, she shooed them away with a sweep of her foot. At Rippa's excited hail, she looked up, and shielding her eyes from the sun with one hand, waved at Rippa with the other. Seeing that he was not alone, she quickly pulled the baby around in front of her protectively and began walking toward Rippa and Briana.

Briana was bothered by the woman's anxiety at the sight of a visitor. She did her best to assuage the woman's worry by putting a warm smile on her face and giving an airy wave of her hand as they came together.

"Hello, Mrs. Tollemy," she said, extending her hand. "I'm Briana Brennan. Sorry to come unannounced, but I met Rippa down by the pond and he thought you might not mind if I came home with him to meet you."

Suspicion lingered in Mrs. Tollemy's stance and in her eyes, but she smiled cautiously and responded to Briana's handshake. "You're welcome here, miss. What brings ye out this way, after all?"

"Well, that's a long story, Mrs. Tollemy, and one that you might also want Mr. Tollemy to hear. Will he be coming in soon?"

Mrs. Tollemy glanced at the sun and then out to the field where her husband continued to plow, oblivious to their visitor. "Rippa, go fetch yer pa and tell him that it's near time for dinner and we have a guest."

Rippa dropped the pole and creel at his mother's feet and raced off. Sighing, Gertrude picked up the fishing tools. She glanced inside the basket and grinned, then beckoned Briana to follow her into the house.

Once inside Mrs. Tollemy stood the gear in a corner and then unwrapped the baby, who had begun to fret, and laid her in a nearby cradle. The cottage was efficiently furnished with the necessities of rural living, nothing more. The large space they were in served as kitchen, dining and living area. A primitive, well-made table graced the room. Sideboard and hutch stood catty-corner against one wall while a huge fireplace for heating and cooking took up the opposite wall, a small fire in its hearth. Built into the fireplace was a crane with several hooks on it. A black iron kettle swung empty on the outside, while another hung closer to the fire with something aromatic simmering within. Other pans and kettles were stored on well-built shelves. One wooden box beside the hearth held wood, another, peat. Shelves along the kitchen walls supported a menagerie of pottery dishes and serving bowls. Baskets of yarn, sewing and herbs were placed strategically around the room. The smell and feel of this homey place wrapped around her. *I could get used to this*, she thought, wistfully. Her future would likely be much different.

Gertrude bustled around, laying the table and filling bowls with food. Briana opened her mouth to offer help just as the door opened and was filled with Rodnner Tollemy, a hulking bear of a man in worn overalls and a slouchy, wide-brimmed hat. His weathered face wore an expression of suspicion, much as his wife's had at the start, but after a glance between husband and wife, the frown reversed and his cautious, narrow scrutiny turned more congenial as he extended his hand toward Briana.

"Our welcome to ye, milady. I know what Rippa here thinks yer doing around here all by yerself, but I would hear it from ye, I would."

"Rodnner," his wife said, setting a bowl of steaming potatoes on the table, "we'll hear the whole story as soon as we've all had something to eat."

Before Briana could respond, the whole family sat as one at the table. Rodnner immediately said, "To Maker we give thanks for this food and for the arrival of our new friend. May all be with us as you will it, and may we ever be grateful."

"And Maker," Rippa added, with the seriousness that only an innocent can impart, "please save our forests and our king." He sneaked a peek at his mother to see if he'd done wrong. She squeezed his hand and smiled reassuringly. His father just sighed and shook his head.

Out of the mouths of babes, Briana thought. *How will they react when I tell them I intend to do just that?*

The food tasted every bit as good as it smelled and Briana must have praised the cook at least five times while she ate. After the dishes were cleared away, the family moved nearer the hearth. Baby Penelope settled in tight to Mama for her meal. Rodnner brought up a seat for Briana next to the fire and poured her a cup of something homebrewed and mellow. The noise of pleasure she made as the foamy liquid slid down her throat was more than enough compliment for its brewer.

"Best in the county," he bragged, as he raised his cup to her. Gertrude slapped him lightly on the shoulder with a wink. "But now that we've filled our bellies with the wife's good cooking, would ye tell us your story, milady? What brings ye out to the country?"

Briana took a deep breath, wondering just how one does tell such a tale. "This may all be very hard for you to believe, but hear me out, please, before you kick me out as some kind of crackpot."

"Crackpot?" Rippa said. They all looked at her queerly, obviously not understanding the term.

She smiled, then went on and told her story from beginning to end. Their faces changed as the story unfolded, from amazement that she came through a tree, to wonder that she was the Mouse of Prophecy, to anger at Shamwa, and ultimately to hope that she could save Uisneach and its king.

For a moment after the telling, everyone was quiet, and then Rippa, screwing up his face, asked again, "But what I still want to know is, What's a 'crackpot'?" The collective laugh that followed broke the serious mood. Briana made a twirling motion with her finger at her temple, making her meaning plain enough.

"Milady, 'tis not enough for me to say that we thank ye for what you're doing," Rodnner said. "I don't know what we can do to help, but our home will always be open to ye for any reason. Whatever we can do to help, ye just let us know. For sure ye'll stay the night with us; there's no reason to return to your journey until the morning."

"Thank you. I'm grateful for your hospitality and your support. To be honest, I have no real plan and don't know what I might need, but I would definitely call on you if I need to."

He nodded, and then grabbing his hat and giving his wife a quick kiss on the cheek, headed back out to the fields, throwing Rippa's hat to him on the way with a nod of his head that said the boy was to come along and help.

Briana spent the rest of the afternoon helping Gertrude with household chores. She was given some bed linens and shown to a little loft area where she would spend the night. As she puttered around the house and garden, she took the time to really think about her plan. She'd pull the map out tonight and plot a course. If the map was going to change at every junction, she'd at least need a general direction. Perhaps Rodnner would have some useful thoughts about this, as well. Unlike Alice's journey through Wonderland, Briana did care where she was going and it did matter which way she went.

The afternoon passed pleasantly. Supper, a smaller but equally satisfying meal, came and went. Rodnner provided information about Uisneach and some helpful advice about things to find and things to avoid. Briana learned more about the Tollemy family as they shared more of the homemade brew. Originally from Cedarmara, they'd moved to the country under King Barclay's subsidized farming program.

"The city was growing so fast at that time. It was no place to raise a family, so we took advantage of the program to start a new life out here."

"Did you build this entire farm yourselves?"

"Sure we did, over time. The missus was young and strong back then. Between us, we put up the cottage, the barns and plowed and planted the fields."

Gertrude swatted at him playfully. "Are ye saying I'm not young and strong now, old man? And what about ye? Yer no spring chicken then, are ye?"

Raising his mug to his wife, he continued. "Overall, 'tis been a good life, at least until Shamwa started his shenanigans. Since then we've spent more time looking over our shoulder for the Gray Military and less time making the trip to Cedarmara to sell our produce. Not easy makin' a livin' that way, ye know?"

She could only imagine. "Where is the army now?"

"Hard to say. They don't stay all together, but are sent off in small divisions to search the land and collect taxes." He sighed. "We've worked so hard and things was so good under the king's reign. Both kings was good men and cared for the people of Uisneach. Shamwa is just plain evil. We'd hoped to build something here that could sustain us and the children as they grew up. Thought maybe other families would move out and farm here. It's so rich and fertile. But no one's movin' anywhere right now. I don't think anyone holds much hope that we'll survive this invasion of Shamwa's. At least I didn't, until now."

Briana offered an encouraging smile. "You'll make those trips to Cedarmara again, Rodnner." She prayed it was true. "Have you ever met either of the kings personally?"

Gertrude answered. "We did once when we was given the title to the land from King Barclay. He was a real gentleman, King Barclay was. The weight of a kingdom on his shoulders, and ye'd have thought he had nothing better to do than to offer us high tea. He said he meant to come out someday and pay us a visit when we had things going, but he died before that happened. His son, King Brath, did come here once, unexpectedly. Can ye believe that? I'll never forget the day, seeing this man ride up on his big horse. He had another man with him. I couldn't imagine who they might be, and was a little nervous. I was home alone with Rippa, who was just takin' his first steps. The bigger man got down off his stallion and introduced himself as King Brath. Handsome man he was – the spittin' image of his pa. You couldn't mistake that dark red hair. He introduced his man as Sigel, his lord marshall. That man, Sigel, was more solemn, real serious about his duty. I remember he had a long scar down the side of his face that was all red and puckered-like, which was too bad, seein's how he was a fine-looking man otherwise. He had hair as black as night, longish, but tied in a knot on his head. Don't know why that particular thing sticks in my memory. The king said he knew of his father's intention to come see us and since his father's death, he was riding around the country to meet the people of Uisneach. Of course I offered my sympathy on his father's passin' and he smiled kindly and thanked me saying, 'I hope I can be half the man and king he was.' Gracious to the core, that one is. His father raised him up right, that he did. Anyway, Rodnner had come home by then and they stayed for tea. I never been so nervy fixin' tea as I was that day. Servin' to the king – oh my goodness, was I ever nervy. One thing I'll not forget is that while I was preparing things, the king was playing with wee Rippa. He had a shiny black coin that he kept flippin' in the air, makin' Rippa laugh out loud. His man, Sigel, was a little less, uh, playful I guess, but he smiled some and was kindly enough. I wonder what ever did happen to him when King Brath was cursed."

The cottage was quiet, everyone thinking about the king and all that had happened. The fireplace lent a protective glow to ward off the shadows, and Rodnner hoisted his fiddle to lighten things up. Rippa joined him, playing a small guitar-like instrument and singing. His angelic voice surprised Briana, his ability to tell a story through song, even more remarkable. *A little bard in the making,* she thought. Some of the songs told the story of this island. Briana grew pensive. Everything was so perfect and peaceful here; she'd never forget this evening with the Tollemys. *This was how life should be – and would be – if she had anything to do about it.*

"Now you rest, milady. Me and the missus will take turns standing watch," said Rodnner.

Gertrude smoored the fire for the night, covering the embers with ash to subdue the flames without putting them out. Brianna said her good nights and went up to bed.

Night settled around the home as Briana buried herself deep into the quilts, content and relaxed for a time. Until she thought she heard the wind picking up in the trees. Maybe it was an animal foraging for food in the straw thatch of the roof that caught her attention, but the hair on the back of her neck suddenly rose and she was wide awake. She listened closely to the household sounds. It was eerily quiet, except for a small scuffling somewhere near her. *Try to relax*, she told herself, and began to quote from fairy tales. Her litany began with Rapunzel, moved to Cinderella and then to a few nursery rhymes. When she recalled the queen wanting to lop heads, she stopped herself. *Oh, this is ridiculous*, she thought, *you're scaring yourself silly, you ninny*. She sat up, grabbing the blade resting under her pillow.

Wrong move. Out of the darkness a cloth-covered hand came across her face, smothering the scream that was just forming. Another pair of hands grabbed and held her feet. Futilely, she tried to kick the intruder. They dragged her violently out of her bed. She began to feel woozy. Through the window, she noticed the waning crescent moon. *Chloroform?* she wondered. It was her last clear thought.

CHAPTER SIX

DUNGEONS AND DEMONS

Returning to a semi-conscious state reminded Briana of the time she woke from anesthesia following the extraction of her wisdom teeth. She heard things before she saw them, and knew things before she knew she knew them. And the first thing she knew was that she was alone in a dark place. The second thing was that her abductors were nearby, because she could hear them.

"Watcha think His Lordship will do with her?" a whiny man asked.

"I know what I'd do with her," a man with a cruelly suggestive voice answered. There was a pause, some disturbing noises and then laughter.

They spoke of inconsequential matters for a while. She started thinking of the whiny goon as Winkle, the other as Wonk.

"Ya think anyone followed us?" asked Winkle. "He won't be happy if sumpin' goes wrong here."

"Nah, the old man's in pretty rough shape. He won't bother us."

Briana winced. If they'd done anything to hurt the Tollemys, she'd make them pay. She was coming out of her stupor enough to realize she needed to come out quicker. Briana began feeling around her. The floor was cold and hard, as were the walls. Stone? *I'm in a dungeon*, she concluded, and felt relieved when she realized she was not bound by manacles or any other device. *Thank God, uh, Maker, for small favors.* Coming more fully awake, she noticed a small window high up in the chamber that let in a glimmer of light as a crescent moon inched into the frame. So probably not a dungeon; it wouldn't have a window. She was freezing, dressed only in an undershirt and leggings. The knife she kept tucked in the leggings was also gone, leaving her weaponless.

As she considered the difficulty – no, impossibility – of getting through the window, the door opened. Light from the outer room backlit a short, bulky man. He lit the rushes. Thick, muscular limbs made up for his lack of stature, making him easily capable of carrying her away from the farm. He lumbered over next to her and she scooted back as far as she could, not out of fear, but to get away from his smell. The man clearly hadn't bathed in some time and the whiff of onion and garlic on his breath was an effective deterrent from any ideas of cozying up to him, which she'd considered, given that neither of them sounded too swift, and might be cajoled into letting her go.

A brutish hand reached out and touched her hair. "His Lordship has no idea what he's got hisself," Wonk mused. She watched the expression on his face and knew he was wondering whether or not he could get away with sampling the wares before "His Lordship" arrived. One of his hands meandered down to the front of his trousers in a rubbing motion. She shuddered.

Any idea of trying to take him on was squashed when Winkle entered. "Don't git no ideas about her," he warned Wonk. "Lord Shamwa could show up at any minute and he'd be pretty mad to find his pris'ner was mussed up by the likes of us. He wants that fun to hisself."

He pushed his way in front of Wonk. "Say, youz the Mouse they all be talkin' about? A course ya are," he crooned. "Do youz believe in the prophecy? You plan on savin' King Brath?" At that, both men laughed hysterically. Winkle bent down until his pointy, features were squarely in her face. "Never happen, girly," he jeered, spittle flying from his lips to her cheek, which she instantly wiped off.

"Shamwa ain't gonna let that happen," he said. "Youz got a dif'rent kind of future now, girly." Winkle and Wonk laughed again.

"Come on, let's leave her stew," Wonk said, grabbing the other by the shoulder, and turning him toward the door. "His Lordship could come at any moment and then we'll get to see some fun."

"You'll see nothing, because rest assured, I will be saved," she finally said, in the most commanding voice she could summon. "And you will be severely dealt with."

"She talks," Winkle said merrily. "Wasn't sure you could. Thought mebbe you was dumb."

"The only dumb ones around here are you two thugs."

"Thugs?" Winkle looked at his partner. "What's that?"

"Dunno, but it can't be good. Think she needs a lesson in manners," Wonk said. He backhanded her across the face. "I'm sure His Lordship won't mind if we learn ya how to behave properly."

"Bastard," she blurted, earning her another, harder slap on her cheek. This time she held her tongue.

"Ah, you gets it," Winkle said, looking pleased. "Youz just sit tight and think about that, cuz for sure, Lord Shamwa will give you more if youz think of misbehavin'."

They tittered their way out into the hallway, leaving Briana in the dark again, cold and more worried than ever. She had to escape. She glanced up again at the window in time to catch a flash of metal in the moonlight and a flutter of black wings lifting in flight.

"Wait!" she cried, but the crow disappeared, along with most of her hope.

She sat on the hard bench, her head in her hands, avoiding the swollen and painful part of her cheek. Considering her options didn't take long, as she didn't have many. *Kill myself? I've got nothing to do it with, since these goons stole my knife. Wait and pray someone would arrive to save the day? Isn't it my job to be the heroine?*

What had the crow been doing here, and who was he? He kept showing up at the oddest times. His appearance had to mean something. Lacking answers to her questions, she moved on to a consideration of what her storybook friends might do. Alice would find a magic potion to make her small enough to shimmy through the window. Peter would send Tinker Bell for help. Dorothy could throw Toto out the window so he could go find help somewhere. Rapunzel could use her hair as a ladder. Queen Elsa would simply make an ice ramp to escape. Standing next to the window, Briana reached up, but even on tippy toes, she couldn't touch the bottom sill. She sighed. *Where was a magical hero when you needed one?*

With each passing moment, she grew increasingly aware that Lord Shamwa might arrive. This became the sole thought in her brain when she heard scratching on the rock outside the window. "Hello. Is someone there?" she whispered.

She didn't expect a response and was well beyond surprised to hear Rippa Tollemy murmur back, "I'm here, milady. Shush now, and I'll get youz out in a couple of shakes."

She was stunned. "Is anyone with you, Rippa?"

"Milady, please be quiet. We don't want thems to hear us, right?"

He was right, of course, so she held her questions. Instead, she paced back and forth between the door and the window, listening for her abductors and trying to figure out what Rippa was doing. A little grunt and the child's scruffy head appeared, silhouetted in the window frame. His arm came over the sill and tossed down a corded rope to her.

"Now, hold on a sec. I'm going back down and tie this tight. Then ye can climb out. Youz can squeeze through the window, cantcha? Yer pretty small; I think you can do it."

"I can, Rippa. Just tell me when."

Not more than thirty seconds went by and she heard him speak again. "All right now, milady. Come on, careful-like."

She wasted no time putting one foot in front of the other onto the knots on the rope. Her training with Jack paid off, and in another few seconds she was squeezing through the window and heading down the other side. She didn't bother to use all the knots on the outside wall, but went down two lengths and jumped lithely to the ground next to Rippa. She squeezed him in a bear hug. He giggled, then pulled away. "No time for that, milady. We gotta get outta here fast."

They sprinted into the darkness as far as their lungs would carry them before stopping, out of breath.

"We did it!" Briana exclaimed. "Oh, Rippa, how can I ever thank you? I can't believe you did that. How did you know where I was? Does anyone know where you are? Did..."

His hands rose up to protest her barrage of questions. "The short of it is that I heard something from the loft and got worried, so I snuck up just as those ruffians was dragging youz out. I went to get Pa, but he was knocked out. Then I seen the crow and he made like he wanted me to follow 'im, so I did. Those guys who took ye, they were faster'n me, but the crow kept flying back and forth between them and me, so he really brought me to youz. What a good bird that'n is."

"Indeed he is," she replied. "Tell me, Rippa, do you know about that crow?"

"Nah, but I thought he was here to help us. Sometimes you just knows these things, know what I mean?"

"Yeah, I do, Rippa. You are so brave to have done this all by yourself." She hugged him again. "I'll never forget this, my friend. I might make you a knight or something when I'm the queen."

He smiled sheepishly. "I don't need no honors. I just wanted to help."

Briana smiled and bowed her head. "Thank you, Rippa. That means a lot to me. Now, we have to go check on your parents, and then I need to leave right away, because I'm sure those goons will come back and I don't want your family to suffer again for protecting me."

"Can't I go with youz?" he asked, hopefully.

She shook her head. "Rippa, I would be proud to have you on this journey with me, but your parents need you and would be heartbroken if I took you with me. You have to go home, but someday you'll come to the castle and there will be a place for you." As the words were uttered, she realized she believed them. She had turned some invisible corner and knew this was her world now, no turning back to the world she lived in as Brianna Edwina Brennan. The girl without a plan, the one with a ticking biological clock, was a thing of her past. She was the future Queen of Uisneach for better or worse, and Rippa's family were not only her friends, but her responsibility. She'd make sure they were safe and well cared for. She'd see him safely home and retrieve the map and her belongings. Then she'd be immediately on her way.

They ran as long as they could, and walked fast when they needed to catch their breath. The first sight of the cottage, lit up like a jack-o'-lantern, made her happier than she'd ever been before.

Rodnner burst out the door. "Where on earth have ye two been?" he yelled. "Beggin' your pardon, milady, but we were worried sick when we realized those ruffians got ye."

They got you first, she thought, wincing at his black eye.

Briana touched his shoulder gently and nodded. "I can only imagine, Rodnner, and I am so, so sorry. I was kidnapped by Shamwa's thugs. Your son rescued me." His jaw dropped and he stared, wordless, at her. She gave him a gentle nudge. "Shall we go inside? We'll tell you the whole story, but quickly. They have no reason to believe I've come back here, and I don't want them to find me anywhere close to your family."

Briana ran upstairs to dress and collect her belongings. By the time she returned, Gertrude Tollemy had breakfast on the table. "I'll not send you out without a full belly," she said. "You'll need strength."

As Brianna wolfed down scrambled eggs, warm rolls and stewed fruit, Rippa told the story of her escape. Rodnner and Gertrude kept looking with amazement and admiration at their little boy.

"I'm so sorry I've endangered you," said Briana.

"Never ye mind," replied Rodnner. "Never in my wildest dreams would I have thought we'd any part to play in saving King Brath and Uisneach, but I see now we do and ye can rest assured, milady, that if Shamwa shows up here, we'll send them as far away from ye as we can. Go with our blessing and our gratitude and our hope that someday, when Uisneach thrives under yer reign, we'll see ye again."

"You will, and when that day comes, you will be rewarded for your loyalty and heroism." She looked specifically at Rippa. "I may not be a queen yet, but all things considered, I think I can claim the power and authority to bestow an official title." She automatically reached for the dagger in her belt, before remembering it was gone. "Thank you," she said as Rodnner handed her his.

"Ye'll need it, milady. I've got another."

With great ceremony, she tapped Rippa on both shoulders and the crown of his head with the knife. "I, Briana, the future queen of Uisneach, confer upon you, Ripparivendar Tollemy, the title of Sir Ripparivendar, Protector of the Queen, from this day henceforth."

Rippa beamed with pride and Gertrude clutched her heart, sighing with delight. "Yer presence in our home is reward enough. Maker bless ye, milady."

Briana hugged them all and left quickly, racing across the Tollemy homestead to find the path just inside the wood line. Five minutes later, she came to a crossroads. Extracting the map from the pocket in her leggings, she studied it in the marginal light of early morning. Both trails led to Tynan Ibor. The narrower, twisting path went through what appeared to be some overgrown orchards; on the map, gnarly trees twisted a little ferociously. *They'll expect me to take the easier route*, she decided. She rolled the map and put it back in her pocket. *The trees might look spooky, but what could they do to her?* She was startled by a sound and saw, perched in an old oak tree, the crow with the shiny medallion.

"Who are you? I know you have something to do with all of this, but I don't know what." The crow blinked and cawed vociferously. "Have I chosen the wrong way? Should I go back?" Crow hopped a bit and then jumped to the next tree ahead. "I'll take that as a sign I'm headed right." The bird flew forward a few more trees, looked back at her, bobbed his head and blinked and then lifted off, leaving her alone again, positive she was going in the right direction.

CHAPTER SEVEN

YOU DON'T WANT ANY
OF THEM APPLES

Briana negotiated a narrow path littered with tree roots and boulders, on grades ranging from flat to hilly to very steep. Her footwear seemed to magically conform to both foot and earth and was quite comfortable. At least she wouldn't be incapacitated by blisters. She was grateful for the gnomes' craftsmanship and wilderness survival skills.

Now, more mindful of the real dangers of this undertaking, she considered different scenarios and how she might react, thinking about resources she might need. She found a piece of flexible grapevine that might serve as rope and hooked it to her knapsack. She now knew firsthand how handy a rope could be. She grew more alert to the tiny noises around her and scanned for the minutest movement in the shrubs. Field mice and tiny birds, thankfully.

When the sun spiked at its zenith, she took some bread and cheese from her pack and ate alongside a brook with cold, clear water.

My mother must be as frantic as the Tollemys were when they discovered me missing, she thought. She closed her eyes for a moment as her throat closed up. There was nothing she could do to allay her mother's fears. If she focused on that, she might well get herself killed.

Briana checked the map again and didn't notice any changes, so she repacked her sack and continued on.

The surrounding trees thinned, allowing sunlight to warm her face, lifting her spirits. She soon found herself in a meadow of spring flowers, their floral essence saturating the air. In what seemed a constantly changing landscape, the path began to climb slightly up stone steps to a ridge. Unable to see ahead, she approached slowly and carefully, mindful of each ancient stone her foot touched. She wondered who'd taken the time to carve these natural stairs into the hill. At the top she paused again, looked around, but observed only an overgrown orchard in front of her. The path seemed to go straight through the grove. Although she remembered the map's image of some unfriendly trees, these stood as serenely as old apple trees usually do. Surely their bent and gnarly trunks and branches were only evidence that they had been around for a long time. A barred owl startled her as he flew out of the cavity of an old oak, hooting his displeasure at her interruption. Other than the owl, she neither heard nor saw anything sinister as she walked casually into the orchard. She came to a small clearing and stopped abruptly when she spied a small herd of deer eating apples along the clearing's edge. They became aware of her and stood to attention. A face-off followed, no one moving for several moments. Briana blinked when she saw them look at each other and begin to whisper something. The largest of the deer, with magnificent eight-point antlers, took a few tentative steps toward her. "Are you the one they call Mouse?"

At first she was too shocked to speak. The stag canted his head and waited patiently for her to respond.

"I... well, yes, I am," she replied. "You can talk." If a deer could raise its eyebrows, this one did. "My apologies, sir. I'm not accustomed to animals talking to me."

He only nodded his acknowledgment. "We assume you travel to Ard Darach to rescue King Brath."

"I do."

"Then we shall do what we can to lead you safely through this orchard. These trees are cursed. If they should awaken and discover who you are and what you're doing, they'll attack you."

"What would cause them to wake up?"

"Picking one of the apples might. We deer know which trees we can approach safely, so they don't bother us much. If you please, walk between us and let us escort you through. It may be enough to prevent them from recognizing you."

At his signal, the other deer nonchalantly moved around her and as one unit they began to move forward along the path. Briana, at the buck's instruction, stopped talking. The herd stopped and grazed cautiously when a tree made a motion or waved a branch. She stood as still as stone, barely breathing. The does moved closer to her in a protective embrace, gently blowing apple-scented breath.

They were within a stone's throw of the orchard's edge when a tree jerked to life, its widespread boughs thrashing. The buck turned to Briana and whispered, "Run, Mouse. Go now!"

The deer tried to distract the tree by splitting up and sprinting in circles through the orchard. Ignoring the tactic, the tree zeroed-in on Briana. It thrust out one leafy branch and grabbed her by the throat, squeezing violently. She gasped, unable to breathe. She tore at the branch with one hand, searching for her dirk with the other. Just as she found the knife, the tree knocked it from her. Her legs were soon bound, holding her prisoner against its rough trunk. Through blurry eyes, she made out a grimacing face in the bark of the tree, with a grim, barky slash of a mouth, its menacing stare blazing into her very soul. *Oh my Maker*, she thought, *these things are really powerful!* Her only recourse was to play dead and hope the tree loosened its clench, allowing her to slip free. She willed her body to relax. As soon as she felt the branch ease up, she took the opportunity to refill her lungs with air before lunging forward, but it was useless. The moment she moved, the branch tightened again. By now all the other trees around them twisted in a frenetic and indeed ferocious dance of anger. She continued to fight and wiggle in an attempt to break away, but believed it was pretty hopeless. Unless another miracle occurred, King Brath would stay in his cursed prison and her mother would never know what happened to her only daughter.

Something whizzed by her head. The tree grunted and loosened its grip. Without thinking, she ripped herself away and ran like the wind. In seconds the orchard was behind her and she knew she was safe. She fell to the ground, trying to catch her breath.

"Milady," a man said, next to her.

She shrieked. Scrambling on all fours, she tried to move away, but the man spoke again, more firmly this time. "Mouse, stop. I won't hurt you. You're safe."

She brushed hair out of her eyes. As soon as she saw his scar and the knot of dark hair at the back of his head, she relaxed. "You're Sigel," was all she could get out, still breathless from her fright and flight.

The big man kneeled next to her. "Yes, I'm Sigel, the king's lord marshall. You must be Milady Mouse." Using hands that were surprisingly gentle for their size, he began to pluck the leaves and branches out of her hair. "Okay, now?"

She nodded, gathering her wits and her strength to stand. While she wouldn't have called him handsome, per se, as Gertrude Tollemy had, he was arresting, with his raven hair and the vivid scar running down the right side of his face into a dark beard that gave him a fearsome look. His eyes, though, were dark and kind. She believed him when he said that she was all right.

"What happened back there?" asked Briana. "What did you do to the tree? Where are the deer?"

"Just a simple hatchet through its branch. It'll live. The deer weren't injured. They ran off."

"Thank you, Lord Sigel. You saved my life. The deer tried to guide me through the orchard without waking the trees. Oh! I didn't thank them."

He looked surprised. "Thank them?"

"Of course. They said they would help me get through the orchard and they did try, but…"

"You talked to them?"

"Well, yes, but they talked to me first. Is that unusual?"

Sigel's eyes narrowed thoughtfully. "It's not unheard of, but very few people have the ability to communicate with animals."

"How did you know I was here?"

He smiled. "Word is getting around. I, and many others, have spent years waiting for you to arrive. Will you allow me the privilege of serving you as I would serve my own king, milady, and let me bring you to Ard Darach?"

Uncertain about the etiquette for interacting with a member of a royal entourage, Briana bent in a brief, clumsy curtsy and nodded. "I'll be grateful for your protection, lord marshall, and your company."

He looked overhead. "We probably won't make it much farther today. We should start looking for a place to camp for the night."

They went only a short way before finding a fairly hidden spot in some pines near a clear running brook.

She watched Sigel dig a hole and then a smaller one beside it that tunneled into the main hole. Inside the larger cavity he piled dried leaves, bark and small twigs. Soon he had a fire going that would give them heat and a little light, but would not be seen by anyone outside their camp.

"I've never seen that done. What's the second hole for?"

"It allows air into the fire and makes it burn hot and almost smokeless. We'll not cook tonight, though," he said, handing her a strip of dried meat. "The smell could attract unwanted attention."

Briana pulled out Genevieve's bread and added that to the evening's meal. While they ate they talked, keeping their voices low. She summarized all that had happened to date and when she finished with her rescue from Shamwa's men, he shook his head.

"They don't sound like Gray Military at all. Shamwa's army is made up mostly of descendants of the Moherians. They're big men, warriors by nature. Not terribly bright, mind you, but there's no one to compare for brute strength. They integrated into Uisneach culture over the generations, but it doesn't take much to spur to war. The chaos created by Shamwa's betrayal was just enough to bring them to his side. The men you describe don't fit; they're just a couple of his henchmen."

"Well, luckily, they weren't too competent." She pulled her cloak a little closer around her shoulders. "Tell me about Shamwa. Why does he hate King Brath so much?"

Sigel leaned back against the rock behind him. "Brath and Shamwa are as different as night and day. Brath wants to take Uisneach forward, build harbors to increase trade between us and other lands, and work with the faeries to bring magic back into the world. Shamwa, on the other hand, believes that by opening borders between lands, we make ourselves vulnerable and risk losing power.

"You have to understand that Shamwa is consumed with the desire to be powerful, and to that end, would levy heavy tax and rent burdens on the people in order to increase his own wealth."

"But that makes the people of Uisneach poorer and ultimately weakens the kingdom instead of strengthening it," she replied, recalling Genevieve Wells' words.

"Exactly." Sigel nodded. "Brath tried every way to Sunday to explain that to him, but Shamwa wouldn't listen. Personally, I think Brath worked too hard to try to get Shamwa to see reason, when he should have just exiled or killed him."

Briana frowned. "That seems extreme."

"Some people who crave power for its own sake will hurt or destroy anyone or anything that stands in their way. Shamwa is one of those people. Had King Barclay not been so determined to include many voices among his advisors, Shamwa would never have gotten this far. I do understand Barclay's and Brath's reasoning, though."

"Keep your friends close and enemies closer."

Sigel nodded. "It's a reasonable approach, but the risk is that your enemy can scheme behind your back and ruin you, as Shamwa did. At the time, Brath didn't really consider Shamwa an enemy, just a…"

"A disgruntled employee," she finished for him. "So why is he after me?"

Sigel looked sideways at her. "Because you represent a possible threat to his plan, for starters. I'm guessing he knows about the prophecy and thinks if he controls you, he controls the prophecy. He'd be able to lift the curse and finish killing Brath. Besides, if he thinks you're meant for Brath, he'll want you for himself."

"He sounds like a real jerk," she said. "He's got another thing coming, if he thinks I can be had that easily. I'm not a piece of property for anyone's pleasure."

He looked down at his lap. "You do know that part of this prophecy says that you are meant to marry the king?"

"Well, yes, but…"

"There are no buts, milady," Sigel said firmly, looking back up at her.

"The prophecy is clear about that point. The Mouse will marry the King of Uisneach and their children carry on the Taranian line."

Shivering, Briana fumbled around in the knapsack for the tent. "Where will you sleep, Lord Sigel? I was given this tent to camouflage myself at night, but do I really need it, with you here? Or…" she was running out of words to get her meaning across.

"I'll sleep by the fire, milady, but I think you should put up your little shelter so you might have some privacy. I'll keep watch."

She nodded and began to unfold and arrange the fabric. Sigel raised the water bag to his mouth. When she climbed in to test it, virtually disappearing, Sigel choked and sputtered. She stepped out again. "Oh yeah, I forgot to tell you – it's a magical tent from the gnomes."

Sigel stroked his beard as he studied the contraption. "Clever fellows, those gnomes."

Not yet ready to sleep, she sat back down and asked him about himself. She learned he had come from a long line of marshalls who had served kings for many generations, and that he'd begun training when he was only four years old.

"Did you never want to do something else with your life?" she asked.

"Never did." He reached for another piece of bread. "This land's been blessed with some great kings and has gone centuries without having a war. Being lord marshall to the king means having an opportunity to help him work on things to keep the land prosperous.

"Were we more warlike, maybe the job wouldn't be so appealing, but I've been honored and happy to be a part of King Barclay and King Brath's reigns."

"If you haven't had any battles, then how –" She stopped, embarrassed by her question, but unable to force her eyes away from the damaged flesh along his cheek. He understood and with a light laugh answered the unasked question.

"It was no big act of bravery that caused the wound, sad to say. My scar resulted from childhood foolishness. When Brath and I were young men, we hoped for a war; all young men do, I suppose. We battled each other to hone our warrior skills. When we fought, we held nothing back. One day, we were dueling with daggers along the castle wall, which was a good fifty feet from the ground. You'd have thought we'd have better sense than to be prancing around and jabbing at each other up there, but like most young men, we had more sass than sense. In the middle of the duel, which I'm very sure I was winning, Brath thrust his knife, and when I jumped to avoid the hit, I slipped off the wall. My fall was broken by a big oak tree. Though it prevented a harder landing, one of the limbs scraped down the side of my face and laid it wide open." He laughed at the memory, but she noticed a glimmer of pain, too. "I screamed like a baby and everyone came running. Blood was pouring down the side of my face. The women thought I'd been killed. Brath came running down around the wall and was shaking all over for fear he'd mortally wounded me. 'I'm so sorry, Sigel, so sorry. Don't die, please don't die.'" His voice dripped melodrama as he tried to portray the prince's angst. Briana giggled.

"It's amusing now, but I can tell you for several weeks after the accident, there was no laughing. The wound became infected and nearly did take my life. Brath and I were both punished, but I know for a fact the punishment meted out by King Barclay was nothing compared to the punishment Brath put on himself. He's never gotten over it. I'm sure that he feels bad every time he looks at me.

"He's got a good heart and a powerful sense of justice. I like to think that maybe our misadventures contributed to his sense of humility and compassion. It's what makes him such an excellent king, and why we have to break this damned enchantment and restore him to the throne."

"When King Brath is freed, what will happen to Lord Shamwa and the Gray Military?"

"Milady, there's only one way this is going to end. Even if you, and probably Brath, find it distasteful, Shamwa must be killed, or he'll continue his efforts to overthrow Brath and control this land for his own despicable purposes."

"Can you kill Shamwa?"

Sigel picked up a small branch lying near the fire and snapped it in two pieces. "Just like that. Brath is brave, but he isn't ruthless. I can be, and I won't hesitate to kill if it means protecting those I care about. I guess that's why I'm the warrior of the two of us, and he's the ruler."

"So why haven't you killed Lord Shamwa?"

"Because of the prophecy. You're the one who is supposed to save the king. Nowhere in there does it say Shamwa is killed before that happens. Besides, we don't know exactly what role he plays in releasing Brath, and I don't want to take any chances until the king is back on the throne. The best I've been able to do is to keep troops together and trained to push the Gray Military back. Shamwa's been off limits until now."

"How much military do you command, Lord Sigel, and, just curious, will they be coming to help us?"

"Our army numbers in the few thousands at the moment, spread across Uisneach to try and keep order. Now that you've arrived, they've been alerted and are on their way. The plan is to meet at the Dromdara Mountains. We'll meet a few small units along the way, and I suspect Silas will be along shortly. We'll recruit more men from the towns we pass through. We want as many men as possible when we get to Ard Darach. It is certain that the prime minister will try and meet us there with his own military."

"Who is Silas?"

"The Royal Bard. He is the only one, besides me, that escaped the castle before the enchantment. I ordered him to come with me to help catch the druid, Artanin, and the rest of the knights to stay and protect Brath." Regret darkened his features. "Anyway… milady, we'll want to start early in the morning. Why don't you get some sleep?"

She nodded. "Sigel, thank you for everything today. I would be dead if not for you. The king and the kingdom should be grateful for such a valiant defender as you."

Sigel had the grace to flush and lower his head. "Thank you, milady. I'm glad I could be there for you. I only hope Maker will see us both to Ard Darach soon, so we can release Brath. I'll say this to you, but deny it to him – I miss not only my king, but my best friend. I must thank you for accepting this quest to save him."

She waved his thanks away. "I'm not sure I actually did accept it. It seems like it accepted me. Lord Sigel, before we go any further, could you do me one favor?"

"Of course, milady. What can I do?"

"My name is Briana Brennan. Could you please call me Briana and not Mouse, and most certainly not milady?"

"But you are the Mouse; why does it trouble you?"

"I've been called Mouse since childhood, but I've outgrown it. And milady is way too formal. I hate being treated like royalty. There's been way too much of that already. Just Briana, if you please."

He rubbed his beard. "You are royalty. You will be queen, and it wouldn't be right for me to address you so familiarly."

"At the moment, we are partners on a journey to save the king. If it turns out I'm actually going to be queen, then I'll reconsider. Besides, you call the king by his first name. I would like the same courtesy from someone who might become my first-in-command." She offered her hand. He took it and the deal was made. It was a nice thought to be this man's partner, and even better thinking they might become friends.

As she stepped inside the tent, she heard him whisper to himself, "You'll make him a wonderful queen."

Her stomach clenched. *I cannot think about that now. One day at a time.*

Oblivion claimed her quickly, but temporarily. She woke to the back and forth hooting of owls and other sounds of night and wondered if Sigel had fallen asleep. She poked her head out of her shelter and saw he was wide awake, stretched out by the fire, with his back against a log.

"A bit eerie, seeing just your head pop out of nowhere."

"Kind of cool, isn't it?" she responded, crawling out to sit next to him by the fire.

He cocked his head. "I'm not sure what you mean."

Briana was reminded that her slang wouldn't always be understood. "Interesting or fun."

"Then yes, I suppose it is rather... cool. Can't sleep?"

"I did for a while, but now I'm awake. I was wondering, do you think the Gray Military can be reintegrated onto our side when we start rebuilding our army?"

Sigel's lips curved in a smile. "Our army, is it lass? Sounds like you're already stepping into the job."

"Oh, I don't know about that, but I certainly want to be on the winning team."

"I think if Lord Shamwa is destroyed, the Grays will simply transfer allegiance back to Brath. The problem is that treachery will always be their tendency. I doubt we can ever trust them." He paused. "Well there's exceptions. Sir Cruahan is a descendant of the Moherians and he is one of Brath's most faithful knights. Nothing and no one could make him betray his king."

She sighed. It seemed that in every world there was an element of terror that plagued whatever good might try to rule the day. She looked into the still, dark night. "Why don't you try to sleep and I'll keep watch."

He yawned and nodded. "Perhaps I could close my eyes for a bit. But if you hear or see anything unusual, wake me immediately. Understood?"

"I will, Sigel. Trust me, I'm no hero. If anything happens, you'll be the first to know."

He rolled onto his side and drew his cloak over him and in less time than it takes to say "kingdom of Uisneach," he was snoring.

As she watched the fire and occasionally threw another log on, she imagined this kind king whom she was meant to save. Sigel painted a picture of a man who was smart, compassionate and humble. Added to the physical description Gertrude Tollemy had provided, she was starting to imagine some kind of rock star. She wondered if the two of them would actually click. Again the jitters danced around in her belly. To distract herself, she took out her map and studied it. *Where are we, anyway?* She could see the terrible orchard on the map. Not too far ahead was another crossroads, and beyond that, Tynan Ibor, the dark forest. Should they go through this wild, dark wood? Luckily, she no longer had to decide on her own. Dromdara was still a long way away. This was no overnight trip for sure, but when they got to the castle and King Brath... her thoughts trailed off with the closing of her eyelids.

CHAPTER EIGHT

BEAUTY AND THE BEASTS

"**M**ilady, Briana, rise and shine. Time to be going."

Her eyes flew open to see Sigel sitting next to her, the pale light of dawn casting a rosy shadow on their camp. "I am so sorry, Sigel. I must have dozed off. A great guard I make."

"You've not been sleeping long."

"How do you know…" she said, then shook her head. "Did you get any rest?"

"All I needed."

"I have another question."

"Aye, what is it?"

"You said yesterday that word was getting around that I was here. How? If everyone is being kept apart, how do people know about me?"

He handed her an apple and some crusty bread to eat as he munched on his own.

"I hope the apple didn't come from one of those nasty old trees back in the orchard?"

"It did. I grabbed a couple before we ran. They owed us that much."

"When you put it that way…" She bit fiercely into the fruit.

"The crows."

"What?"

"The crows are spreading the word. They've been the only source of information between the kingdoms since the curse."

"So that crow I keep seeing is traveling all over Uisneach?"

"Well, you're probably referring to Sir Thomas, the clan chief of Winge Mansion. He's a shapeshifter. All of them can shift when they've a mind to."

She recalled the crow perched in the window of her cell. *Why the hell didn't he shapeshift and get me out?*

"May I have a look at your map?" Sigel asked, waving at the parchment on the ground. She must've dropped it when she drifted off. He pointed to a place marked Tynan Ibor. "Cailleach lives there. We'll stay with her a few days. She can teach you about the prophecy and the history of Uisneach. I warn you, they call it the dark forest for a reason. We'll have to move quietly and stay hidden as much as possible. Ready?"

She nodded eagerly, catching the satchel he threw her.

The path took them up and over ridges, down and around boulder piles, across a stream, straight up and through a minor mountain pass, then flat along some old-growth forest.

She and Sigel chatted easily as they journeyed. Quick-witted and thoughtful, Sigel helped her see Uisneach through his eyes, a homeland he'd die to protect. She learned he was older than Brath by eight years, an age gap that hadn't prevented the brotherhood that grew between them.

"I watched over him when he was in his nappies. As he grew older, we became inseparable, more like brothers. He is truly my brother and best friend."

Briana wanted to learn about Brath, but found her attention wandering, nevertheless.

"Forgive my interruption, Sigel, but there's something that's been weighing on my mind."

"Yes, milady?"

"My mother must be frantic, thinking I was kidnapped or worse. Is there any way we can contact her? I mean, you have magic here. Even some of the animals are magical."

He nodded. "Cailleach is a skilled witch. I think she'll be able to help." He smiled reassuringly. "Everything has happened just as the prophecy predicted, so that makes me believe it's real. You're meant to be here. I can't believe the Maker would cause your mother to suffer in order for us to benefit."

"Thank you, Sigel," she said, softly.

More dried meat and bread for supper, with a handful of nuts Briana found along the way. They shared watch that night by another well-protected fire. She was proud of herself when dawn broke and she was still awake and alert.

He stretched and yawned. "Well done, little warrior." She handed him a chunk of bread and apple. "I'm impressed. Were you accustomed to living outdoors where you came from?"

She shook her head, finishing the bite in her mouth before answering. "I've done some camping, not a lot. But I'm a horticulturist, a person who learns a lot about plants, so I have an idea of what things might grow wild." She explained her work as a landscaper.

"Ah." He grinned. "There just happens to be a garden too long untended at a castle that's gone way too long without a king or queen. Shall we continue on our adventure, little warrior-queen?"

"Let's do this," she said, with a small salute, and helped him break camp.

It was nearly mid-day, under a filmy sun, when a large flock of crows flew noisily overhead. Moments later, goose-like birds covered the sky, and minutes after that, a small herd of deer raced by. Sigel frowned as he scanned quickly around them. He put his finger to his lips, then directed her behind a large blowdown of pines. "Do you hear that?"

She didn't hear anything at first, but when she closed her eyes and concentrated, she realized she heard chopping.

"Let me see the map, please."

Briana pulled it out and handed it to him. He examined it for a few minutes, cocking his head every few seconds to listen, turning it in different directions as if that would somehow change things. More animals bolted past them, clearly startled by something happening to the west.

"What is it, Sigel?"

"I think we should take a little detour. Let's be cautious. If my suspicion is right, then some of Lord Shamwa's minions are about."

That meant danger. *Now is the time to act like a proper warrior.*

They unsheathed their weapons and moved as silently as forest owls, following the sound. Critters scooted by, birds screeched overhead, and soon the buzzing became a little louder.

At a fairly large brook at the bottom of a cascade, they had to choose whether to cross the river or climb up the hill to the ridgeline. Sigel asked for the map again. Human activity showed up in the area that seemed to be the source of the chopping noise, as expected.

"What do you think it is?"

"Probably a division of the Gray Military. Come on, we'll hike up to the ridge. Just before we reach the top, we'll stop and I'll scout." He started up, clearly expecting her to follow.

Steep pitches necessitated the use of sturdy trees and bushes to give them a handhold as they climbed. She lost her footing in one particularly difficult spot, but Sigel was quick to grab her arm and pull her up. By the time they reached the crest, the sun was completely obscured by clouds and a gray fog rolled in, allowing them to see over the ridgeline without being seen.

A group of about ten men dressed in blue-gray uniforms were gashing and hacking two faerie trees. Silvery bells and purplish leaves fell to the ground. No way could faeries live through this demolition.

She was repulsed but couldn't look away. Sigel touched her shoulder and indicated with a slight nod of his head that they should move back down.

Back at the brook, Sigel filled his water bag. "Drink up, little warrior. We need to move fast and put as much distance between them and us as possible."

Briana kneeled down and cupped the cold water to her mouth, letting its pure, fresh taste slake her thirst. Sigel guarded her, scanning the forest for any signs of trouble.

A thin veil of fog wafted through the forest, obscuring the sun and adding to the eerie sense of anticipation.

"Is there anything we can do to stop them?" Briana asked, rubbing the shivery goosebumps from her arms.

Sigel shook his head. "We've got to get our own army together to stop this. At the rate they're moving, there won't be a tree left on Uisneach in a year."

"When did they start?"

"It was one of the first things Lord Shamwa initiated after he cursed the king. He wanted to eliminate any potential resurgence of magic. Come, we've got to pick up our pace and get as far away as we can."

They continued on, Briana matching his longer strides with some effort until they came to a small mist-enshrouded glade. She halted abruptly, seeing a group of gray humps with green mantles huddled together in the center of the open space.

"Sigel?" she whispered. He seemed oblivious to the gathering.

"What is it?"

She nodded toward the gray mass. "Who are they?" she mouthed.

He turned to see what she was looking at, and laughed out loud. Taking her hand, he brought her to the cluster and placed it on what turned out to be moss-covered stone.

"Oh!" she breathed, putting her hand to her chest. "I thought they were people."

"Only their spirits," he said. "This place is called 'Druid's Grove.' Someone thought these stones looked like druids gathering for a ritual."

She nodded slowly. "I can see that."

Just when her heart rate returned to a normal rhythm, the forest exploded with loud screams and a blur of movement behind a stand of pines. They had barely enough time to unsheathe weapons and take a military stance before the Gray Military men fell upon them. She counted four, but it could have been more, as large bodies whirled around them in a frenzy. They tried to grab her. She jabbed and slashed with her dirk at everyone who came near her.

"Cathachurra!" Sigel howled back at them, simultaneously swinging his arm, his sword flashing. One man fell cleanly dead at his feet. Another came at him from the side. He waved his shining silver blade and feinted backward. Moving around sharply, Sigel stabbed the man, missing vital organs, but creating a leg wound that promptly started gushing red. The man screamed and fell to the ground, helpless. A burly brute grabbed Sigel by the neck and pulled a short but lethal dagger out of his pant leg.

Briana had no time to think. She threw her knife with all her might and miraculously hit the attacker's shoulder. He released Sigel, who jerked away and whirled around behind him, sinking his own sword into the back of the man's neck at the base of his skull, ending his life in an instant.

Sigel retrieved Briana's knife and threw it back to her. Stepping back, Briana lowered her weapon, but Sigel yelled at her. She turned to see a bull of a man with a round head, dark, angry eyes and a smashed bulbous nose, reaching for her. Before she could get her blade up, he seized her and held her roughly around the neck. She struggled, kicking him as hard as she could, but her efforts only made him laugh. One beefy arm came near her mouth. She bit down with all the strength she could muster. He howled in pain and for a split second, released her.

Another man called out, "Get down!" She dropped to the ground. An arrow winged so close over her head that she felt the air move through her hair. The arrow buried itself into the forehead of the beastly man, dropping him, too.

Then there was silence.

She moved away from the motionless body behind her, staying low, looking for Sigel. He rose and turned his attention to the man with the leg wound. Quietly and firmly he commanded Briana, "Turn around and look toward the pine trees."

She did as instructed without question. A slicing sound followed by a brief gurgling made her stomach recoil. After taking a deep breath, she turned around and saw that the man breathed no more.

"No reason to let him suffer," was all Sigel said. He pulled the arrow out of the head of the bulldog man, inspected the fletching and then said, "Silas, man, where are you?"

The most beautiful man she'd ever seen walked out of the mist, through the pines, slinging a quiver behind him as he moved around the stone druids and into the circle of carnage. Breath left her body. His knee-high leather boots made no sound as he strode with catlike grace toward Sigel. The kilt belted at his hips, a plaid of gray, rose, and brown, swung gracefully with each step. When the two came together in a hearty hug and some virile back slapping, she noticed he stood several inches taller than Sigel, and was more slender. A chill snaked up her spine. There was something remotely familiar about him.

"What took you so long?" asked Sigel.

"I was held up at Moiria."

Sigel laughed. "I'll bet you were. While you were at it, did you sign up any men?"

"Oh, aye. They'll be on their way to Dromdara whenever you give the word." He spoke with the throaty, rounded syllables of the Irish, the words comforting to her ear.

Civilities exchanged, they both turned to Briana. Sigel flourished in her direction. "Silas, this is the Mouse, or as she prefers to be called, Briana Brennan. Briana, may I introduce you to Silas of Cedarmara, our royal bard."

With courtly elegance, he bowed deeply to her. "And now, fully at your service, milady." His smile, generous, warm and perhaps a little roguish, put her immediately at ease. She responded with a full smile of her own.

"Please, Briana is fine," she said, not sure if she should shake his hand, curtsy or just swoon. His hair revealed every color of blonde in the palette and hung carelessly below his shoulders. Feathery bangs swept across his forehead, edging darker eyebrows. Dark blue eyes, deep pools of soulfulness, drew her in as one is drawn into a good story. Downward curving eyelids made him look a little sad, in spite of his warm smile. A hawkish nose guarded perfectly bow-shaped lips and slightly crooked front teeth. Underneath the light stubble of his beard, she noted a small dimple on his chin. *Old soul*, she decided, *old, drop-dead gorgeous soul*. She realized she might be staring like a schoolgirl with her first crush and was relieved when Sigel interrupted.

"How did you know where we were?"

"Followed the crow. He's been all over Uisneach."

"You can talk to him?" Briana was fascinated.

"Of course, when he's in human form," he replied, studying her as intently as she'd been watching him.

"That's so cool."

Silas looked puzzled. Sigel said, "She means something interesting or fun."

"Oh," Silas said, his beautiful lips forming a perfect circle with the word. "We should be goin'. There are more Grays not too far behind us. I suppose they can tend to their comrades."

Sigel nodded while Briana inhaled the lilting music of Silas's voice. To Silas he said, "I assume you're coming with us?"

Silas glanced at Briana and produced that enigmatic smile as he said, "Of course I am."

Chivalry is alive and well in Uisneach, she thought, as he held out his hand to help her over the log.

Hands touched… eyes connected… a flash… the world tilted. Two bright flames came together in one single explosion of light energy, an awakening of something ancient and eternal.

Her core shuddered when she saw the same soul recognition in his eyes. Destiny had just taken an unexpected detour on this journey.

CHAPTER NINE

A WEE ENDEARMENT

riana felt a stab of guilt as she looked around at the bodies they were leaving behind. But the stab turned into a gut punch when she turned back around and saw Silas' backside as he assumed the lead in their small group. An image exploded in her mind of a blonde-haired archer walking away from her on a battlefield. Her knees wobbled as the air whooshed out of her lungs.

"Milady," Silas asked, seeing her struggle to regain composure. "What's wrong?"

Sigel put his hands on her shoulders to brace her. "It's the shock of what just happened. Let's find you a place to sit and catch your breath."

She couldn't speak, could only stare at Silas in stunned awareness of why he seemed familiar to her. The faceless man had a face... and it was beautiful. *Silas...* she whispered in her heart, the name sounding like the answer to a prayer.

"You're him," she whispered.

"He's who?" asked Sigel.

She met Silas's eyes and saw a calm acknowledgment and something akin to satisfaction in the blue depths.

"He's who?" Sigel repeated, more brusquely.

She shivered and forced herself to look away from Silas. "It's nothing," she lied. This was a revelation meant only for herself and the bard. "You're probably right, Sigel, just a little delayed shock. I'm okay. Let's go."

After a searching look, Silas nodded and moved ahead of her again. Sigel took his post behind her, and they headed down the path.

Silence and stealth provided an opportunity for her to sort out the mish mash of emotions tumbling around inside her. The bard glanced behind with a tender smile, almost as though he knew what she was thinking.

They made their way quietly through the woods, staying a bit off the main path and out of sight. The men exchanged lead positions now and then, always keeping her between them. She compared the way the two men moved through the woods. Sigel, a fairly large man, didn't exactly bulldoze, though he wasn't afraid of whacking down a limb or vine, either. Silas, on the other hand, leapt from stones to logs to the ground with catlike grace on those long, lean legs. The earthy colors of his kilt camouflaged him so that he became almost one with the forest. He frequently found opportunity to take her hand and help her, which she might have resisted from anyone else, but which she readily accepted from him.

Reluctant to show any sign of fatigue, she pushed herself, so they wouldn't have to. When Silas told Sigel he knew of a secure spot near a brook to camp for the night, she offered a prayer of gratitude to Maker. She didn't think there were too many steps left in her.

Their camp was a beautiful, high place on a hill, with good views all around. Stands of trees provided shelter and cover. A small, clear stream trickled by.

Briana began digging a hole for the fire.

"I can do that," Silas offered.

"Thanks, but I'd like to practice what Sigel taught me."

"Then I'll do a perimeter check," he said, and headed through the pines. Sigel stayed close. She finished her fire preparations efficiently and set up her tent while Sigel riffled through his pack.

"I'd forgotten I had this," he said, holding up a bundle of herbs. "Tea would be nice tonight and won't put off too much scent."

She joined him by the fire when the water started boiling.

"Och!"

She looked back. Silas had bumped into her tent, which was practically indiscernible, pitched against some pines.

"Sorry, Silas. I didn't hear you come up, or I would've warned you sooner."

"What in Maker's good earth is that? Me legs been banjaxed for sure."

"Her sleeping tent," Sigel said. "She's got some magic, Silas. Better watch yourself."

"I'll keep that in mind." He rubbed his shin. "How's it work?"

"I don't know how it works, exactly," Briana said, entering the tent and leaving her voice to float over the encampment. "It's gnome magic."

"That's... cool," said Silas. "On second thought, I'm not so sure I like it," he said, scratching his head. "It's rather creepy. Come on out of there, Briana."

She emerged, laughing. "You must admit, Silas, it has its advantages."

"For instance?"

"For instance, I can see what's going on outside the tent, but no one can see in. They don't even know I'm there."

"Unless, of course the poor lad falls into the tent on top of you."

"Well, there is that possibility," she admitted. "But at least I'd be ready for him."

They shared a sheepish glance as she handed him a cup of tea.

He traded her the cup of tea for a wrapped bundle.

"What's this?" she asked, as she unwrapped it, uncovering a generous chunk of cheese. "Outstanding!"

"There's more," he said, handing her a second package. "Mrs. McPhee was determined to fill me pack."

What she discovered was a meat-filled pie. No one would go to sleep hungry tonight.

"I've never appreciated food as much as I do here," she told her companions, breaking the cheese into three sections.

"Well, dried meat and bread do have a way of making you grateful for something heartier," Sigel agreed, as he divided the meat pie in half, and then thirds. Briana wrapped the other half and put it away, in case they needed it tomorrow.

Talking subsided, allowing their bellies the luxury of feeling full for the first time in days.

Twilight changed to dusk and then to darkness. All vestiges of fog and mist dissipated, leaving only the brilliantly studded night sky.

"It's beautiful," she whispered reverently, seeing the vertical sword of the Milky Way stabbing from heaven to earth.

"Aye," Silas agreed.

"No, I mean really beautiful. In my time, there are so many competing lights, you don't get to see it like this."

Stars danced overhead as the bard quietly sang of a beloved king in language that almost made Briana believe she could fall in love with such a man.

She must have drifted off, because Sigel was gently nudging her awake, encouraging her to go to her tent. "I'll post guard first, then Silas will take the morning half. You, little one, are going to have a full night's rest."

"Oh, no, I'll do my share," she protested, with a yawn, but Sigel was insistent.

"Not tonight, Briana. You need some rest. We'll do well enough without you."

She glanced over at Silas, who nodded his agreement and said quietly in the old language, "*Oiche, mhaith a mhuirnin.*" She didn't know what it meant but oh, it sounded sooo nice.

She awoke to full daylight. Trying not to disturb anyone, Briana lifted the flap of her tent, which faced the brook. Silas knelt by the stream washing his face. Shirtless. His back was strong and carved with sinewy muscle, the broad shoulders tapering down to a lean waist. Sitting back, he turned slightly but didn't seem aware of her. She should turn away and allow him privacy, but simply couldn't take her eyes off him. Blonde hair lay softly across the upper part of his chest, tapering down to his belly. On the left side of his chest she noticed a small inked drawing of a tree with crossed arrows across its trunk. His kilt slid down a little on his hips when he moved. She held her breath. Her belly was doing some wild gymnastics and she felt her heart drumming out a loud tattoo. She raised a hand to her chest to stop the flutter, catching his attention. He stared back at her with a look so devastatingly honest that it was all she could do to not go to him. Time held them in an embrace of understanding, both exciting and painful.

Oh my Maker, this cannot happen. I'm promised to another, she thought. Somehow the message, translated through her eyes, perhaps, reached him. He stood and walked away, permitting them both the dignity of recovery.

After her breathing and heart rate returned to normal, she recalled the black medallion with a gold tree hanging from a leather cord around his neck. Her hand automatically went to her own mysterious pendant. *Something they shared, but why?*

Thoughts continued to race around inside her head. *What should I do? How do I act as though nothing happened?*

When she left the tent, luckily, there was no sign of Silas. Sigel bustled around, putting things in packs and readying them to go. "Good morning, Briana. Sleep well?"

"Yes," she responded, woodenly. She tried to appear nonchalant, but the marshall was too observant for her.

"Briana, you okay?"

"Yeah, I'm fine."

He didn't look convinced, but let it drop until Silas wandered back to the campsite, looking equally apprehensive. "Something wrong, Bard?"

Silas shook his head wordlessly, not looking at him.

Sigel glanced back and forth between the two. "Is there something I should know?"

Silas and Briana spoke at once: "No!" Sigel stared thoughtfully at them and muttered, "Let's go. We should be at Cailleach's by late afternoon."

Briana shouldered her pack and sheathed her blade while Silas arranged his quiver and bow, as well as a guitar-like instrument attached to a shoulder strap and a small skin-covered drum at his waist.

The man hauls a lot of stuff around, she thought.

He motioned her ahead of him and she started forward, with Sigel in the lead.

She whispered, "Silas, I..." She really didn't know what to say, and stopped.

He smiled kindly. "It's all right, *a mhuirnin*. No harm done."

She walked a few feet and then asked, "What does that mean, *a mhuirnín?*" Her tongue stumbled over the pronunciation.

Sigel answered her question with an impatient growl. "It means 'sweetheart.' Now, come on you two, can we please just get going?"

She stumbled over the nearest rock and would've fallen if Silas hadn't caught her arm. He righted her and said with a wink, "Just a wee endearment, Briana. Come on, let's go meet a witch."

A wee endearment? She mulled that over for the next few miles. *Was he telling her she had misunderstood his attention?* After a while, the uncomfortable silence was replaced by Silas' soft humming.

They asked her some questions about where she came from, and she discovered that talking about airplanes and television and the internet was a good way to get her mind off the bard. While Sigel had lots of inquiries about technology, Silas was more interested in pop culture and of course, music.

They spent most of the morning following a ribbon of trail along a ridgeline with spectacular vistas. She stopped the men once to gaze out toward the northwest, where the mountains seemed to roll purposely down toward what she imagined was the ocean. Pointing in the direction of her gaze, Silas said, "Cedarmara, where I was born and raised, is that way. A few day's walk."

"I bet it's beautiful," she said, admiring the panorama. "I hope we get to go there someday."

"Oh, we will," Sigel said. "When we release the king and the two of you are married, the king will want to visit all of the island to reestablish relationships with his people, and introduce them to his bride. Of course, all of that while we are decimating the Gray Military and killing Lord Shamwa."

"Sounds like a lovely honeymoon," Briana muttered.

Sigel pointed to the opposite side of the ridge from Cedarmara. "See that valley?" She nodded, though in truth it was still quite far off. "Cailleach's cabins are down there. It will be late, but I think we can make it today."

They walked on. Briana asked Silas about his boyhood in Cedarmara. Nostalgia softened his eyes. "Well, Cedarmara is a beautiful harbor. Me father fished there for a livin'. He and mum worked hard and loved well, each other and me. I was an only child and they spoiled me terrible.

Me father loved to tell stories at night at the hearth, and I took easily to it meself, soon replacin' him as the storyteller of the family. Before long, I was tellin' stories to the whole village. Sometimes it got me in trouble."

"Trouble? How?"

"Oh, once I made up a story about me friend stealin' a lamb from his neighbor. It was quite the adventure and had everyone laughin', but it was completely untrue."

"Couldn't the boy see the humor?"

"Not with his backside burnin' from the beatin' he took when his da thought he really had stolen it. I felt terrible about it, but the apology to his da didn't remove the pain from his bum, aye."

She grimaced, imagining how this might have played out.

His knack for music and storytelling, even as a child, became a local legend and soon attracted the attention of King Barclay. He was commissioned and brought to Ard Darach, where he perfected his craft and was eventually appointed Royal Bard to the House of Taranian.

"I was happy enough, though I missed Cedarmara. Worse yet, was the terrible storm that blew through one winter and took me parents' lives. They were out fishin' when the weather turned fierce and capsized their wee boat."

"I'm so sorry, Silas." Her heart ached for his loss, knowing full well the depth of that particular grief.

He nodded. "Aye, well, I still had me other family. King Barclay and Queen Eleanor were kind and generous surrogates. I grieved, but in time was happy again."

"Were you and Brath friends?"

"Aye, we were – are. He's not dead, just asleep," he reminded himself. "We were – are – not as close as he and Sigel here, but we got along well. He treated me like an annoyin' wee brother, which I suppose I am." He laughed and recalled a few stories about the king. She listened, enjoying the sound of his voice, wishing the day would go one forever.

"One more question," she asked, catching sight of the scar over his eye.

"Aye?"

"How did you get the scar on your eyebrow?"

"Here we go," Sigel muttered.

"Well, lass, it was like this. I suffered the wound in a fight to protect a lass's virtue."

"Oh, my," Briana said, intrigued.

"A bonny lass, but much too young to understand the consequences of her flirtin', she attracted the attention of the wrong man. When he demanded more than she meant to give, there was a tussle and I felt honor bound to step in and give her time to get away from the situation. In the process, the man's knife connected with me head."

"You were lucky he didn't take out an eye."

"Aye, I was, indeed. I like the mark, though. Gives me a rather gallant look, don't you think?"

"Oh, certainly," she said with a smile.

The late afternoon sun began to cast shadows in the forest, accompanied by the usual symphony of noises, but suddenly Briana heard a different sound, like an animal whimpering. She asked the men to stop a moment as she tried to determine the direction of the cries. It seemed to be coming from below them. She followed a trail of crushed ferns that led down a bank to an old birch stump. The whimpering grew louder. She pulled back some overgrown shrubs and was astonished to see a very large dog, its gray fur matted and grungy. "An Irish wolfhound," she murmured, and started to bend down toward it. Sigel grabbed her arm and pulled her back.

"Careful, Briana, he's wounded. He might bite." As if to prove it so, the dog growled. They stood staring at the canine for a few seconds. He was wet, probably from trying to cross the brook beyond, and bloody, with an injured right front paw. He was in bad shape. Sigel looked at Silas and made a motion with his head.

"Come on, lass," said Silas. "Let's go on back up. Sigel will put him out of his misery." He tried to turn her away, but she jerked away from him.

"You'll do no such thing! He needs help, not a slit throat! Sigel, I'm really good with animals. Let me try and tend to him."

Looking skeptical, he moved back a little, staying near enough to intervene if the dog reacted badly. Briana got down on all fours, inching forward. "It's okay, boy, I'll help you. You're a handsome fellow, for sure."

He stopped whining and gazed pitifully at her. She kept talking, and reaching out gently, ran her hands over his head, neck and the rest of his body, seeking any other injured parts. When he seemed at ease with her, she took his big paw in her hand. Beyond a soft whimper, he did nothing as she examined it. There was no telling what had happened to cause the swelling and laceration on the paw, but it wasn't actively bleeding. She thought it must have happened some time ago. Briana sat back on her heels, thinking.

"Can you find me two sticks and some cloth or string we can use to make a splint?

"You're not thinking of keeping the animal? That's a bad idea. He might bark and give our location away, and he'll need food."

Briana paused a moment, looking at the dog, before turning back to Sigel. She couldn't explain it, but she knew this was a special dog. She was certain he was wise enough to stay quiet when needed; in fact, she suspected he would prove to be an important companion. She felt such a connection to him, deeper than anything she'd ever experienced with another dog. More than friendship. Briana channeled her most queenly expression. "He's going to stay with me." Praying he wouldn't argue, she turned back to the injured canine and continued her ministrations.

Her tactic worked. Neither man said another word. Silas went to get the supplies she'd asked for and Sigel stood beside her, "just in case."

Cloth, sturdy branches and twine in hand, she fashioned the supportive device around the foot as best she could. He cried out once and pulled his lips back over his teeth, but she paused in her ministrations, calming him with her voice, and then went on until the dog's foot was firmly bound. He whined pitifully when she helped him stand. The hound took a few tentative steps, then looked at Briana with woeful, wondering eyes.

Silas looked at her with new appreciation, but Sigel was the first to speak. "You've a rare gift, lass."

She shrugged, hesitant to accept the compliment, not finding it necessary for them to thank or praise her for doing what seemed the only humane thing to do.

"Well, anyway, come on, we need to find someplace to rest for the night. This has put us behind and I don't want to arrive at Cailleach's after dark," Sigel said.

The sun had sunk below tree line and the wildwood was hauntingly dark when Sigel finally indicated a good spot protected by a rock overhang where they could make a small fire and spend the night.

Once the dog was settled, Briana made a fire and boiled some water. She'd found some wild herbs along the trail for a nice tea and set that to brewing. The dog seemed to rest comfortably now that he was dry and his hurt paw splinted.

Last night's leftovers eased the gnawing in their stomachs. "Do you really mean to keep the lad?" Silas asked, breaking off a bit of food and handing it to the dog.

"Yes, if he'll stay. The question is, what to name him?" She stared at the hound. "Cedarmara has such a nice ring, but is way too big a name, even for this big guy."

Silas toyed with the word and the letters and said, "What about Dara? I knew a monk once by the name of Dara. He had hair the color of this great beast and was about as hairy."

They all laughed, and the name stuck. "Dara," Briana said, as she caressed the tangled coat along his sides and neck. He looked up at her with trusting amber eyes. "I'll take care of you, Dara."

"More likely, he'll take care of you, once he's well. He's one big beast," Sigel said, before adding a log to the fire and lying down on the ground. "Silas, first watch? Wake me in a few hours." Within minutes he was snoring lightly, as was Dara, leaving Silas and Briana to a peaceful observation of the night sky above. They sat together talking in low tones, trying not to disturb Sigel.

"I don't think I thanked you for saving my life," Briana said.

"Oh, I'm not so sure I saved your life. Had I given you another minute, you'd have probably had him yourself."

"I don't know about that. I don't think the bite would have stopped him for long."

He shrugged. "Maybe, maybe not. Regardless, I had to try and save you, or face the consequences if somethin' happened to you."

"Consequences? What consequences?"

"Well," he replied, "We need you to save the king. And once we do, he's going to want to have his bride all in one piece. He'll have our heads otherwise."

"So you believe the prophecy depends on me marrying the king?"

"Oh, aye, that's the way I understand it."

She searched his face. He returned her stare directly. Neither of them said anything, but looking into his blue eyes, Briana found marriage to the king less and less appealing every minute.

Silas chuckled and made an undecipherable noise.

Stars flickered overhead. They sat in silence until Briana yawned. "Guess I better get some sleep, too. Will you have Sigel wake me when it's my turn to watch?"

"Sleep, *a mhuirnin*, we'll see you safe till mornin'."

She didn't argue, but curled on her side and covered up with a light blanket that provided more comfort than warmth. The sounds of the night and Silas' soft humming were a lullaby to her tired body, and she drifted into peaceful slumber.

CHAPTER TEN

CAILLEACH

"Fresh," Silas said, looking up from a crouched position over a rounded, moist pile of deer droppings.

Sigel nodded. "We ought to bring something to help feed the extra mouths we're bringing. Briana and I could wait here a while if you want to track it."

"You're going to kill a deer?" Briana asked.

"You want to eat?" Silas asked, wryly.

"Of course, but…"

"But nothing, *a mhuirnin*. This is where that lovely meat pie came from, and there's only one way to get it."

She put a hand to her hip. "I know that, Silas. We hunt in Maine, too. I wanted to watch and see how it's done."

Silas and Sigel exchanged a surprised look. "I thought you'd hate the idea."

"I think the death scene in the apple orchard forced me to get over any squeamishness I might've had regarding killing something. Don't you?"

"Well," Silas said, "I suppose you're right, and you probably should learn how to hunt, at least how it's done here. But you and the beastie will have to be very quiet, aye?"

She stared at Dara and tried to communicate something to him. Satisfied that he understood, she turned to Silas and nodded.

Slowly and soundlessly, they searched for deer tracks and other signs of disturbance. The tracks led over a knoll and down through a thicket. Instead of going through the dense brush, Silas led them sideways to the edge. Though the recent misty day had left the woodland floor wet and made stealth easy for both parties, soft blowing gave away the deer's location, just beyond the thicket. The small buck stood about thirty yards out, his four-pronged antlers turned away from them. Bringing his bow around in front and nocking an arrow, Silas looked at his partners, assuring their silence. All three knelt down and Briana put a hand on Dara.

Briana watched Silas study the shot, lift his bow and draw back. He closed his eyes and silently mouthed words before opening his eyes again. Then he held his breath and released the arrow.

The deer jumped with a startled cry and took three great bounds before stopping, stumbling back a few steps, then gently laying down in the leaves, his life's spirit gone.

Hallowed silence and penumbral light filled the woodland cathedral. Finally, Silas stood and headed toward the fallen animal. Sigel nudged Briana and they followed, careful as they neared the animal, in case he wasn't truly dead. A wounded animal could be dangerous.

Silas knelt beside the animal and ran his hand gently down its reddish pelt. "Thank you, brother, for your sacrifice. You honor us with your willingness to die so that we might live. May your spirit now wander among ripe apple trees and clear runnin' streams."

When Silas looked up, tears streamed down Briana's cheeks. "Did this upset you, lass?"

She shook her head. "It was terribly beautiful. And I love that you blessed him after."

"Death and sacrifice are requirements of life, and we should never take them for granted," was all he said before getting down to the business of preparing the body for transport.

When the ministrations were complete, Sigel offered to carry the deer. "You're lugging enough with all your wee instruments and such."

"And the *wee* bow that killed the deer," Silas pointed out, as he hoisted the animal across Sigel's shoulders.

They followed a brook through a forest abundant in fruit and nut trees. Briana collected handfuls of fallen walnuts and put them in her pocket. Low-hanging apples found their way into her pack, as well. The trail led stubbornly through a thick stand of pines. When they came out on the other side, she discovered that the brook they'd been following was actually the outlet of a very large waterfall that fell straight down into a clear pool and then out into the stream. It was stunning.

"Ah," Silas sighed. "Haven't been in that pool for a very long time. Can't wait to have a good bath."

"I'll be right behind you," Sigel agreed. "First order of business after getting Milady Mouse settled."

She growled at the use of her nickname, before shrugging it off. "Are we almost at Cailleach's?"

Sigel pointed to stone steps that led up a gentle slope. Light poured from above, through some pines and directly onto the stairway, illuminating them like a divine wand. "Walk into the light," she murmured, prompting yet another look of confusion from her companions. She led the way up the stairs.

More than a forest hut, it was a gathering of structures. The main cabin, presumably Cailleach's, was a moss-draped, wood and stone structure set against a massive granite slab that appeared to be part of the forest itself. Windows peeked out upon a porch that ran across the front of the cabin, where two simple wooden rocking chairs sat empty. A smaller window, higher up, hinted at a room above the main floor. Tendrils of smoke swirled lazily from a chimney on one side. Next to the main lodging stood a smaller cabin, primitive but complete, and what looked to be a crudely fashioned stall and paddock complete with an idling goat and wandering chickens. A large yew tree (or what had likely been three yews grown together, with the combined trunk size of three or four big men) stood in the center of the croft, creating a natural arbor. A low stone wall encircled the complex. Everything looked as though it had been there eons, covered in moss and old leaves, yet sturdy and alive.

The door opened and a woman stepped out onto the porch with a hawk perched on her shoulder. Her hair fell in a thick braid, with feathers and flowers woven into it. She had an air of mystery and earthy beauty that was captivating. Her long woolen dress was decorated with more natural trinkets, and soft leather boots covered her feet. Along with an amulet of amethyst and wren feathers, she wore a black medallion with a Tree of Life on its face. She was beautiful in a mysterious way. She was a woman of the forest. She was a witch.

By this time, they were at the steps to the porch. Awe kept Briana quiet; Sigel bowed to the woman. "Greetings Cailleach," he said, respectfully, and with poorly hidden affection.

Cailleach's soft, berry-colored lips parted in a smile that made her even more arresting. "Sigel. Silas." She nodded to them both and then turned her full attention to Briana. "And you must be the Mouse." Before Briana could protest, she added, "Or shall I call you Briana? You've grown up to be such a lovely woman, but then, you were a beautiful baby." Her honeyed voice wrapped around Briana. "And who do we have here?" she asked, smiling at the huge gray hound, who stared at her with baleful eyes.

Briana found her voice. "We found him injured yesterday afternoon. I did what I could to set his paw and tend to his wounds, but he still needs rest and some food. A touch of willow bark wouldn't be out of order. I hope it's okay that we brought him. His name's Dara. He doesn't eat as much as you might think, and he never made a sound when Silas shot the deer." Cailleach was studying her with interest and a tiny smile. Briana wanted to smack herself for her nervous blathering.

"Of course Dara is welcome here. Come in, all of you, and bring the gray lad, too. He needs warming by the fire. Sigel, you can hang the deer in the shed. I have tea on. I'll want to hear all about your journey, Briana."

The cabin's single, surprisingly large room was filled with natural light. Having run her own herbal business, Briana first noticed the signs of Cailleach's medicinal work: the racks of drying herbs, small containers of oils and ointments, and baskets full of twine and bark. Near that were other necessities, mounds of colored cloth and fibers, black pots and other cooking tools, and colored glass bottles and pitchers. A variety of plants made the place homey. In the center of the room stood a large wooden table with four chairs, and tucked away in one corner, a small feather bed covered with handmade quilts, and a perch for the hawk. *A place for everything, and everything in its place.* Stairs led to a loft. In the other corner sat a large barrel. The smell and heat of the peat fire was welcoming and cozy.

Cailleach set the hawk on his perch in a grumpy rustle of feathers, before turning her attention to her guests. After inspecting Dara's wounds herself and getting him settled on blankets by the fire, she showed Briana the sleeping loft. They went back downstairs and Cailleach put bread, fruit preserves and some dried meat on the table. She was pouring mugs of ale when Briana remembered the nuts and apples. Climbing the stairs again, she retrieved the fruit and offered them to the witch, who seemed pleased with the gift and set them in a bowl on the table to be shared with the meal.

The men made quick work of the food and drink, while Briana and Cailleach spent more time talking than eating. When Briana told her about coming through the tree, Cailleach asked, "Do you remember being inside the tree?"

"Not really. I remember images on the walls, but nothing specific." She paused, her eyes suddenly drawn to Silas. She shivered, feeling a strange sense of déjà vu, but it passed, so she continued. "I went down and then went up, I do remember that. It wasn't frightening or anything, I'm sure of that. I know I felt safe and mostly curious."

The witch nodded. "And the Wellses were good to you?"

"Oh my, yes. Somehow, they made sure I had everything I needed. Of course, Jack pushed me hard in the training, but now I know why."

They talked of many things, including her parents. Silas asked, "Do you look like your mum or your da?"

Cailleach answered, "She looks just like her mother."

Briana started to ask how she knew that, but the conversation turned quickly to concerns about the Gray Military and the destruction of the faerie trees, and she forgot about it. Differences of opinion developed over how to proceed with the next phase of the journey. In the end, Cailleach's opinion was accepted. They'd stay for several days so Cailleach could finish Briana's education about the kingdom and teach her some new skills. "While we're working, you two might do something to replenish my larders," Cailleach said. "The deer is helpful, but I need other supplies."

Sigel and Silas agreed to hunt and to make the long journey to the mill in Moiria for barley, rye and wheat flour. With these decisions made and their meal complete, the men prepared to go back out and see what other game they might find. They promised to bathe in the pool at the waterfall before coming home that evening.

"Good idea. Now that you mention it, before you leave, could you bring in the tub and some water so Briana can have a good hot bath?" The mere suggestion of Briana bathing had her blushing, but the men did as they were asked.

Sigel arranged the copper tub near the fireplace. "I'll empty it when we return. We should be back just after dark."

Once the men were gone and the tub filled with hot water, the shyness Briana felt about undressing in front of the witch disappeared as the woman moved about the cabin, talking gently, and finding an herbal wash for her hair. Briana wasted no time getting into the tub.

Dara's presence nearby, and the occasional chirring of the raptor, whose name was Merlin, were soothing energies. She slid down into the hot water with a deep sigh.

"Can I wash your hair for you, lass?"

Briana nodded. Cailleach immediately went to work on her long hair, washing, rinsing and pulling out tangles, which reminded her of how much she missed her mother.

"Cailleach, can you help me let my mother know that I'm all right? She must be so scared. I just disappeared without a trace."

The witch's fingers stilled. "Your mother knows where you are, child."

Briana turned and stared at her, thinking she'd heard wrong. "What?"

Cailleach looked at Briana, baffled. "Are you telling me that Katrina never talked to you about Uisneach?"

"How would she know about Uisneach?"

Cailleach explained her visit to Katrina on the day of Briana's birth. Briana was stunned. "Mom knew all along and never told me? Why not?"

"I suspect she hoped the day wouldn't come," Cailleach said. "Or perhaps she just never found the right time."

Briana remembered her mother's comment just before her disappearance that they needed to talk. "She may have started to just before I went through the tree, but it was a bad time, so she said we'd talk soon."

"She should've told you long before then. You could've been preparing for this. Och, well, nothing to be done about it. We'll just have to start from the beginning. Tomorrow. You can have this afternoon to catch your breath. Ready to come out? I think your fingers are turning into old mushrooms."

It was hard not to feel more than a little hurt and angry that her mother had kept this from her for twenty-five years. It would've been nice to have some preparation, if only for the separation that would come.

Except that had I known, *we would've spent a lifetime worrying about when it would happen.* Perhaps it was for the best that Katrina kept it from her.

"I guess she won't worry I've been abducted." With a last long sigh, she stepped out of the tub and into a wooly towel, to dry off.

"Cailleach, what are the medallions for?" she asked, toweling her hair.

"I'm still trying to figure that out. I believe they're important, but we don't know how to use them to unlock the curse. Just don't lose it, lass. It will be critical to our success."

"Silas has one too, and the crow."

"As do I," she said, pulling hers from inside her dress. "Sigel has one, too."

"He does? I hadn't noticed."

"There are five medallions, five keys. Time is running out to discover their magic."

"Shouldn't we hold off on going to the castle until we do?"

She shook her head. "I have every faith that we'll learn what to do at the proper time. In the meantime, we need to get you to Ard Darach."

Briana was sitting by the fire, rubbing an ointment on Dara's scratches, when the men returned with a brace of partridges. They'd bathed and shaved. Briana looked up with a smile, in spite of the slight headache that had begun to plague her this afternoon. *They clean up nice*, she thought. She could see in their expressions a similar sentiment toward her freshly scrubbed appearance in a linen shift topped by a long dress made from flax, dyed cornflower-blue and piped with rabbit fur. The medallion shone black against the pale blue of the dress. Around her waist, Cailleach had laced a wide brown leather belt. The dress was soft and pretty and Briana was glad for the opportunity to feel and look like a woman for a change.

"You look lovely, lass."

"Thank you, Silas," she responded, with a shy smile.

Cailleach interrupted the moment, directing the men to get the birds hung in the smokehouse and take the tub out, which Briana had emptied before their return.

Briana's head throbbed all during supper, so she ate little. She had no idea if she would ever see her mother again; the thought brought a stab of pain in her heart. In the meantime, the affection she felt for these men and this amazing woman was deep and true. The men had proven their loyalty, and though she'd just met the witch, she already felt a strong connection. She couldn't help but feel a reciprocating allegiance.

While the women cleaned up from supper, the men stoked the fire and pulled some chairs around the hearth. Cailleach poured ale from a crock. Silas brought out a small instrument similar to a guitar or mandolin. Settling in, they listened attentively as he began to sing. His clear and emotive voice brought to life the stories of victorious kings and battles hard fought and won. Briana was captivated by both his lyrical voice and his dreamy good looks.

"Silas, would you allow me to play your guitar?" she asked him, suddenly.

"You play?" Sigel asked, leaning forward with curiosity.

"My dad taught me to play. I also took piano lessons growing up. My folks were big believers in the importance of music education. Your instrument is a little different than what I'm used to, but I think I can figure it out."

"Do you sing, too?" Silas asked, clearly pleased by this discovery.

"I can carry a tune."

He handed her his guitar with an encouraging smile, then leaned back in the chair, stretching his long legs in front of him.

She strummed a few riffs, then took a deep breath. "This is a song I've been working on for some time. I couldn't figure out where it came from, or why, but now I know." She strummed a few lines and began, "Across the veil a sign appears. A hero's call to arms. A crown to save and nation free, release from evil charms. A journey made from future times, to ancient royal mound…"

Silas' face was ghostly white and his mouth hung open.

Her fingers stilled on the strings. "Silas, what's wrong? It isn't that bad."

Cailleach and Sigel both looked concerned. "What is it, lad?" Cailleach asked, gently.

Silas reached for his instrument, which Briana quickly handed to him.

Staring directly at Briana, he continued, "Raisin' sword with steady hand, to prophecy she's bound. Duty calls across this fair land, for men and lass alike. Pick up your shield and make your stand, for Uisneach now we strike."

Briana gasped, but when he continued she joined him in perfect synchrony.

"Crossroads coming, make a choice

Remain and die, or fight.

Your hearth to leave, the future calls

Hide no more – your battle cry.

Between the tree and standing stones

Your destiny awaits you.

To save the ways of older days

For Uisneach's sake, we'll try or die!"

The only difference in their words was that when he said "Uisneach," she used the word, "kingdom."

They finished the song together and Silas put the guitar down.

The crackling of the fire and the individual rhythms of their breathing were the only sounds in the room for several minutes.

"How is this possible?" Briana finally asked.

Cailleach appeared to be thinking, Sigel frowned and Silas was starting to regain a little color.

"I don't know," Silas said, "but it seems rather significant, don't you think?"

There were no apparent answers or even theories, at least none anyone cared to share.

Sigel said, "What we do know is that the queen is a bard in her own right. Careful she doesn't steal your job, Silas."

Briana looked down at her hands, limp in her lap.

Better me job than me heart, she heard clearly in her head.

Puzzled, she looked up to meet Silas' equally confused stare. When a strand of hair fell across the side of his face, butterflies rose up in a ferocious flutter in her belly. She wanted to reach over and push the stray lock back behind his ear.

"I once saw a swarm of butterflies rise up as one flutterin' army," Silas said. "It was beautiful."

"What's that got to do with anything?" Sigel asked.

"Nothin'," he replied. "The thought just crossed me mind."

Briana didn't take her eyes off him. *Why would you say that when I was just thinking of butterflies? Are you reading my mind?*

I think so. Ask me a question.

Her eyes narrowed. *What do you think I should name the song?*

"Well, gettin' back to Briana's song. Have you named it yet? I'd call it 'Crossroads.'"

Sweet mother of God, she thought. *What's your favorite color?*

"Or perhaps the 'Green Hills of Uisneach'?" Silas said.

"I like 'Crossroads' better," Sigel said.

We can read each other's minds! How? Why? What does this mean?

I don't know, but I think we should keep it to ourselves until we work it out. And, Briana?

Yes?

You should probably stop starin' at me. Cailleach is watchin' us like a hawk.

Indeed, Cailleach was watching them with great intent and fascination. Keeping her eyes on the witch, Briana thought, *Okay, but one more thing.*

Yes?

I think I'd like to steal your heart.

CHAPTER ELEVEN

THE BOOK OF LEAVES

Briana rubbed small circles over the small of her back as she came downstairs the next morning, feeling as though one cross word would make her cry. Cailleach met her at the foot of the stairs and handed her a bundle, with a look of sympathy on her face. The packet held clean linen cloths, a soft leather garment and small packet of herbs.

"How did you know?"

"Well, first of all, I'm a witch, so some things I just know. There will be little you can hide from me, Briana," she said. Briana had the good graces to blush. "Second, I'm a woman, and well aware of the signs of a woman coming into her courses."

She studied the undergarments as Cailleach explained their use and care. It was a workable solution, as long as Briana could find time away from her male traveling companions. *Speaking of the men…*

"They've already gone out hunting," Cailleach said. "See to your needs. When you come down again, I'll have some toast and hot tea with mugwort and raspberry to ease you."

Tea and toast did, indeed, go a long way to making her more comfortable. Dara was much improved as well, up on his feet and wagging his tail. "I'm glad you're better, Dara." His response was a sloppy lick to the side of her cheek, which made her laugh. "Where's Merlin?"

"Out hunting for his breakfast, I imagine. He comes and goes." Cailleach ate with her while explaining their plans for the day. "You'll spend the morning studying the prophecy. It'll help you to understand why you're here and how important it is that you help release King Brath and become his queen."

Maybe it was because of the time of month, or because her thoughts strayed constantly to Silas and their newly discovered magic, but this statement provoked a rebellious reaction from Briana. "I'm not going to marry a man I don't even know! That's barbaric! What if he's old and hideous?"

Cailleach set her tea down with an enigmatic half-smile. "Brath is five years older than you, Briana, and though I myself may be 'old,'" she paused, looking anything but, "I assure you he is most certainly not hideous."

"Please, give me a dose of hemlock in case I need it."

Cailleach laughed at her. "Oh, Briana, don't be so dramatic. You must trust me when I say that you will not be disappointed by either Brath's looks or manners. He is a truly wonderful man and king, and any girl would be happy to be his bride. Now, let's get down to business. We've much to do today."

Maybe so, Briana thought, *if that girl's heart didn't already belong somewhere else.* She let the thought go and rose to clear away the breakfast things. While she tidied up, Cailleach wandered around the house, picking up this and that, saying they'd focus first on history and then review her knowledge of herbal medicine.

"These are the things that will deliver you safely to Ard Darach, and may save your life and the lives of those who travel with you." She pointed Briana in the direction of a heavily laden bookshelf. "Can you lift that big green book?"

It was hefty, but Briana pulled it out and put it on the table. "How beautiful," she murmured, lightly stroking its forest-green leather binding and the title, which was embossed in a shiny substance like crushed topaz. *The Book of Leaves* was written on top, and underneath, *The Prophecy of Uisneach*. The full prophecy was written on the first page. She began to read the first stanza out loud:

"*When the wheel of the seasons forgets to turn,*

The trees are nearly gone.

From ancient oak a Mouse appears,

A queen is met with cheers.

She'll journey far to save a king,

In castle strong under gloomy spell he rests.

Five keys will lift the curse.

Help arrives from king's right hand,

Rare magic and a map.

Crow and crone lead and teach the future
ordained Queen of Uisneach."

Briana was quiet for a long time. "I'm starting to realize this is much more than a sweet story. It's real. People will live and die by this prophecy, won't they?" Cailleach nodded. "And I'm responsible?"

"Well not solely, but yes, you hold a great deal of responsibility for this, Briana."

"Why me?"

Cailleach shrugged. "Who knows the how's or why's of prophecy? The universe calls who it will, to do what it wants done."

"Tag. I'm it," she said, leaning her chin on her hands, thoughtfully. "Do you think that we're intentionally part of this, or are some of us just in the wrong place at the wrong time?"

"Nothing is ever by accident, lass. The universe isn't that wasteful. Even when people make mistakes, their errors will be used in some way."

"Hmmm…" she read further, but silently, Cailleach giving her time to absorb the text. "Do you understand everything in this prophecy?"

"No, I don't. For one thing, I have no idea who the cat is."

"Wedding day breaks the cat." Briana read slowly. "Hmm…"

"And the 'brown king' is a bit confusing also," Cailleach said, almost to herself. "It must be Brath, but…" She stared intently at the prophecy, as if that would somehow make its meaning clearer. "There are parts I have suspicions about, but shudder to consider."

Finally, Cailleach stepped away. "The rest of the book tells the genealogy of Uisneach, and that is what you need to learn today. I'm going out foraging, so you'll be by yourself for a while. I'll be close enough to hear if you should call me. After lunch we'll work some magic." She stroked the younger woman's hair as she walked by, called to Dara to go with her and grabbed a basket on her way out the door, leaving Briana to her studies.

Turning pages old and beautifully decorated with ancient art, Briana discovered that Uisneach was a fascinating place with a long and magical history. According to *The Book of Leaves*, the island of Uisneach was one of the first creations of Maker. It rose up out of the blue ocean on the breath of dawn. It was a beautiful, green land of shining mountains, tall trees, cozy harbors, sheer cliffs, long sandy beaches, deep and mysterious valleys and a thousand waterfalls. Mist covered the land every morning, and the sun shone upon it every afternoon. Maker's imagination ran wild as flying, swimming, walking and crawling creatures were created to live among the hills and waters of Uisneach. It was peaceful and abundant – Maker's finest creation.

In the middle of the island stood one tree, more significant than all the others, for it was the Uisneach Tree, the Tree of Life, connecting the physical and spiritual domains of Uisneach. Its roots grew deep and wide under the earth and into Otherworld and its canopy of leaves reached far into the sky, toward Maker. It was the center of the world and the source of magic that fed Uisneach. It was believed the faeries came from the Uisneach Tree, and should the tree die, so would the faeries and magic.

Five races would eventually live on the island of Uisneach – the magical folk, faeries and other nature spirits; the gnomes; and the three races with human blood: the Eiriens; the Divine Practitioners; and the Moherians.

The first to make their way to Uisneach were the magical creatures – faeries, pixies, brownies, dryads and nyads and the sort – who came through the tree. They lived for many centuries in harmony. Joyful souls, they contributed much to the beauty and magic of Uisneach. The first king and queen of Faerie, Talisorin and Urelian, ruled peacefully over seven tribes of faeries, each specializing in certain forms of elemental magic to create and care for Uisneach. They inhabited the trees and created some of their own, and also built little hills and carved caves into cliffs. Faeries wove spells to give some of the animals the gift of speech, thinking it would be lovely if they could communicate with them. From the faeries came runes, musical instruments and rainbows. They slept much of the day, but at night they gathered around faerie bonfires, dancing, singing and storytelling.

Then came the gnomes, the first of the non-magical inhabitants of the island (though the gnomes had some wee magics, as Briana knew). The gnomes simply appeared, without evolution or genealogy. A large group from the beginning, all shared the same last name and an affinity for comfort. They loved to garden and got on well with the faeries. Perhaps because it was warmer in the south, or because they loved apple wine (the trees grew abundantly there), they congregated in Appleduir, which in time came to be called Wellsland. A peaceful and pastoral people, they coexisted with the magical beings for thousands of years.

A day dawned when everything changed. Strangers appeared on the shores of Uisneach, humans, much more complicated than the gnomes or magical beings. The other races named them the Eiriens.

The Eiriens gave rise to the kings and queens who would rule the land. Taller, stronger and more determined than the other races, they built many things that changed the way the island appeared and functioned. Land was cleared for villages and cities, the rivers became congested with their rafts and boats, and many of the animals withdrew to the mountains. Overwhelmed by the frenetic energy of the Eiriens, the magical folk hid in little mounds, or sometimes inside trees or watery caves. It was a long time before the humans felt their absence. By the time they did, much as their joyful spirits were missed, a schism had formed between the races, and the nature spirits were rarely seen or heard. (The only exception was one tribe of faeries who would later join forces with the Eiriens to use their magic to fight the Moherians, invaders and enemies who'd find their way to Uisneach's shore.)

The Divine Practitioners were a powerful mixed race of magically gifted people: druids and shapeshifters, healers, musicians, storytellers and dancers. This line arose when Maker sent Olama, a being from Tir fo Thuinn, the land under the waves, to Uisneach. Olama, a great healer and poet, was gifted with many extraordinary powers, including the ability to shapeshift. He married an Eirien. Their descendants, including Oirion, Duirchlann and Amuira, all had special gifts, and seemed destined to live a peaceful existence with the other people and beings of Uisneach. Her mind was transported by the beauty of it all.

But then, the fifth race, the Moherians, arrived. Warlike by nature, they came by sea in huge, tall-masted warships and scattered across Uisneach, bringing their axes upon the heads of Uisneachans of all races. The first wave of them overwhelmed the Eiriens during the time that would be remembered as "The Great Wars." Those who survived became the feudal subjects of the Moherians, and Eirien kings were replaced, in large part, by Moherian kings.

Over time the races blended and spread across Uisneach. They created the separate territories now known as Appleduir or Wellsland; Cedarmara; Dromdara, the ancestral home of the Taranian royal family; Tynan Ibor; and Evalon, the Land of Faeries.

Battles were fought and peace accords signed until the time of King Banniman of the Taranian house, Brath's great-great-grandfather, who brought enduring peace to Uisneach.

The book ended with a terrible battle between two druids, which led to this very time. Peace so hard-won, and so long-lasting, might be broken now, thanks to the evil machinations of one self-serving prime minister, Lord Shamwa.

During the Moherian invasion, the High Priestess Glenamore proclaimed a prophecy. Beginning as an oral tradition, it was later put to paper by a secret order of scribes as the prophecy of the Mouse in *The Book of Leaves*. Buried in the royal library for centuries, it was revealed when Shamwa cursed King Brath. Shapeshifting crows carried copies of it across the land, giving its despondent inhabitants not only hope, but a sense of shared purpose.

Unfortunately, a page of the prophecy had been torn from the book. But they had enough information to know that help would arrive.

They waited and watched for the Mouse to come through the tree, and when she did...

Well, as they say, the rest is history, Briana thought. By the end of the afternoon, her back ached from leaning over the big book. She stood and stretched, trying to ease her throbbing muscles. *What a lineage I'm marrying into.*

A powerful and important lineage, said Silas.

Briana involuntarily looked out the window for Cailleach. Not seeing her, she relaxed. *Silas?*

Have you read all the history?

Yes. I'm trying to wrap my head around being involved in it. I'm puzzled about one thing, though.

What's that?

I wonder about the war between the druids. I get that the evil druid survived, but what happened to the good druid from Evalon?

That's a question we'd all like to have answered. That and the missin' page of the prophecy must somehow be related, but no one knows how or why. Uh oh, Sigel is asking me a question I can't answer because I'm not listenin' to him. I need to go.

She heard him chuckle, then nothing. *How strange this is.* She wondered how their telepathy worked, if they could control it, and what the ramifications were if they couldn't. As excited as she was about being able to communicate with him privately, she also had reservations about the potential lack of privacy. *Could he read all her thoughts?* She wasn't reading his all the time.

Briana mulled this over until she realized by the sun's position that it was past lunchtime. Cailleach should be back by now. Briana put water on the hearth for tea and searched for something to prepare for lunch. She found bread, butter, and strawberry preserves and was looking for more when the witch came in, carrying a basket filled with fiddleheads, some brownish mushrooms and a handful of herbs.

"The fiddlers are just perfect for the picking. You like them?"

Briana nodded enthusiastically. She and her mom went out every spring to collect the tender fronds before they opened up. "Love them."

"I see you have things ready. Good, I've worked up quite an appetite. Is that tea water ready?"

"Just about." Briana set two mugs on the table and dumped the herbs in the kettle. In her own mug she added a bit more of the raspberry and mugwort. Her discomfort was minimal, but it wouldn't hurt to dose herself once more today.

When the brew had steeped, she poured for them both. They sat down to their meal. Briana told Cailleach how far she'd gotten in the book and the older woman nodded approvingly. "Quite a history you've gotten involved with, isn't it?"

"Exactly what I was thinking just before you came in. I don't honestly know how I feel about being cast in the role of savior and Queen of Uisneach, but after getting to know some of the people here, I feel some responsibility for doing what I can to turn things around."

Cailleach looked into her mug. "It's a big burden you bear, Briana, and not one that you fully understand now, but hear this – when all is said and done, Uisneach will owe you a debt of gratitude such as we can never repay. Prophecies never come without a cost, and you will sacrifice much for the sake of Uisneach."

Briana leaned back in her chair and closed her eyes. "This will sound strange, but I keep having this feeling that none of this is news to me, like it's something I've known all along."

"Have you?"

Briana answered in a voice barely above a whisper. "Maybe this is what I've been waiting for my whole life."

Cailleach responded with a half-smile, as she picked up their plates and mugs. "Well then, best you get back to the lessons. We'll work on some basic magic this afternoon."

"When will the guys be back?" Briana asked, nonchalantly, as she pushed *The Book of Leaves* back into its spot on the shelf.

"They'll probably not be back tonight, lass. It's a long way to the mill. They'll stay the night there and come back tomorrow, perhaps in time for supper."

A look of disappointment must have skittered across her face, because Cailleach added, "Just as well. Give us a respite from their foolishness, hmm? We'll have some quiet and get a good night's rest."

After lunch Cailleach began to assess Briana's knowledge of herbals.

"Willow?" Cailleach challenged.

"Pain and fever," Briana shot back.

"Birch?"

"Gout, rheumatism and skin sores."

"Lemon balm?"

"Depression, uh, melancholia."

"Aye, what else?" Briana shook her head. "You want honey, you plant lemon balm," said Cailleach. "It calls the bees."

"Huh. Good to know."

"Horehound?"

Resting her head in her hands, Briana searched her brain for the answer. "Of course! Cough and cold."

"Mint?"

"Stomach ache."

"Comfrey?"

"Lots of things, but most importantly, wound healing and bone mending."

"Rowan bark?"

"Loose bowels, uh, flux."

"Rowan berries?"

"Laxative and sore throats. Of course you can make a jam that also helps with the flux."

"Well done," said Cailleach. "Salvia?"

Stumped, Briana shook her head, but before Cailleach could give the answer, she snapped her fingers. "Milk fever!"

"Excellent. Elder root?"

"Headaches, and encouraging labor pains."

"To stop bleeding?"

"Thistle or oak bark."

"Excellent. Always keep thistle and oak in your bag. What else is oak good for?"

"Leaves and bark for burns, tea for lung congestion, hemorrhoids or female infections." Briana paused and grinned. "Oh, and for getting between worlds."

Cailleach laughed and patted Briana's hand. "Indeed, wee Mouse, indeed."

They went on like this for several hours until both women were satisfied Briana was skilled enough to handle emergencies along the road to Ard Darach.

Shadows had begun to darken the room by the time Cailleach produced a small bag and emptied it of several small, smooth stones on the table. Briana observed for a few minutes as the crone moved the pieces around, her mouth moving in silent incantation. She looked up and motioned Briana to come closer. The stones had different symbols carved on them. Runes.

"I'm trying to send your mother a message about your welfare. Sit down, Briana, and place your hands on the stones while thinking about your mother. What would you say to her if she were here? Imagine it clearly in your mind."

It wasn't difficult to do, but it was emotional. The polished pebbles were initially cool to her touch, but warmed appreciably as she focused on the sensation and her intent. Briana easily fell into a trancelike state. Her eyes moistened as she imagined Katrina sitting before her. *Oh, Mom. I miss you so much.* A feeling of connection with her mother washed over her, and after assuring her mother of her well-being, she thought of everything that had happened to her since coming to Uisneach. She thought of Silas. *I think I'm in love with him*, she thought. That admission jarred her out of the trance, coupled as it was with the fear that Silas might also have heard her.

"Briana?" the witch asked, with concern.

"Something happened." Cailleach nodded. "Mom doesn't have any runes, though. How will she get the message?"

"It will translate to whatever medium she does use, so the cards will offer her the images she needs to receive your intention. You've done this kind of magic before."

It was a statement, not a question, and Briana confirmed it. "I wouldn't have called it magic, but yes, I've used divination cards and imagery before. I once attended a shamanic workshop and the journeying we did felt similar to this."

"What you just did does qualify as magic. But that's tomorrow's lesson. Hungry?"

Dara jumped up from his bed by the fire at the word, making the women laugh. After feeding him and the outside animals, they ate their own supper of ferns, mushrooms and carrots mixed with a little goat cheese, and talked about all that Briana had learned that day. Apple wine, a peat fire, a dog to pet and gentle conversation all worked their own kind of magic, easing the discomforts Briana had felt during the day.

Cailleach seemed to be dozing when Briana's attention was caught by Merlin's chirping. Turning to the bird, she listened for a minute before saying quietly, "I'll look forward to that."

"What?" Cailleach asked, suddenly wide awake and interested.

"Seeing him shapeshift. He said…" Briana stopped, astonished that she had actually heard the hawk say something to her.

"Well, well, Briana. You are full of surprises. That, my dear, is faerie magic."

CHAPTER TWELVE

ABRACADABRA

The next morning, Briana was staring holes through Dara, who stood cocking his head from side to side, when Cailleach joined her.

"You can't force it, Briana," Cailleach said. "Both parties have to be willing."

Briana turned from the dog to the witch. "It can be controlled, then?"

"I think so. I'm not a faerie, so I don't know exactly how it works, but it seems that animals and faeries can communicate telepathically when it's necessary."

Yeah, well, so can Silas and I, she thought. Briana squirmed under the witch's sudden, intense scrutiny. *I need to be very careful that I don't give anything away.* She didn't necessarily want to keep a secret from Cailleach, but she agreed with Silas that until they understood what was going on, it was best not to say anything. "So," she said, smiling and rubbing her hands together gleefully, "are we ready to get into the magic?"

The witch guided Briana to a chair at the table. "Magic is nothing more than the manipulation of energy for a purpose. As long as your intention is good, such as for healing illness, you've more power than you can imagine."

"So if I try to harm someone, then it won't work?"

"Oh, it will work, but that's not magic; it's called evil."

"*Oh*," Briana mouthed.

"Your visualization last night with the runes was an augury of one kind. Wise use of healing herbs and potions is another. The feelings lovers share between them, well that's another kind of spell altogether." Cailleach tittered, triggering Briana to laugh, also.

Cailleach gathered a bowl of water, a candle, several bird feathers and the rune stones. "Before we start, I must advise you not to have terribly high expectations. For some reason, there's been a general lessening of magical power. The protective spell I use around the cabin and forest doesn't last as long as it used to, and some of my enchantments seem a bit weak. I suspect it has something to do with the loss of faerie trees, but I'm not sure. However, you still must learn and practice your skills. Ready to get started?"

Briana nodded, eyes big and excited.

"You know the proper breathing technique, right?"

In answer, Briana sat back and closed her eyes, taking slow, deep breaths, and allowed her body and mind to settle. When she felt ready, she opened her eyes and gave a nod to her mentor.

"We work with the elements because they make up everything in the universe. We are nothing more than a particular form of water, fire, earth and air, you ken? Let's start with water." She pushed the clear water in front of Briana. "Now this is serious work, Briana. I want you to focus as much as you can on the water, remembering it's not just a bowl of water, but many drops of water gathering together. See it clearly. Try to imagine each single drop making up the whole. Focus all your attention and tell me when anything happens. It can take a long time to get this, so don't hurry. We have all day, aye? Do you feel relaxed?"

Briana nodded dreamily and gazed into the bowl, pushing away any thoughts that interfered with her ability to connect with the water. Nothing happened for a time. On some level, she was aware of the witch's presence near her, but Cailleach had more patience than Maker and sat silent and unmoving as Briana studied the element before her. She was about to give up when she noticed ripples spread out across the surface. Subtle colors appeared in the water. A small ahhh escaped her lips at this beautiful miracle.

"Now," Cailleach murmured, "believe that you are one with the water."

Briana journeyed into her own body, mentally seeing blood and plasma flowing through her veins. Vital liquids reaching out to the bowl of water. A wave moved between them, drawing them closer together until they became a single body of liquid. She barely breathed, wanting to hold this unity as long as she could.

"Gaze into the water, Briana, and notice what other images come to you. Don't try to force it, just continue observing and tell me if anything appears."

When Cailleach's face appeared in the bowl, she jumped, breaking the spell. "Oh no!" She turned to Cailleach, surprised and disappointed.

"It can be a bit of a shock the first time. Tell me, what or who did you see?"

"You. I saw your face as clearly as I'm looking at you now."

Cailleach sat down in the chair with an interested, almost smug look on her face, nodding appreciatively. "My, my, you are gifted. I had a feeling you might be."

Briana stared back at the water. "Who knew?"

They worked with water for a while longer before turning to fire. A candle became the locus of Briana's attention. Her confidence and excitement grew as she discovered a similar process to change the tiny flame into a dancing flame, which at one point, threatened to set the cabin on fire.

"Easy, girl, careful with that power. We don't want to magic us out of hearth and home."

Briana delighted in her newly discovered gift and wondered what else could be done magically, especially as it related to Silas.

Reading her expression, Cailleach said, "The most important thing to learn is the appropriate use of magic. Used well, it can be a blessing, but used for one's personal advantage, it can result in unimaginable heartache. Maker has a plan for us all and any attempt to disrupt or alter that plan, tempting as it may be, is most unwise."

"How do you know the difference, Cailleach?"

"That's the hard part, sometimes. You may be called on to use your powers in ways that do seem like interference, but it will be right to do so. I don't believe that Maker intends you to withhold a tool that could ensure the fulfillment of the prophecy. On the other hand, enchantment used to turn the head of a certain young bard would not be a wise use of the gift. Understood?"

"Cailleach, I wouldn't…" She couldn't finish the sentence since that was exactly what she was thinking.

"I'm sure you wouldn't. I'm trying to show you the difference between the proper and improper use of your gift. And Briana, your power will continue to grow as you grow in strength and wisdom."

Briana considered this. "So, is this journey I'm on inevitable? Is there no room for me to decide what I want to do?"

"You have the power to choose. Yes, but with choices come consequences, aye? Maker has a grander view than we do, and though we can always follow a direction other than the one meant for us, things might not turn out as well as they could. Faith is what's required to see this through. Not always easy. Your willingness to make choices consistent with the prophecy is critical to the survival of Uisneach, but know this lass – you won't be alone. There's many of us here to help you along."

"No pressure," she muttered.

The morning flew by. Briana was slicing slabs of bread for lunch, lost in a daydream.

"Is there enough for us, too?"

She jumped and the knife clattered across the table. Silas reached around her and caught it before it could hit the floor. His touch, grazing her waist, raised the alarm for the butterflies who'd set up permanent residence in her belly these days. She accepted the knife with a slight tremble in her fingers.

"Geez, Silas, you scared me! I didn't hear you come in."

"Sorry." He grinned. "Not really."

Louder steps announced Sigel's arrival behind him. She cut several more slices of bread as Cailleach instructed them to put the sacks of grain in the root cellar. They'd also bagged and cleaned a few birds for this evening's meal, a gift that Cailleach accepted with hearty appreciation.

During lunch, Sigel recounted the numbers of men gathering in Moiria. "Now that word has gotten out that the Mouse is here, they're coming out of the stones, ready to fight Shamwa."

"And will we be fighting?" Briana asked, picking at the food before her.

"Hopefully not. Priority one is getting you safely to Ard Darach to release Brath. Then we'll meet the prime minister with a full army and king. And maybe a queen."

Briana refused to react, but couldn't help stealing a glance at Silas to gauge his reaction. He stabbed a chunk of partridge, popped it in his mouth and chewed, giving away nothing by his expression.

"I've ordered most of the troops to stay put until we get there and send only scouts south to Long River. When we get to Moiria, we'll cross the river and head for Winge Mansion, while the troops fan out and make a slow march upriver. They can keep any of Shamwa's troops away from us.

"Sir Thomas will provide horses for us. We can head up the coast and then cut back across the river to the north of the castle. It's a little circuitous, but gives us distance and cover. We'd be too exposed if we went straight across the plains into the mountains. Going through Poet's Gap would bring us way too close to Aurum Castle, Lord Shamwa's residence."

Her world was being crowded with shapeshifters, druids, faeries and witches. Keeping the players straight was a full-time job. However, she replied with the confident cheer of someone who dealt with shapeshifters every day. "Sounds easy enough."

He gave her a warning look. "Nothing about this will be easy, Briana, but if we stay in a small group and move fast, we have a better chance of getting you to Ard Darach before we have to meet an army. Are you going to eat that, or can I have it?"

She slid her bowl of barely touched food to him. "What exactly do you mean by a small group?"

"I mean for the three of us," he wagged a finger at her, Silas and himself, "to get to Winge Mansion and then make a run for Ard Darach. I think we can stay relatively hidden. Our army will create a wall between us and the Gray Military."

He continued to talk about military matters and training the troops as they finished their lunch. When he leaned back with a satisfied burp, Cailleach rose and gathered the dishes. Briana rose to help.

"No, lass, back to the studies for you. You still have to read up on the Divine Practitioners," the witch said, pointing her in the direction of the bookcase.

"Ah, me favorite subject," Silas said, staring at the ceiling dreamily. "In fact, why don't we walk down to the brook and I'll tell you the whole story so you don't have to read it from a dusty old book. We might even catch a few fish while we're at it."

Please say yes, Cailleach, she prayed silently.

The witch looked from student to bard and sighed. "Well, I suppose it would be nice to have some fish, and you do have a knack for finding the good ones. But no shenanigans, you wily charmer," she said, giving Silas a pointed look.

"Wiley charmer? Me? I'm on me best behavior, Cailleach."

Allowing Cailleach no opportunity to rethink her consent, Briana headed for the door, Silas right behind her. When Dara tried to follow, she spoke firmly. "No, Dara. You need another day or so off that foot. Maybe next time." Lowering his head, the dog went back to the bedding, turned a couple of circles and dropped down with a disappointed shudder.

I'm such a clever lad, Silas thought, steering her quickly out of the arbor.

How so?

Well, milady, you'll get your studies in, we might fish and we get to spend time together without a chaperone? I'd say that qualifies me as clever.

She smiled up at him. "Yes, you are. And now, Bard, tell me about the Divine Practitioners."

They walked through an ancient forest that set the stage for the story of Uisneach's magical people. Silas began to recite the thousands of years of history that he'd spent his life committing to memory.

"You'll have read about Olama and his beautiful wife, Princess Amuira?"

"Yes, he came from Tir fo Thuinn to counsel the Eiriens in spiritual and philosophical matters."

Silas gave her an approving smile at her correct pronunciation of the mythical place. "Olama's powers were extraordinary, and his wisdom nearly as legendary. He became second-in-command to the King of Dromdara. When he and the king's daughter fell in love, they were given approval to marry under the Uisneach Tree, a very high honor.

"Their children were blessed with mystical and magical powers and eventually became the race known as the Divine Practitioners, the witches, druids, priests and priestesses, and shapeshifters. Did you read about Oirion, the great musician and storyteller?"

"Yes, the first druid and bard. He had a child with the dryad."

Silas nodded. "Duirchlann. 'Child of the oak.'" He looked down at Briana with a playful smile. "Me great-great-great- and so on and so forth-grandfather. Duirchlann…"

She raised a finger to stop him. "Are you telling me that you're a druid?"

"Oh, aye. From the bardic lineage. How did you think I came to be a bard? It's sort of one and the same."

"I hadn't thought it through that far. Wow! You're a druid," she murmured, gaining new respect and feeling suddenly a little intimidated.

"It's just me lineage, Briana," he said, noticing the look on her face. "I'm just me. But back to Duirchlann. He was very powerful and passed his magic down many generations. Some of his children were great healers, some singers and storytellers, and some fine leaders and judges. Duirchlann married an Eirien woman named Nieve and they had several children, all born with special powers. One of them, Catriona, married the faerie king, Kailen of Evalon, a warrior among the faerie. This union produced a rare and beautiful form of druidism with strong healin' power.

"These bloodlines were passed down a few generations. Those who were more skilled at healin' became witches and could marry if they chose. Most druids did not marry, though there was no prohibition. They simply chose to take on students to carry on the practices."

"Wouldn't the students have to have natural magic?" Briana asked.

"Aye, but in those days, it was likely that everyone had at least a wee bit of magic."

"But some druids married?" She didn't know why this point seemed important to her, but she felt compelled to assure herself that they could.

"Oh, aye. There was one great druid, Atan, who married a witch, Croniana. They moved to the forests of Appleduir and had two daughters.

"Then came the split between the druids and witches. Many of the witches moved to the forests of Appleduir and focused on healin' and divination, only coming into the villages when sought by folk to treat the sick or deliver difficult babies. The druids, on the other hand, became bards or priests and engaged in the seasonal rituals, judgments, and unfortunately, the politics of the land.

"Three schools for druidic craft developed in Uisneach. The first, in Cedarmara, focused on bardic skills; the people there were known to have a deep love of story and song and created the beautiful tales and art contained in *The Book of Leaves*. The second was in Dromdara, and these druids became counselors and judges. The druids of Evalon, the third school, worked closely with the faeries to advance natural magic and healin' arts."

He paused, giving Briana time to absorb the history. "What about the kings?" she asked. "Were they magical, too?"

"Not very magical usually, but in the beginnin', druids and witches held equal power with kings. Workin' together with the monarchy, the Divine Practitioners developed laws, rituals and practices that would contribute to the social and religious order of the realm. Sadly, as time passed, they took a secondary, or complimentary role, and basically served the monarchs as deemed necessary."

"That's a bummer."

"A what?"

"I mean that's too bad."

"Anyway," he continued with a nod, "although the druids were basically the good guys with the best interests of Uisneach at heart, sometimes they got caught up in the power struggles of kings and prime ministers, like Artanin did with Lord Shamwa.

"Do you recall that the Uisneach Tree was the source of all magic? Well, the faeries had done well to hide themselves and the Uisneach Tree deep in the forest. Very near here," he said, grabbing Briana's hand to help her over twisted tree roots and a small boulder pile.

The sturdy warmth of his hand around hers caused a rush of emotion. She stopped. Whether he was reading her mind or body language, he paused with her, not letting go of her hand right away. Words were unnecessary. Until they were.

"Come along, milady. There's more to the story."

Letting go of her hand, he continued. "As I said, the tree is somewhere in this very forest."

She searched the shadowy grove for evidence of the tree.

"The tree was, is, well guarded by the current dryad, Nionon. She and Cailleach have thus far kept it well protected. Shamwa believes that by eliminatin' all the faerie trees, he will become the sole source of power, now that King Brath is incapacitated. He does not understand that when the Uisneach Tree dies, all of Uisneach dies with it."

"Is that really true, Silas?"

He nodded gravely. "The Uisneach Tree is the source of all life, not just magic. It connects the above with the below, holds all things together. What *I* don't understand is why Artanin is helpin' him. Artanin knows very well what will happen if the Uisneach Tree is destroyed. I suppose that's what happens when you become corrupted by evil. You begin to believe you are a god and more powerful than Maker.

"Shamwa must be more worried than ever. They now have you, the Mouse of Prophecy, to contend with. He will surely focus all his attention on gettin' his hands on you, and that's what we must prevent."

As they approached the trail, Briana heard rushing water. Silas led her down the stone steps to the basin of the falls, but rather than stay at the pool, turned her downstream. "Too loud. The fish will be scared and we won't be able to talk."

"The fish won't be scared," she replied, letting him know she wasn't that naïve.

He shrugged. "Well, we do need to finish your lesson and I don't intend to scream."

As they skirted a bumble of tree stumps and roots, odd-shaped stones and an occasional wee salamander, he continued to talk, finishing the genealogy. "And so, the druid, Artanin, came from the Dromdara line of druids. Actually, so did Sigel, though he doesn't put much stock in that part of his ancestry. Cailleach and her sister Ealga the daughters of Atan and Croniana, came from the Appleduir line. Sir Thomas came from the Tynan Ibor line and I'm descended from the Cedarmara line. The great druidic mystery is, as you asked yesterday, What happened to the Evalon line? And the answer is – we don't know."

It was fascinating history and she could appreciate the predicament this kingdom was in. Coming to terms with the idea that she somehow fit into its story and might even be necessary to its salvation was something else. And she still couldn't get past the fact that this man, who sang like an angel but could just as easily put an arrow through a bad guy, was a Divine Practitioner. Her perception of druidism had just been turned upside down.

The moss-carpeted trail led them to a section of brook far below the falls, where the pools entertained only small cascades and offered plenty of hiding spots for brookies. Gnarly trees hovered over the glittering water like ancient guardians over treasure. Finding a spot he liked, Silas reached into his pocket and produced a fishing line made out of a nettle and some hemp fiber, a small hook, and a handful of worms. After instructing her on the correct way to bait the hook, he demonstrated his technique for catching the small fish that lived in the mossy pools.

"You must sneak up on them, aye? If they hear or see you, they won't bite."

He no sooner had the line in the pool than it jerked and spun. With a snap of his wrist, he had a decent-sized brook trout on the bank beside him.

"Wow! That was fast. You don't just have a knack, you're amazing!"

"Your turn." He set her up beside a promising pool, then moved a few paces back and sat on the ground, putting a boulder to good use as a back rest. Briana tried to sit quietly, waiting for something to happen, looking at him from time to time, wondering what was wrong.

He shook his head. "Patience, *a mhuirnin*, patience."

Sun filtered through the leaves of the trees, dancing across Briana's body. It made her feel like a faerie.

What do you think Cailleach meant about us behavin' ourselves?" he wondered, chewing on a fern leaf.

She turned slowly and looked at him, raising one eyebrow. *I'm pretty sure you know what she meant. Silas, we need to talk about this mind-reading thing. I like it, but I don't understand it.*

He slid his foot back and forth across a mossy patch. *I don't, either. I've never heard of it, so it's some kind of new magic, I think.*

"Can you control it?" she asked.

"I don't know. I don't hear every thought you have and I assume you don't hear all of mine." One corner of his mouth lifted slightly.

"Cailleach says that I have a gift for talking to animals."

"Oh? That's faerie magic."

"Um hum. She said that both parties have to be willing to communicate. I wonder if this is similar. Maybe we both have to want to communicate something."

He shrugged. *I need to think about it, but in the meantime, I still think we should stay quiet about it. I don't mean to be hidin' things from them. I'd just like to have a little more time to work it out.*

Something tugged at her line. She whirled around to manage the bite, turning so sharply she lost her balance and fell into the water. Silas was instantly at her side, but it was too late; she was thoroughly soaked. However, she had the wiggling animal still on the line. Grabbing it with both hands, she raised it above her head in victory. "I got him!" They both laughed as he helped her out of the water.

Warm sun and a light breeze dried her dress as they sat beside the brook on a large, flat rock, enjoying the afternoon. Silas captured two more unsuspecting fish while they chatted about everything – their childhoods, the mechanics of hunting with bow and arrow, and music. He was particularly interested in her description of her favorite Irish band, which sang mostly traditional music, performing on elaborate stages with gigantic Celtic crosses.

Their hands were so close she could feel the hair on the back of his hand tickle hers. She felt the heat from his thigh next to hers. Her body was awakening to this man like a new blossom reaching for the radiance of the sun. His sun. She closed her eyes, unwilling to make any sound or movement that would create space between them. His energy seemed so familiar to her that she could almost imagine what his skin felt like, how his joints fused together and where the muscles of his chest were the strongest. *It's like I know every part of you*, she thought, and heard him make a sound of agreement.

Silas, I want to go back to the druids not marrying.

He cocked his head toward her. "That certainly seems to be a topic of great concern to you."

"Why did some druids not marry?"

He scratched his head and didn't answer right away. "Well, for one thing, bein' a healer or a bard is mentally time consumin' work and we need a lot of time alone to do what we do."

That answer wasn't what she expected. "And for another?"

"For another, they don't need to. Marriage isn't required for people to raise a family. For druids, the freedom required for their studies and work often makes marriage seem too restrictive."

"So," she thought out loud, "people don't have to be married to, uh, have a physical relationship with someone?"

"No. Sexual relations are considered natural and nothin' to be ashamed of. That's not to say marriage isn't desirable as a commitment between people, but it's not a law."

Well, that's the best news I've heard since I got here, she thought, a smile spreading across her face.

"Unless of course, you're royalty. Specifically, a queen."

She shot up, outraged at what he was implying. "You're saying that everyone can make love with whomever they like, whenever they like, but I can't?"

He looked rather glum himself. "That about sums it up."

"That's not fair!"

"No, but it's the law. Men are forgiven and even expected their dalliances, but queens are meant to be pure and above such things."

"That's absurd," she said, but realized that this moral code was only beginning to change back home. "And what would happen if someone — like me, broke the law?"

He mimed a rope being put around his neck and pulled tight.

"I can't believe it. I must have surely drawn the cosmic short straw."

He understood what she meant and sighed. "Well, perhaps there were two straws."

She sat down again. They grew quiet; the cheerful sound of birds singing and the water's bubbling melody antithetical to Briana's bittersweet feelings. How unfair that she should finally meet the man she could love, only to have him completely out of her reach? She wanted to help save Uisneach. She wanted to see the evil Lord Shamwa prevented from destroying magic in this beautiful kingdom. But stealing a glance at the man beside her, she also wanted to follow the path their hearts were trailblazing.

He broke the silence. "You said the other day that you would like to steal me heart."

She glanced over at him, a hopeful smile forming on her lips.

"It's yours. It has been since before we met in that glade."

The smile faded and she held her breath, feeling the inevitability of the word "but."

"I've longed for you me whole life. When we met, I was able to give that longin' a name. Briana."

Her name on his lips was a blessing. She nodded, knowing exactly how he felt. He was her red archer, the one who listened to her secrets, held her tears and was the source of her own yearning.

"But your body is not mine, nor will it ever be."

"It doesn't have to be so," she said. She moved her hand a fraction and their hands touched, warm against the cold river stone. Her eyes pleaded and promised. His radiated understanding and regret.

"If there were a way around this destiny, *a mhuirnin*, I'd singlehandedly slay every enemy who stood in the way. But the prophecy will not be denied. Uisneach depends on it, and on you. I must not play the enemy to it." When her eyes welled and a tear fought and escaped, he wiped it away tenderly. "I have pledged fealty to me king and I pledge it now to you. I will be your most devoted friend and your staunchest defender, but that is all I can be to you."

She shook her head. "That's not what I want you to be."

He smiled and gently kissed the knuckles of her hand. "It's not all I want either, but Uisneach needs us. Who knows, we may both discover that friendship and loyalty are the better part, *mo chroí.*"

He looked up at the sun starting to dip beneath the pines. "If we don't get back, for sure Sigel will be out after us." He held out his hand to help her up.

"All things considered," she said, wryly, "I've really enjoyed this afternoon, Silas. Thank you."

"Aye, me, too. There'll be other days to spend bein' lazy and catchin' fish, just maybe not for a while."

Cailleach was thrilled with the offering. After Silas cleaned them, she put the fish in a sizzling pan over the fire. It was a peaceful group who ate that night, enjoying one of the few remaining days of rest they would have for a long time, she supposed.

After dinner, they settled around the fire. Sigel pulled out a game board which Briana quickly identified as a Uisneachan form of chess. "Care for a game of *ríocht*, Silas?"

"Do I look addled? I'm terrible at that game. Why don't you teach Briana?"

"We call it chess back home, and I know the basics, but I'm not that good at it, either."

"Sigel is the champion of Uisneach," Silas said. "No one ever beats him!"

Briana agreed to play and found it simpler and less drawn out than modern chess, though she still couldn't quite get the nuances. "Why do I keep losing?" she asked, embarrassed by her ineptness.

"The game is all about the kings and the queens." Sigel reset the board to show her how she should have played the last few moves. "First you must understand that the queen can never checkmate the king alone. He will always have an escape route. So she must work with her king to checkmate the opposing king. You can do this by moving the queen away from the opposing king, creating a 'knight's shadow.'" He demonstrated by moving the queen in a trailing pattern that literally created a shadow around the king. "You do this until the king traps himself in a corner, creating the stalemate. The queen, if she's tricky enough, then moves away from the king, like she's giving him some breathing space, you see."

"Or playin' hard to get," Silas interjected.

Sigel chuckled and moved the king around the nearby squares. "Now the two kings join in a dance for power until they are in this tight position, at which point, that pesky queen slides right in front of the king to create the checkmate. She is staring the king right in the face, but sadly, he has nowhere to go."

Briana watched intently. So did Silas, his eyes following the pieces as they chased each other around the squares. Sigel continued. "The king can't capture the queen because it would put him at odds with the other king. And that, my dear, would be a bad and illegal move."

They thought Cailleach had fallen asleep in her chair and tried to be quiet. Growling under her breath, Briana moved her queen around, following Sigel's example.

Without opening her eyes, the witch spoke. "Don't be so quick to the end game, Briana. Sometimes success takes a long time, and it always requires patience. Besides, the most important part of chess is not winning or losing."

"Then what is it?" Briana asked.

"It's about strategy, vision and seeing the big picture. You won't win if you don't think it through. Do you remember what you did yesterday with the water and the candle? Try that."

Sigel reset the board. Refocusing her breath and attention on the field in front of her, Briana imagined the arrangement represented the game they were all playing in real time. Everything around her disappeared as she directed her sight more intensely, as Cailleach taught her. Things began to change, mountains rose out of red squares, a river ran through the lines that separated the blocks, and some of them melded into one wide plain across the playing field. The king shapeshifted into a man sitting next to the tower at Ard Darach. The knight's horse, carrying Sigel, reared up and moved nearer the king. Looking to the queen, Briana saw herself drifting back and forth between the two kings. The opposing king, she realized with widening eyes, was Silas.

The image jolted her back to the normal chessboard.

Her friends were watching her speculatively. "Did you see that?" she whispered. They shook their heads.

Eyes still closed, Cailleach advised, "Don't let yourself be so surprised by unexpected turns of events, Briana. That will kill your game quicker than anything. Maintain your calm, at all cost."

Later, tucked in bed, images of the living chess pieces battled fiercely inside her head. In every scene and in her dreams, the opposing king won every time.

CHAPTER THIRTEEN

"NON NOBIS SOLUM NATI SUMUS…"

Not for ourselves alone are we born.
—Cicero, from "De Officiis" ("On Duties")

he heavens roared and water poured from furious skies. Briana considered the glistening spider web swaying precariously in a corner of the porch, its tenant wisely hidden elsewhere. The fire snapped and crackled, its music accented by the clicking of bone needles as Cailleach, rocking in her chair, knitted wool into a sock. Sigel appeared to be dozing, but she knew he wasn't; more likely, he was planning the next leg of their journey. Silas sat nearby, staring out the window, reflection being the primary tool of his craft.

Briana was glad for the storm that had changed their plans. Sigel had wanted them to leave for Moiria at sunrise. It wasn't just that she was still sore from yesterday's grueling workout with sword and oak shield (both made by Sigel for her); like the spider, she wanted to hide away, to stay here, sheltered and content with her friends. Even if it meant another punishing session with sword and shield. Though Sigel said "she'd do," she knew he'd want her to do better.

A coin for your thoughts?

She turned to see Silas watching her with a soft expression.

I was just thinking how happy I am to have another day here.

Aye, it's pleasant, but it won't save the king.

I know.

He raised one eyebrow.

"Briana, let's take another look at your map," said Sigel. She turned to find him and Cailleach watching her and Silas. Again.

She rolled the piece of leather out on the table. Sigel studied it, but shook his head. "I don't see much here, do you?"

Briana closed her eyes and took some slow deep breaths. When the dreaminess came over her, she opened her eyes and stared at the map. Symbols shimmered lightly across Uisneach. A tendril of smoke arose from Cailleach's cabin. Long River flowed normally and the wretched apple orchard stood undisturbed. Three new things caught her attention. One was the appearance of tiny men advancing on Tynan Ibor. She frowned. This meant Shamwa's followers were in pursuit, making their pending departure even more crucial. The second was the image of black birds flying across the realm, and the third was the Uisneach Tree standing just to the north of the cabin. It seemed to Briana that a face was looking at her from within the tree, holding a barky finger to its lips as if to warn her not to mention its appearance. Advising Cailleach and the men about the soldiers and the crows, she kept the persuasive face to herself.

The rain stopped shortly after lunch and left a dripping but sunny forest in its wake.

"One more hunting trip, Silas? I expect Cailleach could use whatever we can find."

"Good idea," he agreed, picking up his bow and quiver.

After the two had gone, Cailleach invited Briana to join her by the fire. Briana was just getting cozy when Cailleach spoke, not breaking stride with the rocking of her chair.

"Tread carefully with Silas, Briana." When Briana didn't respond, she continued, "He's a bonny lad for certain and anyone with one eye for seeing could tell you have feelings for him. Seems he has some for you, too. But it cannot be, and it's best to push those feelings aside while you still can."

Quickly weighing possible responses, Briana chose honesty. "Have you ever been in love, Cailleach?"

"Aye, I have."

"Then you know how impossible that advice is."

The witch studied the young woman. "Is this the first time you've been in love, lass?"

Briana nodded, looking at the fire.

"Then you don't know what's possible. I know it seems unthinkable right now, but for his sake and yours, as well as for Uisneach, you must try and train your thoughts to what your destiny has chosen for you. Trust me, if you don't, your hearts will be destroyed by what you cannot have."

When Briana didn't respond, she continued, "Do you know that I have a sister? Ah, you do know from the history, of course. What you don't know is that we haven't spoken to each other since we were young women and fell in love with the same man."

The witch leaned back in the rocker, but held Briana's gaze. "Borrum was a druid from the Dromdara line. He was handsome, strong and powerful. I adored him. We were inseparable, and I thought we would be wed the fall of that year. I went away to Tynan Ibor to study for several months. After I returned, I went foraging at the river one day and found Borrum and Ealga in a passionate embrace and kissing. They'd fallen in love while I was gone. I felt betrayed and wouldn't speak to either of them. Borrum left our village, hoping his absence would help heal the wound between me and my sister. Shortly thereafter, he was killed by a rare bear attack.

"I blamed Ealga and eventually she left, too. We never saw each other again. Impossible love has caused me years of heartache. I do not wish that upon anyone, least of all you. You and Silas are not meant for each other and you must let him go."

Briana's heart ached for Cailleach and her sister. "Is there no hope of reconciliation between you and Ealga?"

"I don't know. We've lived separate lives for so long."

"You just said nothing is impossible, Cailleach. You're right. The very fact that I'm sitting here having this conversation with you points to that fact."

"I am old, Briana, and thought I'd experienced everything I must to move on from this life. Perhaps I have not. Separation was a steep price to pay for loving deep enough to be hurt, but not deep enough to forgive." She sighed. "I suppose I must find a way to forgive my sister."

Briana smiled and took her hand. "As to Silas and me, I have to tell you, I don't agree that we are not meant for each other."

She told the witch about her resistance to any romantic affairs back home, that sense of longing she'd always had, and even the red archer figurine. "Why would Silas be the answer to all that, if we weren't meant for each other?"

After a few moments of thought, Cailleach shook her head. "I don't know, but I do know you must marry King Brath and that means you cannot have a relationship with Silas. It really is that simple."

"Silas said we could be killed for it."

"He's right, and I'm relieved to hear that he's at least thought about that."

Her tranquility shattered, Briana struggled to get through the rest of the afternoon. Hours passed. When the men failed to return for supper, she and Cailleach ate without them. Cailleach spent the evening knitting while Briana read aloud from *The Book of Leaves*.

Briana yawned and closed the book. "I guess Sigel and Silas aren't coming back tonight."

"They probably decided to camp out and hunt again in the morning." Cailleach rose and smoored the fire.

"I guess I'll go to bed. Good night, Cailleach," she said, patting Dara's head as she walked by.

"Good night, lass."

The cabin was dark and silent, the night held together by Cailleach's rhythmic breathing. Restless, Briana puttered around her room until there was nothing more to putter at. She snuffed out the candle and went to sit by the window. Moonlight illuminated parts of the forest not cloaked in shadow. It didn't take her long to spot the minstrel sitting under the tree, strumming his guitar and singing softly to himself. Her heart ached. *Was he singing about her? A tragedy about a handsome man and a beautiful girl, who, having fallen in love, were held apart by an evil king?* She instantly regretted the thought. By all accounts Brath was handsome, kind and beloved by his subjects, a good man and fine monarch. This was no forced marriage; she had accepted her part in this prophecy. Yet, her heart couldn't help thinking all the things young thwarted lovers think when the object of their heart's desire is unattainable.

Silas raised his head to the window and their eyes met. Time stopped. Attraction, which in daylight must be hidden, was communicated across the land separating them. She prayed this moment would never end, but even as she wished it, he stood, and with one last look of longing that would stay in her heart forever, silently moved into the dark interior of the forest.

Briana fell into a troubled sleep, haunted by the face in the tree, which was telling her to wake up. She did wake, and in a haze, rose and went to the map, unrolling it on the bed. The tree and the face now had a greenish iridescence hovering over them. Emerald spiraled up from the center of the map and found its way to bare inches in front of Briana before moving away, compelling her to follow. Quickly donning her dress and boots, she followed the ethereal entity. Tiptoeing down the stairs, she walked past Dara, who lifted his head and then stood to chaperone her. Trying to stop him would be futile, so she let him come.

The green spiral led her out of the cabin and into the woods. She followed it, with no concern or caution, in spite of Shamwa's men camped not so far away; she could feel the shielding of forest magic. The forest was eerily lit by the quarter moon and unnervingly hushed. Owls and insects alike seemed to be on alert to what was unfolding in their home. Woman and dog moved deeper into the forest to the waterfall and down the brook past where she and Silas had spent the afternoon fishing. She paused, lingering on the pleasant memory. Urged on by the green wraith, she eventually came to an ancient yew forest, the trees' enormous, gnarly trunks and roots spreading out around the massive standing stones placed in a circle. *By druids?* The brook meandered around the ancient rocks, its musical tinkle adding to the spell of this sacred grove, leading her to the tree she had come to be with. This magnificent ash towered majestically through the canopy created by the yews, made more mystical by the moon's light through the leaves. Dara whined and lay down. Tentatively, Briana approached the ash tree. A beautiful face peered out of its trunk. Musical chimes emanated from within it. All was bathed in green light. The tree began to tremble and open, allowing the dryad to emerge slowly, separating herself from the trunk. Briana waited, suspended in the moment, breathing in the essence of the creature.

"Hello, Mouse," the dryad said, in an earthy voice that Briana wasn't certain was actually audible.

"Briana," she corrected automatically, then realizing her rudeness, Briana quickly apologized.

The beautiful female spirit had a laugh like bells. "Briana it is. You may call me Nionon." Now fully formed, she was glorious. Tall and slender, with smooth nut-brown skin and streaming pale golden hair and her branchlike limbs swaying gently around her, she seemed both human and arboreal. Raw, pulsing energy drew Briana into her goddess embrace.

"Is this the Uisneach Tree?" Briana asked, conscious of the peculiarity of the circumstances, yet feeling no insecurity or confusion, only awe.

"Indeed it is, the heart and soul of Uisneach. I am its guardian."

"Could I travel through this tree back to where I came from, like I did with the oak?"

"I don't know, but would you wish to?"

It was a good question. The dryad gave her time to consider.

"No, I don't want to go back. I can't believe I'm saying that. I miss my mother terribly, but this is my home now." Acceptance strengthened her and she asked, "Why did you call me here?"

Nionon's hair danced gracefully about her body. "You're about to embark on an important expedition, one that will challenge you in every way a human being can be tested. I may be able to help prepare you for the journey."

"How?"

"First, we must talk of magic. You're learning that you have some unusual gifts."

"Like talking to animals, manipulating elements and…"

"Mind-reading?"

Briana's eyes went wide. *How does she know that?* She was considering how much to admit when Nionon continued. "Cailleach is a good teacher of the elementals and you are learning quickly. Being proficient is critical to your journey. It may well save lives. Keep studying, keep practicing."

Briana nodded, having heard this before.

"I imagine realizing that you could talk to animals was shocking."

"Cailleach believes I have faerie magic. Is that true?"

"It is," the dryad said cheerfully. "You have that blood in your veins. Your heritage is a key to the reason you are the Mouse of Prophecy. I suspect the faeries will come to you soon and explain this further. What I can tell you is that you are vital to the future of this kingdom. You are the rightful Queen of Uisneach, and its survival depends on you. It's a responsibility you'll need to accept if you are to continue on this journey.

"That leaves the question of the connection you and Silas feel for each other."

Briana groaned. If one more person told her how wrong they were for each other, she'd scream.

"This may be difficult to understand, but the reason you and Silas feel so strongly toward one another is because you share the same soul. That's why you can communicate without words."

Not what I was expecting to hear, Briana thought, flinching as a chill rippled through her. *And yet...* "So, are you saying we're soulmates?"

"Not exactly. It goes deeper than that. Any two people can feel the kindred spirit of two separate souls, but only rarely do two people come together who share a single soul. You feel like you loved Silas the first time you saw him."

"Before that, even," Briana said.

The dryad nodded in understanding. "I have been, in one form or another, with this forest since the dawn of time. And so have you and Silas. Everyone has. We are one with its ever-changing life force. You are eternal and have traveled the Wheel of Life many times, your body regenerated, like the seasons.

"You and Silas are, and have been, inseparable throughout time. Now, you've come together for a specific purpose, to share a difficult path that requires tremendous forfeit. In this season, Briana, you hold the key to balancing the Great Wheel. To do that, you will experience both abiding love and terrible sorrow. Loss and gain. Giving and receiving.

"But you are living the dance, dearest, creating with every moment new alchemy, new life, and new opportunities. You have many partners in the dance. Silas is only one of them, with his own destiny to fulfill. This is only one moment in a long migration of your soul. If you both stay true to the path, I can promise that you will create an enchantment so strong no one can ever harm either of you or Uisneach. Perhaps that knowledge will make your way less painful.

"You must live in the moment while remembering it is only one of many, leading to something more important than a single day or a particular opportunity. Imagine a weaver weaving a tapestry. So many threads must go into the creation. Without every single one, the design would be incomplete. You, everyone you love, and even some you don't, such as Lord Shamwa, are threads in this tapestry."

"How do I stop these feelings for Silas?"

"You don't. You must become more aware of what your soul knows: you and Silas live as one, for all eternity. Sometimes as lovers, sometimes as friends, and sometimes as partners serving a higher, holy purpose. That will help you sort out the perdition of your heart."

"But how?"

"Through love, Briana. Love of not just one person, but love of all. There are so, so many ways to love. The best decisions you can make will be based on the love of everyone and everything in Uisneach, not just you and Silas, and not just in the physical sense. Remember, if Uisneach fails, then there's nothing for you and the bard in this world. Nothing for anyone. You will constantly be called upon to trust in something beyond yourself and your desires in each moment."

"It's a lot to ask of a person."

The dryad acknowledged this with a slight dip of her head. "Knowing all of this, you must choose between acting for personal happiness or the good of an entire kingdom."

The dryad gave her time to battle conflicting desires and emotions. Finally, Briana raised determined eyes to Nionon. "I doubt I fully understand what I'm giving up, but, yes, I believe I came through that tree for a reason, and I must honor my role no matter how much it hurts."

The dryad smiled. "I will not lie to you, Briana. What you've been through so far is nothing compared to what awaits you. Grave danger and staggering amounts of loss and grief are ahead. You must understand that when you leave this grove, but also know you have a good many gifted and powerful beings looking out for you. Cailleach has helped you, but she is not the only one."

"The crow."

The dryad nodded. "For one, yes. Lord Sigel is another. He may end up closer to you than anyone, in the end. Even King Brath will have something to teach you, something that will enhance your soul's growth. Many surprising new friendships and relationships will develop that are meant to help you mature. Be open to the wonder and joy of it, dearest. Perhaps destiny will not seem such an enemy in the end."

It seemed every leaf, nut and drop of water in the forest acknowledged Briana's decision and offered her their loving embrace, bringing a momentary sense of peace.

"One more thing, Briana. Do you see that stone?" Nionon pointed to the largest standing stone, a gray slab at least ten feet high and half as wide, that stood like a sentinel on a small hill. "Go to it and receive its gift. This will be your own source of protection and magic."

Briana walked to the stone, its vitality washing in waves over her the closer she got. The forest seemed to pulsate with life, making her dizzy. Laying a hand on the rock to steady herself only strengthened her connection to the stone. She feared she'd be pulled in. She cried out, jerking away as the surface began to shift. A sword emerged, the likes of which she had never seen, and slid into her hand. The emerald light in the forest intensified. A bolt of lightning struck the granite stave. She cried out, then realized she wasn't hurt. The forest seemed to wrap itself around her as she held the magnificent weapon in her hands, the metal gleaming in the moonlight. Powerful energy moved back and forth between her and the sword. Much larger and heavier than the sword she'd been using, it was not only an impressive weapon, but a work of art, with intricate carvings of the history of Uisneach along its blade. On its point, a faerie tree, then higher, the harbor at Cedarmara with its mighty sailing ships, and faeries dancing in Evalon. Near the hilt was an image of a great castle. Projecting slightly above the center of the pommel was a relief carving of the Uisneach Tree and a mouse. She sucked in her breath.

The dryad now stood next to her.

"It's beautiful," Briana said, faintly.

"It is yours, Briana. Once named, it will become a part of you. No one else will ever be able to use its magic."

Closing her eyes, Briana felt its magic surge through her, and thought of all the Celtic stories she'd read in her life. The one legend that had always resonated with her was about Nuada, the first king of the Tuatha De' Danann, a brave and just king who led the old ones into battle against the Fir Bolg. When he lost his hand in battle and it seemed he would be king no more, his physician created a silver hand to replace the missing one. Nuada resumed the throne for many years. His perseverance and dedication to his people was legendary.

Briana turned to the dryad, lifted the sword above her head with both hands and declared, "I thank Maker for this gift and bestow upon it the name of Nuada!"

The dryad smiled, and Briana felt her slipping back into the tree. "Oh, don't go, Nionon."

"I must and so must you, Briana. You may never have imagined yourself doing what you are about to do, but you will be triumphant. You must learn though, how to protect not only your people, but your own heart. If you cannot do that, your heart will destroy you and bring an end to Uisneach."

"I won't fail," she promised, unsure how she would safeguard both Uisneach and her heart.

The dryad settled into her resting place as she wished Briana Makerspeed, and became once again a part of the tree, her beautiful face the only thing Briana could see in the bark.

The green light began to recede from the forest and with it waned Briana's strength. She knelt on the grass next to the Uisneach Tree, helpless. Dara came to her side and laid his nose and paw on her back. Normal noises returned to the forest, the hooting of an owl, scuffing of tiny paws through ground clutter, a slight breeze through the trees and the addition of one unexpected sound: footsteps. All she could do was whimper.

"It's all right *a mhuirnin*, I have you. I'll see you safely home."

"Silas," she moaned. "How did you... did you see..."

"Aye, I saw and I heard. Perhaps the message was for me as well, aye?

We don't need to talk now, *mo chroi*. It can wait." He pulled heavy twine from his bag, tied Nuada to her side and picked her up in his arms.

"I can walk, Silas, if you help me. Just give me a minute."

He carried her to a boulder outside of the circle and sat, holding her on his lap and stroking her hair as she recovered. She settled into the sanctuary of his arms, reassured by the familiar beating of his heart.

"What happens next, Silas?"

"We save the king and the kingdom."

CHAPTER FOURTEEN

WHITHER THOU GOEST

Daylight was far from breaking but seeing that everyone was up, Sigel had decided they may as well head for Moiria.

"Will I see you again, Cailleach?" Briana cinched the belt holding her sword Nua, her nickname for Nuada.

"Of course. I'll meet you at the castle."

"If I lived a million years I couldn't thank you enough for all you've done for us – for me. I'll miss you."

Cailleach held Briana away from her and searched her eyes. "You're ready."

"I am."

"Go in peace and good health, Your Majesty." She hugged Briana and patted Dara affectionately, urging him toward his mistress.

"Here's your pack, milady," Silas said, easing the load over her shoulders and waiting for her to adjust the fit.

Cailleach's cabin disappeared within minutes of being on the trail. The trio kept a steady pace along a well-hidden trail, heading south for the small town of Moiria.

Silence was easy to maintain in the aftermath of destiny not only knocking at her door, but blowing it wide open. Time for her to put on her big girl boots and get serious about things.

You're awfully quiet.

Thinking.

She was a queen – would be, anyway. Not a job she'd ever desired or even thought about. Even now, it sounded more like a prison sentence than an honor. Yet, she'd agreed to do whatever it took to save this kingdom, including letting go of the man she loved. What she really wanted was to run away with Silas to a nice little thatched-roof cottage somewhere and raise babies. He was a part of her, but a part she'd learn to live without. It had seemed so easy last night, in the mysterious green light of the Uisneach Tree, to agree to accept her role as queen and heroine of a cursed realm, to choose duty over the desire of her heart. In the light of day, with that desire in front of her and the threat of an evil army behind – not so much.

Following Silas along the trail, she enjoyed the sensual, feline grace of his movements as he hopped over rocks, forded small streams and reached for tree limbs to scramble up a ravine. She watched the play of muscle across his back, down to his hips and buttocks. Her mind drifted to forbidden places. The fantasies became more graphic, involving a fireplace and bearskin rug. *Stop it already!* In reality she had committed herself to play Guinevere to Uisneach's King Arthur. The last thing she wanted for Silas was to play Lancelot. *I will let him go. I will forget him.*

Who's Lancelot?

She sighed. *You are.*

He turned and smiled, decimating her good intentions. *I will try to let go and forget.*

The loud sound of rushing water led them to a wide brook. "We need to cross," said Sigel, "but that last rain has made it higher than usual."

"I'll scout upstream and try to find a better place," Silas said, dropping his pack and sprinting away. After only a couple of minutes he was back, looking anxious.

"What's wrong?" Sigel asked.

"That won't be the best way to cross unless you want to skirmish with Shamwa's friends. There's a dozen of them about a half mile northeast."

"We need to move fast then," Sigel said, heading south as he spoke. "Come on, then. We'll find a crossing farther downstream."

Minutes later, he found a manageable section, though Briana had her doubts. The boulders looked too far apart for her to make it across the racing water. She looked at her companions dubiously.

I can't do this, she thought. *I've lost Daddy, Mother and now Silas. How much more must I give up? How much more can I endure?* She stared at the water, rushing along in front of her, threatening to take her soul and carry it far downstream to be released into a fearful, lonely ocean.

"For Maker's sake, Briana, just jump!" Sigel said. "We don't have time for this."

Gripped by fear, uncertainty and loss, she stood rooted to the path until she saw Silas, on the other side, calmly extend his hand. No endless sea to drown her pitiable soul, but the safe harbor of a poetic druid, welcoming and shielding… home. He understood.

"Come with me, Briana."

The faint echo of a Bible verse wafted through her mind: *Whither thou goest, I will go; where you lodge, I will lodge; your people shall be my people.* If Silas led her through the bowels of hell, she'd follow him.

Not follow, my queen, lead. "You can do this. Sigel, can you give her a boost from your side?"

Sigel took hold of her waist, preparing to give her some lift over. She reached for Silas's hand. "I suppose if I can cross a death-defying gorge over a rainbow bridge, I can manage this." With one's nudge and the other's firm grasp, she made it across.

Silas squeezed her hand and gave her an encouraging smile.

A second behind her was Sigel, followed effortlessly by Dara.

"Should we check the map again?" She was already reaching into the bag for it.

Sigel moved out in front. "Be quick about it. We need to keep moving. I suspect they'd prefer to waylay us out here and not come into Moiria after us, so we need to get into town."

Sigel set a fast pace that left no room for ruminations. The trees thinned and soon they were walking through a meadow painted with wildflowers. Exposure forced them to walk a little more warily, the men and Dara keeping Briana well protected between them.

When it was safe and her emotions were under control, she asked about Moiria, eager to visit her first real town since Baigsith.

"What are the people like?"

Sigel talked as he walked. "Mostly like us, though a few gnomes call it home, as well. They're a friendly sort, so much so that in a village of about a hundred folks, you'll find twenty pubs."

"Must like their booze," she joked.

"Nah," he said, "not so much that as they love to socialize. They'd talk the wool off sheep."

"Do they have a doctor?"

"Are you sick, Briana?" Silas asked, with concern.

"No, just curious." She stubbed her toe on a root and swore.

Sigel listed off a few businesses, including a merchandise store, millinery and a bakery. "They have a bookshop, too. You'd enjoy it if we had more time."

"I suppose we'll stay at the Howlin' Wolf Tavern," Silas said, looking sideways at Sigel.

Sigel harrumphed. "They do have the best stew and bread in town."

"I could go for a bowl of hot soup right about now," Briana agreed amiably, wondering why Silas looked suddenly nervous.

"I smell wood smoke," she said to Sigel, who was pulling her back into the tree line. Silas moved ghostlike amidst the pines and closer to the source. "Only a wee farm house," he said, upon rejoining them. "Doesn't appear to be anythin' devious about it."

Nevertheless, they approached the empty yard slowly. Silas hollered out a greeting with no response. He looked back at his companions with a raised eyebrow.

The hair on Briana's neck rose. *With a fire in the hearth, surely someone was home?* Sigel moved in closer to her, keeping her between the two men as they neared the door.

Silas spoke again. Still no answer. He entered the darkened abode. Briana held her breath as she followed him into the eerie emptiness. The fire was nearly burned out, its scent overpowered by something scorched in the pot hanging near the fire. Broken glass littered the floor. As her eyes acclimated to the dim room, she found bedding crumpled and dragged across the floor, an overturned barrel and bloody footprints.

"Where do you suppose the people have gone?" Silas asked.

A whimper came from a dark corner.

Briana stepped in the direction of the sound, but Silas stepped in front of her and moved toward the heap of quilts. Dropping to one knee, he carefully pulled down the edge of the quilt to reveal the terrified face of a woman who shrank back as far as she could.

"It's okay, Missus," he said, softly. "We mean you no harm."

Sigel passed Silas a lit candle. The woman's face was badly bruised, with one eye swollen shut. A thin line of blood trickled from her mouth. When she clenched her arms tighter around her middle, a feeling of dread gripped Briana. That was the move of a woman holding a baby.

"Silas, you better let me," she murmured. When he stepped out of the way, she moved and knelt beside the woman. "I'm Briana. Is your baby okay?" Fearful eyes gazed up at Briana. "We're here to help. Can I see your wee one?"

The woman seemed to relax slightly at Briana's reassuring tone and nodded, allowing Briana to slide the quilt down lower, revealing an infant tucked against her breast. The baby was an ominous blue color, smeared in blood. Lifeless.

"She's not nursing," the woman said, tonelessly.

Briana bit her lip.

Don't cry, a mhuirnin, *she needs your strength and comfort.*

Briana took the limp baby from the woman. The girl had no obvious injuries. *Where did the blood come from?* "Are you injured anywhere besides your face, milady?"

The woman pulled the quilt down to her legs revealing a staggering amount of blood on her gown, from chest to thigh. The sight of it rocked Briana back on her heels. Nothing in her life had prepared her to triage the needs in this cottage, but she intuitively ordered Sigel to get the fire stoked, heat a pot of water and find clean linen to use as a towel. She transferred the baby to Silas with instructions to wash the baby once the water was warm. When the men set about their tasks, she turned back to the woman.

"What's your name, Missus?"

"Mary Keary."

"Mary, I need to examine you. Is that okay?"

Mary made eye contact and nodded, allowing Briana to raise her dress. Bruises painted a vicious picture across her body, as did the heavy blood stains between her thighs. She'd been brutally raped, possibly by more than one man.

"Who did this, Mary?" she asked, quietly.

"Don't know their names, but they was with the Gray Military. I knew by their clothes." A single tear rolled down the woman's battered and probably broken cheek. "They took my man. When he went with them, two came back and... Can I have Evie back?"

"We're going to bathe her."

Ask her about Artanin.

"Did the druid hurt you?"

Mary shook her head. "He came back in and made them stop. But he was the one who wanted to know if the lord marshall had come by here." Her eyes darted to Sigel. "That's you, ain't it, sir?"

Sigel only grunted a response and Briana affirmed it for her. "What did he say?"

Silas handed her a bowl of warm water. She began cleaning Mary's face.

Wincing, Mary said, "We was having breakfast when they arrived – busted inside without a knock. Eight men and Druid Artanin. They asked if we'd seen the lord marshall and a woman. I heard one man say 'the Mouse,' but Artanin hit him and he shut up." The woman's eyes grew wide. "Is that you? Are you the Mouse?"

Briana nodded but kept washing Mary down her throat to her chest. *Please look for a clean dress*, she asked Silas.

"Oh, Maker. Kenneth said he heard you was here. When the druid asked about you, Kenneth told them you'd been here yesterday and headed toward the mountains."

That's why they were going that way, Silas said, handing her a gown.

"They said Kenneth must come with them and join the army or they would kill me and Evie. I begged him not to go, but he told me he loved me and went.

"A couple of minutes later two men came back in and grabbed me. Evie was crying and one of them did something that made her stop. I tried to help her but one pinned me down and... there was nothing I could do, milady. They only stopped when the druid came in and pulled them off me. But he didn't do anything else to help, just left us.

"When they was gone, I went to Evie and been trying to get her to nurse; she be only a couple of months old, but she won't suck and she's awful cold. Will she be all right, milady?"

Briana eased the clean dress over Mary's head. Other than the trauma from the sexual violation and the body bruising, there were no other injuries. Briana took a deep breath and took Mary's hands. "We're going to give Evie to you, Mary, but you must know she's dead." Saying the word was the hardest thing Briana had ever done, but necessary to help the woman begin to accept the reality of it.

"No," Mary whispered, the word full of contradictory understanding. Silas handed Mary the infant, washed and wrapped in a small blanket. Silent tears fell, daring sound to flout the holiness of the moment. Briana sat by, giving the mother all the time and space she needed to begin the grieving that would go on long after she was away from this tragedy.

Sigel, on the other hand, was clearly growing anxious to go. "Missus, do you have family in the village?"

Mary nodded, but clutched the baby tighter. "I can't go. I can't leave my baby girl here alone."

"You can't stay here," Sigel said. "It's not safe."

Shaking her head, the mother repeated, "I'll stay with Evie."

"What's the name of your family in Moiria?" Silas asked.

"Heaney. My sister's husband is Seamus Heaney."

"We're not far from Moiria, Sigel," Silas said. "I could stay here with Missus Keary and you could send her sister to her. I'll meet you later at the tavern."

Sigel agreed. Though Briana was hesitant to leave the woman, she knew they had to move on. The best people to help Mary Keary bury her child and mourn her loss were her own family.

"Mary, I am so sorry for what's happened. I promise you we will do our best to capture Lord Shamwa's army and bring Kenneth back to you."

"You're going to be the queen, aren't you?"

"Yes." Briana was shocked at how easily the response came. "And we will end the terrible pain Shamwa and his men are inflicting on Uisneach."

Giving Silas one last, sad look, she followed Sigel and headed for

Moiria, leaving the bard to put everything else in order in the cottage and offer comfort to the grieving mother.

Once they were a distance from the Keary cottage, Sigel asked, "Are you okay?"

"Fine. Can we rescue her husband?"

Sigel shook his head. "As soon as they find out he lied about us passing by in the opposite direction, they'll kill him."

Briana thought about that for a minute. "Do you think he knew that?"

"Aye, he did it purposely to throw them off track. You see, Briana, you have people all over this kingdom willing to do whatever it takes to protect you and save their king."

The weight of that responsibility crashed down upon her. How could she even consider not seeing this through?

"Come on, we still have a lot to do today. We really don't have time for missions of mercy."

You're wrong about that, Sigel, this entire journey is a mission of mercy.

CHAPTER FIFTEEN

CROSSROADS

Sounds of village life greeted them as they came over a slight knoll and saw Moiria, a delightful hamlet of homes and shops. The path turned to cobblestone as they came into the town proper. In the middle of town was a cheery fountain with a sculpture of three goddesses spouting water from their mouths. Storefronts lined up along both sides of the main street, each boasting a different, brightly colored door. Like Baigsith, a profusion of window boxes and gardens decorated the windows, stoops and terraces of nearly every cottage and shop. Children scampered around the town, playing their games, being spoken to and occasionally cuffed by adults. A few people hailed Sigel.

All of this would have delighted Briana under normal circumstances, but the occurrence at the Keary home had flushed any enthusiasm from her.

"That's the Heaney home," Sigel said, pointing to a small cottage beyond the milliner's.

After delivering the news as respectfully and kindly as possible, and being assured that Mr. and Mrs. Heaney were on their way to help Mary, Sigel and Briana continued to the tavern.

The Howling Wolf was a quaint establishment, built entirely of old lichen- and ivy-covered stone. The tavern's name was painted in bold red letters across a full moon. Carved into the moon was a ferocious looking, gape-mouthed wolf. They walked through a low stone wall that enclosed a courtyard guarded over by a huge chestnut tree. Entering the dimly lit bar, they were welcomed by Hugh and Eleanor McPhee, proprietors. Lots of backslapping occurred between the men. Mrs. McPhee immediately set two tankards of ale on a table.

"Where's Silas?" she asked.

"He'll be along," Sigel said, without divulging any details of what happened. The danger inherent in the close proximity of Gray Military should've been cause for alarm, so Briana was surprised he didn't mention it. Mrs. McPhee was solicitous of Briana even before she knew who she was, but once she was introduced to "the Mouse of the Prophecy," she couldn't have done enough to make her comfortable.

"Oh, my goodness gracious, what an honor to have you here, milady."

"Please call me Briana."

"You will be the queen one day; such familiarity wouldn't be proper."

Briana smiled weakly. A lovely young woman with coppery hair brought a plate of cheese and bread.

"Where's Silas?" she asked, and received a cursory response from Sigel.

Briana rolled her eyes when the third young lady with dark curly hair and a plentiful bosom sauntered over.

"I expected Silas to be with you, lord marshall. Has he lost his way, then?" She smiled provocatively.

"He'll be along, Grania. Go on now, Lady Briana and I have business to discuss."

The buxom girl turned her attention to Briana. An arc of animosity flashed between the women. Holding Briana's eyes, the young woman spoke to Sigel. "When Silas gets here, would you mind telling him I'm looking for him and intend to collect on a promise he made me."

"I'm not your messenger, Grania. You'll tell him yourself."

"Silas sure is popular," Briana commented, wondering how evil it was to wish the dark-haired girl a nasty trip on her way to the kitchen.

"He's a bard," was all the response she got before Sigel turned the conversation to the more important matter of what they were here for.

They hadn't gotten far when they were surrounded by men hearing of her arrival and asking questions about the plan. Briana was introduced and welcomed with a plethora of responses that ranged from surprise to uncertainty to outright goddess worship.

"Some of you will stay behind to protect the town, but we need as many men as possible to join the king's army at Long River," said Sigel. He outlined the plan to what appeared to Briana to be a raggle-taggle group of men, if ever there was one.

Uncertain murmuring traveled around the group. She didn't notice Silas slip in until he was standing beside her, watching her with an odd expression on his face.

How's it goin'? he asked.

Okay. How is Mary?

As you might expect, but her kin are there. Anythin' unusual happen?

No. Seeing the relief on his face, she added, *unless you mean that Ellie and Margaret are looking for you and Grania needs to talk to you about collecting on a promise.*

He choked on his ale. Briana smiled innocently. *I'd make that a priority. She was very insistent.*

"Silas," said Sigel interrupting their silent conversation. "I know it's a lot to ask, but given what's happened this morning, I think it's important to tell the villagers the news, and introduce Briana and get them stoked for their part in this. People are gathering outside to hear you sing."

"Are you seriously going to perform after what we've been through today?" Briana couldn't believe he would be able to switch gears so fast.

"Especially after what happened to the Kearys," Sigel said. "I know it sounds harsh, but if we only tell people what happened at the cottage, they'll be angry, but feel hopeless. If they hear about it wrapped in the story of the prophecy coming to fulfillment, they'll be more motivated to fight."

Briana sucked in her breath trying to imagine how Silas would pull this off.

Silas downed his brew, gave Briana a grim smile and nodded to the door. "Our audience awaits."

She, Dara and Sigel followed him out under the chestnut tree where a large group of people were gathered. Anticipation and uncertainty charged the air. He pulled his small guitar out and began to sing.

"Druid oak, connecting worlds, twilight bears a queen…"

I didn't come at twilight.

Poetic license.

"Holly chants a holy song. Awake Uisneach, your queen is here…"

I'm not the queen.

Yes, you are.

"Crows fly over misty moors."

That's true enough, she admitted.

"Mountains pave her way."

You've quite the way with words, Silas.

"Glen to peak her voice will speak. Awake Uisneach, your queen is here.

"Your queen is here, good people of Moiria. Lady Briana, the Mouse of Prophecy is here and she has witnessed a terrible thing today, at the hands of Lord Shamwa!"

He told of the atrocity that was done to one of their own and vowed, on behalf of the Taranian House, that this reign of terror the prime minister was inflicting on them all would stop. "We need to save the king, and to do that, we need the support of every single person in Uisneach. Will you stand with us?"

Amidst muttered anger, concern and questions, shouts of a hometown militia rising, and oaths to fight for the Taranian house, could be heard.

Sigel moved in closer and put an arm around her shoulder, whispering in her ear, "Do you see what he's doing?"

She nodded without looking at him. "They're on fire, listening to him."

"Not quite, but they could be." She turned to him and the glint in his eyes terrified her. "You could do that – ignite them."

"Me? Not likely."

"I disagree. Remember that song you sang to us in Cailleach's cabin about the crossroads? If you and Silas could sing that together, it would set them on fire."

She gulped. Catching Silas's eye, she had the distinct impression he knew what Sigel was saying. "Sigel, I've never done anything like that in my life."

"Then use your magic. We need men. Only you can set the wheels in motion to end this. We need Brath and we need you."

Her mouth fell open. Silas nodded as he continued to sing. She paced in small circles, breathing deeply and trying to call on her power. With deep intention, she created an image of them performing together, envisioned the scene in her mind, all the people raptly watching them. *I do this for Mary and Kenneth, for the poor baby who didn't live, for the Tollemys and for everyone who has felt the cruel reach of Lord Shamwa.* Feeling ready, she took a position at the side of the stage, waiting for Silas to finish. On the last note of his ballad, Silas looked at her with a slight movement of his head and a question in his eyes. She nodded sharply. Those gathered barely had time to catch their breath before they heard her pure, ethereal voice from the side of the patio, sing out, "Across the vale a sign appears…"

Silas responded, "A hero's call to arms…"

Briana put one foot upon an empty chair and leaned toward the audience. "A crown to save and nation free –"

"Release from evil charms," Silas replied, fiercely.

Back and forth they called to each other before turning together to ask the audience, "Will you come?"

"Yes, we will!"

Silas hesitated for a moment, then leaped onto the short wall. Eyes shining, he spoke to the audience in a low, mysterious voice. "A journey made from future time, to ancient royal mound."

Briana stood before them, planting her feet wide. Drawing Nua swiftly from her sheath, she held it high above her head, its metal flashing in the sunlight. "Raising sword with steady hand, to prophecy she's bound." Wild cheers rose up before the blade quickly went back into its sheath.

Silas jumped down facing her, posing the question, "Will you raise?"

He was magnificent. "Raise we will!" she assured him boldly.

The staccato rhythm of the song mesmerized everyone. Silas raced around the courtyard like wildfire. Briana sprang onto the wall, graceful as a deer, and dashed across it from one side of the courtyard to the other.

"But come we now, our lives to give…"

Silas sang to her and to the audience, "No longer wont to wait."

She hopped down and knelt before a venerable old woman with a dreamy look in her eyes and crooned to her, "Crossroads coming, make a choice…"

From behind her Silas challenged, "Remain and die, or fight."

Briana and Silas went back and forth, asking each other and the audience what the future held and what their responsibility was to preserve it. As they came to the end, Silas made his way to Briana. Pulling her backward into his arms, they sang the last line together. "Rise up brave lads, your queen to serve, and victory is won!"

For an instant all was silent. Then, a roar of assent assaulted her ears. "Sweet Maker," Briana gasped. Sigel was right. Moments later a long line of men and a few women stood ready to pledge their support.

Briana was breathless. Silas grinned from ear to ear. "Well done, lass! Well done!"

"Did you know Sigel was going to ask me to sing with you?"

"No, but when I saw him talkin' and the look on your face, I thought it might have been that. It was the perfect time. And that move with Nuada was bloody fantastic, *a mhuirnin*."

She shook her head in amazement.

"A little help here?" Sigel called, and they realized he was bombarded with village folk wanting to talk about the plan to rescue King Brath and destroy Lord Shamwa. *Guess it's time for the meet and greet*, Briana thought, and headed into the crowd to do her part.

Sharing her story with these good people turned out to be more enjoyable and useful than she imagined. She learned more about how the imprisonment of the king and Shamwa's destruction of the land had affected them. Eleanor McPhee, the tavern owner's wife, told her that their oldest son, one of King Brath's knights, was inside Ard Darach when the curse was cast.

"We can only hope he's still in there and able to return to us."

"We'll find him, Mrs. McPhee, and when we do, I'll send him home to you."

Eventually, the party dispersed enough that Sigel, Silas and Briana found themselves near enough to talk to one another.

"That went well!" Silas commented cheerfully, bringing a smile to Briana's face.

"I think so, too," Sigel said, before giving his attention to Briana. "Why don't you go have a rest before supper? I'll send someone to fetch you later."

"It has been a hell of a day. I would love to lie down just for a few minutes."

"Lady Briana, if you would come with me, I'll take you to your room," said Mrs. McPhee.

☙

Mrs. McPhee's knock at the door woke her to a darkened room. "Come in," she invited the woman, who fortunately entered with a candle and lit the one in Briana's room. "I can't believe I slept so long."

"It's not been so long, milady, but Lord Sigel is downstairs and bids you come down for some soup. I've got a little something for the lad, too," she said with a nod at Dara.

"Thank you," Briana replied. "Please tell the lord marshall I'll be right there."

When the older woman left the room, Briana splashed cold water on her face, ran her wooden comb through her sleep-mussed hair and slipped into her dress. A glance in the oval mirror told her that she didn't look too bad, all things considered.

Candles did little to light the main room of the pub, but she found Sigel and Silas sitting at a table, already tucking into their meal and having a conversation about why Artanin stopped the rape of Mary, something they apparently thought was out of character. She sat across from them.

"Feelin' better?" Silas asked.

"Infinitely." She nodded when coppery-haired Ellie asked if she'd have the stew.

Sigel handed her a slice of fresh buttered bread. She started to take a bite when Grania sashayed up next to Silas. With obvious familiarity, she slid an arm around his shoulder, pressed herself into his side and leaned down to plant a kiss on his cheek.

"Hello, Silas. I've missed you," she said in a voice honey-sweet and full of promise.

"Hello, Grania." Silas said, staring at his plate.

"I believe we have unfinished business," she said sweetly into his ear, in tones low enough to be thought private, but loud enough to make sure

155

Briana heard. Briana wanted to slap the hand that was stroking his arm and shoulder with such intimacy.

"I think we should have this conversation somewhere else," Silas said, standing. He led her outside.

Briana bit her lip and tasted blood. Unconsciously, she started to rise from her chair.

"Sit," Sigel ordered firmly.

She sat.

"You are a queen. Queens do not get into catfights with tavern maids over bards."

"Queens also do not have to sit by and be made a fool of," she retorted, her eyes shooting daggers at him.

"The only person who could make a fool of you right now is yourself."

She stared at him, wondering how fast her heart could beat before coming out of her chest. She wondered if anyone else in the room could hear her labored breathing. Red and green emotions battled for supremacy until purple rose up and vanquished the others. Raising her head up and setting her jaw, she lifted the tankard in front of her and took a purposeful drink.

Sigel raised his glass in wordless acknowledgment of her small victory.

❧

Briana?

Ignoring him wouldn't work. *Yes?*

I am so sorry.

About?

You know what about. I didn't know how to warn you that might happen.

You don't owe me any explanation, Silas. I never thought to ask if you had a girlfriend or wife.

I would have told you if I had either of those. Grania is not my girlfriend. I made that clear to her tonight.

The less-than-queenly part of her smiled in satisfaction. The queenlier Briana responded. *Silas, you have every right to be in a relationship. I'm going to be married and your queen. Whatever we might feel for each other has to be forgotten.*

A moment of silence.

Forgotten? Can you?

I have to, and so do you. No answer. Weary of even thinking about the subject, she asked, *Silas, why were you and Sigel so interested in what Artanin did?*

Another pause.

He's not a good guy, Briana, and I can't see him caring one way or another if soldiers rape a woman or smother a baby. It's just an odd detail.

Maybe he isn't as bad as you think?

Yes, he is. He's the one who poisoned Brath, remember?

She sighed. *I have to tell you, Silas, for the first time in my life, when I saw that poor woman and her baby, I wanted to kill. This kingdom is turning me into a woman I don't even know. I used to say that violence doesn't solve violence. Now, I'm not so sure.*

I don't know much about Maine, but this is a harsh land, Briana. At least it has been for the past ten years. Vengeance and justice are not pleasant, but sometimes necessary. Shamwa cannot be allowed to continue his tyranny, and I only know one way of stoppin' him.

You sound like Sigel.

Well…

She lay on her bed, counting wisps of thatching on the ceiling. The day's events, from the horror at the cottage to the thrills in the tavern, continued to parade through her mind. She wrestled with the conflicting emotions of wanting to be the queen they thought she was and her desire for a much simpler future as the wife of a bard.

This has been an awful day. I'm so tired.

Go to sleep, Briana.

Silas?

Yes, a mhuirnin?

Can I cry now?

He didn't answer but a moment later, she felt a presence, strong and comforting, wrap around her. Curling into invisible arms, she abandoned the fight and let the tears of sorrow, responsibility and loneliness melt into the healing beat of another's heart.

CHAPTER SIXTEEN

A STORM IS BREWING

When they reached Long River, Sigel ordered the Moiria recruits to fan out on a slow march east. Urging Silas and Briana across a sturdy bridge,, they headed south toward Winge Mansion, moving fast, keeping quiet under cover of the forest.

"Gonna rain," Silas said, looking up at the darkening sky. On cue, the first rumble of thunder rippled over them.

Sigel and Briana studied the map. Briana looked confused and Sigel uneasy. "We should be able to go straight," Sigel pointed, "but are you seeing what I'm seeing?" he asked Briana, who nodded.

"Looks like men to the south, moving in our direction."

Silas asked, "Want me to take a quick scout down there?"

Sigel didn't answer right away. "What's that to the east, Briana? I can't quite make it out."

"There's a storm – you were right about that, Silas – heading in from the east, and I think there's a cave near the lake, but the crows are gathering there. I don't know what that means."

"It means that's where we should head. I think they're trying to warn us. Silas, why don't you go see what the Grays are up to, and meet us at that cave at Lake Ardghal."

He nodded, adjusting the placement of his bow and sword.

"Please be careful, Silas," Briana said, trying to maintain a facade of camaraderie and professional concern.

You'll not get rid of me that easy. I'll be back before you know it. He squeezed her shoulder. "I'll be fine. See you in a couple of hours." With that, he sprinted toward the small brook heading south. Sigel wasted no time leading her down the eastern, less-traveled trail.

When they were away from the main route, she glanced at the map again. Silas and Shamwa's men seemed to be moving toward each other, and the storm was picking up in intensity. Black birds flew frantically from the lake to Winge Mansion. Her stomach clenched. "How far is it from here to the mansion?"

"About a day's walk. But the terrain is rough and the nasty weather will cost us some time."

The path grew more challenging, meandering through a hanging valley underneath a prehistoric moraine. Briana scrambled over boulders and around other glacial debris, then up a slippery talus slope that demanded concentration, balance and the use of every muscle in her body. Bony trees provided occasional handholds. They hiked over a steep slab, the trail practically invisible. Briana stopped, catching her breath and collecting her wits. From far below them a reservoir peered up, made ominously dark as it reflected the thunderous clouds developing overhead.

"Is that where we're going?" she asked.

"Eventually, but first we have to pass beside the cliff and back into the woods. We'll wait in the cave for Silas." She watched Sigel pale by degrees.

"You okay?"

"I'm fine. Let's get across this section in front of us and find the cave." He headed before her with the stern warning, "Be careful, Briana. This is a narrow, dangerous section with no room for error."

She tightened the straps on her pack, and on Nua, patted Dara encouragingly and followed in Sigel's footsteps along a knife-edge meant for adrenaline junkies, a trail no more than a foot wide. It was a drop of several hundred feet to the churlish water below. The trail curved around the side of the mountain, bringing them in sight of a magnificent water-fall. They'd have to cross the brook inches away from the head of the falls. *Okay, I'm officially scared out of my wits,* she thought, but that didn't begin to cover the expression she saw on Sigel's face. He'd gone ghostly white, with sweat beading his forehead. His mouth was tight and his eye pupils dilated to the size of turkey platters. *He's terrified*, she thought, remembering the fall that scarred his face. It took her a second to reconcile the strong, fearless man she'd known every day of this journey with the one standing before her, who could barely take the next step. *You can do this, Sigel*, she mentally encouraged him with all the strength and magic she could muster. He turned to look at her and with a deep breath, looked back at the narrow ridge and stepped forward. She could almost feel his legs trembling as he picked his way across the precipice. Her own fear of heights kept her diligent as she trailed behind. It seemed like an hour before they made it safely across the rock face. The sound of falling water intensified as they neared the cataract, and they had to use hand signals to communicate. The trail skirted the precipitous edge; loose stones in the stream increasing the risk of slipping and being carried down the falls to a certain and agonizing death. Sigel was more confident in his ability to rock-hop and pointed to the stones best suited to making it across. The stretches were not too wide, so Briana jumped between the rocks without help. Dara took a more direct route and beat her to the opposite bank. Sigel found a boulder to sit on.

"Good job, Sigel," she said quietly.

He grunted in response.

"Where's the cave?"

"A few minutes up there," he said, pointing.

Before they left the nightmarish landscape behind them, Briana dared one glimpse out across the vista and the lake. "It's beautiful," she remarked, taking in the valley framed by the steep bowl-shaped hollow of the cirque, made more dramatic by the stormy sky above.

Sigel followed her gaze. "Aye, but we best get moving. This storm will break any minute." Even as he spoke, lightning split the sky and rain poured out of the blackness. The wind whipped at their clothing. They ran, receiving little cover from the trees, and were soaked when they reached the cave. Sigel instructed her and Dara to wait under a nearby yew until he inspected the dwelling to make sure there were no man-eating animals denned up in it.

She waited, shivering, and fretted about Silas' safety. The trees around her were black with crows, hunkering and silent in the rain. The big crow with the medallion – Sir Thomas, she corrected herself, though she still had a hard time wrapping her mind around the idea of him as a shapeshifter, for real – was not among the assembled. Sigel returned and led her inside the cave, now lit by a single torch. It was large enough for a small army to camp in, musty, but dry. Chirruping echoed in its shadowy upper vaults. *Probably bats*, she thought, *but they'll take off as soon as we get a fire going.* Dara ran his own inspection, nose to the ground, then came to stand beside Briana with a snort. Someone had left a sizable pile of wood, a boon, as all the possible sources in the forest would be soggy now. She removed her sword and backpack while Sigel quickly built a small fire. As she suspected, a line of furry creatures fluttered out of the cave. He handed her a large woolen wrap. "Here, get your wet clothes off and wrap up in this. Your clothes will dry faster if we can hang them by the fire."

"Huh? You want me to take off my clothes with you in here?"

"For Maker's sake, Briana, obviously I'm going to turn my back." Which he did, the moment she accepted the kilt from his hand.

She'd never changed so fast in her life.

"Okay, I'm covered," she said, tucking the edges of the garment firmly around her as he came back to the fire. "What about you? You're soaked through."

"Aye, I am," he said and pulled off his own shirt, hanging it and her clothes over a couple of sticks near the fire.

Firelight dramatized the tapestry of Sigel's bare back. He was a wellbuilt man, large, rugged and ripped with muscle, a marvel to behold. But her eyes were riveted by the multitude of scars that crisscrossed his back, from shoulder to waist.

Hearing her sharp intake of breath, he turned around and realized what she was looking at.

"Compliments of Lord Shamwa."

"What happened?"

"Turn your back. I'm getting out of these trousers."

She whipped around and heard rustling cloth. "Three years ago, Shamwa captured me."

"What!" she caught herself before turning all the way around.

"We'd received word that the Gray Military was pushing into Tyan

Ibor toward Moiria. I led a small militia around Art Aron and up the western side of the Dromdara Mountains to stop him. You can turn around."

She found him swathed and belted in a yellow-and-black plaid kilt. He motioned her to sit beside him as he continued his account.

"We were ambushed at Poet's Gap and split up. I had the misfortune of being overpowered by some Gray Military men and held captive to await the pleasure of Shamwa.

"He tried to talk me into joining his army as his own lord marshall. Of course, I promptly spit in his face and told him he could... well, never mind what I told him."

"I know what I'd have told him."

Sigel shuddered. "I pray to Maker, Briana, that we can protect you from ever having to speak to him at all."

"Anyway, he wasted no time in tying me between two trees and taking the whip to my back. I think I stuck it through fifty very brutal lashes before passing out. The next thing I knew, Silas was beside me, cutting the ties and helping me slip away from the camp. The man really does move like a cat. I never heard him coming. Shamwa had apparently gone back to his castle and the soldiers were all sleeping. Except for the one who had received a new red necklace, courtesy of the bard.

"The trip to Ratskillen was misery, but we made it. I heard that Shamwa had that entire unit of men killed when he found out I'd escaped. He's a cruel, evil man, who pleasures himself by torturing and killing things."

"Sounds like a real psychopath," Briana said, rubbing a hand across her forehead.

"I don't know about that, but he's definitely crazy."

"You have good reason to want to kill him," she reflected.

"I want to kill him, but not because of what he did to me. I want to kill him because of what he's done to this kingdom and what he will continue to do if he is not destroyed."

She nodded. "How long do you think it's been?"

"About three hours."

"He said he'd be back in two."

"So I'm a little late," Silas said, entering the cave, dripping. Briana jumped up and then forced herself to sit back down. "Thank Maker you're okay, Silas."

"All of us together in one piece. You made it across, huh, Sigel."

"Aye," he said. "And you, what did you discover?"

"Wait a sec," Briana intruded. "Silas, you're soaked to the bone. You need dry clothes."

He talked while he was pulling his kilt from inside his pack. Cocking his head at Briana, he said, "I really don't mind if you watch, milady, but…"

Reddening, she quickly turned her back.

"Aye, well, not such good news, I'm afraid. Shamwa's men are marching up along the river between Sir Thomas' and Moiria. I think they expect us to come that way. We'll have to bushwhack around the loch to get to the crow's place."

Sigel nodded. "If they're heading north, our men are going to come up against them at the river."

"Probably, but there's not so many we can't easily take them. Okay, I'm decent, Briana."

"We'll leave at first light," Sigel said. "In the meantime, we keep the fire low, eat some of this delightful bread Mrs. McPhee sent along, and try to get some sleep."

Throughout this conversation, something had been bothering Briana. "Why doesn't Sir Thomas just send horses?"

"Horses wouldn't cross that cliff trail," said Sigel. "Do you think we're making things more difficult for you on purpose?"

"No! Of course not. I just wondered."

"It's a good question, my queen," Silas assured her quietly. He glared at Sigel, who hastily murmured an apology.

After dinner, Dara stretched beside his mistress, staring into the tiny fire, looking like he was thinking deep dog thoughts. His comrades joined him. Silas broke the silence.

"By the way, Briana, could you take a look at somethin' for me?" He turned his back to her and pulled his hair to the side, revealing a large knot of briars tangled in his hair and a nasty cut from his neck running down to the upper part of his shoulder. Briana gasped. "Silas, why didn't you say something before? What happened?"

"Ah, it's not so bad, but might need one of your wee ointments. I tripped over a tree root and fell down an embankment into a patch of thorny buggers." She rose to her knees and moved behind him to examine it more closely. It was a brambly mess. She palpated the skin around the wound.

"Is it painful?"

"Just a bit."

She reached into her bag and pulled out a small pot of comfrey salve and a tiny bottle of willow tincture. "I wish I had some alcohol to wash it off." She was about to reach for the water bag when Sigel handed her his flask.

She smelled the contents. Whiskey. "This will do." She hoped.

"It was to be a surprise for us tonight, but if you need some for the lad's cuts, although for the life of me I can't see why, you're welcome to it."

"I only need a small amount of antiseptic…" Both men look confused. "To clean out any germs," she explained. Now they look more confused. She gave up. "Adding a drop of willow will make you more comfortable, Silas." As she cleaned and medicated the cut, she directed her thoughts to its healing, visualizing the skin returning to its normal integrity. She tied a piece of fabric around his shoulder and under his arm to keep the area covered.

"I can't be wearing this contraption," he complained. "It'll drive me crazy."

"Just for tonight, to allow the salve to soak in. I'll remove it in the morning. Now, to the nettles." Reaching into her bag again, she pulled out her wooden comb. Sitting back against the wall, she spread her legs apart and patted in between them. "Sit here, Silas, so I can work on your hair."

He looked at her with a raised eyebrow.

"It will be easier for me to reach."

He scooted between her legs. "How's that?"

He turned to look at her and winked wickedly. She slapped his good shoulder lightly with the comb and turned him back around.

With Dara sitting beside her, his head on her upper thigh, she began to tease Silas' hair apart and pull out the tiny burrs and knots. She tried to remain impassive, but the feel of his hair in her hands and his body settled so intimately against hers was hard to ignore. Eventually she gave up the effort and allowed herself the guilty pleasure.

Sigel took a long pull from the flask and passed it around. "We'll have to go easy with this, kids. We still have to stay alert."

Silas took a swig. "Maker, that's good. Where'd you steal it?" He offered the whiskey to Briana.

"Hugh McPhee made sure I had some for the road."

"Well, I'm grateful."

Briana stopped her work for a moment and tipped the container to her lips. Honeyed spice burned going down. "Nice," she croaked.

Her companions laughed.

"Not much of drinker are you?" Sigel asked.

"I enjoy a beer or glass of wine with the best of them, but I've not had much whiskey, though I could get used to it, I think."

The whiskey created a warm, companionable silence in the cave. Silas kept letting his head fall back against her, occasionally eliciting a growl from Dara until she pushed him forward again. When the burrs were removed, she combed out his hair.

Mmm, that feels good, a mhuirnin.

Her heart lurched and a shiver ran through her body. She kept combing and stroking long after the tangles were gone and Silas had fallen asleep.

I wish we could stay like this forever, was her last conscious thought.

CHAPTER SEVENTEEN

THE BATTLE OF ARDGHAL

Briana sat up and shivered in the cold. Silas slept a chaste distance away under his kilt and Sigel hunkered like a gargoyle at the entrance of the cave, barely visible in the gray mushy light of another overcast day.

Hearing her move, Sigel turned. "Well, it's not pouring," he said, without lowering his voice.

"Huh, what?" Silas mumbled, stretching his long limbs.

Briana smiled at his tousled hair and sleep-heavy eyes. When a lock of hair fell across has face, she fought not to push it back.

"Silas, let me take a look at that cut and hopefully take the dressing off," she said instead, getting to her feet and stretching out the kinks in her own body.

"No hopefully about it. It's comin' off. I can't stand it."

"Oh, stop whining," she teased, as she moved next to him and eased his hair away from his neck. Lifting the bandage, she saw it had healed a lot last night. Healthy pink tissue without a sign of infection. *Medicine or magic?* Either way, it was healing well, so she rolled the bandage and put it in her bag, hoping to wash and reuse it another time. Things like bandages didn't come easy in this world.

Sigel handed them each fruit and bread and offered Dara some dried meat, which went down in two gulps. She stroked the dog fondly. "Stay with me, Dara. No running off."

She caught the men's anxious glances. "Aye," Sigel said to Briana. "Pay attention and be ready for anything."

She did her best to present a sober and battle-ready demeanor. "We will." She patted Nuada. Sigel studied her, searching out something in her eyes. "I'm okay, Sigel. Really. I'm ready."

He took a deep breath. "Maker, I hope so."

The trail away from the cave grew narrower and narrower, winding down the side of a ravine to the top of Lake Ardghal. Briana struggled a little, trying to balance the need to focus on small details, like finding tree limbs strong enough to hold her as she scrambled down over steep sections, with the need to be vigilant about everything else in her environment. It was like trying to blend monocular vision into binocular vision, and she found it tiring. Dara also became a source of concern to her. She kept looking back to find him.

When they reached a flatter spot and stopped for a moment to rest, Silas came up behind her. "I've got my eye on the gray lad; you look after yourself." She smiled her appreciation and they kept going. Sigel led. She and Dara followed in the middle, with Silas behind them. Switchbacks took them down the side of the mountain, offering occasional glimpses of the deceptively beautiful valley below. Nothing happened as they continued the descent, but when they found themselves at a gap between two mountains, the hair went up on the back of her neck at the sight of another heart-stoppingly narrow trail, this one a couple of hundred feet above the lake. Falling would be fatal. The ridge would put them out in the open and unprotected. Silas lifted his bow and nocked an arrow.

Something else was wrong; she could feel it.

"I don't know what's out there, but something doesn't feel right," Sigel said. "We need to cross this and find the fort. Cath Ardghal isn't much, but it's the best defensive position nearby. Have sword and shield at the ready. I'll go first. Briana, you follow, as quickly as you can safely, and do not stop. For any reason. Understand?"

"Yes, sir." She was already untying her shield and finding the balance with it and the sword in her other hand.

"Silas, you and Dara will come last, aye?"

Silas contemplated Briana with concern.

"Stop worrying about me or it will slow us down," she said. "When the time comes, I'll be ready and so will Nua."

"You think so, Briana," Silas replied, "and I admire your ferocity, but if you've never seen battle, never seen violence and death, you don't understand. And everythin' happens so fast. You haven't the experience for it yet, so I am worried."

"I have seen battle. If you recall, that's how we met."

"A skirmish. This might be much worse."

"Well, it's a moot point, isn't it? We must keep going and hope I can manage."

"That's about the truth of it," Sigel agreed impatiently. "So, let's move."

She and Silas exchanged a look.

You better not die today, she thought.

None of us dies today, a mhuirnin.

"Ready?" asked Sigel. He took a deep breath and moved out on the cliff trail. She could only imagine what this felt like for him. She went deep into herself to call up protection, which came in the form of imagining a solid ledge, much wider than the one they crossed. She willed Sigel across this ledge easily and unharmed. Once across, he turned to her, his face pale and unreadable, and beckoned her to come.

She glanced back at Silas, who held his bow steady, aimed over and ahead of her. He was totally focused but managed an encouraging wink. "Go quick, *a mhuirnin*; don't stop."

Filling her lungs and concentrating on the ground under her feet, she dashed out and made her way across as speedily as she dared. In the middle of the traverse, her foot hit a stone, which sent her a bit off-kilter. She dipped dangerously toward the edge. Gulping, she righted herself and continued on with no more than a second's pause, Dara right behind her. She held her breath when Silas headed over. He darted across like a mountain lion, sweeping his bow in front and up as he ran. While it had taken Sigel and Briana a full minute to make it across, Silas made it in seconds. As his foot touched solid ground, a whizzing sound broke the silence and a spray of blood shot out from his shoulder.

"Silas!"

"I'm fine! Keep moving! Shield up!"

She obeyed, staying close to Sigel as they headed for the protection of the trees on the other side of the ridge, trusting that Silas and Dara were behind her.

They ran down the steep trail as fast as they could. Sigel paused. Briana caught up to him, gasping. Before she caught her breath, Silas joined them. Briana started to turn back the collar of Silas' shirt to see his injury, but he waved her off.

"I'm fine, just tore some skin. We'll deal with it later."

Sigel nodded. "We haven't time now, Briana. They're close behind us."

Briana had no idea of the range of a typical archer. Two hundred yards? A hundred? Less? *Too close.*

They'd finally reached level ground, on the north side of a large field that was about a hundred yards from north to south and perhaps a little wider. A stone outcropping bordered the eastern edge with trees circling the rest of the field. There, about halfway down the western edge of the meadow, stood Cath Ardghal. Or what remained of the ring fort. The ruins wasn't much larger than a house. Briana guessed there was enough stone to provide some cover from all directions.

The glade was growing misty with a fine drizzle. Sigel scowled. "Watch your step, Briana. The grass will be slippery. Silas, you head for those rocks and give us cover. I'll get Briana across. We'll meet up in the woods, near the trail."

"Aye," said Silas.

"Briana," said Sigel. "See that spot where the rocks are crumbled?" He pointed to a slight opening on the northern curve of the fort. "Aim for that. Run fast as you can, on my say." He nodded at Silas.

The archer shot out into the meadow, heading east toward the outcropping. Briana wanted to close her eyes, but couldn't. *Maker keep him safe.* Her heart pounded until Silas jumped over one boulder and disappeared behind a larger one. He waved at Sigel.

"Now, Briana!"

Sigel and Briana ran west toward the fort. She slipped on the wet grass. Sigel caught her by the arm and hauled her up and forward, nearly tossing her over the stones into the fort.

"Damn, I wish I could raise a protection spell, but I haven't gotten that far."

A gaping hole on the other side of the fort had probably once held its stout door. There were four narrow vertical windows, more like slits, one in each direction. Sigel took a quick look out the window on the northern side, then pushed Briana to the ground.

"Stay here and keep Nua ready. If they find you, swing, stab, cut, do whatever you must, to defend yourself."

A horde of men burst from the trees on the north side of the field. Not the foolish goons who tried to steal her from the Tollemys' farm. These were big fighting men, and lots of them. Their Pictish screams were bone-chilling. Silas loosed three arrows in about eight seconds, taking out their archer and two others. *Damn, he's good,* she thought, pride checking her fear and giving her courage.

Projectiles came one after the other from Silas' hidden spot, taking out several combatants. "Do not engage them! Stay put!" With those orders, Sigel ran through the fort's doorway and plunged into the fray, his sword swinging, with a yell that rocked her.

Silas emerged from the boulders with his sword at the ready. The sound that issued from his throat paralyzed her and she momentarily forgot who he was. Wielding the heavy metal blade side to side, he gouged, sliced and separated limbs and tissue from one man after another.

Sigel and Silas cut down every man who got close to her. Suddenly, all was quiet except for the wheezing, whimpering sounds from those not yet cold with death. Briana stared through the narrow window on the northern side at the carnage. Sigel looked toward her, his sword dripping, his face bloody and wet from the rain. He said something she couldn't hear. Her eye caught Silas walking away from a man whose head lay neatly beside him. Something about the quiver swaying gracefully behind him called up a sense of déjà vu and nausea.

She noticed a gray ripple move inside the trees behind Sigel. She screamed his name as a second wave of the Grays poured onto the battle-field from the north.

Silas was engaged with two of them when Sigel raced back into the fray. Dizzy with rage and fear, Briana found her own war cry. Nua flashed in the sun as she burst out of the fort into the conflict, Dara beside her. Trying to keep her shield up, she ran toward the man in front of her but was knocked sideways by another.

"Briana, get back!" Sigel yelled desperately.

"Too late," she yelled back, before ramming Nua like a spear into the soldier reaching for her. When another came at her, she ducked, right before his weapon found her body. He somersaulted over her and landed gut-first on his own spear, the end sticking out through his back. There was no time to be amazed at this grisly acrobatics. A giant of a man came at her. Using both arms, she swung Nua with all the power she had. He deflected her swipe and jumped away. He dropped his weapon to grab her. *Did he think she couldn't fight?* Her next move unfolded like a game of chess. She let him advance. When she felt his fetid breath on her face, she raised Nua above her head, blade pointing straight up. She kneed him hard in his crotch. He dropped down to his knees, howling. She jammed Nuada's hilt as hard as she could on his head. Bone cracked as he fell.

There was no time to view the result of her move. A beast of a man appeared out of nowhere, his sword drawn. Their swords clashed a few times before she retreated and stepped aside, using a move Sigel taught her. His momentum carried him beyond her. She swung Nua, connecting with one, if not both, of his hamstrings, dropping him.

She outran one man and made her way toward the stone escarpment where Silas was having a go at a huge bear-faced man. Blow after blow was exchanged, but Silas moved faster, and swung more accurately. The man was repeatedly disappointed. A glance in the opposite direction showed that Sigel was managing well enough, two bodies at his feet and a third about to be dispatched. Dara was doing his best to keep men away from his mistress, currently pinning one terrified man by the throat to the ground. The man's gurgling scream stopped, and Dara instinctively turned on the next man to come near her.

A large shadow crossed overhead and she looked up to see the crow, the black medallion hanging from his neck. *How's he going to help?* The air changed perceptibly and she grew light-headed. The light went from spectral to shimmering, giving the battlefield a dreamlike quality. Sir Thomas touched down just feet from her and began spinning, twisting, and bending. Wings became arms and stick-like bird feet became a man's long legs. The crow's round black eyes and narrow head turned beautifully human. He was impeccably dressed, in black. A dark angel who wasted no time in securing a sword from the nearest lifeless hand.

Elegance did not disallow fury and skill and this Victorian-looking warrior was every bit as efficient with his weapon as Sigel and Silas. The luxury of shock vanished when a loud grunt drew her attention. Briana turned. Silas dropped to his knees and then to all fours, blood covering the side of his face. She didn't know if the blood was his or not, but she wasn't waiting to find out. Bear-face stood over the back of Silas, sword raised, his intention clearly to run him through the back of the neck.

"Silas!" she screamed, as she leaped from the ground to a rock behind his attacker. She flipped Nua upside down, preparing to drive her into the back of the man's neck. A split second before she connected, Bear-face, responding to her scream, whipped backward and brought his blade up vertically. As hers drove down into his throat instead of the back of his neck, his connected with the inside of her leg, ripping up. Then he lay still, blood gushing out of his neck when Briana yanked Nua out. Everything around her seemed to sharpen somehow. She heard the cries and screams as men delivered blows and received them. She smelled the reeking bloody drain of vicious wounds. She observed Sigel in hand-to-hand combat, sunlight glinting off metal as they clashed ferociously. She noted the flash of alarm on his face when he glanced her way. Dara now stood protectively in front of her on the rock, teeth bared. She stared at the man she had impaled, lying face up in front of Silas, still, blood jetting from his neck. Nua hung at her side, dripping blood, her work done for the moment.

Silas turned toward her with a look of pure rage that turned to fear when he looked at something on her lower body. Her eyes followed his. The inside of her left leg was splayed open from above the knee all the way up to her groin, her trousers practically filleted off. She stared as though the mangled mess belonged to someone else. *Oh no! I might not be able to save Uisneach after all.* She looked back at Silas. *But at least you're alive.* Then, the world spun wildly out of control and went black.

～

Sigel's face was bathed in blood. She cried out and reached for him.

"Be still, little warrior. It's mostly not my blood. I'm fine. Silas is, too."

"I'm here, Briana."

"You were cut," she said, looking for the injury.

He showed her the slice along his jaw, not as bad as she imagined. "A wee grazin'," he said, his voice trembling.

"Make sure you put some of the comfrey salve on it tonight."

Behind the men were the boulders they had been fighting on. They must have pulled her out of the way. She made a move to try and stand. "Let me get up and –" Pain shot up from toe to hip.

"No, no, Briana, don't!" Silas held her back with gentle hands. "The only one of us who is severely banjaxed is you."

She recalled the flash of a knife and pain in her thigh, and mustering the courage to do so, looked down and wondered, *How in the hell did I survive that*? "I think I killed a man," she said, sounding like she had asked for two cubes of sugar rather than one.

"Several," Sigel corrected. "You did very well, Briana. You fought as hard and brave as we did. In fact, you saved the bard's life, you and Nua." His calm was reassuring, a sharp contrast to the scene around her – bodies and blood everywhere.

"Are you mad at me, Sigel? You said to stay hidden, but…"

"Shhh… you don't listen worth a damn, but I don't see you had a choice," he said.

"The black angel… where'd he go?"

"Black angel?" Sigel said. "Do you mean Sir Thomas?"

"I watched him… shift."

"A bit of a shock the first time, I imagine. But not the only shock of the day, aye?" Silas said, quietly.

She looked again at her leg and for the first time since the assault started, she felt scared and started to shake. "I think I'm going to be…"

Silas held an empty helmet to her mouth. When she emptied her stomach and wiped her mouth, he threw the headgear into the woods.

"We need to get you to the fort for the time being, until we figure out what to do next. We're going to put you on this blanket and carry you. It'll hurt like hell. Think you can be brave a little longer, *a mhuirnin?*"

She nodded, not really sure she could. She couldn't help but look again at the unholy chaos around her. *Did I seriously just do that?* At that moment a searing pain split her in two as they lifted her. She gritted her teeth to keep from screaming. Wave after agonizing wave assailed her until finally the world went blessedly black again.

When she came to, she was settled inside the ruins of Cath Ardghal near a fire. Sigel sat beside her.

"Where's Silas?" she asked in a panic.

"Just gone for some water, lass. We need to clean you up a little."

Pain nearly tore her apart but she spoke stoically. "How bad is it, Sigel?"

He grimaced. "Bad. He laid you wide open."

"We'll need to take these pants off," she said, reaching below, only to discover her legs were bare under the cover of a kilt. She looked up questioningly.

"We had to check for other injuries."

She nodded, laying back and closing her eyes. She opened them again when Sigel said with some amusement, "You know, Mouse, other than the huge gash running down your thigh, you have very nice legs."

She managed a weak chuckle. "Well, thank you, Sigel. And since they are all I've got, do you think we can save them?"

"I fail to find any humor in this," Silas muttered, returning with the water.

She understood the trouble she was in. The laceration was long and deep. The bleeding had stopped, but exposure to mud, blood and other unsavory elements ranked her risk for infection high.

"It needs to be stitched," she said, knowing full well they didn't have access to anything like medical sutures and needles.

"Can you do anything with your magic?" Silas asked.

She shook her head. "Visualization will help, but I can't heal this fast enough to make traveling feasible. We'll do the best we can with honey and comfrey. How am I going to get to the mansion?"

Sigel was already boiling water as she'd taught him, to prevent infections when dressing a wound.

"Sir Thomas is going to send horses here," Sigel said.

"Once this is wrapped, find me a walking stick and we'll go. We can meet him on the way," Briana said, trying to exhibit a bravado she didn't feel.

"Briana, you can't walk!" Silas snapped.

"I can try!" she bit back.

They stared at each other, then looked away sheepishly.

I'm sorry, Briana. But you can't walk.

I know.

"So then, all we can do is clean and wrap your leg while we wait for help." Sigel poured some of the hot water into a bowl, swished it around, threw it out and poured fresh water into the semi-sterilized bowl. "Ready?"

"Yes, let's do it." Wanting to give Silas something to focus on, she asked, "Silas, will you help me with some magic while Sigel does his thing?"

He knew exactly what she meant and what she needed. Clasping hands, they focused on each other and began the process of visualization. She imagined the extremity in her mind, free of germs and building new tissue. When Sigel poured the sterile water into the wound, she winced. Silas, back in control of himself, kept helping her focus. He rubbed her hands and provided the distraction that helped her stay calm and tolerate Sigel's ministrations. *There are worse things than having to stare into your beautiful blue eyes,* she thought. Something in their blue depths carried her away to another place altogether. They were lying in a sun-drenched, flowery meadow, arms wound around one another, as lips sought and found their pleasure. His hand slid down her arm and moved to stroke her hip and then back up the side of her rib cage to her breast. The intimacy was breathtaking, and as her lips parted in a tiny sigh, she actually did gasp, which made Sigel think he'd hurt her.

"Sorry, lass, almost done."

"Please don't hurry," she said softly, keeping the connection with Silas' eyes.

Sigel looked up from his work. "Is there nothing to stop the two of you from ogling one another?" he remarked, dryly.

"I doubt it," Briana whispered, wishing Sigel would shut up and leave them to their reverie.

Me too, Silas agreed, but the vision faded, much to their mutual regret.

Sigel finished. He and Silas repositioned her on the blankets, built up the fire to keep her warm, and allowed Dara to curl up next to her. She faded in and out of consciousness, waking at one point shivering uncontrollably, in spite of the fire.

"I'm so cold," she murmured, "and thirsty."

"There's nothing else we can cover her with," Silas said, bringing a cup of water to her lips, but only allowing a sip. He edged away from her and she heard disagreeable muttering and then, "You know what she needs, Sigel. Either you do it, or I will. It matters not to me, as long as she is kept warm."

A deep, resistant growl, then the muttered words, "two poor choices" and the rustle of fabric. Silas' warm body slid under the kilts with her, on the opposite side of the dog. He took her in his arms and drew her as close as he could without moving her leg. Eventually, between the warmth of Silas and Dara, her shivering began to subside.

"My great cat," she sighed, into his chest.

"What?"

When you raced across the ridge today, all I could think of was a great mountain lion. And watching you fight those men... You made me so proud, Silas.

He snorted in response. *I didn't do much to protect you today. I'm sorry Briana, more than you'll ever know.*

Stop, Silas. You and Sigel both said it could've been any of us. I think maybe today was my chance to pay you back for saving my life last time. Consider us even.

Finally relaxing, he scooted a little closer and hugged her, whispering, "Well, we're even, then. Now, you can go to sleep, *a mhuirnin*, trustin' that tonight I will keep you safe."

"I know you will, Silas."

CHAPTER EIGHTEEN

WINGE MANSION

Briana drifted in and out of sleep all night, but come morning, opened her eyes to find Sigel resting and Silas puttering with his inking supplies. He was crafting lyrics in his head.

"Come closer, come closer, till our hearts beat as one, from the rise of the moon, till the break of the sun. Whispers and touches, laughter and tears, you're my love, forever, biding the years."

He caught her watching him, and she smiled at the dreamy look in his eyes. *Beautiful.*

He opened his mouth to say something but closed it again and returned his attention to the tools in his lap.

Where did you learn to tattoo? she asked.

Once, a long time ago, a came to Ard Darach. He created brilliant tattoos and taught me the skill. He made the one on me chest. She imagined her fingers tracing tracing the outline of the crossed swords on his chest. Though he continued to look down at the box of powders and needles, she saw his lips curve. She looked over at Sigel, dead to the world, then back at Silas.

Make me one, she asked.

His eyes flew up to meet hers in surprise. *A tattoo?*

She nodded.

He studied her. *Not a great idea*, a mhuirnin. *What would the king say about that?*

She shrugged. *Make something he wouldn't question or that he could misunderstand, but that has meaning to us. Perhaps a tree to symbolize the journey?*

"Or a mouse," he said, softly.

No mouse. I want something from you that no one can take away.

You already have somethin', he said, touching his heart.

You know what I mean.

He studied her a moment longer. *You want me to mark you?*

Please, Silas.

He hesitated.

If something should happen to me…

"You're going to be fine," he whispered. "We won't let anything happen to you."

"Just in case," she insisted.

No. Briana, you're in a vulnerable state and I won't take advantage of that and do so somethin' you might regret.

I won't regret…

However, I could create your own personal insignia and paint your shield. I can't think of any reason why anyone should be upset over that.

I want it on my body.

Let's start with the shield, he said, firmly, reaching for water to mix the ink. *If someday you still want the tattoo and it won't get you killed to have it, I will happily oblige you.* He mentally described a design, which she approved, then went to work while she dozed to the relaxing sound of his humming.

"Briana?"

"Hmm," she murmured, opening her eyes.

"Do you like it?"

She drew in her breath at the beautiful artwork. A glorious oak covered the shield. In the center of the trunk was Nuada, in bas relief, with a small mouse at its base. "It's beautiful."

I'm not finished. I want to hang two feathers from Nua's hilt.

Immediately grasping the significance of two feathers, she smiled. *Can you intertwine them, wrap them around each other?*

An hour later, two exquisitely drawn feathers entwined in ivy, wrapped around Nua: a raven feather, symbol of magic and healing for any goddess worth her salt, and a swan feather.

Swan? She raised an eyebrow. *I've always thought that was the symbol of bards, music and poetry. That might give the king pause.*

Aye, but also symbolic of travel between worlds. Ambiguous enough, I think.

As they admired his work, Silas rubbed his thumb along the side of the design. *You know the symbolism of the feathers. The ivy represents affection... fidelity... and wedded love.*

She frowned. *That sounds more like an allusion to Brath.*

As it should be. This emblem represents both the hope of your soul and the hope of a kingdom.

Sigel woke up while they were admiring Silas' handiwork. He studied the art, the artist and Briana carefully. She could tell he wanted to find fault with what Silas had done, but it *was* ambiguous and all he could do was shrug his shoulders.

"She should have had the Taranian herald," he said, gruffly.

"Many queens have had both the house banner and their own insignia," Silas pointed out, matter-of-factly.

No more was said; Silas put away his inking tools and went for more water. Briana fell asleep.

Briana woke to find the two men staring at her. "What's wrong?"

"Nothing." Sigel's voice was nonchalant, but the tightness around his mouth gave him away.

"Tell me."

Silas replied. "You look flushed. Your skin is hot to the touch. We're worried your wound is going bad."

She touched a hand to her forehead. Hot was an understatement. "Damn," she muttered, peeling off a section of the bandage.

"What are you doing?" Sigel reached out to stop her.

"I just want a peek to see if it looks infected." She pulled back the makeshift dressing and groaned. The skin was inflamed and ugly. She lay back, thinking. They could take the wrapping off, clean and re-bandage it, but they didn't have any more supplies, so would only be putting dirty dressings back on. In her weakened condition, she couldn't even muster any magic to help. The only thing to do was wait for help and take care of it when they got to the mansion and she said this to her companions, who nodded their agreement. In the meantime, they began to bathe her face with a cloth and cold water.

Sigel pulled out her map and handed it to her. While she interpreted that help should be arriving soon, the men made a crude splint, which they attached to her leg to keep it as still as possible during travel.

"We can make a litter," Sigel said.

Briana cut him off "Not! I am not being hauled behind the horses. I will ride like everyone else."

"Briana, that would be painful and awkward," Silas said.

"I don't care. I'm not being trussed up and dragged along. I'll manage on a horse."

"Maker, you are a stubborn woman," Sigel growled.

Rummaging through their three packs, he was able to find a few hard biscuits and some dried fruit and meat.

"You two have mine. I'm not hungry," said Briana.

"You need food, Briana, whether you want it or not, to keep up your strength." Sigel forced the bread into her hand. She choked down a couple of bites before handing it back.

"I just can't, Sigel, but I could drink some water." Silas offered her his cup and she drank her fill. She tried to lay down but shot right back up as a wave of nausea overtook her. Lightheadedness and confusion followed. She should know where they were but somehow couldn't put things together. "I don't feel so good."

"Hang on, *a mhuirnin*, a little longer."

Hoof beats announced the arrival of help. She beheld three groomsmen on big black horses, leading three other riderless horses and a litter. *Correction, two groomsmen and a woman.* They wore matching formal equestrian wear, bright white shirts and red ascot ties, urbane for groomsmen. In Briana's feverish state, the woman resembled a Persian goddess, with ivory skin, dark, depthless eyes and inky black hair that fell in a single braid down her back to her calves. *That must be murder to wash*, she thought.

The lead rider dismounted from a black giant of a horse and came toward them. She recognized him from the battlefield, but he still took her breath away. Sir Thomas was at least as tall as Silas and slender, with the longest legs she'd ever seen on a man. Obsidian hair stylishly cut to shoulder-length, feathered back at the temples, with not a hair out of place. He had high, arching, black brows atop charcoal eyes, an aquiline nose and elegant lips, not too full, but not at all thin. Sculpted cheekbones and a flawless fawn complexion complimented his darkness. He was attired from head to toe in black, sophisticated and polished. And sensual.

So, like are all the men in Uisneach drop-dead gorgeous?

Silas chuckled and whispered in her ear, "Should I be jealous?"

"Never," she managed to croak out. The shiny, black medallion the man wore around his neck confirmed his identity. "You're the crow – I mean, Sir Thomas," she said, weakly.

"Yes, Lady Briana, I'm the pesky crow that's been following you around, and I am so pleased to finally meet you in person, though we might have chosen better conditions."

"Not pesky. Without your help, I'd have been lost or dead several times already."

"I did what I could, milady, and it was my pleasure to do so. But now, you appear to be in a bit of quandary."

"You could say that." Her ability to maintain civilities was growing more limited by the second.

He watched her with concern, as did Silas and Sigel, but she couldn't find the words to question anyone about it.

Silas took the reins of a gracefully built chestnut horse. "I'll mount, then the two of you can lift her up –"

"Certainly not," said Sir Thomas. "The litter is safer."

"Our future queen prefers to ride," Sigel said, with a dour expression.

And that was that. Silas, being the most nimble, was chosen to ride behind her. He'd be able to mount without jostling her.

Not bad, thought Briana. *There's something to this queen stuff.*

Sigel and Sir Thomas went to each side of Briana. "This is probably going to kill you, but we'll be as quick and easy as we can," Sigel said. "Ready?"

She nodded and took a deep breath in preparation. They counted to three and lifted her. She cried out once before things once again went dark.

She was semi-aware that they were traveling. She heard someone say

Cailleach would meet them at the mansion. *Good*, Briana thought, *she'll fix this bloody leg.*

"You all right, Briana?" Silas asked.

"No, but it's worth it," she said, keeping her eyes closed.

"What do you mean?"

"Worth the pain to be in your arms." His heartbeat against her back was a comforting lullaby in a sea of pain.

⤚

Silas muttered, "Thanks be to Maker, we're here."

Briana opened her eyes. She inhaled sharply as they entered the beautiful and mysterious oak-lined avenue whose ancient trees reached across the lane, creating a passageway of green and brown. This opened to a spectacular view of Winge Mansion, beautifully situated on the southern coast of Uisneach.

"Downton Abbey," she mumbled.

"What did you say, *a mhuirnin*?"

"Nothing… tell you later." She didn't have the energy to talk but she did marvel at the palatial manor, with its stacked walls of massive white marble stones. At each of the castle's corners stood black marble towers pinnacled by imposing statues of crows. More black stone was inlaid around the front door and windows. Above the front door was a stone crow, wings spread out imperially. Several people waited in front of the castle, all dressed in black, and like Sir Thomas, supremely beautiful. *This is going to be very interesting at some point*, she thought.

Briana was eased out of Silas' sheltering arms to Sigel's, who carried her inside. From within her foggy shroud, she noticed the immense, opulent foyer resembling a giant chessboard. An enormous chandelier suspended from the skylight illuminated the space with brilliant light from thousands of tiny candles and almond-shaped pendants.

Along the walls were sculpted tree trunks rising up into a series of wall sconces shaped like nests, upon which crow candles perched. Glass sculptures of crows sat on pillars and tables and one huge figure, wings outstretched, stood in the center of the hall. Light flashed off the crystal, reflecting all around the room. Opposite the front entryway, a sweeping black marble staircase led to the second floor. Sigel carried her up, following the graceful lead of a classically stylish woman with onyx hair swept up in a chignon at the back of her head, wearing a floor-length gown of black and red silk covered by a day jacket. Dara trotted along faithfully behind them. Briana was taken down a long corridor and laid gently on a soft bed.

The stylish woman moved forward. "Hello, Lady Briana," she said, her tone a comforting blend of confidence and grace. "I'm Lady Isabella Winge, Sir Thomas' wife. I wish we could offer you a finer welcome, but I believe the more important thing is to clean you up and try to make you comfortable. Cailleach will be here very soon to mend your leg. One of our young ladies is going to bathe you and change your clothing. Your friends will refresh themselves as well, and then they can come back up. Silas, please take the dog with you?" Her kind, but firm tone eliminated any argument, so Briana gave herself up to the relief of being safe and cared for.

Silas nodded. "Don't worry about Dara, Briana. I'll tend to him." *Rest easy*, a stór. He watched her face for a moment longer, then, calling the hound to his side, left the room.

Lady Winge efficiently issued orders to a young woman with long black hair tied back in a feathered band, who was gathering towels and water from a kettle hung next to a warm and heartening fire. Briana gave herself up to the blessed relief of oblivion, assured they'd take care of her, praying Cailleach could repair her injuries.

She stood in front of a throne in the middle of a great hall, alone and afraid, surrounded by cold, gray stone. A noise echoed behind her. Whirling, Nua raised in defense, she observed one of the Gray Military soldiers coming at her, his own sword poised for attack. No time to respond. He cut down through her like a knife through butter, dropping the two halves of her cleanly to the floor. Searing pain coursed through her split body, but she didn't die. Sigel burst into the room, and after swiftly running his blade through the evil swordsman, came to Briana. Looking down at her, he seemed unsure what to do. Finally, picking up one-half of her, he set her on the throne and put the jeweled Taranian crown on her head. Silas came into the room in a druid's cloak, wearing a crown of oak leaves. Sigel handed her other half to Silas. With that half of her face, she looked at Silas and begged, "I just want to be whole. Make me whole."

Eavesdropping wasn't a habit of Briana's, but from this other-worldly abode, she couldn't help it. As from afar, she heard Sigel talking to Cailleach.

"I have concerns about her and the bard."

"Then do something. Separate them."

"I would, but for two things. One, I need him, at least until we join the rest of the army. And two, he is the Royal Bard, and her story is as much his responsibility to tell as Brath's."

"There will be a different story to tell if they go astray. Sir Thomas will provide men to accompany you if you need them, or he would go himself. Your call, lord marshall, but remember that our primary objective is to get her to the king, free him from the curse and see them married and her pregnant. It really is that simple. If it makes you feel any better, the possibility of her falling in love with Brath is not so far-fetched."

"I hope you're right, Cailleach."

Wind swirled around Briana like the tornado in the Wizard of Oz. She was tumbling and twirling around in an endless downward spiral. Fighting men appeared, their swords cutting and jabbing as she did her best to move out of the way. Cailleach floated by, her face a rippling mask of water. Her mother, crying in the garden, blew past her, beyond her reach. The horrid green face of the Wicked Witch of the East leered at her, cackling, coming closer. She turned from green to blue, until it was no longer the witch of Oz, but Lord Shamwa of Uisneach. He repeated over and over, "I'll get you, milady, and the gray lad, too!" Dara jumped in front of her, teeth bared, but Shamwa struck a blow, cracking the wolfhound on the head. Dara fell dead in front of her. She cried out repeatedly until she felt strong arms wrap around her, those of a mountain lion. And then the mountain lion turned into the man she loved. "Silas," she whispered into the darkness. The steady, reassuring beat of a heart filled the blackness with love. Quiet. Peaceful. Healing. Then a rush of cold air jolted her out of the sheltering cocoon. Metallic clouds grabbed at her as she and Silas were ripped apart. She stared helplessly, racked with tears and sobs as he rode away into a storm on a chestnut stallion. "Mother," she cried, "help me, please, help me."

CHAPTER NINETEEN

HINTERLANDS

The room was lit by a crackling fire in a black marble fireplace. A lovely young woman with long dark hair sat beside her bed doing needlework by the light of a single, stubby candle. Disoriented, Briana surveyed her surroundings. Unfamiliar, but luxurious in both its size and décor, royally furnished with heavy blankets, brocade curtains, brilliant tapestries, wool rugs, a round wooden table and two hand-carved chairs. Upon the table sat a small basket of greenery, and a pewter pitcher and goblet. Across from the fireplace was a walk-out balcony with ornate doors, currently closed against the chill morning air.

Beside her bed stood Nua and the shield with her new insignia, but she couldn't find Dara. Frantic, she jerked up on one elbow.

"Easy, milady. You're safe," said the girl, setting aside her embroidery to touch Briana's arm. "You're safe."

"Who are you? Where's my dog?"

"I'm Claire, your lady's maid," she said in a voice like warm cinnamon cookies and hot cocoa. "The hound is out in the hall with your guard."

"My what?" It was coming back: the battle, the injury and the trip to Winge Mansion. Briana lay back down, letting her breath out. "What time is it? How long have I slept?"

"It's the wee hours, milady; three days after your arrival here."

Briana came back up on one arm and tried to sit up, but dizziness forced her back down. "Three days? Are you serious?"

"You must lie still, Lady Briana. Cailleach has been working on your leg and said you shouldn't move too much. I'm to fetch her when you're awake, so let me…"

The door to her room opened and a familiar head poked inside. "She awake?" Silas asked, softly.

"I am," Briana replied, yawning. "No need to whisper. Come in, Silas."

The bard stepped into the room. Dara loped in behind him and planted a sloppy lick on her face. "Just for a moment. Then I'll find Cailleach."

He came to her bedside. Briana noted Claire's vigilance beside him. "I've been asleep three days?" She asked him, as though needing to confirm it with someone else.

"Aye. You've been very ill, milady. Cailleach's stitched up your leg as best she could and used magic to hasten the healing. It's comin' along, but you've a ways to go yet before jumpin' out of bed."

Milady?

We must be proper here, Briana. In fact, I shouldn't even be in your room.

Briana frowned, not liking the sound of this one bit.

"I'm relieved to see you awake, Lady Briana. I'll go fetch Cailleach." He winked and turned to leave.

Briana watched him go in silence, sensing things were about to be radically different between them.

"You've been well looked after, milady," Claire said. "Either the bard or the lord marshall have stood guard since the day you arrived."

"They're guarding me? From what?"

"As the queen, you must be protected at all times."

"I'm not the queen yet."

Claire shrugged, as though that were inconsequential.

Briana sighed and closed her eyes. When she opened them again, Cailleach stood at her bedside.

"So you've come back to us, hmmm?"

"Good morning, Cailleach. I didn't expect to see you so soon."

Claire slipped into the room with a tray and set it on the table beside the witch, who poured a steaming cup of something that smelled like beef broth, then added a small amount of white powder to it. "Drink up. It's healing nicely, your leg."

Briana took a sip as Cailleach poured a cup of tea.

"I think I owe thanks to you for that. I understand you've been working on it for a few days. I guess I might have died without your help."

"It's a nasty wound, girl. Quite the story of courage in how you acquired it. Perhaps Silas is also lucky to be alive?"

Briana couldn't quite tell if Cailleach was impressed with this or angry at her, so she changed the subject. "How did you get here so fast?"

"Merlin. He shifts and I ride."

"No kidding! I mean, I knew he shapeshifted, but big enough to fly you around? Wow!"

"Speaking of magic, let's take a look at the leg." She slid the bedcovers off Briana's leg to reveal a well-bandaged limb, which she deftly undressed.

Sutures crossed over a mending laceration with pink, healthy skin on either side of the wound, and no sign of infection. It was not completely healed, but insanely close to it. Briana lifted her leg and winced. "Well, it still hurts, but I'm amazed. You did this all with magic?"

Cailleach shook her head. "Magic and a little ordinary medicinals. Now you can continue the process."

"You want me to do... what?"

"Magic, of course. Visualizations of healing. I'll continue to dress the wounds for you." The witch prodded around the sutures. "You could've done most of this yourself at the fort."

"You think I own that kind of magic?"

"I believe you do. Let's get busy, aye?"

They spent an hour practicing, Cailleach instructing, coaxing and encouraging while Briana visualized and spoke gentle healing words of affirmation to her injured leg. At the end of the hour, she was sweating and exhausted from the intense concentration required. Cailleach patted her good leg.

"Enough for today. Well done, Briana. I want you to spend the next few days resting." Picking up her supplies, Cailleach headed for the door.

Briana nodded, closed her eyes and drifted off before the door closed behind the witch.

Three more days passed in a miasma of practicing magic and rest. "I feel like Jesus in the tomb," she complained to Claire on the third day. "I'm not alive, but I'm not dead, either."

"Who is Jesus?" Claire asked, as she put away the dresses that the local seamstress, Jemeny, had altered for Briana.

After the CliffNotes edition of the story, Claire asked, "Why did his father let him die if he was such a great man?"

"People have been asking that question and fighting over the answer for thousands of years. Far be it from me to pontificate. The more important question at the moment is, When can I leave this room?"

"Cailleach says maybe tomorrow. Would you like to play another card game?"

"No, I would not." What she wanted to do was go find Silas. His absence since the first day of her awakening was troubling. Was he staying away on purpose? Was he not allowed to visit her? Sigel and Sir Thomas had each been in once, Cailleach and Lady Isabella every day.

On cue, there was a rap at the door, and Lady Isabella poked her head in. "May I speak with you, Lady Briana?"

"Of course. Come in."

The lady of the manor moved across the room like a swan on a pond, her long gown flowing behind her as she came to sit beside Briana. "Cailleach thinks you might be ready to join the rest of the household the day after tomorrow. I hope to take you around to meet the rest of the staff here."

"Will I be staying here long enough to make that important?"

"It's been decided," Lady Isabella spoke carefully, "that you would stay a few more days to learn the rudiments of managing a household. It would be a privilege to assist you in the endeavor."

Glancing at the line of dresses in the open wardrobe, she should have guessed. The "it's been decided" rankled. Too many things were being decided for her, but she pasted a smile on her lips. "I will be happy to learn from you, Your Ladyship, but I don't see myself as the kind of queen who spends her days ordering servants about."

Lady Isabella stiffened and tipped her head. "Oh? What kind of queen do you want to be?"

Great question, Briana thought as she realized how unkind she'd been. "I didn't mean to suggest..."

Waving off the apology, Isabella nodded to the chair beside the bed. "May I?"

"Please do," she said, face still pink from her faux pas. She had been paying attention to the way Lady Isabella managed her household, at least from the limited vantage point of her bedroom. Watching the older woman operate with such grace and efficiency, Briana did hope she could become half as proficient when she had to manage a castle.

"This must all be so strange for you, Lady Briana."

"Briana is fine," Briana said, knowing by now it would make no difference.

Lady Isabella sat back in the chair and folded her hands in her lap. "No, it isn't fine. One of the strange things about being a queen is that people treat you with a deference you may be uncomfortable with, but you must learn to accept milady. It comes with the position.

"As does managing a household. There are many things that must be done to keep a home running smoothly, and in the case of royalty, even more, as you will be receiving and entertaining people constantly, at all hours of the day and night. It's essential that you provide the leadership and oversight necessary to make Ard Darach the pride of Uisneach."

Briana nodded. "I understand, but I have had some leadership training and I know if you hire the right people and make your expectations clear, they will do the job you want them to do."

"And you can be free to run about the countryside with the army, fighting Lord Shamwa?"

"That is our mission."

"That is King Brath's mission. As his queen, your role is largely supportive. That means assuring a standard of excellence in his castle that allows him to come and go without fretting about what's happening at home." Seeing the expression on Briana's face, she patted her hand. "As I said, this is all strange to you, but let me help you. You are bright and talented and as brave as any soldier. But bravery has many playing fields, not all having to do with blood and guts."

Part of what Lady Isabella said was reasonable, but Briana had no intention of being a housewife. She'd learn what she needed to learn and find the right staff to run the household. She didn't intend to be left out of the adventures of her husband's more active life.

The conversation moved to other things and Briana came to

understand this was a woman she could trust, someone who'd experienced her own share of joy and sorrow and wasn't just spending her days "ordering servants about." She and Sir Thomas had two children, a son who was "away" at the moment, and a daughter who died while trying to shapeshift into another time.

"Shapeshifting can be dangerous, especially when one is attempting to enter another world. Leieria was in love with a man from the world you come from. In her endeavor to be with him, she was flashed during the transformation process."

"Flashed?"

Isabella's hands made a swift, fluttering movement into the air.

"I am so sorry. I can't imagine what you must have gone through."

Sir Thomas' wife squeezed her hand. "Losing a child is a terrible thing, but it was a long time ago, and the pain of it has dulled. Don't let anyone ever tell you that you'll get over the loss of someone you love. You will not, though the pain does soften. You find ways to keep going. But then, you know all of this."

Memories of her father surfaced. Her mother, too, who, though not dead, was still as lost to Briana. She missed them both terribly, but she was coping. *Yes,* she thought, *it does soften. Will I be able to say the same about Silas someday?*

"Well, my dear, I've kept you chatting far too long, and you need a rest, I should think. I'll leave you, but I have truly enjoyed getting to know you a little better. Please, don't hesitate to call on me if you should need anything." She rose with prim elegance and walked over to the fireplace, where she added another peat brick to the fire.

"Thank you, I will," Briana agreed. "And Lady Isabella, I will do my best to learn my duties."

"I'm certain you will. Rest now, milady." She left the room, the silky black train of her dress floating behind her.

Sigel showed up after lunch with a wooden box.

"Up for a visit and a game of *ríocht?*"

"*Ríocht,* maybe, a talk with you, definitely."

"Oh?" He didn't look at her as he set the box on the table and began to set up the board with beautifully carved wooden pieces. "Something on your mind?"

"I understand you gave orders for me to stay here for a few days."

"I don't know if I'd call them orders, but that's the plan. There are some things you need to learn that Lady Isabella is particularly suited to showing you." He continued to set up castles, rooks and knights.

"I thought we needed to hurry up and get to Ard Darach?"

"We do, and had you not butchered your leg…"

"I didn't exactly plan that," she said, acerbically.

"…we'd be on our way. Since you're not ready to travel, it occurred to me that learning a bit about the domestic side of queendom would be to your benefit. I'm trying to help you, Briana. White or red?"

"Red. It suits my mood."

He grinned. "Are you cranky?"

"You might say that. I'm stuck here. People are planning my life and forcing me into things I'm not ready for. Silas is being kept from me…"

Sigel put up a warning hand. "He is not 'being kept from you,' Briana, and I would be careful how loudly you say that. Silas is busy doing his job and you need to focus on doing yours."

She waved at her lower extremities and around the room with a questioning look. "What am I supposed to do from here?"

"Practice your magic, learn what you can from the people around you and prepare yourself to take on all the tasks of being a queen." He moved a soldier and she followed suit automatically. A couple of moves were made in silence.

"The middle game," he said, moving a rook, "is where the game is won or lost. We can reach the castle and rescue Brath, but if you don't know what to do once that's done, everyone loses. A queen is both something you do and someone you are. This is a good place to learn what you do, and Lady Isabella is a perfect example of how to be."

While they played, he offered an update on the status of Shamwa, who hadn't been seen, and the Gray Military, who remained near Long River. Thoughtful silence prevailed over the rest of the game, which Briana lost – again. She sighed. "I'm tired."

The *ríocht* pieces went back into the box and Sigel gave her one last look. "You are ready, Briana. You only need to be sure it's what you want. You aren't a prisoner and no one will force you to finish this. Say the word, and I'll take you back to Baigsith as soon as you can travel."

"Really? You would?"

He nodded, tucking the box under his arm. "I find it hard to believe the prophecy could be so wrong, and I have every faith you can be the queen this kingdom needs, but not if you don't want it. You're a free woman."

"Not exactly," she muttered, to his exiting back.

If resting was what they wanted her to do, they had a funny way of showing it. Streams of visitors poured through her room all afternoon. Shortly before dinner, Cailleach came to help her take her first steps since the injury, which she did tentatively, but without pain.

"Okay, I'm all better. I can go down for supper."

"One more day, Briana, please. We don't want to undo what's been done." To prevent further argument, she gave Claire orders to fetch Her Ladyship's dinner.

The witch's visit was cut short by the first visit of the mansion's Mistress of the Hunt.

"Hello, Lady Briana. I'm Epona. I was with Sir Thomas when you were rescued, but you probably don't remember me." She patted Dara affectionately as she came into the room.

"Of course I remember you," Briana said, awed again at the Persian goddess before her. "Please, won't you sit down?" With less than a full measure of hope, Briana asked, "I don't suppose you'd prefer to call me Briana?"

"Absolutely! I find titles so pretentious, don't you? I'm sorry it took me so long to come and visit, but it's been quite busy in the stables, getting horses ready for the rest of your journey. You do ride, right?"

"I do, both English and western. I rode competitively as a teenager."

"Those terms are unfamiliar, but I'm glad you know your way around a horse. When are they going to release you from your cell?" she asked, looking around with a shudder. "I'd go batty stuck in here for days."

"Tell me about it." Briana smiled at her newfound kindred spirit. "Cailleach says I'll be released tomorrow, but I'm not sure about riding yet."

"Excellent! Silas will be happy."

Alarm bells went off in Briana's head and her smile disappeared. "Silas? Why would he care?"

"Really, Briana. You are looking at the romance expert extraordinaire. I watched the two of you all the way from Cath Ardghal to Winge Mansion, and even in your loopy state, it was pretty obvious there's a connection. I'm not saying anyone else noticed it, but I make it my business to notice these things. Don't worry, your secret is safe with me. I am well aware you are King Brath's intended. Not sure how you'll pull this off, but I wish you luck."

Briana was stunned and clueless as to how to respond. She knew it would be dangerous for anyone to guess their feelings, and yet the idea of having a friend to confide in was appealing. But she barely knew Epona. "You must be mistaken this time, Epona. There is nothing between me and Silas. I am betrothed to the king."

"Whatever you say, Briana. If ever you want to talk, I've got your back. I'm all about impossible love."

Yet another knock at the door interrupted further discussion. Claire arrived with dinner.

"I suppose I best go downstairs," said Epona. "I do wish you could come. Silas is going to entertain us tonight. Can't wait. A voice to die for. See you later."

Releasing a breath she didn't realize she was holding, Briana turned her attention to her dinner. After days of broth, tea and light fare, the roasted chicken, potatoes and asparagus made her stomach growl in anticipation.

All was quiet in her room, while everyone else dined downstairs, entertained by the bard.

Minutes turned to hours. With nothing else to do, Briana fell asleep.

Briana?

She woke instantly, hearing his voice in her head. *Silas?* Claire was sleeping soundly on the couch, one arm flung across her face, the other clutching a blanket.

Hi, he said.

Hi. Where are you?

Outside your door. I'm on guard duty tonight.

Really? After a night of storytelling? They work you too hard. Come in.

Can't. But we can talk.

Where have you been? I haven't seen you in days.

I know, I'm sorry. Been busy.

A vague answer, which she let go. *So what's happening out in the real world? I feel so isolated in here.*

Only a wee bit longer, a mhuirnin. *Are you feeling better?*

Well enough to be out there with you. She looked again at the lady's maid and wondered if she could sneak out without disturbing Claire.

Not a good idea, but I have another. Would you help me write a song?

Sure, she said, glumly. *Is that my consolation prize?*

It starts like this: I love to see you swimming in our enchanted sea, finding treasures in the surf and in the sand. You make me believe in magic, long past when I should. He stopped, as though thinking.

I want to swim beside you, she thought.

Come take me hand, he added.

Come, my love, and swim with me,

In this beautiful, magical sea.

They both went quiet, immersed in the imagery.

Silas, I don't know how not to feel the way I do for you. I try not to… She trailed off, lost and uncertain what she should say. *I want to do what's right for Uisneach, but I'm afraid.*

Afraid of what?

That I can't do it, can't be that queen, can't follow through with the marriage. She paused. *Can't stop loving you.*

He didn't respond.

Silas? Are you still there?

I'm here, a mhuirnin. *I wanted to hold that thought in me heart for a minute. I don't think we can stop lovin' each other, but we must try with all our might not to act on it. I confess, I'm afraid I don't have the strength, which is part of the reason I stay away. If I'm not near you, it's a wee bit easier. When I'm with you, I lose me senses.*

That's a wee bit of a problem, isn't it, since we work for the same king?

More than a wee bit, a mhuirnin.

CHAPTER TWENTY

OUR ENCHANTED SEA

Briana stood on the balcony drinking in the warm, spring night. The moon was just past full but still poured its glorious white light across the courtyard. The newly born leaves of an ash tree waved in the breeze next to the balcony, their music blending naturally with that of the bard's drum somewhere below her. Briana contemplated the tree's wild limbs. *Would they hold her weight?*

"I can't stand being cooped up in here anymore, hovered over like the crown jewels," she said, scowling at Claire.

"Tomorrow, milady. Cailleach said…"

"Tonight, tomorrow morning, what difference does it make? I want you to pull out the best dress in that closet and take me downstairs."

"But milady…"

"Claire, I've been walking around this room for two days, just fine. There is no reason I can't go sit downstairs and listen to music. Don't make me pull rank; you know how I hate that."

Finally, the girl smiled. "Okay, but if I get in trouble…"

"How can you get in trouble when it's an order from the future queen?"

Claire growled. She held up a green dress. Briana wrinkled her nose. "Too stuffy."

A gold brocade came out next. Briana shook her head. "Let me see that black one?"

Claire sighed when she pulled out an elegant black floor-length gown with a dipping sweetheart neckline and beaded bodice.

Briana's eyes lit up. "That will do nicely."

It didn't take long to transform herself from convalescent to near-goddess. Claire swept part of her hair up in a chignon while leaving tendrils around her face and down her neck. A humble string of stones sparkled around her neck and wrist. She wore matching teardrop earrings.

"Ravishing," Claire said.

Briana took a deep breath and with her lady's maid at her side, made her way down the hall and stairs to the salon, where everyone was gathered. No one noticed her at first, enthralled by Silas' singing and the wild movements of his body as he spun and gyrated with the bodhran. She listened for a moment. The song seemed to be about one of Uisneach's epic battles. He saw her and came to an abrupt halt, the expression on his face changing from surprise to pure delight.

Everyone else turned to see Briana looking every inch a queen. Sigel stood and came to her side. "Welcome downstairs, milady," he said, leading her to the empty seat at the head of the table.

"Please continue, Silas," she said, trying to sound nonchalant, though her insides were quivering. "I want to hear how it ends."

"Somehow a song about warriors and battles seems amiss at this moment. Perhaps somethin' more enchantin'?"

She inclined her head and tried not feel self-conscious at the stares she felt around her. Cailleach, seated next to her, whispered in her ear, "Can you never do as you're told?"

Briana gulped and stared at the woman, relieved when she noted the sparkle in her eye. "You're not upset?" she whispered back.

"Tonight, tomorrow morning, what difference does it make?"

Great minds think alike. Briana turned her full attention to Silas, who picked up an ancient precursor of the Uilleann pipes and began to play a heart-wrenching tune. When he had every eye in the room bright with sentimental tears, he traded the pipes for his guitar and began to sing.

"I love to see you swimming in our enchanted sea,

Finding treasures in the surf and in the sand.

You make me believe in magic, long past when I should.

I want to swim beside you, come take me hand.

Come, my love, and swim with me

In this beautiful, magical sea.

Heart to heart, we dive and dart,

Through the waves of our enchanted sea."

Briana found it impossible to hold back her tears. Fortunately, she was not alone. Every woman in the room held a hanky to her eye. Sigel handed her his as Silas continued with another verse.

"You make me believe in mermaids bathing 'neath the stars.

Moonlit dolphins dance in joyful wonder in the waves.

We set our sails, batten down and ride on waves of love.

Knowin' some will gently swell, others drive us under.

Come, my love, and swim with me,

In our beautiful, magical sea.

Heart to heart, we dive and dart,

Through the waves of our enchanted sea."

Briana's heart swelled with love and with a longing deeper than the words the bard sang. She closed her eyes and let the song flow over her.

"I dive into the watery depths, rise up with a pearl,

Set it on your finger, the promise of a dream.

With every foamy wave that breaks upon the rocky coast,

I hold you close and love you, in our enchanted sea."

If only.

When she opened her eyes, Briana found all eyes on her. With perfect grace, she stood to face Silas. "That was lovely, Silas. Thank you for taking us all to such a beautiful place."

Everyone else stood, applauding the bard, who bowed deeply, but kept his eyes on Briana.

The pleasure is mine, a mhuirnin.

Hours later, as the mansion settled into silence and Claire into sleep, Briana returned to the balcony and contemplated the evening's performance, especially the songs that had been meant just for her. She sighed. *It's nice to be in love with a bard,* she thought. Only it wasn't all that nice when you couldn't be together.

Suddenly, she saw him crossing the courtyard in the direction of the garden. He seemed in no hurry and even stopped to gaze up at the moon and smell a flowering bush.

An idea began to form in Briana's mind. She gauged the proximity of the ash tree to the balcony. *Very close. Not too far from the ground, either.* Claire snored softly on her couch, tucked into her blankets. Since Silas was outside, Sigel likely guarded her door. Briana's heart beat faster. Tiptoeing to the closet, she eased it open and pulled out her trousers and tunic, then slipped into them. She warned Dara with a finger to her lips. *Not a sound, okay?* The hound gave her a complicit look, laid his head down and shut his eyes. *Good lad.*

Standing next to the tree, she closed her eyes and focused on the image of her sliding easily from limb to limb to the ground below. She couldn't reinjure her leg. They needed to get on with their mission, and she'd go crazy if forced back into that bed. When she felt ready, Briana raised herself onto the railing and reached for the first limb. Easing the rest of her body up and over, she put a foot to the next lower limb and tested its sturdiness. Smiling, she transferred all her weight from the railing to the branch and with the ease of an eel, slid down through the leaves until she could drop the last few feet to the ground. When her feet touched grass, she looked up, making sure she could return. With a quivery smile and racing heart, she followed the path Silas had taken.

Silhouetted against the cliffs and the ocean, he looked mystical in the moonlight, a druid communing with his source of inspiration. She paused, wondering if she should interrupt his solitude.

Come on then, you made it this far.

She hurried next to him. He still faced the ocean. Luminous white light streaked a path across the water to the rocks where the waves crashed loudly. The occasional groan and phoof of air from a whale's blowhole reminded her that there was a whole other world below the water.

Our beautiful magical sea. Come, swim with me.

Did he mean it literally? She peered over the edge of the cliffs to see if there was a way to get down to the beach.

Silas chuckled. "No, *a mhuirnin*, we'll not swim in the ocean tonight, though I'd like that very much. I was referrin' to this journey we take together."

She remained quiet, not sure what to say to him now that they were actually together, away from the intense scrutiny.

"You shouldn't be here. How did you get past Sigel?"

She explained her subterfuge. He glanced down at her leg. "It's okay. Nothing happened to my leg."

He turned toward her and caressed the side of her face. She leaned in and closed her eyes. "Ah, darlin' you take such risks for me. I wish you wouldn't, but I can't help but be proud that you have."

Unbidden tears sprang up.

"Why do you weep?" he asked, pulling her against his chest.

His heart beat steadily against her ear. She whispered, "This – you – it's all I ever wanted and I don't know whether to be happy or sad."

His arms tightened around her.

"Sigel told me today he would take me back to Baigsith, back to the tree, if I didn't want to go through with this."

Silas pulled away and searched her face. "What did you answer?"

"I didn't. I don't know what to say. I don't want to be a queen, guarded and hovered over until I go out of my mind. I don't want to marry a man I can never love. If I can't have you, I would rather go back home and live my old, boring life in a place where I can at least have a hot shower."

"Would you really? Are you willin' to give up on Uisneach?"

She shrugged. They stood quietly, searching for answers in each other's eyes.

"Maker help me, but in this moment, it would be worth dying for," he said.

"What would be?"

"Kissing you."

Her lips fell apart in surprise. He claimed them. The instant their lips touched she went weak, drowning in their own personal enchanted ocean. His body became her life preserver as wave after wave of pleasure and joy washed over her. Weakness turned to strength and she swam with him, drinking in the taste of his love, smelling the salt of the sea upon his skin, thrilling to the music his own passion made against her ear as his mouth traveled from soft, eager lips to ear to arching neck and back to lips.

Diving and darting among the waves of desire and connection, they were the mermaids he sang about. Hands wound in each other's hair, then searched the treasures of each other's bodies. Breathing became impossible, so they stopped breathing until the need for air made them rise and take it in great gulps.

"I want you, *a mhuirnin*." *I can't live without you.*

"I need you," whispered Briana, trembling against him. *Please, Silas, love me.*

"I do love you, Briana. I've always loved you and will continue to love you regardless of who you marry or where we live. Our love is not dependent on circumstances. It exists in a place beyond that. I don't want you to leave. Even if it means seein' you wife to another man, I want you to be here. Not just for the sake of Uisneach, but for our own sake. I want to watch you govern a kingdom, have babies and grow old."

He studied her face as though memorizing each curve and line. "I'll remember this moment as long as I live: your hair blown about by ocean breezes and," he swept his thumb across her kiss-swollen lips, "the way you look when you've been loved." After a few moments, he guided her head to his chest, holding her firmly against his body. "I do love you, Briana and that love means I will protect you, even from me love. You must make your decision knowin' that this moment was a gift, never to be shared again. If you choose to stay, it will not be to find times and places for forbidden kisses and lovemakin' that will destroy you as a queen and get you killed."

Never kiss him again? Would she spend the rest of her life missing his kiss, his touch and dreaming dreams that could never come true? *Will I regret this for the rest of my life?*

Briana reconsidered. Silas was right. It was a gift, beyond anything she could've imagined. A pearl. She set it in her heart, where it would remain forever protected.

"I don't know why Maker brought us together under such impossible circumstances," Silas said, "or why we were given this magic to communicate silently, but I do believe there is a reason. We must trust, *a mhuirnin*, and follow our destiny to the end."

CHAPTER TWENTY-ONE

TO BE OR NOT TO BE

Cailleach finished bandaging Briana's leg. "Now you're ready to go down to breakfast."

Wending their way slowly downstairs, Briana had the time to really take in the glamour of the mansion. Everything sparkled, the polished black-and-white tiled floors, the crystal crow statues and magnificent chandeliers, even the glass dishes of blood-red stones and glass twigs on tables and in corners. Briana thought they looked like magical nests.

Cailleach pushed open the double doors and motioned the younger woman in, then quietly shut the doors behind them. *Odd*, Briana thought, but didn't question it. The scent of Earl Grey tea and freshly baked bread made her stomach growl. Sigel stood at the sideboard pouring tea into a cup. He greeted her with a warm smile.

"Good morning, Briana. Ready for some breakfast?" He set his cup down and reached for another to pour her a cup.

She couldn't help but smile at his cheerful welcome. Then she saw Silas standing near the window, a cup of tea in his hand. Her heart melted at the sight of her golden cat bathed in the rays of the morning sun. Their eyes met across the room and she smiled tenderly.

"Good morning, milady."

"Good morning, Silas."

Last night's kiss added a layer of unmistakable intimacy to the greeting. Sigel's head whipped up sharply, his eyes narrowing.

"Oh Maker!" he growled. "What have you done?"

"Nothing," they answered in unison.

"Something happened. I want the truth."

"Sigel, it's kind of personal between..." Silas started to say, but Sigel cut him off.

"Nothing is personal between you and her!" he roared, slamming his fist down on the table, knocking over his cup. Briana jumped, startled by his anger. Silas remained unruffled, staring back at Sigel coolly. "She's the bloody Queen of Uisneach!" said Sigel. "Do you think I'm blind? That I haven't seen you," he said pointing at Briana, "mooning after him with doe eyes! And you," he said, turning back to Silas, "looking at her like you've forgotten where your loyalties lie!"

Silas straightened, his eyes turning to blue glints of steel. "I've forgotten nothing. My loyalties lie with my king *and* my queen."

"Sigel," Briana said, adopting an authoritative tone, which by the look on his face, didn't impress the lord marshall in the slightest. Ramrod straight, she met his glare. "Sigel, I am not married yet and though I am aware *potential* queens are not allowed to have... a physical relationship with anyone but the king they *may* be betrothed to, there is nothing in the law that says kissing is illegal."

"You kissed her?" he thundered at Silas. "You realize you could hang for this?"

Silas held his gaze. "I do."

"What the hell were you thinking?"

"I think it would be pretty obvious, sir," he said. "I love her. I know," he said, when Sigel opened his mouth to protest, "I have no right to love her, but me heart doesn't quite understand that."

"I fail to see how risking each other's lives is an expression of love," Cailleach said.

Silas shrugged. "Passion got the better of me. It was completely me fault and it won't happen again."

"No, it won't," Briana echoed. "We decided that last night. In fact..."

Sigel held a hand up to stop her. "Not another word."

"Sigel, be reasonable. It's not like I cheated on my husband."

Silence cast a deathly hallows over the room Sigel stared at the overturned cup, seemingly unaware that the tea was flowing over the table edge to the floor. When Sigel looked up, Briana was surprised at how devastated he looked. "Is that how seriously you take this? Let me enlighten you. The law does not outline which acts of 'passion' are allowed or disallowed. However, it is the intention of the law that no one, other than the king, has physical contact with the queen. Married or not, 'just kissing' the bard could get you both killed."

"Well, then you have a bigger problem, because where I come from, even sex is legal, and I have kissed many men!"

Have you now?

Well, not that many.

She could see this argument stumped Sigel, so she pressed her advantage. "And furthermore, you will not kill Silas."

Briana, be careful.

"No? Why won't I?"

"Because if you do, I *will* go right back through the tree to a place where they are less barbaric. That would mean your king stays in suspended animation and the kingdom dies."

"Briana, you would not do that," Cailleach said.

Briana didn't take her eyes off Sigel, but inclined her head toward Silas. "Yes, I would."

When no response was forthcoming, she continued. "At the moment, there are only the four of us who know this happened. I suggest we keep it that way and let life go on as before. We've promised it won't happen again."

Waiting for Sigel's response was agonizing. The space was filled only with their collective breathing and Dara's scratching at an itch.

Finally, Sigel turned to Silas. "Pack your things and head to Ratskillen. Mobilize the men there and head for Poet's Gap. We'll meet you at Long Bay in two weeks."

"That's not fair and not necessary!" Briana objected, her whole body rigid.

"It's fair, milady," Silas said, softly. "And for the best. Providence may be showin' her face."

"He's the bard, Sigel. We need him to tell our story."

"Now there's something you should have thought of before last night."
Sigel snorted. "We'll tell him all about it when we meet him at the castle."

"Don't you understand anything about love?"

Oh, my Maker, Briana, you have no idea what you've just done.

Sigel staggered back with a ragged breath. Momentary sorrow clouded
his eyes. "Aye, lass, I do. But I also understand duty and responsibility."

"Who will you take to help protect her?" Silas asked. "You don't plan
to be her only guard?"

"Probably Sir Thomas."

No one seemed to know what to do next until Cailleach put her hand
to Briana's elbow. "Let's go back upstairs."

Briana looked at Silas, who smiled encouragingly.

I'll miss you, but I'll be fine.

I'm so sorry, Silas. This is all my fault. If I had just stayed...

*No regrets, mo chroi. I will gladly pay the price for last night and I would
do it again — well, no, I won't do it again. I promise. I failed to protect you,
but I won't fail you again.*

A not-so-discreet cough interrupted their communication. Silas took
a sip from his tea and headed for the door. Cailleach led Briana out behind
him as Sir Thomas appeared, dressed spotlessly in black.

"Good morning, milady. Cailleach."

The women acknowledged the greeting but continued on their way.

Mild discomfort in her leg necessitated a slow pace through the halls
and up the stairs to her room. Valets and maids hopped around with brisk
efficiency, all with black hair, black eyes and black uniforms. Everyone
greeted her with a bobbing curtsy and inquired if there was anything they
could do for her. Cailleach instructed them to tend to the spilled tea in the
dining room and bring up a breakfast tray.

As soon as they entered Briana's room, Cailleach told Claire to leave.

Briana walked to the balcony, still trying to calm the fury inside her.
How ridiculous this all was. Over a bloody kiss. A splendid orange and
black butterfly flew to the railing, interrupting her angry thoughts. "Look
Cailleach, a monarch butterfly."

"Unusual to see them here. Ironic, isn't it, that one would appear now."

"What do you mean?"

"You have a choice to make, Briana."

The seriousness of the witch's tone refocused Briana on the situation at hand. "You're mad at me, aren't you? I've disappointed you, yet again."

"I'm not mad that you kissed Silas. It was just a kiss…"

Not exactly, thought Briana, catching her breath at the memory.

"I am concerned about a queen who would put her own desires above the needs of her kingdom."

Though the words were spoken gently enough, Briana felt as though Cailleach had slapped her. Tears welled.

"You must decide what you're going to do and then commit to it. Any faltering, any indecision, could result in the death of people you care about. Don't think for a minute Sigel decided to send Silas away rather than kill him because of your threat. He's already given you the option of leaving. It was pure grace and love for both of you that made him weak. You dare not tempt him again."

"Weak? How was that weakness?"

"Under any other circumstance, he would order the man to be executed."

"Over a kiss? Ridiculous."

Cailleach shrugged. "I didn't make the rules. Sigel is responsible to the king before anything or anyone else."

Silence filled the space as Briana thought about what the witch said. "I understand, Cailleach, and I don't want to fail, but what you need to understand is that I've waited for Silas my whole life. He's lived in my dreams. My soul has talked with him. It's not so easy to dismiss the love of my life."

"And this kingdom has waited your whole life for you," she replied, lifting her eyebrows meaningfully. "There is something else you should know about Sigel.

"He was married once. Molly was a kind and beautiful woman who died in a tragic accident." Her eyes filled with grief. "She and Sigel had been in love their whole lives. Her death left a hole in in his heart I doubt anyone could fill. So, when you said what you did, I imagine it was a like a knife ripping through his heart all over again.

"You must learn to be more careful, Briana. You can heal or you can wound with your words. I know that you would never intentionally hurt someone like that."

Briana bit her lip and closed her eyes to prevent tears from flooding out of her. *Oh, Maker, is there nothing I can do right? Can Sigel ever forgive me for that thoughtless remark?* "I might as well leave Uisneach now," she said. "I'm making a mess of things."

"You've not done anything irreparable yet," Cailleach said. "But you do have to make a choice and then either go back, which I do not encourage, or work on becoming a true queen."

Feather-light, the butterfly fluttered around her and landed on her hand. Briana smiled at the small, perfect creature, amazed that it allowed her to stroke its satiny wings. She would've sworn she heard it speak to her. *We are kindred spirits. We are queens.*

"I will make this right, Cailleach, just as soon as I get over being angry at Sigel."

"Get over it quick, please. Wounds fester when left untended. We don't have time for indecisiveness. We need a strong queen who can do what needs to be done." She stood at the door, preparing to leave, but paused and looked at Briana with an unmistakable twinkle in her eye. "So, how was it? The kiss?"

Briana closed her eyes, and sighed. "It was beautiful and perfect," she said dreamily. "More wonderful than I could ever have imagined."

"A gift to be treasured always and never repeated."

Briana nodded.

A light knock ended the moment. Cailleach admitted Claire, who placed Briana's breakfast on the table. At a look from the witch, she turned and left.

"You have much to think about, Briana. Don't keep us waiting long for your decision," Cailleach said, as she closed the door behind her.

Briana picked up the cup on the tray and took a sip, but ignored the food. Two decisions to be made. *One, would she stay and accept the role of Queen of Uisneach? If she did,* what kind of queen would she be? The butterfly wafted by, leading her to the balcony. Silas was riding away on a chestnut stallion.

How do I live without you?

He turned and looked up at the balcony window. *You will never be without me. Remember what Nionon said. We share the same soul. I'm never away from you in spirit.* He offered up a wave and turned back to the road before him.

When he was out of sight, she curled up in the chair beside the fireplace. Now she understood the depth of the sacrifice asked of her. *I feel like such a failure. How do I honor the promise I made in the grove?* She leaned her head back, closed her eyes and cleared her mind of all thought except one. *Will I stay?*

Blue-gray stone surrounded her as she passed through two heavy wooden doors to a large hall. In front of her, flanked by colorful banners, sat two thrones. One was empty. On the seat of the other rested a monarch butterfly. She walked to the thrones, past two lines of people she knew and loved: Cailleach, Genevieve and Jack Wells, young Rippa, Sir Thomas and Lady Isabella and Sigel. At the end of the line on one side stood her mother, smiling and nodding. Across from her stood Silas, his eyes bright with love and pride. He nodded to urge her forward. The butterfly rose up and she took its place on the throne. Unfamiliar energy dwelled in the throne beside her, without form, but strong and trustworthy. An ermine mantle settled across her shoulders, then a hawthorn crown descended upon her head. Heavy at first, it became lighter as she grew accustomed to the weight of it.

The vision ended.

Bittersweet determination thickened her throat as she made her decision. The butterfly glided around her in apparent approval.

Her belly rumbled. She nibbled on the oat bread. *So, what kind of queen do I want to be?* She finger-danced with the butterfly while running through the merits of all the queens and female world leaders she could think of, the wild Irish Boudicca, the Queen Elizabeths, and first ladies of her own country, until she rested upon the one quality that defined the great ones. Sacrifice.

Am I willing to sacrifice my personal desires for Uisneach, or will I be the catalyst for its demise? If I choose to continue on this journey, I will have to fully accept that I can never be with Silas in the way I want to, to believe we were brought together and given this telepathy for some purpose other than to live a bucolic life with me as his wife, bearing his children.

Aye, that would be lovely, Silas said, *but it will have to wait for another time. Just be yourself, Briana, and the rest will fall into place. I'll do me part to help and not hinder your victory.*

When her thoughts finally settled upon one course of action, Briana leaned back in the chair with a deep, satisfied breath. The butterfly circled around her once more before floating out the balcony door to be carried away on the winds of fate.

CHAPTER TWENTY-TWO

FROM THE FRYING PAN INTO THE FIRE

"There are hundreds of acres here and three training rings," Sir Thomas told Briana as they walked toward the stables. "You're free to ride wherever you like, with guards, of course."

"Of course," she replied, with only the barest trace of sarcasm. It was her first time outside since coming to the mansion, and she was awed by the splendor of the home and its stables, and the amazing view of a seriously sheer cliff dropping down to the ocean. Briana turned around to gawk at the mansion again. Hundreds of crows perched on the roof, all along the ridge and dormers.

"Is there a purpose to all the crows along the roof?" she asked.

"Watchers. All are capable of shapeshifting in the event of a threat upon Winge Mansion, but for the most part, they simply alert us to any visitors."

"A self-contained army," she murmured.

"Quite right."

Entering the barn transported her to another time and place: horse, hay, leather and liniment evoked pleasant memories from her youth. Her eyes grew accustomed to the shadowy interior, revealing a spotlessly clean aisle that was easily wide enough for three horses abreast. Along both sides of the aisle were ten stalls, enough for twenty animals and, if the sounds emanating from the boxes were any indication, they were full. Except for one, presumably the chestnut Silas had taken. The nickers, whinnies and soft chatter were music to Briana's ears. The chatter, she discovered, was Epona talking to a horse she was working with.

"Epona?" Sir Thomas called out.

A delicate head with a long dark braid swung out of a stall. "Briana! You're here! Wonderful! One second, and I'll be right out."

Briana and Sir Thomas wandered down the aisle. He introduced the magnificent blue-blooded equines. One big black stallion had his head over the wooden door, making spirited, blowing noises at her. She moved toward him, and then paused, noticing a clear warning in his eyes.

"You, sir, are very handsome."

His ears twitched and he snorted. Dara stepped forward, a tiny growl forming in his throat. Briana pulled him back and stroked his head reassuringly.

"Meet Dorian Gray, my mount," said Sir Thomas. "Don't go too near until he knows you. He's a bit of a beast."

"Or so you'd like us to think," Briana crooned at Dorian Gray, keeping her distance.

The stable housed a red mare, a matched set of bays with four perfect black stockings, a smaller white horse, a black mare much smaller than Sir Thomas' stallion, and an assortment of other horses. At the last stall, Briana found the horse that called to her soul, a beautiful dappled gray mare with a black mane and a black tail flowing almost to the ground. She had the delicately dished head of an Arabian, but on a larger body, like an Andalusian. Strong and powerful, her body was clearly made for battle, but there was a contrasting gentleness in her manner that spoke to Briana. She slowly raised her hand toward the horse, who nuzzled her.

Breath like hay and apples tickled the skin on the back of Briana's hand, bringing a smile to her lips. The horse's dark eyes met Briana's and an instant kinship was established.

"Meet Banrion," Epona said, as she came up beside Briana. She pronounced the name "Ban-reen." Briana repeated it under her breath. "Isn't she gorgeous?" Briana could only nod, so taken with this lovely, strong creature. "Do you like her?"

"Oh, yes," Briana whispered. "She's beautiful."

"Good, because she's yours."

"What!"

"Sir Thomas told us to select a mount for you, and this is the one Silas chose for you," she said.

"Silas?"

"Is an excellent horseman and thought she would be the perfect mount for you," Sir Thomas interjected. "The Taranian stables will be a good home for her."

It was almost a full minute before Briana could respond. "You want me to keep her? I couldn't."

Epona turned to her. Placing one hand on each of her shoulders, she said, "Briana, you will be the Queen of Uisneach." Her tone was firm. "Gifting this horse to you is the least Sir Thomas can do for you." He turned away.

Embarrassed? Angry? Briana wondered if she'd ever get the hang of being a queen.

"You must graciously accept her," said Epona. "Besides, the two of you are obviously soul mates. Silas chose well for you." She gave Briana a conspiratorial wink.

Banrion pushed her muzzle gently up against Briana's cheek, sealing the deal with a horsey kiss. The women laughed. "Well, Banrion, I guess you and I are a team," Briana said, stroking her velvety nose and bonding with the animal.

"When Cailleach clears you for riding, Epona will take you out," Sir Thomas said, "but we best return to the house for lunch. Epona, will you be joining us?

The woman shook her head. "I've a mare foaling. I want to stay here."

After checking on the mother-to-be and determining that it might be a while, Sir Thomas urged Briana to come with him, promising that Epona would alert them when the mare foaled. Briana hugged the Mistress of the Hunt, and left with Sir Thomas.

Briana's stomach grumbled at the aroma of oyster stew and warm bread being laid on the dining table. "I guess I'm hungry," she said, smiling, as she took her seat.

Until Sigel walked in. Seeing him reminded her that for no good reason, Silas was gone.

There is a good reason, a mhuirnin. *Let it go. He did what he had to do. Hrmph…*

"Lady Briana." Sigel bowed formally.

"Lord Marshall."

She could not let it go. Neither could she express her anger. Instead, she turned her attention to Lady Isabella. "I want to thank you for Banrion. I can't say I'm comfortable accepting such a gift, but your husband insists I must."

"As do I. It is the least we can do for our future queen."

Briana forced herself to avoid looking at Sigel. "Thank you. Also, following up on our conversation from yesterday – is there more we need to discuss about staffing issues?"

Lady Isabella lips parted in a pleased smile. "Why don't you plan on spending tomorrow morning with me?"

Briana agreed. "Where's Cailleach?" she asked, suddenly noting the witch's absence.

"Out for a walk," Sigel answered, between mouthfuls of soup. "She said to tell you she'd come this afternoon to check your leg."

Briana nodded and turned to her meal. No further words were exchanged between the two of them, though Briana was careful to keep her expression and behavior neutral. The conversation was friendly and informative. Briana learned all she could about the day-to-day operations and atmosphere of Winge Mansion.

Cailleach met her in her room after lunch and wasted no time in assessing her leg.

"It's all but completely healed. I think you can start riding in a day or two, but I'm going to recommend to Sigel you remain here for another week."

Briana spent the afternoon lighting candles with magic, changing the flow of the breeze coming through the balcony doors and trying to make a goblet move. Claire gasped when it slid an inch. The energy it took to do these things exhausted Briana, so she decided to try a simple scrying in hopes she might find guidance about her recommitment to the prophecy.

Once centered and relaxed by some breathing, she gazed into the bowl of water. Letting go of any unrelated thoughts, she reached a place of receptivity and was not surprised when ripples skittered on the surface and rearranged themselves into an image of a golden castle. Details emerged: a tree beside the fortification, locked windows, a little person curled up by a fireplace, books and papers strewn about on the floor. A face flashed before her, a man with ice-blue eyes and long blonde hair. *Handsome. Cruel. Enemy.* Split-second thoughts dashed through her mind. The minutia of the room disappeared, replaced by a fast-flowing river and a boat. The image lasted only a couple of seconds before her mother's worried face appeared.

Use your power to save yourself, said her mother.

I'm okay.

Lastly, Silas's face emerged, strong and reassuring. *My great cat.*

The vision left Briana more confused than satisfied. "Claire, would you please hand me my pack out of the wardrobe?"

Briana found the map and unrolled it. A lone figure with bow and arrow made his way to Ratskillen. No other figures appeared to threaten his journey. *Well, that's good,* she thought. Shimmering gold drew her attention further north. Aurum Castle. A tight line of gray figures encircled the castle. *Coward,* she thought, wishing the prime minister could hear her. *You don't have the guts to meet us face-to-face.* Ard Darach remained under a blue haze. *The sooner we get there, the sooner this comes to an end, and the sooner I can get on with my life, whatever that means.*

She sat back in her chair, yawning. A rap at the door erased any idea of a nap. "Come in," she said, wearily. When Sigel walked through, she stiffened.

"I wish to speak with milady, Mistress Claire. Alone."

The girl looked at Briana, who nodded, then left, closing the door quietly behind her.

"Cailleach tells me you'll be ready to leave in a week."

"Yes."

"You'll be riding tomorrow?"

"I hope to, yes." She wished he would come to the point. Maintaining a pleasant expression and finding more than obligatory words was proving to be a challenge.

"Then we'll leave a week from today. My question to you is – are we going to Baigsith or Ard Darach?"

They stared at each other until Briana finally said with as much queenly dictum as she could muster, "We ride north."

"Good. You have a few things to do before we leave, which will keep you busy enough, I suspect."

"I do. I'll be working with Lady Isabella, hopefully riding with Epona and I know Cailleach wants to go into Derryfeeny for supplies. You may want to plan on accompanying us on the trip."

He nodded. "I'll speak with her about it."

An awkward silence hung between them. He turned to go.

"Is there anything I should know? Any word on Shamwa?"

He frowned as though confused by the question.

"I'd like to have a report each day about what's happening. If I'm going to be the queen, I would appreciate being treated like one. I want to be involved in the planning and decision making from now on."

"Ah, I see. Well, perhaps you're right, milady. You will have the privilege as you earn it."

She gritted her teeth, wanting to argue, but forced herself to stay calm. Resentment didn't provide an excuse not to correct a wrong on her part. "Sigel?"

"Yes, milady?"

"I'm sorry for what I said to you earlier, about not understanding love."

He nodded. "Apology accepted." He turned his back to her and left without another word.

Briana had plenty to keep her busy over the next couple of days. She spent the entire next day training to run a large household. She went through the tedious process of approving Mrs. Churchill's menus and making sure the head housekeeper had everything she needed. She approved staffing changes, answered questions about what to do with dingy linen, rotten meat, chimneys that needed cleaning and cracked wineglasses. By the end of the day, Briana was exhausted from plain boredom.

"Do you think you're ready to take on Ard Darach?" Lady Isabella asked her.

"In my sleep. However, I should tell you, the first thing I'll do as queen is hire someone to do it for me!"

"I should have guessed you might."

Evening brought relief from the tediousness as they enjoyed an elegant meal and interesting conversations. Sigel managed to include information that would serve as a report without having to directly address Briana. Silas' singing and storytelling was missed by all, she was sure, but no one mentioned it. Also unmentioned was the tension between Sigel and Briana, until Epona quietly voiced her opinion.

"I don't know why he did it," said Epona, "but it was a stupid move. He needs Silas to get you to the king. What was he ever thinking?"

That he needed to separate us, she thought. Briana said, "Sir Thomas is coming with us, I think." As much as she liked Epona, she wouldn't feed her curiosity about what prompted Silas' banishment.

"Well, Sir Thomas is capable, but he's not anywhere near the warrior Silas is. I hope he plans on taking a murder of crows with him."

Lady Isabella asked Briana a question, saving her from further discussion. The evening ended pleasantly.

When the last candle was blown out and Briana was tucked into her bed, she called out to Silas. *Where are you?*

I'm sittin' in a tavern in Ratskillen drinkin' ale and missin' you.

Is drinking ale what we pay you for? she teased.

I suppose it's better than what I'd rather be doin'.

They talked about the day's events. Briana shared her determination to find someone to carry out domestic duties at Ard Darach. He described Ratskillen to her in homey images.

Sounds cozy.

It is when there's not the threat of Gray Military breathin' down your neck. Now, go to sleep, a mhuirnin. *For sure they'll have you busy tomorrow.*

She was dozing off when she felt a light kiss on her cheek and smiled into the darkness.

The next morning, a knock at the door interrupted her as she was dressing. "Lord Sigel says for you to come to the training ring with your sword and shield," said Brigit, one of the housemaids. "He said to leave the hound behind," she added, eyeing Dara with some trepidation.

"That's odd," she told Claire after dismissing the maid and reaching for Nua. "We've barely spoken to each other these last couple of days and I haven't even been riding yet."

Claire handed her shield over.

"Will you keep an eye on Dara while I find out what this is about?"

"Of course, milady."

Briana left, Dara whining but obeying the order of his mistress to stay with Claire.

Sigel stood talking with Sir Thomas in the ring, which was nothing more than a fenceless circle of dirt. The lord of Winge Mansion nodded at Briana and stepped outside the circle.

"Sword practice?" Briana asked, tension spreading across her chest and shoulders.

"When we head north, you need to be prepared to fight and protect yourself. I can't risk you getting injured again. Epona is admirable with a sword, but every man – *and* woman – needs to be battle-ready."

"Epona? She's coming?"

"We can't leave Winge Mansion without any men. The grooms can manage the stables."

Without warning and with complete control, he brought his sword up toward her. Instinctively she deflected the assault and jumped into fighting mode. Legs apart for balance, she swung Nua at him, struggling for the same control he had.

"Don't worry about me, just fight. I doubt there's anything you can do to hurt me."

Really, she thought, anger rising up in her. *We'll see about that.* Dropping to one knee, and clenching Nua's hilt with both hands, she swiped sideways toward his knees. Grinning, he neatly stepped away as Nua sliced through air. Still on her knees, she gave a grunt when he pushed her to the ground with one foot. Uninjured but furious, she started to rise, but he jumped over her, his own broadsword pointed at her chest. She was breathing heavy when he took a step back away, letting her stand.

"Again," she said, through clenched teeth.

He shrugged and advanced, thrusting his blade in her direction. She parried. The clacking of swords filled the ring. She swung hard over his head. His steel met hers. She drew back, stepped aside and swung again. Nua met cold steel. She couldn't get at him. She moved back a few paces to give herself a chance to breathe and think. What was his weakness? She faced him, waiting. He looked at something to her right and her eyes travelled in the same direction, leaving her momentarily defenseless. When his blade came at her head, she ducked and lost her balance. He laughed and sauntered away.

"Have you learned nothing? You're fighting like an amateur. You're unbalanced, vulnerable and fighting blind."

Anger turned to rage. She jumped up and ran at him with blade lifted. A stranger took hold of her body and she meant to plunge Nua into his back. Before she could, he turned and blocked her attack.

Sweaty, gasping for breath and on the verge of tears, she continued to fight him.

"Don't you *dare* cry, Your Majesty," he taunted her.

"What the hell is goin' on?" asked Silas.

What is going on is that I am going to kill Sigel. Leave me alone. I need to concentrate.

Briana tried desperately to remember what Sigel had taught her about offensive tactics. Scanning her surroundings provided little she could use to her advantage, except for the sun that seemed intent on illuminating her failure. They traded strikes and she circled away, forcing Sigel to face the sun.

"Better," he said, as though he were teaching her the alphabet.

Her arms ached. Her heart was pounding. Trying to focus only made her more conscious of her mistakes. He seemed to sense her weakness and came at her, forcing her to match his thrusts and swipes. She experienced a brief moment of panic and then utter calm.

Step back and breathe. See clearly how and where to strike, she thought.

Everything disappeared except the warrior in front of her. Emotionless, she saw the challenge as a game of *ríocht* and knew what to do. Feigning defeat, she crouched to her knees, letting Nua fall to her side.

"Really, Briana? You're giving up?" Sigel asked, as he walked to her, letting his own blade drop.

Seizing the opportunity, she rose up with Nua in one clean, poetic movement and cut across his arm before putting the point in the hollow of his throat.

Chest heaving, she dropped Nua on the ground and stared at Sigel. Blood covered his forearm where she'd cut him. He swore. Surprise and something else registered in his eyes. She enjoyed a split second of victory before the horror of injuring him overwhelmed her. She wanted to apologize but had no air left in her lungs to do so.

I will not cry.

"Bring that fierceness to Lord Shamwa and the Gray Military," he said, "but leave the tears, and for Maker's sake, focus much earlier."

Fury, confusion and exhaustion created a storm inside her that demanded privacy. Sir Thomas picked up her sword and offered it to her. She took it and walked alone to the mansion, dismissing Claire and another servant who were arranging her clothes in preparation for dinner.

She sat alone, shaking and sick to her stomach. *Why did Sigel do that?* There was too much emotion and not enough instruction for it to be practice. *He wanted me to get angry. He wanted me to beat him, and I did. I beat the best swordsman in Uisneach. I wonder if he let me?*

I doubt it, said Silas. *Are you okay? What happened?*

I just technically beat Sigel in combat.

A heavy knock at the door prevented her from telling him more. Sigel stood there, a rag held against his arm.

"Would you mind tending to this for me?"

"Where's Cailleach?"

"I'm not asking Cailleach. I'm asking you."

She stood aside and swept an arm to indicate he should come in.

"Your leg okay?"

She nodded. In fact, it looked even more healed than this morning. Magic was working, and fast.

He sat in the chair while she rummaged in the basket of supplies for dressings. Setting ointments and bandages beside him, she pulled away the rag he held. The four-inch gash was ugly, but not deep. Sigel was inspecting it, also.

"It's not as bad as it looks," he said.

She bit her lip and set about cleaning the wound and applying ointment while simultaneously applying a liberal dose of healing magic. The bleeding stopped and the wound began to instantly improve. When the laceration was wrapped, she finally had to look at him.

"Why?"

"You needed it. Maybe I did, too."

Understanding dawned on her. "I'm so sorry, Sigel, for everything. I never meant to put you in a bad position and I never meant to hurt you."

"Well, you did, but I expect you'll not do so again. If you've learned anything from it, I'll count myself lucky to survive with a scar from the magical sword of Uisneach's queen."

CHAPTER TWENTY-THREE

MR. JONATHAN STARK

Briana and Cailleach walked through the oak-lined lane on their way to Derryfeeny. She did her best to ignore Sigel, Sir Thomas and the dozen guards that walked close behind. "It's like a portal to another world," said Briana, stopping a moment to turn around for the view of the mansion framed by the intertwining limbs. "You could almost imagine a procession of druids on their way to a fire ritual to sacrifice a virgin."

Cailleach hooted derisively. "Druids don't sacrifice women, girl. That's a myth."

Briana shrugged, glancing back at her entourage. The men were militaristic in their uniformity, dressed head to toe in black with gleaming black sabers at their sides, their dark eyes constantly scanning the environment for any threat. The efficient troupe of shapeshifters missed no details, but otherwise remained silent, a fact that mystified her. Crows were not known for being quiet.

She faced the road again. "I rode Banrion this morning."

"Your leg okay?"

"Perfect. I was careful to start, but it never hurt at all, and I checked afterward and didn't find a problem. You did a great job of healing that wound, Cailleach. I can never thank you enough."

"You're welcome. That was a nasty gash and I don't mind saying now, you're lucky to have survived."

"Well, luck might have played a part, but it was the excellent care you, Sigel and Silas provided that kept me from dying."

The sun warmed their faces as they walked. Briana didn't know how old Cailleach was, but she was amazed at how fit she seemed to be. She never seemed to tire, and Briana often had to pick up her own pace to keep up with the older woman. Dara frisked about chasing rodents in the woods, happy to be away from the castle. Twice, Briana had to call him back when he'd run a little too far.

Before long they reached Derryfeeny, a quaint little village where most of the supplies needed by Winge Mansion were purchased. Though the local butcher made weekly visits to the manor to take an order from Mrs. Churchill, they stopped in his shop to admire the marvelous assortment of meats and fish. The blacksmith, Mr. Murray, also a frequent visitor to the Winge stables, waved as they walked by. Today was the day for the weekly farmers market, and Derryfeeny bustled as people bargained for fruits and vegetables, as well as soaps, candles, honey and other everyday necessities. They were greeted, hailed and sometimes stared at (no wonder, given her guard), as they passed by the vendors on their way to the apothecary. Briana couldn't wait to meet the proprietor, Hapgood Broomesly-Wells, whom Cailleach often spoke of with great admiration and fondness. She instructed Dara to wait outside and he dutifully sat, catching the eye of several nearby children who came over to pat or speak to him. He loved the attention. Briana didn't feel the same way about the attention she received from her military escort.

"Can't you find something for them to do, other than stand around and look threatening?" she whispered to Sigel.

"Well, then there wouldn't be much point in having a security detail, would there? Besides they don't look threatening," he said, touching her shoulder lightly.

"They do to me," she said, smiling.

Knowing she wouldn't win the argument about security, she gave up and followed Cailleach into the humble apothecary.

Scents of lavender, sandalwood and sage wafted around them as they entered. Cailleach introduced Briana to the gnome, who, she'd been told, had moved from Wellsland to Derryfeeny as a young man to serve the medical needs of the people here. He was a portly gentleman, even by gnome standards, and gregarious. Briana liked him immediately and felt a tug at her heart, remembering the Wellses.

"Oh, Your Ladyship, it's an honor to meet you." He nodded a greeting to Sigel, who accompanied them into the shop and took a post near the window.

"The honor is mine, Mr. Wells. Cailleach has told me all about your extraordinary shop and I've been looking forward to visiting."

"Oh, please do call me Broomesly. Everyone does. What can I do for you today, Cailleach?"

The witch and the apothecary went over her list, pulling this and that out of bottles and jars. Briana complimented Broomesly on his excellent selections of product. When Cailleach had everything she needed, they bid the practitioner good day and left.

Outside the shop, Briana noticed a young man hovering near the corner of the building. She was struck first by his sea-green eyes and curly blonde hair, then by his deplorable condition. As soon as he caught her looking at him, he darted behind the corner. Frowning, she called to Dara and joined Cailleach, who stopped at a cloth vendor for material for dressings. While Sigel carried on a conversation with the vendor's husband, Briana strayed a little ways, the crow detail not far behind, and paused at a jeweler's table, eyeing his exquisite pieces of carved stone, metal and even bone. A bone pendant hanging from a leather cord captured her attention. It was actually one bone that had been carved into two connected hearts that couldn't be separated. "This is beautiful," she said, fingering the polished bone. "What is it?"

"It's called warrior bone. Legend says that it comes from the bones of men who've been killed by heroes on the field of battle. Murder to carve, but once done, it won't break on you. You like this one?"

"Very much. What are you asking for it?"

"For you, milady, a gift."

"Oh, no. I can pay you. I intend it for someone else as a gift." He stated a ridiculously low price, and she paid. He was wrapping it in a square piece of cloth when a flash of blonde caught her eye. The boy she saw earlier was skittering behind a food vendor. She hoped he managed to steal an apple, as she feared he wouldn't allow her to offer him food. She thanked the jewelry maker for the purchase and thought about following the lad when she heard Cailleach call her name. Briana quickly tucked the jewelry in her pocket.

The witch stood at the table of a woman who sold candles, looking intently at the crying infant in her arms. "Briana, what do you think about this girl?"

Along with the congested, barking cough, the baby's nose was practically closed shut with green mucous. She could barely breathe. Briana reacted intuitively, reaching for the baby, whom the woman gladly handed to her. She cradled the child in her arms, raising her head.

"What's her name?" Briana asked.

"Dauphne. She's born just this spring."

"What a pretty girl, Dauphne. Not feeling well?" Briana crooned to the child, not at all daunted by her cries. "She's croupy and terribly congested. Do you have some water and a something to wipe her nose?"

"I think so, milady," she answered, reaching under the table for a jug.

"Here, Briana," Cailleach said, handing her a clean cloth.

"Good girl, Dauphne, let's get this icky stuff out of you," Briana murmured, imagining the infant well as she wiped the crusty green gunk from her nose, allowing her to breathe a little easier. "Ma'am, this child ought to be taken home and put under steam." She explained how to make a steam tent to push moist air infused with cinnamon, cloves and thyme into the baby's lungs to clear up the infection. "Cailleach, do you happen to have any elderberry with you?"

"Well, doesn't everyone carry that around with them?" she said, offering a small vial of syrup to the mother.

"Give her a few drops three or four times a day," said Briana, "and in between, try and get some diluted tea with chamomile and honey into her. That will make her more comfortable. You should also try some warm compresses with pine needle oil on her chest."

"I have some of that," the mother said.

"The cough will be worse at night, so keep this up for a few days. She ought to be right in no time."

The woman nodded, her face bright with awe. "Of course, milady. Thank you."

"You're welcome, Mrs...."

"Jenks. Martha Jenks."

"Good day to you, Mrs. Jenks. I'll see you next week."

They left the market, Cailleach saying nothing until they were well away from the crowd. Finally, she stopped and turned to Briana. "You did a nice job with wee Daphne, Briana. You were using a combination of medicinals and magic."

Briana nodded. "I hope it works."

"It will. You are a healer in every sense of the word. It's your gift, your magic. I just watched you calm and comfort that mother and her child, beyond what the herbs and steam baths could do. Your presence is a powerful tool when you use it to the good."

Briana was speechless at this unexpected compliment from her mentor.

Before she could respond, the blonde boy darted from behind the vendor. Now she saw more than youthful curiosity in his oceanic eyes. "Sigel," she called, letting her tone indicate the potential threat. Dara, sensing her anxiety, moved closer to her.

Sigel was at her side in an instant, his eyes going dark and dangerous as he scanned the location for whatever had troubled her. She quickly explained her concern. A second later, she and Cailleach were surrounded and hustled out of the market.

When Sigel and Sir Thomas joined the group along the road, they reported that the boy could not be found. The local militia would continue the search as they headed back to the mansion.

"Maybe I overreacted, but there was something off about that kid," said Briana. "He seemed to be everywhere I was and the last time he looked like he meant to cause trouble."

"The crows are on high alert, as well as the rest of the staff. He won't penetrate Winge Mansion."

Dinner that evening went on as though nothing happened. Everyone dressed formally and shared brandies in the salon before sitting at the dining room to eat their way through oysters on the half shell, Beef

Stroganoff, molded salad, and pudding. She noticed Sigel declined the offer of a whiskey after dinner, odd, as he generally enjoyed the nightcap.

"Are you worried about the boy?" she asked him.

"No one in Derryfeeny recognized his description. If he's not local and he's interested in you, then he has to be working directly for Shamwa."

She could tell there was more he wanted to say. "What is it, Sigel? What else?"

"Probably nothing, but the groomsmen reported seeing some unusual tracks before dinner. They haven't found anyone yet to account for them. You'll be guarded well tonight, milady."

She nodded. "I'm not worried. I feel overprotected anyway. At least this time, it's with good reason. And Sigel, I appreciate being told this information."

"I debated whether or not to tell you, but the simple fact is, for all intents and purposes, you are the queen and you have not only the right to know, but the authority to determine what's done about any developments."

They shared a look that said the storm between them was over. Briana's shoulders relaxed and she yawned. "The day must be catching up with me. I think I'll go up to bed."

Sigel followed her up to guard her for the first half of the night.

Claire bustled about in her room arranging things for the morning. Briana would never get over the awkwardness of this ritual. Her night clothes were laid out on the bed. Claire waited, ready to help her change.

"Thanks, Claire. I can manage from here. I've been dressing and undressing myself since I was three. I would prefer to continue the practice, but I promise I won't hesitate to ask for your help with some of the more difficult gowns. Fair enough?" She smiled warmly, trying to reassure the young girl that she'd done nothing wrong. Claire smiled back, relaxing.

"I'm happy to help you with anything you like. So you don't need me anymore tonight?" The girl couldn't quite hide the yawn trying to escape her mouth.

"No, thank you. Go on to bed, Claire. I'll see you in the morning."

Once the girl was gone, Briana changed into the light cotton nightgown and pulled her map out, checking it again. Silas was in the mountains near Poet's Gap. There was no indication of anything unusual around

Winge Mansion. She set Nuada beside her bed, just in case. Briana crawled into bed, blew out the candle and slipped into a dozing sleep. She tossed and turned, had a strange montage of dreams that involved images of Lord Shamwa, her mother, Banrion and of course, Silas.

Silas. She awoke to a storm outside. Rain lashed at the window and occasional flashes of lightning momentarily bathed the room in eerie silvery light. Her body hummed with desire from chest to groin. She lay still, willing the throb away, but it would not be ignored. Her body was asking for Silas. She got up and walked around the room in the dark, but the ache grew more insistent. Sliding back into bed, curling on her side and matching her heartbeat to the rhythm of the rain, she called to him.

Are you awake?

I am now. Are you okay?

Yes, but…

Briana, are you all right?

I was only wondering what the limits to our telepathy are? Are we only allowed to be friends or can we be lovers?

Oh. That's an interestin' question. Since I've never had this experience before, I don't know, but if you're thinkin' what I think you are, there are two sides to that coin. On the one hand…

Silas, I wasn't looking for an essay.

You want to see what happens if we make love in our heads?

I've felt you touch me before, telepathically.

But we'd still be breaking the rules, he said.

I don't think the same rules apply if it's just in our minds. We can't get caught and no one gets hurt.

Perhaps not right away, but what about…

Silas, can you please stop talking and just touch me?

A few seconds passed before she felt arms reaching around her. A strong, warm hand curved to her breast, sending shock waves through to her sensitive core. Two soft moans, one from either side of the veil, echoed into the darkness. Light squeezing and stroking only increased the ache below. His hand slid to her belly, caressing, making small circles around her navel and lower. She groaned, on fire for him. She moved back against him, feeling his strength against her back.

So nice, he whispered into her ear.

Oh, Maker, Silas. That feels so…

Her door opened, and light from a candle spilled into the room.

No, she thought desperately, *please not now, please not now.*

"Briana, wake up! We need you downstairs," said Sigel.

She groaned, apologized to Silas, and rose from the bed.

She donned a robe on and grabbed Nua before following Sigel to confront whatever catastrophe had now occurred.

Sir Thomas joined them in the hallway. Sigel told them the grooms had found one of Shamwa's men lurking around the stables. They captured him and brought him to the house. Halfway down the staircase, Sigel stopped. Turning to Briana he said, "With the king incapacitated, you're in charge, Briana. You'll decide on his behalf what's to be done."

"I don't know the king. How would I know what he would do?"

"Briana, this is going to be your kingdom. Now would be a marvelous time to start thinking about how to run it. Come on then; let's go. And for Maker's sake, think like a queen."

Think like a queen. Right. Raising Nua, she took a deep breath. *Okay, my friend, protect us from those who would harm us this night.*

She strode down the stairs, with her robe askew. Her hair floated around her, and Nua flashed in her hands, like some wild Boudicca. Dara stood next to her, adding an extra measure of menace. Somewhere between the twenty-fifth stair and the library, she became the warrior-queen who killed men near fortress ruins. She was prepared to do whatever was necessary. Already in the room stood Cailleach, Lady Isabella, the stable grooms and the intruder.

Whatever she'd imagined, it was not the dirty young boy who stood defiantly in front of her, hands held securely behind him by one stable groom, while a second groom held an axe, presumably the boy's weapon. The boy from Derryfeeny! A wild cap of curly blonde hair framed sea-green eyes. He had barely enough facial hair to shave, couldn't be more than fourteen. His small frame was no match for the stable hands, never mind a real warrior. "He's only a child," she muttered to Sigel under her breath. *Her spirit tryst with Silas was interrupted for this?*

"A child wielding a battle-axe," he reminded her.

She took a breath and thought three things. First, she should not let his angelic appearance pull at her heartstrings. He was in a place he shouldn't be, with a weapon he shouldn't have. Second, it would be just like Shamwa to try and fake her out with a cute young boy. For all she knew, this might be Shamwa cloaked in a charm. Third, even if he was just a boy, what she did next would determine his fate. She could order him killed as a threat to the kingdom, or try and turn him around to their side. In either case, she needed to be strong and regal, and appear prepared to kill him.

He looked around at everyone but her, his eyes flashing murderously, lips clamped shut.

She walked closer to stand in front of him. "What's your name, boy?"

He said nothing.

"Are you able to speak?"

"He spoke plenty, out there by the horses, where we caught him," a groom said. "I think he knows every curse word from every village in Uisneach."

She took the boy's jaw firmly in her hands and lifted his head to face her. His green eyes were mesmerizing. With a slight shake of her head, she refocused. "I'll ask one more time. What... is... your... name?"

Still, he held out.

"So that's how you want to play, huh?" She took a step back, whipped Nua up and pointed it at his chest, its steel flashing in the candlelight. Several gasps issued around the room. "I've killed men with this sword and I will not hesitate to kill you, if you don't start being a little more cooperative."

For the first time, she detected fear in his eyes, which eliminated one possibility in her mind. He was not the evil prime minister in disguise. Shamwa would never show fear. Moving one step closer to him, she repeated in a more menacing tone, "What... is... your... name?"

He swallowed. "Jonathan Stark."

She narrowed her eyes. "A fine name for a small boy."

Eyes blazing, he thrust his jaw out. "I'm not a boy! I've passed my sixteenth birthday."

"Yeah, right, and I'm the Queen of England."

He looked at her, confused. The rest of the household was speechless. Sir Thomas was trying to hide a smile. She turned and winked at him. "Sir Thomas, bring me a chair, please."

She pulled it extremely close to the boy and sat down, laying Nua in her lap, her hand tight to the hilt, letting the Stark boy believe she would run it through his chest in an instant. She pulled his face up to hers and stared hard at him, forcing him to meet her eyes. Like magic, a change came over the boy and he became malleable. The defiant edge was replaced with awe. She began the interrogation again.

"What were you doing out by the stables?"

"I wanted to see if the Mouse was here?"

"Why?"

"Lord Shamwa gave me some money to spy on her. Are you the Mouse?" he asked, his tone now full of boyish curiosity.

"I am the Queen of Uisneach." *Or I guess I will be*, she thought. "Where did you get the axe and what did you intend to do with it?"

"It's my father's." He puffed up. "I was going to kill whoever I needed to, if they got in my way."

"Is that right? That doesn't seem to have worked out too well for you." His stomach growled. Her eyes narrowed again. "When was the last time you ate?"

"I'm not sure, a couple of days ago, I guess. So what?"

"Did you work for Shamwa before this job?"

"Why do you care?"

"Is he nice to you?"

He made a rude noise. "He isn't nice to anyone."

She sat back and let him stew as she purposefully stared at him, as though considering his fate. She turned to Sir Thomas. "The prudent thing would be to execute him."

"Quite right, Your Majesty. That would, indeed, be the sensible thing. Would you like to do it yourself, or shall I order Ivan do it?" He directed his look at Sigel.

Sigel growled menacingly.

Oh, sir, well played, she thought. Sigel did, in fact, present a terrifying figure.

Briana fingered Nua, letting the blade slice a thin line of red along her finger. The boy flinched, as intended. She sucked the blood from her finger. "What do you think, Mr. Stark, should I do it, or let the monster, Ivan? He loves killing things, but he does it more slowly than I would."

"Would you be willing to negotiate?"

It dawned on her that this young man's language and demeanor were reasonably cultured, indicating a good education. "Who are your parents?"

"None of your business."

He's protecting them. She wondered what his big secret was. "What could you possibly offer us?" Her look spoke volumes about his chances of survival.

"I'll tell you what you want to know about Lord Shamwa."

She exchanged a surprised glance with Sir Thomas. "That might be worth something. Perhaps I won't let Ivan kill you, then."

"Could I work for you?"

"You would turn traitor to Shamwa? What kind of loyalty is that? How would I ever trust you?"

"No one works for Lord Shamwa out of loyalty. If you are the queen, then that means you are the Mouse, and that means you might be able to save King Brath and do something about what's going on in Uisneach."

She leaned back in her chair, impressed with this boy-man. Apparently thinking his chances had improved, he relaxed and now stared at her with the appraising eye of a pubescent boy. She glanced down and noticed the slightest hint of chest peeking above her ribboned nightgown. *It doesn't take much at that age*, she thought. Or maybe this nightgown, which she considered frumpy, was racy by his standards.

Briana rose and walked over to stand next to Sir Thomas. "I'll give it some thought. Put the boy in a locked room under guard."

Color flushed Jonathan's cheeks as he his gaze swept boldly up and down Briana's body before meeting her eyes. "I'm willing to make the deal, but I am not a boy, and I wish you'd quit calling me one."

Ignoring the comment, she nodded to Sir Thomas, who nodded to his groomsmen. They hustled the boy out of the room.

When they were alone, Sir Thomas bowed to her. "Blimey, I wouldn't have missed that performance for the world! Briana, you never cease to amaze me. King Brath himself couldn't have handled it any better. Perhaps you'll make a good queen, yet."

Cailleach clucked her tongue at Sir Thomas. "She already is a fine queen." She gave Briana a look that sent a shiver all the way down Briana's spine.

A bit unnerved by Cailleach's proud reaction and uncertain if she could live up to the admiration she secretly wanted, Briana turned aside for a moment. "Well now, if your queen is just able to plan meals and make sure the chamber pots are emptied, all will be well in Uisneach."

"And direct the lady's maids," said Lady Isabella, with a twinkle in her eyes. "Don't forget all the maids."

"How could I," she responded, grinning. She was becoming fond of Lady Isabella. "Thank you all. Shall we dress for Round Two? Do you have anything that looks formidable, my lord?"

"Indeed I do."

Briana smiled. "Excellent. Lady Isabella, could you impose on Mrs. Churchill to whip up something for us to eat? This has been a long night." She glanced out the window. *Maker, it's already past dawn.* "We need food, and he needs to stew for a little while."

"Consider it done, Your Majesty."

Sir Thomas, Lady Isabella, and Cailleach left. Briana fell into a chair and held her hands over her face for a moment. *I did it. I really did it. I sounded pretty queenly, didn't I?* She grinned like a fool. *Don't get too cocky, Queen B*, she reminded herself. *This was just the warm up; the main event hasn't even begun.*

Sigel urged her back to her room for a short rest before breakfast. The rain had stopped, but the air was still heavy with energy and heat. Briana removed her robe and went to the balcony. She reflected on this young man who had so bravely, if foolishly, been stalking her. There was something special about him. *He's going to play an important role in Uisneach's story.*

She returned inside and lay down on her bed for a moment.

Everything all right?

She smiled. *Everything is fine. Long story… tell you later. The queen still has some work to do.*

Oh? She felt a soft brush against her cheek and an arm around her waist. Light stroking on her hip.

Mmmm... nice. Reaching a long leg lazily down, her foot caressed another foot on the other side of spirit.

Tell Her Majesty that her man awaits her pleasure. Don't work too hard, a mhuirnin.

Briana smiled. Then sighed. He wasn't her man, was he? The longer they pretended he could be, the worse it would hurt when they had to stop.

An hour later, when Jonathan Stark was brought into a windowless, cold, prison-like room, it was the warrior-queen he saw, dressed in leather pants, a belted linen tunic and knee-high boots, with Nua strapped to her side. The room was lined with crows who had shapeshifted to human form for the occasion and stood as silent sentries, their black sabers flashing in the candlelight. Sir Thomas was equally intimidating in his dark perfection, as was Sigel, dressed in battle gear, hair pulled back to expose the scar on his face. His sword hung at his side, but it was the boy's own battle-axe that he held crossed in front of his chest. Cailleach stood by to ferret out any potential charms or spells in the boy or his story.

The boy was shoved into a chair next to a table. His gaze travelled around the room. He swallowed hard.

"Mr. Stark." She straightened her own spine for the interrogation. It wasn't easy, when his angelic looks made her want to smile.

He glared at her. "You locked me up."

"Of course I did. You're a prisoner of King Brath."

"King Brath is a prisoner himself; how can I be his prisoner?"

"His state of incapacitation is no reflection on his authority as the ruler of Uisneach. I'm acting on his behalf."

Briana nodded to the woman who stood in the doorway. She entered the room silently, as instructed, and placed the boy's breakfast in front of him.

"Eat," Briana commanded.

The boy glanced suspiciously at the food, and then at each adult in the room. His stomach growled. He bit his lip.

No one said a word.

It didn't take long before Jonathan picked up a sausage with his fingers and popped it in his mouth. He chewed only once or twice before gulping it down. Three more followed, as did the eggs and bread, and in only a couple of minutes, the plate was empty. Briana frowned, wondering how long it had been since his last meal.

"Still willing to deal with us?" asked Briana.

He nodded.

"Then I need you to be honest with me about some things. Like why you agreed to help Shamwa in the first place."

The combination of the show of force and compassion worked its magic. Everything came pouring out. His parents were wealthy merchants in Cedarmara, but, times had been tough, and business poor. His mother was ill and his father unable to work and feed them. Desperate, he sought out Lord Shamwa for work. The nefarious monster paid the child a fair amount of money to travel to Tynan Ibor and find the woman traveling with two men.

"He didn't call you Mouse, or milady, just 'the woman,' but I knew who he was talking about. Everyone is talking about you. Anyway, I found you at Moiria and started following you. Only I got lost after that big fight at Cath Ardghal. You sure got sliced up there. I thought you would surely die."

She made a rude noise under her breath. "Well, if you were there, then you know I have killed men." He shrugged. "And as you can see, the injury hasn't slowed me down any."

He nodded again, respect evident in his eyes. "So, why didn't you report my whereabouts to Shamwa? Why are you still hanging around?"

He blushed and looked down at his feet. "I was trying to work out what to do. If I told Lord Shamwa where you were, he'd come after you and maybe hurt you." He paused. "I didn't think I wanted him to do that."

"Where is Shamwa?"

"He's at his castle. He never leaves the castle. People go to him and he sends his military and spies out to do the work."

Sir Thomas nodded. The boy was speaking true. Shamwa hadn't actually been seen outside of Aurum Castle since the curse was placed on Ard Darach.

"But I can show you the way into his castle."

Briana's heart skipped a beat. She glanced at Sigel, who was staring at the boy with an odd expression on his face. She turned back to Jonathan. "That would be helpful, yes."

He took a deep breath, met her eyes, and for a split-second she recognized the man he would become. Her stomach pitched. He had a destiny in Uisneach, she was sure of it, and Maker help the woman who would fall in love with him and those killer eyes.

"Your Majesty." He spoke with passion. "I decided the minute I saw you kill that man who was going to kill your friend that I wanted to work for you, not Shamwa. I just didn't know how to go about it."

"You can start by telling the truth," Sigel said.

Briana shot him a surprised glance. So did the boy.

"I know well who your father is," Sigel said, "and it isn't a merchant in Cedarmara."

Briana looked hard at the lad, squeezing Nua's hilt. "Not a great way to solicit my trust in you, Mr. Stark," she said, disappointed in his deception.

He looked at the floor and said nothing for a few moments. Then he looked up and met Briana's stare. "My name is Jonathan Stark and I did come to you from Cedarmara, but not originally. The merchant and his wife that I told you about are not my real parents, but the people who took me in and raised me when my mother was murdered by Lord Shamwa and my father made a prisoner at Ard Darach."

He paused long enough for Briana to close her mouth, which had dropped open in shock at this revelation. "Please, continue."

He resumed his story with more confidence. "My father is Sir Jameson Stark, knighted for his superb horsemanship and victory in jousts, but also for his loyalty to King Barclay. When the senior king died, he stayed on to serve King Brath. My mother was from Cedarmara, said to be the most beautiful woman in Uisneach, with hair like corn silk and eyes as blue as the sky. Her family disowned her when she eloped to Ard Darach with my father, whom she met when he came to Cedarmara for a jousting tournament. I've been told they fell in love at first sight and nothing would keep them apart."

Briana's gut clenched, but she remained focused on the boy's tale.

"I was two years old when my mother took me to Ard Darach to be with my father. That was the night that Artanin and Shamwa poisoned King Brath. My father stayed at his side, to protect him."

Out of the corner of her eye, she caught Sigel's hands curl reflexively at his side, and watched him bite his lower lip.

"When mother tried to take me out to safety, Lord Shamwa grabbed her, ripped me from her arms and threw me over the wall, before doing whatever he did to her. I don't know the details, but she died. I should've died too, I'm told, but did not."

Squirming in his chair, the boy reached a hand to his eye, pretending to scratch an itch. Briana didn't miss the shiny wetness of traitorous tears. She turned away to allow him some dignity. After a few seconds, he continued.

"One of the merchants visiting the castle, Colm Connuckle, took me back to Cedarmara, intending to turn me over to my mother's parents. Sadly, they were also killed, in a separate incident with the Gray Military, so there was no one save Colm and his wife Deidre to raise me.

"They were kind to me, and I love them very much. My leaving had nothing to do with them. Mum – that's what I call Mrs. Connuckle – is sick, and they do need money, as Pa – that's what I call Mr. Connuckle – has not been able to make much of a living with his wine business since Lord Shamwa started torturing everyone. I did think the money he offered would help, but that isn't the real reason I decided to follow you and turn you over to him."

"It was to find your father," Sigel said.

"Right. Once I knew you were going to the castle and once I saw Lady – well, when I realized you could help me as easily as Shamwa, it seemed the better way to go."

"Why didn't you just tell me the truth?"

"I didn't think that would persuade you as much as me telling you I could find Shamwa."

"Is that true? Can you get into his castle?"

He nodded. "I was taken there by the druid. He was nice to me, Shamwa I mean, but I know it was because he wanted me to do this for him." Turning to Sigel he asked, "So, how did you know, Ivan?"

There was some confusion at the name until Briana remembered.

"Well, Mr. Stark, we also told a wee lie. This man's name is not Ivan. He is Lord Marshall Sigel."

The boy's mouth gaped. "Sir," he said, in a hushed, clearly awed tone. "I've heard so many stories about you."

Sigel grunted something unintelligible. "Your father and I are friends. Your eyes are unquestionably his. Must get your fairness from your mother, though."

"I don't remember either of my parents, but Mum and Pa told me all kinds of stories about them. Is it true my father was the best jouster in Uisneach?"

"He is, indeed," Sir Thomas said. "Sigel, do you remember the tournament at Moiria the year before the Great Wars began?"

"You mean the one where Sir Jameson almost killed Sir Cruahan? Cruahan's mount bolted, throwing him into the path of Jameson's lance. Only your father's lightning reflexes allowed him to pull the lance away in time. Great jouster and a good man with a horse!"

The boy smiled, pleased to hear such praise for his father. "We'll get him out too, right?"

Sigel nodded. "If he's in there, you will be reunited with him."

"Did you know my mother?"

"A rare beauty and a kind woman," said Sigel. "I remember you as a babe. Your parents loved you very much, lad."

A hush fell, allowing the young man to reflect on this information about his parents. After a time, Sigel broke the silence. "Now, in the future, you must promise to tell the truth. One of the most important things about being a member of the king's, or queen's, detail is that we need to trust each other. Understood?"

Queen's detail? She sensed a connection with this boy. Some special energy flowed between them. Jonathan had the heart and soul of a knight. The kingdom could use another brave defender. She could use such a shield.

"Mr. Stark," she finally said. "I think you're a good man," he smiled at her reference to his manhood, "who has gotten himself into a dangerous situation. My Maker, you could have been killed several times while you followed us. This is no mere childhood adventure, and Shamwa does want me dead. We are, at this very moment, gathering troops to defeat him. You are young," she put a hand up to stop his automatic protest, "but you seem to possess some brains and a good heart, and would be welcome to train for the king's army. What do you think?"

The boy looked dumbstruck. "I'd like that, Your Majesty."

She smiled. "I'm going to take you off house arrest, but the eyes of every person in this mansion will be on you every second. There is no way for you to leave without us knowing, and should you attempt it, you will be dealt with severely. Am I clear?"

"You don't trust me," he said, sounding disappointed.

"Not yet, I don't. You've got some proving to do." She avoided looking at Sigel.

He nodded solemnly.

"Well, then, Mr. Stark, when we get to Ard Darach, we'll see about getting you trained."

She turned to Sir Thomas, who'd said nothing during the interview, but whose expression communicated respect and approval. "Do you have anything to add, Sir Thomas?"

"Only that if this young man proves his fealty to us, then he should be a fine addition to King Brath's defense."

"Your Majesty, if he's to join your retinue, he must be bathed and properly clothed," said Cailleach. "Shall I see to that?"

"Yes. Thank you, Cailleach. I will trust you to do all that's necessary." *In case I forgot anything.*

The witch and the groomsmen escorted the boy out of the room. A moment later, Briana let out a deep breath.

"Well done, Lady Briana. King Brath could have done no better," said Sir Thomas.

She sighed deeply. "Would he have taken a risk on that boy, do you think?"

"He's Sir Jameson's son. Of course he would," Sigel said.

"What did you mean by him being on the 'queen's detail'?" she asked.

"You need someone specifically trained as your personal guard and escort."

"A squire?"

"Yes, but he'll serve you, rather than one of the knights. He's young, and smart. I can see a bond forming between the two of you. You want someone you can trust absolutely and I think he's your man – or boy, at the moment. He'll grow into the position, and quickly, I imagine." He put a hand at her back to lead her out of the interrogation room. "You did well with that, Briana. Sir Thomas is right. Brath couldn't have handled it any better."

She might have done a fair job of faking it as the queen in front of a boy, but this was serious business, and she needed to be totally focused on the job.

She also realized there was something she needed to do to prepare for the next part of their journey. Now that they all had such fine steeds, it would be idiotic to continue on foot. She needed to spend some time in the saddle to brush up on her skills and make sure she could keep up with the men. And she needed to talk to Silas.

"I'm going to the barn," she said.

While she brushed Banrion, Briana filled Epona in on everything that had occurred with the Stark boy.

"It sounds like you discharged your queenly duty quite well. The boy was lucky to have run into you. Lord Shamwa would undoubtedly have killed him once he got what he wanted from him."

"I must say, Epona, there's something about him. I'm glad he came here." Banrion kept pushing sideways into Briana and nuzzling her hard. Briana smiled. She and the mare also shared a connection. So many pieces falling into place.

"Let me saddle her for you."

"I'll do it," Briana said, heading for the tack room. In a matter of minutes, Banrion was saddled, bridled and ready. Briana put her left leg in the stirrup and slowly started to push herself up on her right, wanted to test the pressure on the newly healed wound. It felt fine. The mare was responsive to Briana's slightest command of voice or body and had a relaxing, easy gait, a rider's dream.

Epona stood at the fence, smiling as Briana came around at a lope. "Silas was right. She's perfect for you."

"I'd like to take her out on a trail." For sure they'd be going over some rough ground. She wanted reassurance that she wouldn't lose her seat.

"I'll join you."

"Might as well get used to riding together," Briana said, grinning.

"I know. Isn't it exciting?" Epona assumed a very serious look. "I promise, Your Majesty, that I will do my utmost to protect you from all evil villains and wayward bards."

Looking around and finding no one present to overhear the last part, Briana laughed. "You really do have to cut that out, Epona. You're going to get me in all kinds of trouble."

Epona saddled a black mare named Aquila, and the two of them rode along a trail around a pond where swans paddled regally by. From the top of a hill, Briana saw the nearby villages of Derryfeeny and Glengorrin.

"What a beautiful view. How long have you been here, Epona? How did you ever come by this work?"

"My father was the Master of the Hunt for a long time. He was an amazing horseman and he and Sir Thomas were best of friends. I loved horses; it was the first word I learned to say. My father loved having me with him in the stables, so I rode before I walked. I worked side by side with my father until the day he died, in a riding accident, if you can believe it. He took a jump over a low stone wall. The horse caught her hoof on the wall and fell on him. He hit his head on the wall. It killed him instantly. I was right behind him and witnessed it." Her eyes welled, recalling the day.

"I am so sorry, Epona." Having lost her own father under tragic circumstances, Briana knew there wasn't much else to be said.

"Well, Sir Thomas said there was no other person he would even consider to manage the Winge horses, and so I became the Mistress of the Hunt at the ripe age of sixteen."

"Have you ever wanted to do anything else, go anywhere else?"

Epona shook her head. "This is my life and I wouldn't change it for the world."

"What about a husband? Children? Have you ever wanted a family, ever been in love?"

A shadow crossed Epona's face for a fraction of a second. "I've not met the man who can compete with my horses. If I did, and if he accepted my life, I'd be happy to marry and have babies, but I'm not really looking. I'm happy the way things are. Now, if I met someone like your Silas…"

"He's not my Silas," she broke in. "You must put that idea out of your mind, Epona. It's dangerous."

"Just because you might not be able to marry him, doesn't mean he isn't yours. If ever two hearts were meant for each other, yours are. Besides, you never know what the future might bring, do you? Don't give up so easily, Briana."

Briana gazed upward through the leaves of an apple tree. "There's nothing to give up on," she said, realizing for the first time in her life, that she was losing her belief in fairy-tale endings. "Epona, could I have a few minutes alone, please?"

Her friend scanned the area around them and nodded. "I'll be over there. We'll head back when you're ready."

With the Mistress of the Hunt out of the immediate vicinity, Briana took some deep breaths and called Silas.

I'm here, he responded.

Where's here?

Along the banks of the Long River. Nothin' to report. All's quiet. How about you?

She updated him on the interrogation of Jonathan Stark, as well as the plan for his future.

Sir Jameson's boy. Well, I'll be damned. I do remember he had a wee laddie with his eyes. It sounds like he'll make a good squire for you, Briana. And what are you up to now?

Riding with Epona. I'm alone right now.

There was a pause. *Why do I get the feelin' this is serious?*

Because it is. I've been thinking about last night, this morning, whenever it was.

Aye, me, too.

Her stomach flipped and rolled in agonizing waves. *Silas, I think you were right. I'm worried that allowing ourselves to go down that path is a mistake.*

You regret our lovemaking last night?

I don't regret our loving each other. But we're leaving here in a couple of days. It won't be long before we're at Ard Darach, and then what? I love you and want you. I have to admit that I would find a way to get to you and make it more real. That hardly seems honorable or fair to any of us.

Lasting silence made her nervous.

Silas?

I'm here. I'm thinkin'.

I've hurt you.

Of course it hurts. Doesn't it hurt you?

It kills me. But it's the right thing, isn't it?

It is.

This is probably the most cliché thing ever said, but do you think that we can still talk to each other, but as friends?

Of course.

Frustration replaced nervousness.

Silas, this is feeling like a very one-sided conversation. Don't you have anything else to say?

I'm sorry, Briana. I just wasn't expectin' this and I want to respond properly. So this is what I think – of course we'll be friends. We share the same soul. We are friends, lovers, confidants and anything else soulmates can be. We can't be otherwise. And I love you. So, if not talkin' to me, or being intimate, helps you do what you need to do, then we shall say good night and not speak like this again. However, your role will be a lonely one, at least until you and Brath establish enough of a bond that he becomes your confidant. If you need a friend, I will be there for you. Always.

In the silence that followed, all Briana heard was the wind blowing through the leaves above and the sad beating of her heart. She was humbled by his unselfishness and his love.

It seems you've come to terms with your future and you have my full support, he said. *When you marry Brath, you will be his wife and my queen. I accept and honor that and will do nothin' to compromise you. But there is somethin' between us that no one else can share, and I won't deny it. I will do whatever you need me to do. I'd appreciate you keepin' me informed of anythin' important. Otherwise, maybe we should try not to keep each other awake at night.*

His words were exactly what he should say, and what she needed him to say, so why did she suddenly feel boxed into a corner she might want to get out of? Why did things have to feel both so right and so wrong? *Silas, why do you think we were brought together and given this magic?*

*As I said before, the night I kissed you on the cliffs, I believe that sharin'
the same soul means that we share the same destiny. That destiny is rescuin'
Brath and savin' Uisneach. We play different roles in the prophecy, but we're
on the same side.*

*I'm not sure we can control the telepathy. It may be somethin' our soul just
naturally does. But we have minds that can make choices, and as much as I
wish it otherwise, I think you're makin' the right choices for both of us. Now go
on and do more queenly things, a mhuirnin.*

And he was gone. She scrunched her eyes to fight the tears and took
a deep breath. Sitting taller on Banrion, she waved to Epona. "I'm ready.
Let's go home."

CHAPTER TWENTY-FOUR

DRUIDS

With Claire's help, Briana spent the next morning packing for their journey. While she would've happily left that afternoon, Sigel insisted on following Cailleach's recommendation about her recovery. They'd leave in two days.

From her room, Briana watched Jonathan working on his sword skills in the courtyard with Sigel. *He might have done some damage with the battle axe if he'd decided to use it*, she thought. No wonder Sigel warned them not to be too complacent about him.

A knock on her door interrupted her thoughts. "Pardon me, milady, but Cailleach would like you to meet her in the library," said the butler.

"Thank you, Ballynickle." She followed him downstairs. Entering the library, she found the Winges in a deep discussion about some household matter, which gave her an opportunity to wander around the room. Shelves of beautifully bound books lined two walls. She fingered one volume, The *Ancient History of Uisneach and Tales from a Magical Past*. The book's velvety green binding with ornate gold lettering was compelling, but she put it back on the shelf. *I'll read it one of these days*, she promised herself. Gilt-framed portraits of the Winge ancestors lined another wall. Wide doors in the fourth wall opened to a patio and a stunning English garden. She studied the portraits. Midnight-black hair was the familiar feature, but some kept it long, while others were stylishly cut. Ebony eyes were common, though several had emerald-green or icy-blue eyes, and one particularly mysterious-looking man had topaz eyes, slanted like a cat's.

She wandered across heavily embroidered and exotic-looking rugs to the fireplace, in which a hearty, crackling fire behind crow-shaped andirons warmed the room. Above the mantle, a detailed map of Uisneach (sans the magical activity of her smaller version) caught her eye. On this map, a castle stood in Winge Mansion's current location. *I hope I remember to ask Sir Thomas about this.* From floor to ceiling, the room held treasures and trinkets befitting the grace of the manor. *Pure unadulterated elegance*, she thought, tracing a design with her finger on the black marble table positioned at one end of the room.

Cailleach swept in with Sigel beside her and took a seat at the round marble table. Everyone else followed suit. Four of the five keepers of the medallions sat together. *Why did they all wear the necklaces?* What were they supposed to do with them? Cailleach posed those very questions to the team.

"There has to be a clue written in *The Book of Leaves*," Briana insisted.

Cailleach agreed. "So we must figure out what we hold in common. We are all part of saving King Brath and Uisneach. That's a given, but why the five of us? Silas…"

"Who's not here," Briana couldn't help muttering under her breath, earning a frown from Sigel, who sat next to her.

"Sir Thomas, Sigel and I are descendants of the Divine Practitioners, but you are not," said Cailleach. "Four of the kingdoms are represented at this table, excluding Evalon. Two women and three men? No idea what that indicates. Warrior, healer, witch, bard and shapeshifter… magic?"

"Except the warrior doesn't have anything to do with magic," Sigel pointed out. "It's a different kind of druidry."

Sir Thomas spoke up. "Warrior you are, Sigel, but the marshalls are not only military."

"The druids from Dromdara acted more like counselors or judges," Briana recalled from *The Book of Leaves*, "or, in other words, civilian law. Sigel, you must be from the Olama bloodline! Like Shamwa!"

"Maker forbid!" he said, horrified. "I'm nothing like Shamwa!"

"Of course you're not. The history doesn't say everyone in his line was evil. Perhaps you're the good druid who went missing after the battle."

"No, not the missing druid," Cailleach chimed in. "That one came from Evalon and might have gone through the tree to protect the bloodline. Catriona was the head of the Evalonians. Wait a minute! Catriona is similar to Katrina."

"Different spelling of the same," Briana confirmed.

"By Maker, I think you've discovered the link," Sir Thomas said, with a huge grin on his face.

Briana stared blankly at them. "What is it?"

Sigel patted her head. "Sometimes you can be a little slow, Briana. What Cailleach is suggesting is that you and I are both druids. I'm from the Dromdara line, and you're from the Evalon line."

"It makes perfect sense," Cailleach said. "The Evalonians were famous healers and gardeners. Catriona came from that line and married the faerie king, Kailen. Faeries are the only ones who can communicate with animals. I've seen you do that a few times, Briana. You must have some faerie blood in your heritage."

She was stunned. "No way! I'm not even from around here!"

Cailleach looked at her with new eyes. "Your mother was likely named in honor of Catriona. By your reckoning, you must be Catriona's great-granddaughter..." Cailleach frowned in concentration. "It's hard to be sure. Time in Uisneach and your world isn't perfectly aligned.

"I'd wager this is explained on the lost page of *The Book of Leaves*. For some reason, Catriona stayed in your world, and raised their children there. Perhaps the faeries wanted to protect their bloodline."

Sir Thomas said, "So that's the common denominator: we're all druids. Now, the question is, what do we do with the medallions?"

Quiet settled over the group for a time. Then Sigel said, "It explains something else, Briana."

"What's that?"

"Why it's so important for you to marry Brath and give him a child. It will reconnect the druidic line with that of the monarchy, like Olama did with Princess Amuira. You are the only druidess of childbearing age, the only one who can do that."

Briana, stunned, stared at Sigel for a long minute and then stood. "Excuse me, I need some air."

She hardly noticed the smell of new blooms or the bright colors on the petals along the walkway. She stood looking out over the ocean, trying to wrap her head around what they had discovered. She wished she could discuss it with her mother. A descendant of the druidess Catriona and the faerie king, Kailen? If this was true, Uisneach was truly her land. No wonder she felt such a powerful need to protect it.

Familiar energy settled next to her.

I thought we weren't going to talk to each other.

I know, but I can feel that somethin's happened. I can't just ignore you, milady. I promise not to touch you.

Fair enough. She brought him up to speed on the meeting.

So, you're a druidess. I'm not surprised.

Hmm... I have mixed feelings.

What are you thinkin'?

That I could take this medallion off and throw it in the sea.

Aye, you could, but you won't.

He was right, of course. She loved Uisneach, the people, her new family and most of all, she loved Silas. The end of Uisneach would be his ultimate end. She was torn.

At least now I understand why it has to be me. Before, I kept thinking if I saved King Brath, someone else could marry him and carry on the line.

He waited.

But I don't want it. I want my happily-ever-after with you.

You might change your mind when you meet him.

Never. Only you, Silas. Only you.

You have a rich heritage and an important role to play in the history of Uisneach. Be proud, Briana. As proud as I am of you.

Gulls screamed overhead.

I need to go back in. I'll let you know if anything else happens.

I'll be here.

She waited a moment, but felt nothing. *Damn,* she wished he had touched her. From the other side of the veil she heard a chuckle.

Don't think I didn't consider it.

The druids spent another hour ruminating over how the medallions might be used to remove the curse, but drew no conclusions. They agreed that all must be present and the answer would likely become obvious when the time came.

"I'm going to rest before dinner," Cailleach said, yawning.

Briana, needing solitude of her own, followed the witch upstairs.

She closed the door behind her. Claire spoke, startling her. "Milady, your dress is ready for this evening," she said, pointing to the garment laying over a chair.

"Fine, Claire, thank you. I'm going to rest for a little while, but would you come back in an hour and help me with my hair?"

"Of course, milady," she said, fluffing Briana's pillows. She set a woven blanket across the bed for her.

When she left, Briana did lay down, but was unable to fall asleep for the whirling of her mind. *Mother and I are druids. And part faerie. Go figure.* Shocking news, but it made sense, given their love of nature, her mother's gift of healing, her ability to travel through the tree, and their appreciation of anything remotely magical. How she longed to share this newly discovered heritage with her mother.

It seemed no time had passed when Claire returned to prepare her for the evening. The last wrinkle was smoothed from the emerald-green gown and last pin pushed into her hair, when there came a knock at her door. She opened the door to find Jonathan Stark, dressed nicely in a new suit, his hair combed neat. Again, she saw the man he would become. Sigel stood stalwart and silent behind him.

"Mr. Stark, what are you doing here?"

"I came to escort you to dinner," he replied, with a confidence verging on cockiness.

"I see. Well, thank you." She took his arm, trying to match the seriousness of his duty.

Smiles met them as they entered the salon and Jonathan was treated with the same respect due any member of the queen's entourage.

Conversation that night did not focus on the druidic connection, but upon horses, preparations for the continuing journey to Ard Darach and other more mundane topics.

Servants moved in and out effortlessly. She hoped the staff at Ard

Darach would be so efficient. Over sherry, Briana found an opportunity to ask her host about the castle where Winge Mansion now stood.

"That was Corvid Castle, which stood on these grounds until my great-great grandfather had it torn down to build the current home. He had a terrible case of phasmophobia and the old castle was utterly haunted."

"Phasmophobia?"

"Fear of ghosts."

"Ahh." She nodded and took a sip of her sherry.

Epona sailed in, late as usual, looking gorgeous in a black pantsuit and long tunic. She gave her daily report about the stables. The mare had foaled in the middle of the night; mother and babe were doing fine. No further evidence of intrusion noted around the grounds, confirming that Jonathan had no confederates.

The two young woman found time to chat near the end of the evening.

"Riding tomorrow?" Epona asked.

"Yes, I'd like to get one more ride in before we leave."

"I'll ride with you," Sigel said. "Jonathan will accompany us so we can see if he's half the horseman his old man is. Do you have a mount for him, Epona?"

"I have one in mind."

"Paying for the horses Winge Mansion has provided is going to break the royal coffers," Sigel said, wryly.

"Consider it our tithe to the kingdom," Sir Thomas said, lifting his glass to the lord marshall.

Chapter Twenty-five

Heritage

The next day, after conferring with Lady Isabella about a few last-minute concerns, Briana hurried to the riding ring, where Sigel and Epona were watching Jonathan put a small black gelding through his paces. There were two wooden fences in the middle of the ring, one low, one with three rails, for jumping.

"Do you have any concerns about him coming with us?" she asked Sigel. "He's so young. I worry he won't be able to keep up. He might be distracting. I also wonder if we're putting too much trust in him, too soon."

Sigel grinned. "You thought of all of that over breakfast?"

Actually, she'd tossed and turned all night worrying about it, but she wasn't about to admit that.

"He's Jameson Stark's boy. I'll bet my last coin he has the same level of integrity. I believe he just found the only way he could to reach his father. He can manage a weapon somewhat, and he's courageous. If he can sit a horse, he'll do well enough. I'll have to look out for him, but what's one more inexperienced warrior to deal with?"

She bristled until she saw the smile lurking in his eyes. Standing as tall as her stature would allow, she replied, "I'll have you know, I can hold my own with the best warrior and I have the scar to prove it!"

"That you do, and I deeply regret it."

They watched the boy for a few moments.

"Guess he can ride," she conceded.

"Got his father's genes, that's for sure," Sigel said.

"Milady, look at the horse Mistress Epona gave me! His name's Andromeda."

Her throat thickened at the excitement in Jonathan's voice. His eagerness was admirable, but she worried about his safety.

When Sigel was done with the lad, his attention switched to Briana. "Ready?"

"Yup!" She was already settled into her saddle with Nua sheathed in the leather baldric slung across her shoulder.

Sigel mounted Orion and pranced into the ring across from Briana. "Pay attention, lass."

"Yes, sir," she said, sitting taller in the saddle, eyes trained on her teacher.

He made several solo passes to demonstrate technique, waving, jabbing and slashing with his massive broadsword. Mrs. Tollemy would probably faint to see Sigel in full warrior mode. With the top of his dark hair pulled back in a topknot and the lower lengths hanging free, it made his scar more obvious, and also made him more formidable. *I'd hate to meet him in a back alley somewhere.* He, the horse and his weapon were a single, fearsome entity.

She let Banrion lead the charge, while she practiced swinging Nua to either side. The heavy blade took all her strength to manage, and she had to stay on the horse, as well. It was tricky. Without warning, Banrion jumped over the three-rail fence. It seemed to Briana that time unrolled in slow motion. Nua flew straight up in the air, sunlight glinting off her carved steel. Briana flew off Banrion, landing on her back under the rails, pinned. She looked up in time to see Nua falling, point down, toward her head. With eyes wide open, she willed the blade to change trajectory. A split second before impact, the sword swerved violently to the side and stabbed harmlessly into the ground beside her head. Silence. Briana breathed out at last, eased herself out from under the fence and stood shakily. Looking at the terrorized expressions on the faces of her teacher, friend and protégé, she smiled brightly and said, "Thank Maker for magic!"

Epona's usually joyful face was white as snow and her eyes dark saucers, filled with fear. She wrapped her arms around Briana. "For a second I... I saw my father, jumping over that wall. It took me right back to that day."

Briana hugged her tightly. "I am so sorry."

She declined Sigel's offer to end the lesson for the day, and mounted Banrion again. This time, it went smoothly. Two hours later, she held up a hand. "I'm sure I'm not going to be able to move my arms by tonight, so I guess we better call this done for today." She dismounted and handed the reins to Epona.

"Briana, I want to braid her mane and tail for when you leave. It'll make it easier for both of you, if she doesn't have hair flying in her face all the time and you have less to groom. I'll do it this afternoon."

"Thank you, Epona. You all right?"

"Yeah, I'm fine," she answered, in her usual vibrant voice.

Briana turned to find Sigel watching her thoughtfully.

"You're ready. We leave tomorrow morning at dawn," he announced.

Her last night at Winge Mansion was spent quietly. After a lovely dinner, some discussion about the details of their trip and a reading from *The The Ancient History of Uisneach*, everyone retired early.

Night faded quickly into day. Horses were saddled, loaded and ready to go. Dara paced, wagged his tail incessantly and occasionally tried to jump on Briana, Epona or Sigel.

The plan was to head for Ratskillen, spend the night and then head east past Art Aron. This would be the trickiest and most time-consuming section of the journey. The mountains provided a certain amount of cover, but were not without spots of treacherous climbing, especially on horseback. If they got around Art Aron, they could make it to Shannon Abbey the next night. The abbess would feed and shelter them. The third day would be a hard push to Ard Darach.

"Cailleach and I will rendezvous with you in a few days," Sir Thomas said, as he embraced her. "Be careful, Briana, don't take any chances, will you? You are the..."

"Future of Uisneach," she finished for him, patting his smooth cheek. "I know, Sir Thomas. I'm not worried; I have three of Uisneach's finest at my side. I'll be fine."

Lady Isabella kissed her cheek. "Our home is always open to you, and I certainly expect to get an invitation from the castle."

For my wedding. Briana chased the thought away. "Thank you again for everything, Your Ladyship. I hope I haven't driven you too crazy."

"Not at all, Briana. You have been a joy."

Briana hugged Claire one more time and said goodbye to the rest of the staff. Cailleach was last and smiled as Briana went meekly into her outstretched arms. As always, when she and Cailleach embraced, Briana allowed herself a moment to breathe in the comforting scent and aura of her mentor. She missed her mother, but she had Cailleach, and for that, she was grateful.

"Please check on Mrs. Jenks for me in a day or two. I wanted to do that before we left."

"I will. Hardly any reason to say goodbye, but I will tell you to be safe, Briana. And behave yourself."

"I couldn't do otherwise," she said, mounting Banrion. She leaned down to whisper to the witch, "There's no one to misbehave with."

Cailleach swatted her lightly, trying to hide a grin.

The sunny day was excellent for beginning an expedition. The horses whinnied and Dara barked. Following the road along the sea as far as it was safe to do so, they headed for Glengorrin, hoping to make Ratskillen by nightfall.

Not halfway there, the heavens opened. They decided to stop briefly in the village of Glengorrin to escape the downpour and rest the animals. The travelers also received a tankard of ale from the tavern owner, Broduer Pinkins. There was no new information on Shamwa's whereabouts, but Sigel advised them that the Grays might be roaming around, looking for Briana or the boy.

The publican nodded. "We've posted sentries 'round the clock. Some of our men are getting ready to head for Ard Darach as soon as we receive word from you, Lord Sigel."

"I'd rather you send small groups to different locations along the river over the next couple of days, in case we need your help," Sigel said. "We'll all try and stay hidden while making our way north. Lady Briana, can you check the map once before we leave, please?"

She opened the cloth and spread it on her lap. Seeing nothing, she shook her head. "Nothing. Not a stick figure anywhere."

"Mr. Pinkins, we'll meet your men in a few days," said Sigel. "Take care and stay alert. We don't want to lose anyone."

Then they were back on the road again, traveling much faster with the horses than they had on foot. They did their best to move quietly. On a lonely stretch of road somewhere between Glengorrin and Dun Lura, a sudden shiver snaked up Briana's spine and a voice whispered her name.

Briana. Come.

She halted Banrion and peered into the forest beside her. Mysterious energy flowed from the woods and surround her. "Sigel, hold up a moment, please. Did you hear that? Someone or something called my name."

Sigel paused, frowning, and placed his hand on his sword. "It could be a trap."

"I don't think so. It feels... benevolent... trustworthy. I think I'm meant to follow." *What am I thinking? Look what happened the last time I followed a sound into the woods.*

What happened, indeed? Magic and destiny happened, a kind, tinkling voice responded.

She didn't wait for Sigel, but turned Banrion between two pines. Sigel and Epona followed, their swords ready. Briana didn't touch Nua. Dara padded behind her.

Green light filtered through the forest like sun through stained glass. Banrion moved through the numinous grove and Briana drank in the serene beauty. Mushrooms sprouted in rows along dead trees and in chaotic masses on living trees, their pungent, earthy aroma filling her senses. Dewdrops hung precariously from fern fronds and shards of light glinted off the tiny cascades of a nearby brook. Yew trees spread out in a gnarly community of primordial grace. She expected any second for a faerie to appear amidst the tangled roots of the trees.

In the center of this arboreal enchantment, mantled in spectral light, stood a faerie tree, its purplish-black leaves bathed in pink mist, the little mauve and silver bells shiny with dew. The apparition took her breath away. Briana stood perfectly still, willing the emergence of a faerie, but no spritely face or body appeared. *Where are the faeries?* An odd energy floated between her and the tree, making her dizzy. She recognized an inexplicable sense of kinship with the entity. Dismounting, she stepped across cushioning moss to the base of the tree, growing more light-headed the closer she got. Her breathing slowed and deepened. Uilleann pipes issued a summons.

Pulsating waves radiated around the purple and silver leaves, drawing her in. She felt the slow drumming of a bodhran, the tree's beating heart.

"I have to go," she said, sitting beside the tree and laying a hand on its skin.

One minute she was outside the tree, and the next she was stepping through a door and into another world. Circles of pearlescent stone spiraled down a verdant hill into a world of extraordinary color and light.

"Oh, my Maker," she whispered, stepping off the last disc onto a mossy carpet in a whimsical forest, to the continued sounds of pipe and drum. Wobbling a little, Briana made her way through patches of four-leaf clovers and a wild array of mushrooms with bright caps to a green marble bench next to a sparkling pool of water over which hundreds of dazzling lights danced exuberantly. A profusion of colorful flowers with heady scents, ferns, bushes and trees vied for her attention. In the background, a full golden moon lit the sky, and music filled the air. Sensing another presence, she turned. Sitting beside her was... *Tinker Bell?* Well, not actually Tinker Bell, but an enchanting sprite in a short, form-fitting opalescent gown, whose body radiated light. She was pretty, with spiky, silver hair and round, cornflower-blue eyes.

Briana looked down to discover that she also glowed with a shimmering energy. Her clothes had been replaced by a long trailing gown of midnight-blue silk. She wore a necklace and earrings of peacock feathers, and a sterling crown etched with magical symbols. Her hair curled around her shoulders and down her back, decorated with tiny sparkles. Her toenails and fingernails were painted midnight blue.

"Who are you?" asked Briana.

"I am Teaguen." Briana started to introduce herself, but Teaguen held up a delicate hand to stop her. "I – we know who you are," she said, with a twinkle in her eye. "In fact, I know more about you than you do! We've been waiting for you.

"You are Briana, great-granddaughter of Catriona of Uisneach and King Kailen of Evalon. Welcome home to Evalon." The music stopped, the lights ceased their flight over the pond and Teaguen smiled, encouraging all the other faeries to show themselves.

Briana choked. "Evalon! How did I get here?"

"All faerie trees lead to Evalon."

All faerie trees lead to Evalon. She was stunned… then thrilled. She was… home. The word entered her mind as natural as breath. Evalon was her home and the land of her ancestors. Joy turned to anxiety.

"Where are my friends?"

Teaguen laughed, a sound like summer rain on a rooftop. "Right where you left them, and there they shall be when you return."

Assured of their safety, Briana whirled around, taking in the color, sounds and spirit of Evalon. Ethereal wasn't the right word to describe it, though it was ethereal. Otherworldly came close, but not quite. It was magical. The hovering glimmers were now landing all around her, assuming more solid, but shimmery form. Beautiful beings of various ages and appearances, all with a soft glow and joyful faces, congregated, eager to greet her. Flocks of silver-winged, snow-white birds with azure-blue eyes flew overhead, honking excitedly, dipping their wings in salute as they passed. Graceful black swans greeted her in English as they glided by on the pond. Red and black foxes with kits tumbled playfully, crazy-colored caterpillars crawled and butterflies with kaleidoscope wings fluttered by. A roly-poly porcupine with a bright red bow around his neck waddled by, and two cinnamon-colored bears jigged arm in arm on a gargantuan, moss-covered tree stump. Nothing in her previous life could have prepared her for this place of such extraordinary beauty. It made the *Wizard of Oz* seem flat.

"What am I doing here? Why was I called?"

"Evalon heard your wish to save the trees and we want to help. We are delighted to welcome you, High Lady Briana, Tuathla of Evalon."

"Thank you, but I can't stay. Since you're familiar with the prophecy, you're aware I need to go to the castle. And what's a Tuathla?"

"All in due time, dear one." Teaguen patted her arm with the affection of an old friend. "We'll not keep you long away from your objective. However, it's important for you to understand all the reasons for agreeing to your part in it. Uisneach cannot be saved without including Evalon, the source of all magic and beauty in the kingdom.

"It has been rumored for centuries that one of King Kailen's offspring might come back, but no one knew if it was myth or truth. But, here you are and we believe you are that descendant. The tuathla, a princess of our people."

Briana's jaw dropped. "I'm a faerie princess?"

"Yes. But do not worry, we have not spirited you away to live with us. You have a much bigger part to play in Evalon and Uisneach history. You are the one who will reunite us all."

"What do I need to do?"

"There will be much to do in the days ahead, but first things first, Your Majesty. We would like to properly greet you and give you the opportunity to meet those who will be helping you in your mission." She waved her hand around. Tables appeared, the pipers and drummers who had been playing all along stepped forward, along with a small pixie in a green suit, carrying a fern-shaped fiddle.

A celebration ensued. Briana was offered little goblets of a fruity wine, as well as a smorgasbord of fruit, nuts, sweetbreads with icing and some petite sandwiches made from faerie cheese and summer vegetables. Several of the glamorous beings drew her into the unfettered dancing of Evalon, twirling and dipping, spinning and clapping, letting their bodies move in rhythm with the music.

Begging a break from the stout gentleman who repeatedly took her arm, she wandered away from the merriment to catch her breath. Teaguen accompanied her to a pair of ornate gilded chairs beside a small circle of crystal water. Gazing into the watery mirror, Briana was startled at the woman who stared back.

"Who is she?"

"You're looking into a soul-reflecting pool. It shows you the essence of who you really are. Do you see?"

A most unroyal snort burst from Briana. "I no longer know who I am, so much has changed. I used to be a woman who loved nature and books. Period. Now, I find myself playing the part of healer, warrior and queen-in-training."

"Those are only roles you play, masks you wear. You must let go of the expectations of others, take off the masks and be who you are, regardless of what service you are called to perform. Look again."

The vision peering back was stripped of all labels, titles, duties and impersonations, leaving only the essential nature of herself: a masterful palette of personality and emotion, features strengthened by bravery, hardened by determination, made vulnerable by fear and softened by love.

"That is who you are, Briana," Teaguen said, softly. "If you're true to who you are, all else will fall into place. You will meet any challenge, master any role and conquer any fear using love as your guide. As in all things, milady, it must be balanced with virtues like responsibility, nobility and respect."

"Well, that complicates things."

"Humans are nothing if not complicated, but remember, you also carry our blood, which gives you the ability to go beyond the limits of human consciousness. You have magic, Briana that you are not even aware of yet. There are things you will discover about yourself and your abilities that will surprise you. Nothing is impossible, but everything must be weighed against the law of love and justice." She gave Briana a knowing look. "Also timing. Maker has a way of working out all things in the fullness of time."

Teaguen linked arms with her and led her farther away from the party to a quieter spot underneath a moon tree, named for the little silver discs dangling from its leaves, each revealing a silent, unique and beautiful face.

"So, now that you know about your heritage, we wonder, Lady Briana, how you plan on bringing the kingdoms together and saving the faerie trees?

"To be honest, I don't know. The first step is to defeat Lord Shamwa and Artanin. Stopping the destruction is our primary objective. I'm hoping you can help us figure out what else we can do to repair the damage."

Teaguen nodded. "They are evil men, to be sure, and must be stopped. You cannot replace the faerie lives lost, but at least no more will be taken. Perhaps we can restore magic to the kingdom."

"And restore the trust between Evalon and Uisneach," Briana added. "Wouldn't it be great to have faeries coming and going as they pleased?"

"It would, indeed," the sprite agreed. "I promise you, Evalon is ready to help in any way we can. We are so grateful that you've come and want to help us. We would like to respond by gifting you something in return."

"That's not necessary."

"Oh, but it is. You see, what we're giving you will help you restore the trees." She held out her hand to reveal seven purple, eggplant-shaped pods. "These are faerie tree seeds, imbued with our magic. When the time is right, you are to plant these seeds wherever you like, but we suggest in places across Uisneach. They are our only hope. Well, that and the Evalon Runes."

"Runes?"

"Enchanted runes were taken from Uisneach. They must be returned for magic to be fully restored. You'll learn more about that later. The focus now is on saving the king and stopping the destruction of the faerie trees. Protect those seeds, milady. They are the future of a united Uisneach."

Briana stared at the seeds with wonder. She held the hope of Uisneach in her hand. If only other things could be resolved so easily.

Teaguen smiled, her blue eyes warm with compassion, "Remember, it's all in Maker's timing. More important now is the focus on your heritage and purpose in restoring the kingdom. King Brath will help you with that."

A frown creased Briana's face.

"Try not to worry so much. All will be well. Time for you to go back now. Are you ready?"

"I think so, but one question. Is the Evalon in the other world this place?"

"Good question. The answer is no, it is not. The Evalon you refer to is only a human name attached to that parcel of land. This Evalon is the magical place beyond the physical realm. Faerieland, if you like."

"Will I be able to come back?"

Teaguen shrugged. "Perhaps. It is Maker who gives light and energy to his great web and opens the door for all possibility."

"Then I won't stop praying for an opening." She reached over and placed a kiss on the faerie's cheek.

Passing by the reflecting pool, Briana looked one more time. She saw not only the reflection of her truest self but a second image behind it. *Silas*, she thought reverently, as the face of her brave, loving and equally as vulnerable hero assimilated into the reflection.

"Ah, so he is a part of your own soul," Teaguen said, her eyes twinkling.

She heard Plato's words echo in the hallways of her mind, "...when one of them meets the other half, the actual half of himself... the pair are lost in an amazement of love and friendship and intimacy and one will not be out of the other's sight... not even for a moment." Now she understood why those words had burned a hole in her heart when she'd read them years ago. Bittersweet arms of longing wrapped around her in shades of mauve and gray. Their love remained no matter the circumstances. Smiling, Briana followed her friend back to the hill and the portal she'd come through.

Teaguen stopped at the foot of the pearly stairs. "Good bye for now, High Lady Briana. Maker be with you."

They embraced. "I could never imagine a place like this or someone like you. I wish we didn't have to say good bye."

"We are always in your heart. When you speak to us, we hear you."

"Good to know. Good bye, Teaguen, and thank you."

The faerie nodded. Briana tritzled up the steps and back through the door, leading to her other home.

She stirred and opened her eyes. Sigel and Epona were looking down at her. Jonathan was nearby, holding the horses. Dara stood at her head, a whining sentinel. She looked down at her body, at the plain trousers and tunic she wore, and made a disappointed noise. "Damn! I so wanted to keep the dress."

"What dress?" Epona asked.

She clasped the hand that was offered to help her stand. "I went to Evalon! I danced with faeries! I have faerie tree seeds to plant."

"You did what?" Epona asked, while Sigel watched her with peculiar intensity.

"All the faerie trees lead to Evalon! Hundreds of faeries live there, some big and others very small. I met one named Teaguen, who is pretty and wise and she told me… How long have I been out?"

"About a quarter of an hour," Sigel replied.

"Fifteen minutes? It seemed like hours. Did you know, Sigel, that I am already a Tuathla of Evalon, a faerie princess? It is my heritage and part of my responsibility is to unify Evalon with the rest of Uisneach."

His usual sternness vanished momentarily as he considered her words. "I don't doubt it. Unifying the kingdoms is Brath's goal, as well."

"Really? I'm glad to hear that." She meant the words, but knew they lacked enthusiasm.

"One day at a time, Briana. I may still call you that, I hope. Or must I now start calling you 'Your Ladyship'?"

She grimaced. "I'll never get used to being called by any title."

"Well then, Briana, we need to leave if we're to make Ratskillen by nightfall."

"I know, but can I please just have a few minutes to myself to process all this."

He surveyed the lengthening shadows in the forest. "Ten minutes, and then we need to move."

He and Epona moved far enough away to give her a sense of privacy, yet close enough to aid her if needed. She tucked the precious seeds into a hidden pouch in her trousers. The gnomes had thought of everything. No one would find them there. She sat on a mossy stump and Dara laid his head on her lap. Closing her eyes, she called Silas.

Middle of the day you're callin' me? I hope nothin's wrong.

I'm a faerie princess. I went to Evalon and met a faerie and she explained my ancestry and how I'm meant to help bring peace and cooperation between the faerie realm and Uisneach. She described the day's travels to him, the party and the gift of faerie tree seeds, ending with, *Can you believe it, Silas? You've kissed a princess.*

Well, princess or not, it was the best moment of me life, so far. You will make both Evalon and Uisneach proud, a mhuirnin. Where are you, anyway?

Oh, not too far from Ratskillen, but Sigel is on a tear to get there and this little side trip cost us time, so I best go. I'll tell you tonight how we make out in Ratskillen. Bye.

Quiet ruled for an hour until Briana decided she'd had enough of it. "I love being on the road."

Epona smiled, and Sigel made an undecipherable noise. Jonathan rode tall on Andromeda, never taking his eyes off Briana or the road and scenery around them, his hand glued to the small blade at his side. Briana studied him, wondering about his background and what it was that made him so determined to be her guard. As much as she hated thinking about her destined role as Queen of Uisneach, she supposed she was blessed with such dedicated people at her side. If these three were any indication of the quality of people who would defend Uisneach's interest, then Uisneach was in good hands. She only hoped its leader was of the same caliber.

"Are we getting close to Ratskillen?" The words had barely left her lips when three horses cantered around the bend of the road with unfamiliar men atop them. They pulled up in front of Sigel aggressively, weapons purposely visible. They were not Gray Military, but they could be brigands, so she and her companions put hand to hilt. Briana was immediately encircled by her protectors.

"State your business," one of the men, the larger of the two, demanded roughly.

Apparently, Sigel knew who they were. "I am Lord Marshall Sigel. We journey to Ard Darach. We're looking for a place to spend the night. Captain O'Rourke will be expecting us. You may stand down and welcome your future queen."

Their demeanor changed swiftly as they bowed respectfully to Briana.

"Why the armed greeting, friend?" Sigel asked.

"The Grays are about," the smaller man informed them. "There was a skirmish to the north yesterday. No one injured, but they got away and today, a troop of about ten men has been spotted along the river. We're putting together our own force now."

"Let us see milady settled and we'll come and meet you and your men," Sigel said.

They nodded but before turning to leave, the older, brawnier man urged his horse a step forward, toward Briana. Jonathan's sword flashed a warning and the man raised his hand peaceably.

"I appreciate your position, sir, but I only mean to express our greetings to milady and assure her, and you, that while you are in Ratskillen, we're at your service. You will be safe here."

Jonathan lowered his weapon and Briana responded. "We are grateful to you, sir."

Scores of people materialized from the houses and shops along the main lane through town, hoping to see the Mouse of Prophecy. Dara was, once again, a big attraction for the children, who petted and teased the big dog unmercifully. Ever the ambassador, he accepted the attention patiently, with an occasional sloppy lick or cheerful bark. Ratskillen was a much larger community than Derryfeeny or even Moiria, so it took a while to get from one end of the village to the other. Old men sat on benches in front of their shops smoking pipes, mothers shouted at errant children and vendors hawked their wares. Two young lovers hid behind a tavern sign wrapped in each other's arms, enjoying a passionate kiss. There was a tavern for every dozen buildings. Briana wondered why they'd been sent to the Seven Hearths Inn specifically. Sigel told her it was because that was the largest lodging in Ratskillen, the only one with rooms enough to put them up. Briana smiled, waved and spoke to the villagers, feeling like a bit of a rock star, until they reached the inn. Jonathan jumped off Andromeda and stood beside Briana, ready to assist her off Banrion. She graciously took his outstretched hand.

They were received by the oddest-looking woman she'd ever seen. Mrs. Thacker was not much taller than the gnomes, and twice as wide. Her hair, a wild mass of every possible color in the book, looked like she'd done a few jolts of electricity. Her eyes were different colors, one light blue, the other a mix of emerald and amber. Her nose, likely broken more than once, splayed out over her face. Surprisingly, she had the most beautiful mouth, full of shockingly white and perfect teeth. She appeared to roll, rather than walk, at an alarmingly fast rate, shouting orders as she bustled around the place. She stopped long enough to be introduced to Briana and the men, then ordered a tall, lithesome girl to show them their rooms.

Sigel allowed Briana only enough time to wash up. She quickly re-secured Nua to her baldric, tucked errant wisps of hair behind her ear and stood straight. *Time to act queenly*, she coached herself.

Captain O'Rourke and his local militia of about twenty men was gathered in the tap room, which was lit only by candles. It was a raucous group as the men, attended to by a handful of serving girls hustling about with ale and bread, were doing their best to out-joke, out-lie and out-laugh one another. Talk ceased the moment Briana walked into the room, and all eyes focused on her.

She curtsied and smiled, taking her place next to Sigel at the head of the table. Jonathan sat next to her. Dara tucked himself between the two. Epona sat next to Sigel.

"We should send scouts to keep an eye on Shamwa's army, instead of going after the prime minister directly," Captain O'Rourke said.

"Agreed," Sigel said. "Defend rather than go on the offensive. You hold them back and we'll sneak Lady Briana out under the cover of night."

"A contingent could go toward the Plains of Leanach to throw him off track."

Sigel nodded. "Excellent idea."

"When you're on your way, we'll send the rest of the companies to hold a line between yourselves and Long River."

"Lady Briana," said Mrs. Thacker in a husky voice, "please allow me to serve your supper. We have a delightful roast beef and roasted potatoes."

Watching the serving girls make their way around the tables with food for the other men, Briana smiled. "It smells delicious. Thank you, Mrs. Thacker."

Sigel and Jonathan were already swallowing their first mouthful when she bit into the succulent beef. Her unqueenly noise of appreciation elicited an agreeable chuckle around the table. Wasting no time, she tucked into the potatoes and fresh bread with gusto.

"I appreciate a queen with a healthy appetite," Captain O'Rourke said.

Briana paused in her chewing. *Maybe I'm supposed to eat like a bird.* Deciding it was a kind and not critical expression, she relaxed. She swallowed the bite, then said, "It would be foolish not to enjoy such a fine meal after a long day of travel."

Heavy, fruit-laden cake with cream completed the meal. "Well, if we don't eat for another couple of days, I think I'll be fine."

Mrs. Thacker grinned at the offhand compliment and started to pour more ale in her cup. Putting a hand up to stop her, Briana said, "No, please, Mrs. Thacker. There is no more room in my belly."

"Not to mention there won't be any time to sleep it off," Sigel said, drily. "Mind checking the map once more?"

She pulled it out and scanned for new activity. There was an obscure vibration due north, nothing specific. Briana frowned and showed it to Sigel. It had no shape, no usual markers of Shamwa or Gray Military, but it was troubling.

"I'll send some men to scout," Captain O'Rourke said, rising from his chair.

Sigel nodded. "Advise me of any concerns. Briana, let's get you upstairs for a few hours of sleep. Jonathan, you, too. I'll be right outside your door, Briana."

"I can have one of my men post watch, Lord Marshall, so you can rest, too."

"I'd prefer to stay awake until I'm certain all is well."

The groups dispersed and Briana was escorted to her room. Dara stretched out on the floor beside her and was snoring within seconds. Stripping off her pants, she lay on the bed in her tunic, blew out the single candle beside the bed, pulled a blanket over her and curled on her side. She imagined Silas' arms around her, holding her as she slept. Did she really feel a warm weight settle around her?

An abrupt knock jolted her awake. Sigel entered, holding a candle. "Briana, you need to get up and dress. We've got to leave now. There's a fairly large group of Shamwa's men just outside of town. We need to get going. Jonathan's getting the horses." He didn't bother to leave as she threw back the blanket and slid into her pants. He handed Nua and her shield to her.

"Ready," she said, trying to update Silas telepathically as Sigel was giving her the information.

Be careful, a mhuirnin, *and keep me posted.*

I will.

Lifting her pack, she followed Sigel out of the Seven Hearths and leaped atop Banrion, who stood waiting in the dark. A stiff wind had developed along with the earthy scent of impending rain. None of this bode well for their chances of getting to Long River without incident, but staring at Epona and Sigel's back and knowing Jonathan Stark would give his life to protect hers, she felt prepared and secure. At Sigel's command, they followed the road out of Ratskillen and into a dark forest.

CHAPTER TWENTY-SIX

AURUM CASTLE

Ominous rolls of thunder and a moon obscured by clouds threatened to complicate their journey, though Sigel knew the trail even in the dark.

"I wish we could see what's happening on the map," Sigel said.

"Hold up a minute," she said, unrolling the map. Shutting everything out of her mind but the blankness before her, she smiled when a firefly-like light began to glow around the map. Her smile faded when nothing close to clarity followed. Some kind of glamour vibrated over the map, confusing the images. She shook her head. "What is that?"

"No idea," Sigel replied, frustrated. "There's no choice but to move on. Stay alert. Anything could happen."

Jonathan instinctively moved closer to one side of her and Epona bumped knees with her on the other. She heard the sound of metal sliding out of leather.

Carefully tucking the map in its pouch, she followed Sigel into the dark unknown. Animals felt the coming storm and hunkered down. An eeriness stole over her. "Are you okay, Mr. Stark?"

"Fine, milady. Don't worry about me." A hint of nervousness belied his bravado.

Nua started bumping forcefully against her leg. *Odd,* she thought, glancing down at the sword. She released the strap to pull the sword out. Suddenly, she became woozy. She tried calling out to Sigel but the words wouldn't form. No matter, he slumped over Orion's neck. Dara dropped motionless beside her. Paralyzed, she couldn't even turn to check on Jonathan and Epona. Nua slipped out of her hand. *No*, she thought desperately. Her vision narrowed as though she were seeing everything through a spyglass.

Out of the darkening tunnel, a man appeared, dressed in a long brown robe with a cowl neck. A common, not-so-monstrous face peered out through the hood, and she knew this was the druid, Artanin. He moved with purpose toward her. Beside him, a small, rugged-looking man in a dirty tunic and woolen breeches fiddled with a rope.

Briana could only watch in fear and anger as the man picked her up and carried her off into the woods, where two horses waited. She was unceremoniously dumped over the saddle of the smaller man's horse. He swung up behind her. With a vicious kick to the horse's ribs, they raced off. Not one word was spoken; the sound of silence was overwhelming and otherworldly. Forcing her mind to focus, she did the only thing she could in her state of physical incapacitation.

Silas, help, she thought, as she succumbed to oblivion.

Gold. The room was bathed in shades of gold with splashes of red and black. Not elegant, like Winge Mansion. Garishly extravagant, very nouveau riche. A solid gold chandelier lit the room, still shadowed by early morning. The fireplace was surrounded by gilded stonework etched with black writing in an unfamiliar language. Empty gilt vases sat on shiny golden tables. An ornate desk and chair stared at her from across the room. The lounging chair she reclined on was gold and red silk. A heady, musky scent perfumed the room, sensual and dizzying in its excess. She rubbed at her temples, aching from what? The smell? The heat? Effects of the enchantment? Was she hit on the head? Not feeling any bumps or bleeding, she decided on a combination of those factors. Her throat was dry. She looked longingly at a golden goblet of red wine sitting just outside her reach.

"Ah. You're awake," a smoky voice said. "Welcome to Aurum Castle."

Lord Shamwa's castle. Briana tensed. Drawing on every ounce of queenliness she learned at Winge Mansion, she said, "I don't believe we've been properly introduced." *Lady Isabella would be proud.* "I'm Lady Briana."

"Hardly necessary to tell me," he responded wryly, "but since you insist, Lord Shamwa, Prime Minister of Uisneach." He accented the title as he bowed over her hand and kissed it.

The warmth and gentleness of his lips on her skin were confusing. *How could this guy be such a bastard?*

Whatever she imagined Lord Shamwa to look like, it was not this. Herculean arms crossed a broad chest covered in a red silk shirt and jacket, open at the neck. Honey-blonde hair hung in feathery layers to his shoulders. Crystal-blue eyes scrutinized her. Someone should have warned her that evil can lurk behind a facade of beauty, that it could be extraordinarily sexy. She needed a moment to adjust.

He sat in a chair near a balcony door. When her eyes traveled to the possible route of egress, he leaned over and jiggled the locked door handle. "Locked. Sorry, my lady," he said, his expression showing nothing akin to sympathy. She met his stare and was struck by the intelligence and intensity projecting from his face. However, behind the mask of desirability lurked a coldness; his smile lacked authenticity and failed totally to reach his eyes.

He stood and moved toward her with stallion-like grace. Of course he had long, strong legs. Picking up the goblet, he held it out to her.

"It's not poisoned," he assured her.

This was a man against whom a sword would be useless, not that she had one. She vaguely recalled Nua dropping to the ground. Intuition told her she needed to be as cool with him as he was with her. She must offer no threat, rather, the hint of understanding and collaboration. He would appreciate interest and respect. Having little of this for him made things challenging, but she would put on her own mask and play her part.

Briana smiled and accepted the cup.

Maker, protect me from danger in this wine, she prayed, and took a sip. It tasted divine and eased her parched throat. Shamwa sipped from another goblet.

"Lovely home," she said.

"Thank you. It's... comfortable."

He continued watching her but offered little in the way of engaging discussion.

"Well then," she said, refusing to be intimidated, "you've kidnapped me and I assume you hold some purpose in mind. Shall we get to the point?"

His lips parted in a restrained smile. "If you like. The *point*, milady, is that you have been misguided about, well about everything, and I intend to enlighten you. Perhaps when you know the truth, you will see another way of leading Uisneach forward."

"If it involves beating up women, burning down the homes of innocent people and practicing treason against your king, I assure you, my lord, you will have a hard sell."

"What can I say? Sometimes progress is messy."

"You call what you've done to this kingdom progress? I fail to understand your methods or your reasons, but by all means, do try to enlighten me."

He cocked his head and his smile widened. "You know, I think I like you. Direct, daring and a bit cocky. I honestly hope I don't have to kill you."

She made a rude noise.

Cerulean eyes flashed a warning. "Now, now, none of that." He continued after a moment, eyes calm again. "Are you hungry? I could have my servant," he looked toward a corner of the room, "prepare us a light meal."

She followed his gaze to a bundle in the corner near the fireplace, a gnomish creature wrapped in a shawl. Briana couldn't tell its gender or age, but she could see the fear in its eyes. Briana gave Shamwa a disgusted look. "I'm not hungry. What do you want from me?"

"I just want you to hear me out and decide for yourself what's best for Uisneach. I'm sure they've convinced you King Brath's way is the only way, but I offer another perspective."

She looked out the balcony doors just as the sun was rising over the Dromdara Plains. Fatigue begged her to close her eyes, but there was not the time for that. She had to pay attention and think about possibilities for escape. She knew roughly where Aurum Castle was on the map. *The map!* Her hand automatically felt at her side for the pouch. *Gone!* He couldn't use it, but she would need it when she escaped. Surveying the room for possible clues to its location, she settled on the desk. *It must be in there.* Shamwa's mild chuckle told her she'd been too obvious. She adjusted her position on the recliner. "I'm listening."

The prime minister paused as though thinking about where to start.

Briana, where in Maker's name are you?

Sitting in the salon of Aurum Castle, getting ready to hear Lord Shamwa's side of things.

Sweet Maker! Has he hurt you?

I'm perfectly fine. Artanin put some kind of spell on us and kidnapped me, but no one's hurt me. In fact, this wine is excellent. And by the way, why did no one tell me how handsome he is?

Briana, don't for one second take this lightly. He is brutal and will not blink about doin' terrible things to you. I'm on my way.

Silas, don't come too close. Let me figure out what's happening here before you risk anyone else's life. Send someone after Sigel, Epona and Mr. Stark. I'll keep you posted.

"Let's start with the supposed prophecy and the story that you are meant to save Brath from some enchantment and become his queen."

"You don't believe it?"

He rolled his eyes. "Hardly. Anyone could have written it to advance an agenda. Don't you find it interesting it appeared only after I incapacitated the king?"

Briana wasn't about to tell him that Cailleach had the prophecy and *The Book of Leaves* long before she shared it, just in case he could use that knowledge against the witch. She shrugged.

"Somehow you arrived here. That much I don't deny. And now that we've met, I believe you might make a splendid queen for Uisneach, but not necessarily Brath's queen."

Her eyes narrowed. "You aren't suggesting I should be yours?"

He looked her up and down. "It is one possibility."

Well, the idea might keep me alive long enough to devise a plan to escape. She kept her face blank.

"I'm getting ahead of myself. Let me tell you what happened and why I believe it's essential to remove the Taranian whelp from the throne. Uisneach has been mismanaged for a long time. King Barclay had the potential to be a great king, which is the only reason I agreed to be his prime minister. I had cause to refuse, but I truly thought he would be a strong leader. He was a brave warrior and," he paused, his jaw clenching, "a good friend, once. The problem was he believed the myths about magic and wanted to lift the restrictions placed on Evalon to encourage the faeries to take a more active role in Uisneach."

"Why is that a bad idea?"

"If you allow faeries any role, they'll take over. There will be no Uisneach, but some kind of magically-enhanced kingdom of Evalon, without any real leadership."

"Sounds like you hate magic."

"Magic twists people's minds and makes them weak. What this kingdom needs is not some whimsical, feel-good ideology that makes it vulnerable to outside forces, but strong warriors capable of protecting our borders and preventing anyone from attacking us and taking control.

"We're weak in other ways, too. The Taranian reign has been inconsistent on so many levels. On the one hand, they want to let magical faeries run rampant, but on the other hand, they adhere to an antiquated code of morality that stifles any new blood from strengthening the royal lineage."

Briana nodded slightly. She'd made similar statements to Sigel about the archaic morality codes of Uisneach. However, she felt a little queasy realizing that she and this evil man agreed on anything. "Yet they want to 'modernize' trade policies and be more politically open to other lands. Absurd. The former kings and queens of Uisneach worked hard to build our military power and make us unconquerable. In two short generations, it could all come tumbling down. I'm not about to let that happen."

"Did you present an alternative to King Barclay?"

"Repeatedly. But Barclay wouldn't listen to me. He thought he had all the answers, and he could charm everyone else into believing he was right. I tried to talk to Eleanor, but she wouldn't listen to anyone but Barclay."

Hatred darkened his eyes. He walked toward the balcony.

Eleanor? So, he was on first-name basis with the queen? That look comes from more than just a disgruntled employee.

Silas, was there anything between Brath's mother and Lord Shamwa?

I remember hearin' that when they were young, Shamwa courted Eleanor, but once she met Barclay, he was her only love. Why do you ask?

It could be one reason he hates the Taranians so much.

Hmmm... makes sense.

Shamwa returned with his emotions under control. "Brath would give away everything to curry the favor of the people of Uisneach, including the power of the monarchy. He invited the riffraff to offer their opinion on every decision. Can you imagine that? Servants were treated like best friends, villagers like royalty. Ahh, everyone loved King Brath, but the coffers were dwindling down to nothing and he lived in an old, cold castle with barely a tapestry on the wall and a log in the fire. Is that how you want to live, Briana? Or," he waved a hand around the room, "would you prefer a little more comfort and style?"

"I like comfort as much as the next queen, but surely you attract more flies with honey than with vinegar?"

"Oh, Maker, you sound just like them. Can I save you from yourself? What you invite is the usurpation of your power. I hold the power now, not because I coddle the tenants of this land. I hold them accountable to the law."

"Through fear and victimization?" She saw the bruised and frightened body of Mary Keary in her mind and rage began to surface in her. *Stay calm*, she coached herself.

"It's far more effective than how the Taranians operate."

"I think they tried to build trust and cooperation by building relationships, by making themselves available and visible to the tenants."

"That's what stewards are for. No one respects a king who can't control his country. People respect me because they fear the consequences of not following the rules. People have what they need, and I have what I need. Borders are secure and we are making sure Evalon stays underground. I'm not the only one who believes we need to prevent the interference of faeries. I do have some powerful allies."

I need to find out more about that. I wonder who these "powerful allies" are?

"You have some valid ideas, my lord." *Well, not many, but maybe I can find something to work with.* "What if I could guarantee you a place at the negotiating table?"

He laughed out loud. "Oh, sweetheart, you are bold and delightful. However, you are not in a position to offer me anything. Nor would I be interested if you could. I will not tolerate King Brath's survival. He is single-minded, narrow-minded and too young to understand the consequences of opening Uisneach to foreigners. You really only have two choices here. One, you agree to be my consort and live in the lap of luxury as the Queen of Uisneach, or two, I kill you and end this." He sat beside her on the recliner and placed a warm hand on her knee, sending a cold shiver up her spine. "The former sounds much more attractive, don't you think?"

Being so close to him was unsettling. Everything about him exuded virility and power. *And yet,* she thought, *the only power he has is what he controls through terror and the druid's magic. I, on the other hand, have no sword and no protector, but I do have magic.* She smiled. "Let me give this some thought."

He leaned over and kissed the spot his hand had warmed. She involuntarily moved away. "Very well. In the meantime, perhaps you'd like to clean up. My druid will escort you to your room. I'll meet you back here for breakfast in an hour."

He rang a bell. Artanin entered, his hood down.

"Artanin, accompany Lady Briana to her room and make sure it's secured." No "please" or "thank you" as Shamwa left the room.

"Milady, follow me, please."

"So, you're Shamwa's flunky?" she said, stepping in front of him. He said nothing, but his menacing glare was enough to silence her. She glanced at the creature in the corner, who smiled, with a promising glint in its eyes.

The druid led her into a room with a lavish canopied bed in red and gold, marble table and thick carpets across the polished stone floors. Artanin swept around its perimeter, his robe trailing, making silent incantations. She watched, impressed, as a seal formed around the single window, making the chamber inescapable.

"A room fit for a queen," she said. "Not my style, but nice." He showed her the private latrine, its walls lined with stone.

"Do you speak?" she finally asked him, curious.

"All I have to say to you, Your Majesty, is things are not always as they appear. Be very careful with what you say and do." With that cryptic warning, he whirled and swept out of the room, the sound of a lock clicking reminding her she was a prisoner.

After using the latrine and washing up, she explored the room, coming to a massive oak wardrobe. Inside was a row of elegant gowns that looked to be a perfect fit for her.

You okay? Silas asked.

So far, so good. He said I can be his consort instead of Brath's. He doesn't like the kingdom's rigid moral code. If I were to take him up on his offer, you and I could probably be lovers.

I do hope you're not seriously considerin' it.

I don't know, Silas. He's pretty easy on the eye and I suspect quite charming when things go his way.

Briana, this is no jokin' matter.

I know. Sorry. Where are you?

Headin' your way. How the hell did he get past our men at the river?

Excellent question. I didn't think to ask it, but I will. That reminds me, Artanin said I should be careful and things are not always as they seem. He also addressed me as 'Your Majesty.' Don't you find that odd?

I do. As much as I'm terrified for you, a mhuirnin, *it sounds like you're holdin' your own. Just keep tryin' to get information and I'll be along to help you.*

Between the sleep deprivation and the lingering effects of Artanin's magic, she was feeling logy. A nap might improve her concentration, make it easier for her to think about how to get out of here.

She was jostled awake by Lord Shamwa himself. "Wake up, beauty. You were sleeping so soundly that I didn't want to wake you. But you haven't eaten all day. Come, join me for dinner."

She sat on the edge of the bed, rubbing her eyes. Stars twinkled in a clear night sky over the Dromdara mountains.

Damn, I never meant to sleep that long.

"Here, why don't you choose one of the gowns I had made for you?"

"That's not necessary."

"Oh, but I insist," he said, pulling a red creation from the closet.

"How could you have known what size?"

"Your first inept captors described you to me."

"Winkle and Wonk," she said. "Where are they now?"

He shrugged. "Somewhere the other side of hell, I imagine. I do not tolerate incompetence."

"You killed them? Because I escaped?" She was horrified.

"No great loss. I'll step outside and give you a minute to change."

She had no choice. She slipped the dress over her head and found a way to slide the pouch with the faerie tree seeds and the warrior heart necklace in her undergarments. Now, if he didn't rape her, she'd be able to keep them safe. When she was ready, she knocked on the door.

Opening the door, Shamwa stood back and took a long look at her. "Lovely," he said. "I will enjoy continuing my efforts to persuade you to my side."

She said nothing but preceded him into the salon. The table was laid out with candles, wine, and an assortment of enticing foods.

Lord Shamwa, now formally dressed in a white shirt, bow- tie and black coat with long tails, held the seat for her. She dutifully sat down as the gnome plated her food and the prime minister's without a word. When Shamwa wasn't looking, the gnome winked at her. *An ally? Oh, that would be perfect.* Yet Artanin warned her things were not as they seemed. She wasn't sure who to trust.

She stared unbelievably at the lobster and scallops nestled on a bed of greens. "How on earth did you come by fresh seafood in the mountains?"

"Power and wealth will get you anything you like, any time you wish it. I promise you, King Brath would never be able to provide you such a life."

"Actually, he would. He lives beside the ocean."

"I didn't mean the lobster."

She took a bite of the crustacean, which went down her throat like a rock. "I've been thinking about your proposal. Let me make sure I understand. You want me to agree with your plan on how Uisneach should be run, accept your proposal to be your consort, help release Brath from his deep sleep – I assume you agree I hold some power over that – so you can kill him and take formal control over Uisneach."

"Precisely."

"It seems you need me more than I need you. Without me, your plan can't move forward."

"Without me, you don't get to live."

"So, if we were playing a game of *ríocht*, we'd be at a stalemate."

"More like I have you checked."

"Or I, you."

As they ate, she wondered what her next step was and how much time she had before things headed south. The ever-present gnome curled in the corner. The door would certainly be guarded at all times. There were weapons galore, candlesticks, books, even a sharp letter opener. Without Nua, she was no match for his physical strength.

When they were done eating, Briana walked to the balcony. It seemed the only route of escape, but was secured by Artanin's magic. Maybe her magic was stronger. *Interesting view.* A very old and gangly-limbed beech tree stood next to the balcony. *Why he left this so close to the castle is beyond me*, she thought, seeing it as a simple get-away plan. Beyond the court-yard was a well-kept English garden, complete with hedgerow maze. From her vantage point, she found the way through the labyrinth to its exit. A wide expanse of field separated the garden from a small river. *Oh, and how lovely, there's a boat tied to a tree.*

"Beautiful garden," she said.

Shamwa moved behind her and she held her breath when a hand slid around her waist. "Uh, we don't know each other well enough for that," she said.

"And you are stalling for time. Princess, there is no rescue for you. Your knights, so to speak, will not break through the protective spell Artanin put on this place."

"I am not a princess, Your Lordship. I am a queen." His breath caressed the back of her

He chuckled. "You're spirited. I like that. In fact, I find you quite remarkable, which is the only reason I haven't satisfied my more basic urges. You're a woman who deserves more care."

"Then I am thrilled to have impressed you."

"I won't wait long, though." To prove his point, he put a long, well-manicured finger to her collarbone and slid it down toward the neck of her gown.

She heard his intake of breath and for the first time since arriving, felt real fear that she might not be as much in control as she thought. His lips parted and she thought he was going to try to kiss her. Briana stepped back. Her heart raced, waiting for his reaction. Lord Shamwa picked up his goblet, holding it up to her in salute.

Okay, Silas, now I'm nervous. I need to move a little faster here. What's your plan?

She told him about the river and her idea of escape. *I just haven't figured out quite how to use my magic to make it happen.*

Crows are flyin' all around, but are stopped by some spell at the mountains near Aurum Castle. You'll need to break through that barrier.

There was a knock on the door. Shamwa opened it.

"Sorry to trouble you, Your Lordship," Artanin said, "but there are…"

She couldn't hear his mumbled words.

"I'll be back, beauty," Shamwa said. He swept out without so much as glancing at the druid.

Briana was shocked when the druid met her gaze. "There's a reason King Brath is not dead," he mouthed. Artanin let his eyes travel to the balcony door with an almost imperceptible nod. Again he spoke silently. "You are the future of Uisneach. Go!"

What the hell? What's his role in this? Did he just suggest that he protected Brath?

I believe he just indicated an opportunity for you to leave, said the gnome, in a light and distinctively feminine voice. *Her telepathic speech startled Briana. Don't forget your map.* The gnome looked at the desk. Angry voices seeped through the door. With her heart racing, Briana moved to the desk. Nothing on the top. She tried the drawer. Locked. No key. Taking a deep breath, she willed the drawer to open, which it did with ease. Grabbing the pouch that held her map, she pushed the drawer closed and turned back to the gnome. "Are you…"

No time, Lady Briana. Use your magic and go!

Briana went to the balcony and tried the door. It was unlocked! She was free to make her escape.

A full-length gown was not the most conducive apparel to shimmy down trees, but she focused all her attention on success and was on the ground in seconds. There was enough moonlight to aid her footsteps, but not enough to make her a target. Imagining how the garden was laid out helped her to the maze. She offered silent prayers for guidance as she entered the stiff hedges. Recalling its pattern, she forged ahead, heedless of the scratching branches and leaves against her. Forward. Turn. Stopped in her tracks by a dead end. Go back. Stop. She let out all her breath, closed her eyes and imagined the faerie lights of Evalon. When she opened her eyes, tiny lights fluttered before her, and the way through the maze became clear.

After what seemed like an hour but was likely only minutes, she exited the green maze to the grassy field. Pouring on the speed, she made it to the river in minutes. *Where's the boat?* The hoot of an owl drew her attention. Focused on the owl, she nearly fell over the tiny vessel, wrapped in the shadow of the beech tree in which the owl was perched.

"Hurry milady, you don't have much time," it said.

The boat was tied so tightly to its mooring that she couldn't free it. She'd need magic. Harry Potter would've just thrown out a *wingardium* something or other, but she didn't know any such spells. Frantic and frustrated, she simply commanded, "Release the knot!" To her shock and awe, the rope slid open and fell to the ground. *Awesome*, she thought. *Simpler than I thought.*

Voices raised in alarm came from the castle. Briana wasted no time in climbing into the boat and shoving away from the bank. "Thanks for your help," she called to the owl, who hooted out an acknowledgment.

A fairly robust current took her immediately away from the bank and downstream. Unable to see much around her, and having no earthly idea where she was going, she could only visualize momentum, breaking through any potential barriers and enchantments to freedom. Ignoring the chilly night air and pushing away any dread that might distract her from reaching safety, she knelt in the bottom of the boat, holding the sides, looking and listening for clues to her location.

Briana?

I'm away from the castle, Silas, on the river. The current is pretty fast, so I don't think they can catch me.

The river will flow into Long River eventually. There are rapids, Briana. Try and steer to shore before you reach them.

Two problems there: one, I can't see much, it's too dark; and two, I have nothing to pilot with.

No oar?

Nada. Nothing.

Silence.

I can try and manifest light but I'm not sure how long I can sustain it. That doesn't help me steer, though.

You'll be fine, a mhuirnin. *I'll help you.*

How?

Don't know yet, but I will.

They ceased talking and she settled back, using magic to create a light source. As she suspected, she couldn't hold it long. Deciding to use it only as needed, she surrendered to the dark journey. The steady motion of the water calmed her. She allowed herself a moment to appreciate the infinite perfection of the stars. *I'm trusting you, Maker. Please help me.*

A mighty rushing announced the rapids. Briana imagined herself protected. The sudden cawing of many crows brought some comfort. *At least someone knows where I am,* she thought, before she was dowsed with a frigid splash of water over the side of the boat as it spun and dropped down a watery grade. Drenched and breathless, she was knocked sideways when the boat hit protruding rocks.

The bow snapped forward before spinning backward, forcing her down against the floorboards. The stars above, so peaceful before, swirled chaotically as the vessel jerked, twisted, rose and dove in the rapids. She focused on light and then wished she hadn't when she saw a huge boulder in the middle of the river. It was the size of a small house. And she was heading straight for it.

Silas!

Impact. Flying. Shocking cold. Wet. She entered another world, one in which she could neither think nor breathe. The inevitability of death settled over her. *No!* her mind screamed. *I will not die!* Forcing her legs to kick, she struggled to break the surface, and did for a moment. A great gulp of air energized her momentarily. A small beacon appeared, illuminating the mossy bank in front of her. She flailed toward it, but another swirl of water dragged her under. Fighting with every ounce of strength, Briana tried to surface again. Her dress caught on a branch underneath the water and she was held fast. No amount of kicking and twisting would unloose her. Perhaps it would be best to relax and let go. *I'm sorry, Silas. I'm sorry I couldn't save Brath and Uisneach. I did my best. I love you.*

She focused on the light and the sense of calm that now cocooned her. Suddenly, she was dragged upward by her hair. *I didn't think it would hurt,* was her last conscious thought before she entered the tunnel of warm, bright light.

CHAPTER TWENTY-SEVEN

BLISS

loating. Peaceful. Forever. Wings of pure, lucent light enveloped her. Carried along a stream of bliss so radiant she wanted to cry. Longing, anticipation, peace and joy exchanged places willingly in the dance. Free and fearless, she relaxed into the journey, allowed the luminous to fill all her empty places and heal the wounds from a life lived in earthly form. Settling. Soft. Her vision was filled with the beauty of a place beyond what she could have imagined heaven to be. No streets of gold, no pearly gates, no judging God. Her body lay in unadorned perfection on a mossy bank beside a stream, its gentle slope home to majestic oaks and verdant apple trees. Such a feeling of welcoming grace. Ambient birdsong and the tinkling of the stream pleased her senses. Fear held no authority here. Languid, she turned her head to see Silas move gracefully to her side and lay down, stretching his length to fit hers. She knew him to be a part of herself. His radiance matched her own. Effortlessly, they became one in an embrace that transcended any kind of human joining they might've wished for on Earth. Warmth flooded her body and the sound of his heart beating against her ear brought wholeness. Blue eyes, dark with love. She smiled and reached a hand to the side of his face. A long endless kiss brought them home. Soul recognition. Soul unity. She sighed as his energy covered hers, their separate sparks becoming one united flame. Ecstasy. Release. Relief. Completion. No, not the end.

We cannot stay, he told her.

I won't leave. I want to stay here with you.

We must return. Our purpose is unfulfilled.

Knowledge and understanding surged through her. She saw the past, present and future as facets of one reality. Briana felt sorrow for the corruption her soul would face when she returned to that other place. At first, she resisted the return, not wanting to feel the longing her soul would experience when separated from its other half. Those feelings were replaced with agreement and resolve. Silas smiled encouragingly. She separated herself from him, already feeling the chill of that world returning as her bones reformed.

Chapter Twenty-eight

Unbroken

arkness replaced the light. Bone-deep cold seized her body. She swam up from the watery depths until she felt the solidness of earth beneath her. Shadows danced against stone, a small campfire creating these ghostly personas. She was wrapped in a wool kilt, within Silas' arms. Yet even though he held her, she felt separate from him. Briana began to cry. "I didn't want to come back," she said.

"I didn't, either."

"You really were there with me?"

He nodded.

"How?"

"I followed your heart."

She curled into him, then realized something wasn't quite right. Lifting the kilt away from her chest, she saw she was naked underneath. Silas was biting his lip, waiting for her reaction.

"I'm naked."

"I'm sorry, Briana, I had no choice. Your clothes were soaked and you would've frozen to death. Your gown is drying by the fire."

"Wasn't I already dead?"

"For a moment, I believe you were, but I breathed into you, and you, uh, resurrected. I remembered this cave wasn't far. It's well-hidden and safe enough to make a small fire. I didn't look any more than was necessary, Briana." *But, sweet Maker, you are lovely.*

"I, we, did anything..."

"Not here, it didn't. Your virtue is intact, milady, though Maker knows it hasn't been easy," he said with a devilish grin. "Thankfully, I'm never been one to take advantage of half-drowned, recently dead and vulnerable women."

She pulled the kilt tighter around her and snuggled against him for comfort and warmth. "What happened?"

"The long and short of it is that I figured out where you should be and met up with you in time to watch your wee boat catapult into the sky. You were thrown in the river, miraculously near the bank where I was standin'. You were underwater for much too long, but I did manage to pull you out. You weren't breathin'. Oh, Maker, you scared me. Once I got some breath into you, you recovered. You've a nasty bump on your head, but otherwise, no injuries. Rest now, *mo chroi*. We can take some time for you to regain your strength."

She nestled against him, remembering the journey to the other side and what she learned. The crackling of the fire and Silas' humming relaxed her, but she could not sleep before telling him.

"Silas, there is only one reason I came back."

"To fulfill the prophecy."

She nodded against him. "I find myself in the ironic position of being alone with you, naked in your arms, and knowing that nothing is going to happen between us. I'm meant to go through with this, marry a man I haven't even met, and become the queen of this kingdom. It is my destiny. *He* is my destiny."

Silas's arms tightened around her, protective and reassuring. "Sleep, *a mhuirnin*, and when you wake, we'll be off."

⌇

"Briana?"

"Hmm..." Awakening meant they would leave, ending this precious togetherness, so she resisted his efforts to rouse her.

"When is your birthday?"

"March seventh," she mumbled, turning her head into his chest to avoid fully waking.

"Let's see, in Uisneach time that would be…"

"Near the start of the Wren Moon. I celebrated it about two moons before I came here, and I turned twenty-five. My mother's is in March also, the twenty-first." She sighed. "I'm awake." She looked up, slid one arm out from under the kilt and touched his face. "You need a shave."

"Mmm. Well, I've been a wee bit busy, chasin' after you, to be thinkin' of groomin' meself."

She continued to study him and he returned her gaze, sharing something deeper than words could express. She clutched the wool around her and eased herself out of his lap.

"I guess there's no point in postponing the inevitable," she said, somberly. "Would you be kind enough to…"

He was already up and heading to the front of the den. "I'll saddle Aldebaran."

Watching him walk away, she was suddenly gripped with uncertainty. *What have I done?*

The right thing, he reassured her.

Before she changed her mind and threw herself into his arms and begged him to make love to her, she grabbed the once-elegant gown and put it on. She rummaged around and frowned, not finding the map anywhere, though she still had her pouch. Shaking away the image of him undressing her, Briana checked on the faerie tree seeds, which were slightly wrinkled but safe, and the necklace, intact and still swaddled in cloth.

When he returned, Briana said, "You asked about my birthday. I wonder why we never talked about that. When is yours?"

"The second day of the Archer's Moon. I'm twenty-five seasons also."

She brought her arm from behind her back and handed him the gift. "I guess it's too late for a birthday present, but I found this and thought of you."

He grinned. "A wee present? How thoughtful of you, lass." As he glimpsed the necklace, his cheerful grin turned into an attitude of reverence. "Oh, my. Briana, this is beautiful. Warrior bone."

"You've heard of it?"

"Oh, aye, and it's quite rare. Hearts that cannot be separated," he said under his breath, rubbing his finger across the polished bone. "Will you help me put it on?" He turned away and pulled his hair aside.

She tied the cord securely, the mere brush of her hands against the skin on his neck sending thousands of tiny, pleasurable shocks through her. "There – turn around."

The sight of the hearts took her breath away. Theirs were two hearts held together by an amaranthine bond, stronger than fate.

"Come here, *a ghrá*." She curled into his open arms; now their position matched the connecting hearts he wore around his neck. "This means more to me than you will ever know. Thank you."

"Well, I may be destined for a king, but my heart is bound to a bard and unbreakable."

He placed a chaste kiss on the top of her head. "Remember that, Briana. No matter what happens or where this journey takes us or what storms we must weather, we will remain unbroken."

After a moment, he eased her out of his arms. "Now, on to more practical matters," he said, reaching into his pack. "I don't have much food to offer you, but here's a bit of bread and a handful of dried berries and nuts. When we get to the abbey, they'll feed us a proper meal."

Between bites, she asked about the map.

"I'm sorry, Briana, but I didn't find it. It's not so important now, anyway. I know where we are and where we're going and I also have a pretty good idea of where the Gray Military are. We don't really need the map."

"I guess, but it was nice to see what was going on around Uisneach at any given moment. I'll miss it."

"Aye, it was a clever thing. Time to go, but I want you to wrap this around you." He handed her the kilt. "That lovely red gown will make you stick out like a redbird in snow."

And then there was nothing left to do but leave. Fire doused, they shouldered their belongings and mounted Aldebaran, Briana riding behind Silas, contentedly hugging his waist.

"Once we leave this thicket, we'll be in danger of runnin' into the Grays," he told her. "We can't go straight up-river because I know for a fact they'll be coverin' that route. Instead, we'll go to the abbey and take sanctuary till we can get word to Sigel."

He led her away from the cave through a grove of trees, into a dark hedgerow. They emerged next to a crumbling ruins, an old castle that had been conquered by moss and ivy. An old wooden door hung precariously over the entrance. Nearby, she thought she saw the remnants of a well. Wide stone steps led between larger boulders. Silas let Aldebaran pick his way down the steps. Briana was crushed against his back.

"Sorry, for the rough ride," he said.

"I'm not complaining."

"Neither am I," he replied, with a laugh.

When the landscape leveled out, he urged the horse to a canter, his eyes scanning the forest, looking for something.

"Ah, there you are," he muttered, turning into the woods again. She could just make out a trail.

"Are you sure you know where you're going?"

He turned and gave her a cockeyed look. "Briana, are you seriously questionin' me ability to travel through these woods?"

"Well, this path doesn't appear to have been used much."

"Which is exactly why we're takin' it." He shook his head in bewilderment. "You should've learned that much by now."

She hugged him. "Go wherever you like, Silas. I'll just snuggle in for the ride."

"Why don't you tell me a story?"

"You're the bard, not me." She blew a strand of spider's web from across her face, pulling the pine branch it clung to from her hair.

"I want to hear the story of what happened to you in Shamwa's castle."

"Oh, well, hmm... where should I start?"

"From the beginnin'. I know the bits and pieces you told me from inside, but put the whole story together."

"Well, it started when Artanin put some kind of sleeping sorcery on us. Maker, I hope Sigel, Epona, Mr. Stark and Dara are okay."

"I'm sure they are. We'll probably rejoin them tomorrow."

She hoped so. "Anyway, when I woke up, I was in the salon of Aurum Castle with His Lordship. That place is dripping in gold." She grimaced against his back. "Insanely gaudy."

"But he is, what was it you said? 'Easy on the eye.'"

She laughed. "I had him pictured as a cartoon character, but he's more like an action hero."

"He's no hero, milady."

"No, he's not, but he does have a few arguably valid points."

"Whether he does or not, his methods are invalid. You'll recall Mary Keary?" Aldebaran sidestepped a jutting tree limb, momentarily unbalancing Briana. Silas' arm swung back to prevent her from falling until she could reseat herself.

"I do. I wasn't swayed in the least, Silas. I'm just saying that he isn't any more insane than most of the politicians of my own time. And I think he was terribly hurt by Queen Eleanor's rejection of him and her marriage to Barclay."

"That doesn't justify..."

"I'm just saying."

Raindrops pelted them from a slate sky. She finished telling him everything that occurred in Aurum Castle. He tensed when she told him about Shamwa's amorous attention.

"That alone makes him a dead man," he stated, vehemently.

"He didn't actually do anything, Silas. But, I'm not sure he can be rehabilitated, either. I begin to wonder if there is just some evil in the world that must be eliminated."

"There is," he said, without hesitation.

"You know who might be a hero? Artanin."

Silas turned his head. "How so?"

"He's the reason I escaped. I'm certain he removed the locking spell off the door. I think there's more to Artanin's role in this than we realized. And I still wonder if that gnome was a faerie in disguise."

While she related her river adventure, rain began to spill in sheets, as cold and gray as steel. After ten minutes, Briana thought the rain felt as hard as steel, too.

Silas groaned. "One bloody thing after the other." He urged the chestnut stallion faster.

"Are we almost to the abbey?"

"No, but there are dolmens not too far away, where we can stay dry and let the storm pass. You don't need to be soaked again."

"You keep looking at the sky. What are you looking for?"

"Crows. I find it odd that we've not seen a single crow since I left the river to find you."

"A spell was cast over the area surrounding Aurum Castle. Lord Shamwa mentioned that no one would be able to get close."

"Umm… but we should've seen somethin' out here. They should have crows everywhere lookin' for you."

"And that, dear man, is why the map would be handy," she said, pointedly. "Maybe they're focusing along the river."

"Perhaps, but I imagine they'd fan out. Likely the bloody weather is a hindrance."

In fact, the weather was becoming more ominous by the minute. Gray mist blanketed the forest, making it hard to see the way ahead. She thought perhaps getting wet was a moot point, when she heard him mutter something.

The mist parted and she beheld an awe-inspiring cluster of megalithic structures spread out across a field. Some of the stones stood tall and ghostly, while others formed a crude table, with a flat slab perched across three shorter stones. Silas headed for the largest structure. Closed-in on three sides and topped by a massive granite slab, it was big enough to shelter the two of them and Aldebaran.

He pulled the wool kilt out of his pack and sat down, patting the space beside him. When she was settled, he covered them both with the kilt.

They sat in silence for a while, listening to the rain and occasional claps of thunder. Meditative breathing relaxed her enough to help her appreciate the tranquility of her shelter and the cool, earthy smell of the drenched ground. Then she felt a hairy spider on her shoulder and yelped. Silas swept it away.

"I hope no other family members are waiting to pounce."

"I hardly think spiders are capable of pouncin', milady. But if it will take your mind off the thought, perhaps you'd care to tell me the story of King Arthur and his lusty queen."

"I've told you that story. Besides, why am I the one telling all the stories today? Isn't that your job?"

"I'm tired."

"What! Do you think I'm not?"

He gave her leg a conciliatory pat. "Come on, Briana. I love to hear you tell tales."

"Fine," she grumbled, secretly happy that they had this time alone to tell stories. "Once upon a time, a king built the perfect kingdom. It only rained at night."

"For sure they didn't live in Uisneach," he interrupted, staring out at the downpour.

"Do you want the story or not?"

"Please, continue."

"The king was good to his subjects, made good laws, provided for his people and protected them from outsiders. All was perfect except that he needed a queen. He knew of a woman, the daughter of another king, and took a hankering to making her his wife. The woman was brought to Camelot to marry Arthur and they did fall in love."

"That's nice," he said, gruffly.

She smiled. "But then this drop-dead gorgeous French knight shows up and Guinevere falls in love with him."

"Sounds like a fickle lass, if you ask me."

"You know very well, Silas, the heart goes where it will. Now, be quiet and let me finish."

She wound a tale of love and intrigue that was far too reminiscent of their own story.

"So, what happened to her?"

"There are many endings, depending on who's telling the story, but it seems she ended up in a nunnery."

"And here we are going to an abbey."

"Can we please not make any comparisons between Camelot and our own circumstances?"

Aldebaran snorted and they laughed. "He agrees," Silas said.

Silence followed until Briana said, "Are we going to be here a while?"

"Maybe, why?"

"I have another story I want to tell you, actually, a dream." She shivered and he wrapped his arm around her, pulling the fabric snug around them both. "Before I went through the tree, I had this recurring dream about being on a battlefield in a place like Uisneach. I was hiding in some trees and I saw a man with red hair coming at me with a sword and a crown." She felt Silas shudder but he remained silent. "I didn't know if he was a good guy or a bad guy. I was going to fight him, but he seemed to be trying to help me. Then I saw a blonde-haired man and wanted to follow him, but before I could, I was attacked and stabbed by a man in a gray uniform. He was just about to strike again when I woke up. I thought the dreams kept occuring because I spent a lot of time..." She stopped.

"Spent a lot of time what?"

"It's embarrassing."

"I promise not to laugh."

"I had these action figures, uh, kind of like dolls. "A king and queen, several warriors, a dragon and..." She paused and looked at him. "And an archer."

"Hmm..."

"He meant something to me, something beyond what he should have."

He cocked his head.

She held his gaze and swallowed. "I talked to him. I imagined us as lovers. He was the reason I never could connect with any other guy."

Silas didn't bat an eye. "It was me you were waitin' for."

"Yes, and now I see it was a premonition of what was to come. But Silas, the archer always walked away. And the man with the crown always came to me and tried to give it to me."

"You never saw yourself take it?"

"No, but maybe that was because I wasn't ready to make that choice."

He took her hand underneath the kilt. "Are you now?"

"I am, Silas. I must."

He nodded, staring out at the dismal field of rain and fog.

"I don't want to hurt you," she said, quietly.

"We'll both hurt, *a mhuirnin*, but it will get easier in time. I hope."

They stopped talking for several minutes, just letting the stark reality of their future lay lonely between them.

"Thank you for not laughing," she finally said.

"Aye, well, I can't say I talked to any dollies, but I always knew someone waited for me."

"And here I am, but promised to someone else."

He gave her a wry look. "Maker has a warped sense of humor to make the woman I fall in love with the Mouse of Prophecy."

"He must be a sick bastard."

"Hush, Briana. Don't say such a thing."

"What, you think I'll be struck by lightning?"

A terrifying crack of thunder and jagged line of lightning rent the sky. They both jumped. Briana laughed but Silas shuddered. "It's no jokin' matter, Briana."

She burrowed deeper into his body for warmth. "Let's stop talking about it and just be grateful for this time, which is likely the last time we'll ever be alone."

Close to him and warm, the patter of rain and lack of sleep lulled her into a light doze, though not so deeply she couldn't hear him humming, then softly singing.

"Your heartbeat and mine, solace we find, next to the firelight.

Feathers and ivy, the ties that bind, shine in the moonlight.

Your arms, they hold me, while hold-ing a line, in ruins at twilight.

Stay here, my heart, don't leave me lonely, forever in midnight.

Unbroken, one soul, given forever.
Unbroken, one life, living together

You ask will I wait, I promise I will. If you'll only remember."

All too soon, the sun broke through scattered clouds and their respite ended. Silas gently nudged her awake. "We've got to go, *a mhuirnin*If we hurry, we can make the abbey by dinnertime."

He took them back in the woods where they would be less visible, should any Gray Military be on the hunt. Sunbeams dappled the forest, making the rain-drenched tree limbs sparkle. Residual clouds of mist floated by, wildwood spectral journeyman on their last breath. An odd peace surrounded Briana and Silas. Talking seemed irreverent somehow, but occasional, half-formed thoughts wafted between them, memories of lovely moments shared, worries of what was to come, vows they meant to keep.

The path they followed wound around a pond and through flowering rowan trees at the edge of another opening. Silas pulled up sharply on Aldebaran's reins. *Stay quiet, Briana. Do you see that?*

She wasn't sure what to be more shaken by: the abbey that stood in front of them, or the line of gray-uniformed warriors that surrounded it.

CHAPTER TWENTY-NINE

SHANNON ABBEY

ilas backed Aldebaran into the trees to camouflage them while they watched the regiment.

"Shannon Abbey is supposed to be a protected sanctuary," he said, keeping his voice low. "I don't understand how Shamwa's men are able to get this close." A woman cloaked in religious vestments appeared. She talked with a man in a hooded cloak near the front of the abbey. "I can't tell who he is. Probably Artanin, but I can't be sure." He turned to Briana. "What's wrong? You look like you've seen a ghost."

She felt confused and wobbly, as though she had one foot in one world and one foot in another. "I don't know how this is possible, but I have – had – a picture of this place hanging in my bedroom in Maine."

"Are you sure, Briana? I imagine most abbeys look similar."

The limestone cruciform abbey surged out of the green earth enshrouded in mist, ghostly. The rectangular main part intersected with two matching arms, with a tall square tower spired up out of the middle. The part of the church that housed the altar, with its three long windows, was much grander now than in her world and time, when it had fallen into a sad state of disrepair. It was larger now, too, because of the rooms and walkways around the cloister, none of which remained in her time. Archways and buttresses were ornately carved with symbols and geometric designs, a beautiful piece of architecture that had absolutely no reason to be in Uisneach. Smoke spiraled up from chimneys, its woody scent drifting over the landscape to Briana and Silas.

"No, it's exactly the same, except this one is intact and the picture I have is of ruins. I fell in love with it when we went to Ireland. I didn't understand why it meant so much to me, but it called to my soul." Resting her forehead against her hand, she willed herself not to cry.

The abbey was situated on a plain so much like the one in Tipperary, she expected to find the Rock of Cashel behind it. The hill was there, all right, but Cashel didn't exist, just as this building standing in front of her should not exist. On top of the mound stood the most magnificent circle of standing stones she'd ever seen. Some of them stood thirty feet tall with none less than fifteen feet high. Eight in all, she assumed to mark solstices and equinoxes. She could only shake her head in disbelief.

"Listen, Briana. We'll figure it out, but at the moment, we've a bigger problem. As long as those men are guardin' the abbey, we're stuck."

They watched as the woman and man carried on a heated discussion. Then the woman turned and went inside.

"Hmmm… will you look at that? Whatever she said, they're leavin'."

In fact, the hooded man, (Artanin, she was sure), gave orders, and the troop began to march away from the abbey to the northeast, past the standing monoliths and down the other side of the hill.

"We'll stay here a while, to be sure no one comes back," he said.

Waiting gave Briana time to absorb the shock of seeing Hore Abbey, Shannon Abbey in this world, resurrected in perfect glory.

"I think it's safe." He pulled his bow around in front of him and reached for an arrow. "Just in case," he responded, to her questioning eyes.

They wasted no time getting across the field, still wet from the rain. Silas tied Aldebaran to a post. Before they could knock on the door, it opened, and a petite woman in a gray habit greeted them. "Come in! Oh my gracious, what's happened to you?" she said, taking in Briana's somewhat bedraggled appearance.

"Thank you," Silas answered. "Is there a stable for my horse?"

"Of course. Sister Deidre will tend to him when she goes to feed our little Nellie."

"Thank you, Sister. I'll go down with her and tend to my animal."

They stepped into a vestibule. Briana put a hand to her mouth. A peat fire burned in the small fireplace, with rushes lighting the walls. Adornment was minimal, but so beautifully crafted that it needed nothing other than the occasional carving along a lintel or archway. She stared in fascination as Silas related their circumstances to the woman who'd introduced herself as Sister Clare. Briana wondered why he hadn't been more circumspect, but he seemed confident.

"You are welcome here. We shall not worry about Lord Shamwa as this is a place of peace, protected by the Maker. He and his minions will never come to the abbey. Let's get you dry, fed and rested. You both look about done in."

Briana and Silas exchanged glances.

Are you nervous about the nun's wee lie? asked Briana.

Uh huh. But we'll follow along and see what happens. I hope nothin' till we're fed.

At least you have your priorities straight, she said, wryly.

The tiny woman hustled them along the passageway. Silas leaned over to whisper to Briana, "The poor lady is going to think you're a mute if you don't say somethin'."

Rolling her eyes in embarrassment, she said, "Sister Clare, I'm sorry for my poor manners. I seem to have been overcome by this beautiful place. We're grateful for your help."

The girl stopped in mid-stride and smiled broadly. "Not to worry, milady. I thought you looked a wee bit gobsmacked. The abbey affects some people that way." She turned back and continued down the walkway, leaving Briana to stare at Silas.

Gobsmacked?

Aye, well, she probably hasn't been a servant of the Maker her whole life.

They were taken to rooms and advised they would be collected in an hour for supper and to meet the abbess.

"We must go to our prayers, but you shall have dry clothes in a few minutes. You can rest a while, until I come for you."

"Thank you, Sister," Briana said, before going into the room and shutting the door behind her.

The room was small and sparsely furnished with a narrow bed and plain wooden table and chair. A homey fire crackled away in the hearth, suffusing her body with its warmth. She wandered to a small window which looked out over the stones. It looked so different without the massive castle of the high kings of Ireland commandeering the hill.

Silas? Are you warm enough? I've got a lovely fire going in here.

Aye, I think we took their rooms. Very kind, these religious people.

A knock at the door stalled their conversation. An older woman, dressed in the same garb as the others, with hair the color of carrots, shuffled in, with a more spiritual demeanor than Sister Clare. "Hello," Briana said. The nun handed her a garment that matched the one she wore. "I'm Lady Briana."

"I'm Sister Enda. You may use this robe while your clothes are drying. Would you like me to take them for you?"

"Oh, no. I can hang them over this chair next to the fire, and they'll dry in no time."

The woman nodded. "Just don't set them too close. We can't have the place catching fire."

"No, of course not. I'll be careful."

The woman left briskly, offering no other instructions or friendly chit chat. Once the door closed, Briana shed the wet clothes and after arranging them over the chair, stood naked in front of the fire, allowing the heat to pull the chill from her body.

Briana?

Silas! What are you doing? She instinctively reached for the robe before she realized he couldn't see her. She heard him chuckle.

I was going to ask you not to laugh when you see what I'm wearin'. Some kind of religious robe. I look ridiculous.

A vision rose up in her mind and she smiled, feeling the slight pinch to her midsection. *Ouch.*

I said no laughing.

Rap… rap… rap. She knew it was Silas and opened the door. Laughing was the last thing she wanted to do. Druid he was, sexy and a bit intimidating. She wondered whether to ravish him or kneel before him.

"My goodness, Silas, there's nothing funny about how you look. I'm thinking you should conduct a ritual and sacrifice a virgin or something."

He shivered. "I don't find that funny."

"Hmm. Now that you mention it, I agree. Not funny at all."

"I'm takin' Aldebaran to the stables. I'll meet you later."

Sister Deidre, a plump young woman who hardly looked like a stable hand, arrived beside him, Sister Clare, right behind her.

"Are you ready, sir?"

"Lead the way, Sister."

Sister Clare took Briana to the dining room, where she waited alone. Briana explored the room and catalogued every aspect of it in her mind. Silas and Deidre returned, along with the other five sisters, who'd gathered for the evening meal. They were introduced to Sister Chloe, Sister Colleen, and Sister Ambrosia. The door behind them opened again and the abbess entered the room, shrouded in the folds of a hooded white vestment, the cowl pulled up over her head, preventing Briana and Silas from seeing her face clearly. The sisters all stood until the woman waved them to sit. She came to stand in front of Silas and Briana, her face hidden in shadow. Briana felt something oddly familiar about the woman and nearly collapsed when the woman slid back the hood. She looked like Cailleach's twin.

"I greet you, Lady Briana, and Silas of Cedarmara. I am Mother Ealga, the abbess of Shannon Abbey." Seeing their shock, she knit her brows together. "She hasn't told you about me."

"She… did tell… me about… you," Briana stammered. "She failed to mention you are twins."

"No, not twins, but we certainly did look alike. Do we still?"

Briana nodded.

The abbess sighed. "What brings you to Shannon Abbey?"

Don't say anything about the Grays. Let's see if she tells us, said Silas.

"The lass got herself lost," Silas said, casually. "I found her near-drowned, and this was the closest place we could come for shelter. We mean to catch up with the lord marshall and the king's troops."

"Is King Brath revived?"

"No, but we mean to do so, as soon as we reach Ard Darach. We hope to rely on your hospitality for a meal and a good night's rest. We'll be off in the morning."

"Of course. The sisters and I will be happy to help in any way we can," the abbess said, smiling.

Do you think she's sincere? Briana asked Silas.

I honestly don't know what to think just yet. I do wonder why she hasn't mentioned the Grays.

The abbess was much like Cailleach, not only in appearance – they shared the same storm-gray eyes, cream-and-earth skin and salt-and-pepper hair – but also in attitude and presence. There was a commanding quality, a palpable sense of power, common to the two women, inviting respect and deference from others. The anchorites obviously held her in high regard, attending her with the reverence of those who feel called to sacred and honorable service. It was only after they received some kind of consent from her, which Briana missed, that food was served.

"I'm starvin'," Silas declared, the moment the savory scent wafting into the room.

"Me, too," Briana concurred. "I could eat a horse."

"No horse, milady, but perhaps I can ease your hunger with a cut of lamb," said Sister Colleen in an airy voice as she came around the corner, carrying a huge platter of meat.

Silas took the heavy dish from her and set it on the table. "Lamb will do fine, Sister. Smells wonderful."

Heaping plates of vegetables and a sweet cake were set out, accompanied by excited chatter from the women around the table.

"We rarely feast like this," said Sister Chloe.

"Thank Maker for visitors!" Sister Deidre exclaimed, snatching a carrot chunk that had started to slip off the platter. She popped it into her mouth.

When the food was properly blessed, the sisters began to eat in silence.

"This is wonderful," Briana commented to the all the sisters, unsure who actually did the cooking. Her compliment was met with pleased, silent smiles. She ate two thick slices of fresh, warm bread and Silas ate three. When she swallowed the last bite and finished the last drop of ale, she sat back with a gratified yawn.

The dishes were cleared with graceful efficiency. The abbess focused her attention on her two guests. "Follow me, if you please." She didn't wait for a response, but turned and exited the room, her voluminous robes flowing behind her.

Silas put his hand on the small of Briana's back, ushering her out ahead of him. They followed Mother Ealga down a long walkway and past the chapel, before entering a larger room, a library, with the biggest granite fireplace Briana had seen so far. A hearty fire blazed, and Briana, still shivering from her river misadventure and the constant rain, walked over to stand near it. She moved closer to the hearth, trying to get a better look at the design and inscriptions on the mantle and undermantle, which were carved with primitive designs.

Briana traced some of the shapes with her finger as Mother Ealga poured steaming cups of tea from a pot mysteriously waiting on the table. Briana sat beside Silas, who was already seated with his legs stretched out languorously in front of him, as though he hadn't a care in the world.

"I don't know what Cailleach has told you…"

"She told me of the rift between you over Borrum," Briana said. "I was sorry to hear it, especially since it tore the two of you apart."

"Cailleach blamed me for his death. I stayed in Appleduir for almost a year, trying to gain her forgiveness, but she never softened her heart toward me. Eventually, I joined the cloister here, where I have lived ever since."

Briana said, "I am sorry for your losses, Mother Ealga. Perhaps Cailleach would be more open to reconciliation now."

Ealga shrugged. "It's been a long time."

They moved on to an accounting of their own tale, and how they came to seek refuge at Shannon Abbey. Mother Ealga said, "Lord Shamwa won't come here, rest assured on that score."

"Why not?" Silas asked.

"Because the collective magic of the women who live here would be too powerful for him. There's an eternally protective kind of, well, not spell, really, but power, nonetheless, that pushes him back before he ever gets close. The abbey truly is a sanctuary."

Briana glanced beside her to gauge Silas' reaction. His face was expressionless.

"Good to know," he said. "I'm a bit concerned Lord Marshall Sigel has not been by yet, or at least a contingent of crows."

Mother Ealga didn't respond. A cat-and-mouse game seemed to be underway. Briana waited quietly for the next move.

"Well, at any rate, we'll be off in the morning to find them," Silas said.

"A wise plan. We'll make sure you have food for the journey," Mother Ealga said, before excusing herself to prepare for evening devotions. When she was gone, Silas turned to her, his eyebrows raised.

What do you think?

She shrugged, clueless.

I don't suppose there's anythin' we can do about it tonight, but we do need to leave at first light. He stood and ushered her out into the corridor toward their rooms. They paused at her door.

"Briana," he said, but followed with, "Never mind."

"What?" she asked, wondering why he looked both sad and worried.

"Nothing. Good night, *a mhuirnin.*"

"I hate it when you do that."

"What?"

"Start to tell me something and then don't."

"I was just thinking tomorrow could be messy, and it could also be the day we reach Ard Darach. I want to deliver you there safely, but part of me wishes we would never have to see those castle walls." *And I wish I could kiss you good night.*

"Why don't we agree not to think too far ahead. We've enough in the moment to keep us occupied. I'll count myself lucky if we escape with our lives. The rest we'll take as it comes."

"You're right." He took a deep breath and turned to walk away.

She closed her eyes and imagined them, a normal young couple, kissing good night at her door. She visualized their arms winding around each other, their breaths mingling and sighs of contentment floating between them. She heard his response and opened her eyes. His eyes were shut and his mouth lifted in a pleased smile.

"Good night, Silas."

When sleep finally came, her dreams were troubled by nuns, soldiers, poets and kings. Her tossing about finally woke her before dawn. She lit the candle beside her bed. She kept wondering why Ealga had lied about Shamwa's men at the abbey. Finding a bowl of water for washing, she set it in front of her and stared into it, slowing her breathing until she was focusing solely on the water. As it had in the past, the water rippled until an image appeared. Two images manifested, side by side. One of her sweet Cailleach, washed in light, and the other of the abbess, surrounded by darkness and sinister energy. Nothing more.

A warning, she thought. *Not specific, but Ealga is not to be trusted.*

The picture faded, replaced by an image of the stone circle. She was standing beside Silas. It felt so real, it filled her soul with joy.

You're not the only one to have visions, Silas whispered in her mind. *I would marry you, Briana, here in the stones, witnessed by the ancestors and Maker.*

She gasped at the images that shifted and flowed before her eyes. A gathering of everyone she loved, including her mother, surrounding and blessing her and Silas. A vision of them making love, surrounded by the ancient columns, took the breath from her body.

She left the bowl and turned to the window. Meager light filtered through receding clouds, draping the stones with mystical light. Silas stood among the stones, alone. She considered joining him, but knew it would only hurt them in the end. If, and when, his vision came to pass, she would have joy beyond words, but their vow to honor the prophecy and their king would remain intact this night.

The sisters will be up soon for mornin' prayers. We best be ready to leave.

Silas, we should leave before they wake, or risk not leaving at all.

I'll come for you.

Silas, it was a lovely vision. If I could, I would gladly marry you, any-where you like.

She dressed quickly and already had her pack on her shoulder when he rapped on her door. They made it as far as the communal room when Mother Ealga entered, fully robed and prepared for the day.

"I didn't realize you planned to leave so early," she said, forcing a smile.

"Neither of us could sleep, so we decided we might as well get going," Briana told her.

Silas nodded. "Yes, Mother, we should leave as soon as possible."

The abbess searched their faces. "At least wait and have breakfast. You can't go into battle on an empty stomach."

And she knows we'll encounter troops how? Silas asked.

Oh, she knows.

"Thank you, Mother. While we're waiting, I'll saddle me horse."

"Very well. I'll wait here with Briana."

In other words, she understands you won't leave without me. Maybe you better make a run for it, and get help.

That's not happenin'. Be right back.

Sister Clare ambled into the dining room, rubbing her eyes and yawning. Seeing them, she stood to attention. "Milady! Oh, Mother Ealga! Have I overslept?"

"No, Sister. Silas and Lady Briana plan to leave earlier than we expected. Will you please bring breakfast?"

The abbess made small talk, which Briana had a hard time concentrating on. She apparently managed to supply the correct responses, but her heart was pounding by the time Silas returned. Clare brought tea, and then oatmeal and bread. She served but did not join them to eat. They ate in silence. When bowls were empty and bellies full, Silas turned to her.

"Ready?" he asked, rising from his chair.

She nodded, and stood. Mother Ealga led them down a corridor, collecting a gaggle of sisters in gray robes along the way. She held the women back at the door to a room. "Come with me, please," she said to Briana and Silas.

Wonder what this is about? Silas thought, flashing a concerned glance at Briana. His hand went to the hilt of his sword.

Do you think she's going to kill us?

Not likely, in the chapel. But she's up to something devious.

They were ushered into a cavernous, mostly empty room. Pearlescent morning light cast mystical shadows through the three panes of glass at the end of the chapel. Mother Ealga lit a pillar candle on a stone altar in the center of the room. Briana waited for strains of Gregorian chant to fill the air. No music, but the scent of lavender and meadowsweet from the candle made her feel suddenly peaceful. The change frightened her.

"Don't worry," Mother Ealga said. "I only intend to ask Maker for a blessing upon you."

Covering their hands with her own, she closed her eyes and spoke words in a language different from anything Briana had heard in Uisneach.

Can you build a wall in your mind between her words and your heart? asked Silas. *You need to protect yourself.*

I think so. She imagined a steel door crashing down between her and the abbess. For good measure, she envisioned one for Silas, too.

"*Domini arto, bin screbo nondura mo cardo,*" the abbess incanted. Pausing, she wove a sign over their hands and added, "*Eternio son magor mo cardo infernium.*"

What's she saying? asked Briana.

I think it's the ancient language of the Eiriens. Somethin' about Maker writin' on our hearts. Uh oh. I think the last part means the eternal burnin' of our hearts.

A silver shimmer rose and hovered over the altar. Briana's eyes widened. She might've jerked away, except Silas tightened his hold on her. Only a few moments passed before the gleaming mist dissipated.

"The words I spoke were to bless and protect your hearts as you do what you must to save Uisneach."

Righto, Briana thought. *Let's get the hell out of here.*

Uh, huh.

The abbess led them to the front door. "It goes without saying that you are in our prayers."

The sisters all took a turn hugging the sojourners. As Briana and Silas walked Aldebaran away, their angelic voices floated after them like heavenly protection, up the hill to the circle of stones. It would have been a beautiful sendoff if not for the ritual that came before it. When they were among the stones, Briana finally dared to speak.

"Why do you suppose she let us go?"

"Because she thinks she has cursed us."

"Doesn't she know we've already been cursed?"

He frowned at her words but said nothing. Mounting Aldebaran, they left the protection of the granite sentinels into the world that would tear them apart by the end of the day.

CHAPTER THIRTY

A LONG GOODBYE

"Silas, I need pants and a shirt. I shudder to think about fighting in this dress."

"There's a village not too far from here. I know a family who can help. In the meantime, stay quiet and alert for any movement. I'm not convinced yet that the troops aren't lurkin' about." He patted the sword at his side and the bow attached loosely to his shoulder. "If anythin' happens, hand me an arrow from the quiver."

He urged the horse to a lope as they crossed the field behind the hill and headed once again for the cover of forest.

Briana tried to focus on her more hopeful emotions, but more often succumbed to grief at their imminent separation. She found it difficult to follow her own advice of not thinking too far ahead. Sighs rolled out of her when she considered a life without Silas, a life with a man she didn't know and couldn't imagine ever loving, a life weighted with the responsibility of a monarch. *I never asked for any of this.*

They rode for the better part of an hour before any words were exchanged.Silas patted her leg and spoke, keeping his voice low. "Did I ever tell you about me first trip out on the ocean in a boat?"

"No, I don't think you did," she said, dully.

"Well, I was a wee lad of about four years old when me father took me out on a ship. A big beauty she was, with great white sails that flapped in the breeze once we were out of the harbor. I loved the wind on me face and the rollin' of the boat on the water. It was a very pleasant experience and I thought to meself, 'I'm going to be a sailor when I grow up.'

"Well, that thought lasted until we found ourselves in the middle of a wicked squall. The men sailin' the ship used every ounce of muscle they had to save us from sinkin'. I had been put down in the hold, out of harm's way. I was scared out of me mind and cried like a baby. It was an awful tempest and I thought for sure we'd all die and I'd never see Mum's pretty face again.

"It seemed like the storm lasted forever, but then the winds died down, the sun came out and Da came for me. Seein' me so upset, he took me in his arms and said, 'Silas, lad, storms will come and go throughout your life. They never last. Eventually, the sun comes out and all's right with the world. But, whenever you have to go through one of those storms, remember how much your mother and I love you, and trust us to do whatever we can to keep you safe.'"

He swiveled in the saddle. "I never forgot those words, *a mhuirnin*, and they've helped me more than once to weather the storms in me life."

She swallowed a rising sob and looked at him with plaintive eyes. "I'll try and remember that, Silas, really I will, but I'm having a very hard time imagining this storm will ever end, or that the sun will ever shine again."

"I know. Me, too. I'm recallin' the story for both of us, but trust that even in the storm, I love you, and will do whatever I can to protect you. Here we are," he said, brightly, "we've come to the wee village."

In the clearing nested half a dozen simple cottages, a few sheds, a large communal garden and fenced-in areas for animals.

"Not exactly a village, Silas. More like a compound."

"The O'Braoins, Finnans and Higgins would disagree with you."

Two small boys, twins by the looks of it, tumbled out of one of the cottages and raced toward them.

"Silas! You're back!" they exclaimed. "Mum's washin' clothes, but she will be happy to see you."

"Where's your Da?" Silas asked, tousling their curly black heads.

"Gone after the soldiers," said one boy, proudly.

"They was here a little while ago," said the other, chancing a glance at Briana, as she dismounted. "They was asking about the Mouse of Prophecy. Is that you, milady?"

Briana curtsied. "And so I am," she said, smiling, before giving Silas a more concerned look.

A noise turned everyone's attention to the doorway of the dwelling. where a woman stood with an arm of wet clothing and a fearful expression on her face. "Silas. Happy I am to see you, but you're not safe here." She turned to Briana. "Milady," she said, with an over-weighted dip. Briana nodded and reached to help her with the clothing.

"Oh, no, milady." The woman dropped the bundle in a basket by the door and wiped her hands on her skirt. Loud barking interrupted the greeting and a hound nearly as large as Dara bounded around the corner and jumped on Silas, knocking him back a step.

"Down, Oision," he commanded, pushing the dog back.

Briana watched the happy chaos, wistful for such a simple, homely life. *Oh, to be the wife of a minstrel and not a king. To spend days growing vegetables, washing clothes, cooking meals for a family...*

Her reverie was broken by Silas' introductions. "Máire, this is Lady Briana. Milady, Máire O'Braoin and her boys Garrit and Glendon."

"I'm pleased to meet you, Mrs. O'Braoin," Briana said, politely.

The woman produced a hurried smile and nod. "But, Silas, truly, you can't stay. Lord Shamwa's men were here not two hours ago. We sent them north. Malachy has gone the other direction to alert the king's men along the river."

"That's where we're headed, too," he told her, "but Lady Briana needs some proper clothin'. The dress is a bit cumbersome for the travels we take." His look said he knew the danger they were in.

Máire took in Briana's appearance and ushered her into the cottage. The woman wasted no time in producing a pair of trousers and tunic from her apparently not very large husband. While Briana changed, Máire dug around a trunk and produced a pair of boots, which were a bit too big for her feet. Briana waved off the woman's consternation and focused her mind on the boots becoming smaller. Almost imperceptibly, they shrunk to exactly the size Briana needed.

"You've got magic!" Máire whispered in awe.

"A bit," Briana affirmed. "It seems to be there when I need it, anyway."

After a brief pause, the woman scuttled around, pulling bread and meat together in a bundle, which she handed to Briana. "You'll have to eat on the run, but at least you'll have something for your bellies."

"Thank you so much, Mrs. O'Braoin, for the clothes and food. And please, thank your husband for taking the risk to warn our troops."

"I will, ma'am. I pray that you and the king will be able to stop the terror we've been under for so long."

Briana nodded. "We'll do our best."

When they went back outside, warrior-queen Briana met an approving smile from Silas, who was watering Aldebaran at a trough and talking with several people from the other families living in the "village."

He made brief introductions with an apology for their abrupt departure. The tenants offered bits of advice and encouragement for the journey ahead. After a warm hug to the O'Braoin boys and thank you to their mother, he swung into the saddle and assisted Briana up behind him.

"Feel better?"

"Much."

Then they were off again, on high alert for the danger they knew was "lurkin' about." They rode through a mature forest of old oaks, tall ashes and old tangled yews. Up ahead she could see younger trees and some evergreens among the ancients, with an occasional thicket of rowans, the scrubby kind that was more bush than tree. Silas pointed to the rowans.

If you need to hide, go in the rowans. They provide good cover, but you won't get tangled up in them if you're chased.

Briana nodded, sobered by his warning. After a few moments, she asked, *Should we tie up our hair?*

Good idea. He stopped Aldebaran. Briana hastily knotted his hair and then secured her own.

They heard the battle before they saw anything: blood-curdling war cries, screams of pain and rage, metal clanging against metal as swords and axes met. "An arrow," Silas prompted, and she pulled one out and passed it to him. He reined in Aldebaran, picked up his bow and nocked the arrow. He looked at her. "You have no weapon."

She shrugged. "I'll find one."

He looked worried. She shook her head. "Don't. We'll do the best we can."

With that, they raced through the trees into an open meadow and utter chaos. Expecting a staggering imbalance between the Gray Military and their own army, she was stunned by the number of men who now fought for Uisneach. The noise was deafening, the ground littered with a tangled mess of blood and bone. The overwhelming stench made Briana's eyes water.

Off to their left, on the meadow's western edge, a large rock outcropping near a few scattered pines and a thicket of rowan would provide good cover. Two more outcroppings directly ahead of them, one almost due north, the other off to the right a bit.

See that opening in the woods over there? Silas asked, gesturing with his chin to the northwest. *That's the way to Ard Darach.*

With more fighting to the west, Briana thought it would be safer to take the long way around, using the two boulder piles as cover. She was about to suggest that to Silas when a group of Grays over to the west shifted, revealing Captain O'Rourke.

A Gray head-butted the captain and rocked him back on his heels. Briana grimaced. The captain rolled out of the way as the soldier's broadsword stabbed the earth where he had lain dazed a split second before.

There! Straight ahead! said Silas.

Heavy fighting in the center of the field kept her from seeing whatever it was that Silas had pointed out for several minutes. Then a man dropped to the ground, and she saw Sigel fighting a Gray.

"He's got Nuada!" she exclaimed.

Silas gestured toward some bushy rowan trees off to their right, not far ahead. "Wait in there, and I'll get your sword."

She swung down and scrambled into the thicket, which obstructed her view, but hid her from the enemy. Though frustrated, she promised herself she'd wait a full five minutes before figuring out a way to join the battle. She was just about to leave her hiding place when Silas spoke. She tore her way out and gripped Nuada's hilt as he handed it to her. Instant heat and strength traveled up her arm and through her body, settling in her core.

"She's glad to be reunited," Silas said, as the shimmer of energy raced down the sword into Briana. When it settled, he gave her the shield. "I can't find Jonathan or Dara, but Sigel says they're here somewhere."

"What about Epona?"

"She's over there." He pointed north, near the middle rock outcropping and a large pine tree. Again, Briana had to wait for a break in the battle to spot Epona, who was holding her own against a soldier twice her size. Silas gave a command to Aldebaran, who stepped away and stood quietly. *Follow me*, he said, circling around to the right, just as she thought they would. Pulling Briana between two pines, he said, "Stay behind me. We'll keep a position here for as long as we can. Watch me back, aye?"

She nodded, raising Nua to protect him. Silas released arrows with rapid-fire precision. Several men dropped, grabbed limbs, screamed or just fell instantly dead. There was horrible beauty in his skill; she thanked Maker he was on her side. Briana scanned the battlefield and the surrounding woods for her young protector.

"Damn it," Silas swore, throwing his empty quiver on the ground, "I'm out of arrows. We've got to use swords." He gave her a concerned look. "We've no choice, darlin'; I can't leave you unprotected and I can't stay out of this. We fight together. Ready?"

"Absolutely," she said with more conviction than she felt. "I beat the lord marshall, remember? I can do this."

"Aye, you can," he agreed, sounding less convinced than she. His battle yell chilled her as together, they flew into the conflict. Sword swinging, he connected with a man on either side of him, taking one's head clean off and creating an abdominal gash in the other that would surely send his soul to hell before the end of the day. She copied his example with less precision, but fortunately, fewer targets. Nua's magic saved her more than a few times. With gore flying all around her, and worry over her comrades consuming her, it took all her presence of mind to continue the search for Jonathan.

Instead, she found Sigel, spattered in the red, brown and gray muck of battle, up against two beefy, screeching men. Briana reacted instinctively. Leaving the protection of Silas' sword, she snuck up behind them and plunged Nua into the back of the one trying to run a dagger through Sigel. Shrieking like a banshee, the wounded man gyrated in her direction, close enough to tear a slice in her forearm. Wincing at the sting of the slight flesh wound, she ducked to give Sigel the opportunity to embed his blade into the wounded giant. Sigel kicked the man loose to the ground while simultaneously ducking underneath the axe of the other man. In a pirouette that would honor the most prima of ballerinas, he came around the soldier's rear, stole his weapon and cut him off at the knees with his own sword.

"Thanks, Briana, now get the hell out of here!" he shouted, fiercely, but there was no mistaking the look of relief in his eyes at seeing her in one piece.

For a second, she was tempted to head toward Epona, but the other rocks were closer, and she had to keep herself safe. Without her, they'd fail. Briana sprinted for all she was worth, her heart pounding. Once safely behind the rocks, she had a moment to think. *What's the best thing I can do here? Magic*, she thought, *but I've never done a protection spell before. It can't be that hard, right?* Not daring to close her eyes, she imagined the battlefield as a real-time *ríocht* board, with each one of the king's men moving through with a veil of protection over them. *Let safety surround us and justice guide us. Let our swords swing true and evil be turned away. May it be so.* She had no idea if the words would help or not, nor if the protection would last for more than a few minutes, but she allowed them to flow through her mind along with a silver light surrounding Sigel, Silas, Epona and all the others, so dear to her. Except one, whom she could not find anywhere.

Where are you, Mr. Stark?

A familiar bark caught her attention. Dara stood near the rock formation across the field, to the west. She covered him in protection, as well. *Had he found Jonathan? Was the poor boy injured? Why had she let Sigel convince her to bring him along? He was only a child! Back in her time, they'd call this a war crime, forcing a child to be a soldier.* Briana couldn't stand it. Taking a deep breath, she advanced through the melee toward the dog, praying she'd find Jonathan, too.

Waylaid by several Grays, she was relieved that no matter how hard they tried, their weapons did not penetrate her enchantment. At least for a time. The skirmish waged on around her, forcing her to deflect and counterattack repeatedly, while attempting, with little success, to revive the enchantment.

A deep growl alerted her to danger. A bullish man was coming at her on a dead run, axe swinging, murderous intention blazoned on his face. She raised her shield in defense, but had no time to respond. A flash of curly blonde hair swooped in front of her. Jonathan Stark screamed, his battle cry boyishly high-pitched, as he flew at the giant with his small weapon.

"Jonathan!" Briana screamed as the huge axe came down on the boy and he fell. Dara soared over her head. She shrank from a spray of blood. The hulking monster took a few more steps before he also fell, in a heap at her feet, with Dara's teeth sunk into his neck. She had no idea whose blood covered her, or who was dead and who alive. "Back, Dara," she yelled, as she shoved Nua into her trousers, tucked her shield under her arm, and began pulling Jonathan toward a copse of rowan trees beyond the rocks. Dara, for the first time ever, ignored her command and took the boy's shirt in his mouth, helping Briana pull him out of the fight. Three men from the Ratskillen contingent formed a protective barrier between them and the combat. They made their way through the young trees to a group of dense bushes. Once safely hidden, she rolled the boy over on his back. A sharp gash bled down the side of his face, horrible, but not life-threatening. More worrisome was the bump on his head and the fact that he was not conscious.

"Jonathan, wake up!" She lightly slapped at his good cheek a couple of times before his eyes fluttered open. He tried to sit up, but his eyes lolled back and he sank back down.

"Got to go back and help," he moaned.

"You'll help best, Mr. Stark, by staying still. You saved my life – there's nothing more for you to do."

The young man smiled dreamily. She wished she had ice to put on the rapidly swelling contusion and worried that this would progress to a more serious brain injury.

Briana, where the hell are you?

In the woods with Jonathan, behind the big rocks on the western edge. I think I need some help here.

On my way. Don't move!

Waiting wasn't an option. The boy needed help now. Hearing the sound of a brook, she poked around the copse until she found it, only about fifty feet from where he lay unconscious. A few scraggly bushes along the bank would offer a bit of cover. If she could drag Jonathan there, she could position his head in the cold water, which might help. She glanced at the slice on her arm and shook her head with both relief and irritation. It was nothing, but she washed it and tore a piece of cloth from her tunic to tie around it, to prevent infection.

Briana went back to the boy and looked through the trees at the field at the fighting, which raged on with no sign of stopping. Sigel looked to be making a good dent in the number of combatants they had to deal with. Silas was fighting his way through to her, but by the looks of it, it would take him longer than she wanted to wait. No bad guys were paying attention to the woods. *If the protection spell lasts, I could probably do this myself.* Briana stared at Jonathan thoughtfully. *Was there a better way to move him?* This time, she laid her shield on top of the boy's chest and Nua on top of it. *Close enough to reach, if necessary, and she wouldn't have to drop her shield to draw Nua.*

"Dara, do you think you could help me drag him again?" She motioned the dog next to her, and he gently took the boy's shirt in his mouth. Slowly, vigilant for trouble, they hauled Jonathan to the brook, where she positioned his head in the water to relieve the swelling. His eyes opened intermittently. She kept talking to him, trying unsuccessfully to keep him awake. She also visualized his healing, imagining the bump reducing and the gash closing. Briana cleansed the slice on his cheek and realized it would heal fine without stitches but would leave a nice scar, one he would no doubt be proud of, as a symbol of his bravery in saving the queen. She studied him, her heart full of love for this man-child, and prayed she would have the chance to see him grow to manhood. Clashing swords and resounding screams echoed in her head, but she remained focused on Jonathan.

A lone combatant stumbled into the copse. She settled into a ready stance and raised Nua to strike. He didn't see her at first, seemed more concerned with running from the fight than searching for any of the king's men. He looked shocked when he saw her, then afraid.

"As well you should be, traitor," she said.

Without preamble he ran at her, sloppily swiping his sword in her direction. Nua responded, its energy coursing into Briana's body as the full length of the blade glowed. One fierce arc with Nua took his head and ended his treachery. Briana twisted aside in time to miss most of the jetting fountain of blood from the bloody stump atop his shoulders. The body dropped in front of her. Briana stared, amazed and sickened by what she'd just done.

"Sweet Maker, woman, why can't you ever just follow directions?" Silas asked, as he rushed to her side, his sword pointed at where the man's head would have been. "Did I, or did I not, tell you to wait?"

"Couldn't," she said, breathlessly. "Needed to get Jonathan to this brook. You... were... busy." She looked grimly at the mangled corpse in front of her. "I hate doing that."

"Aye, well, I'm glad you did." He looked over at Jonathan. "He's not..."

"He's alive, but probably has a concussion." Noting Silas' look of ignorance, she started to explain the effects of blunt-force trauma to the brain. "Never mind," she said, realizing they didn't have time for a first aid lesson. "He'll be fine."

"And what about your arm?"

"Just a scrape."

As they were talking, the boy began to moan and opened his eyes again. "Milady, are you all right?" He sat up, hair dripping.

"I'm fine, sir. You, on the other hand, took an awful whack to the head." She moved next to him and examined the area, pleased to find the knobby bump somewhat reduced.

"I'm sorry I didn't stop them from kidnapping you. It's all my fault." He ran a hand through his hair and winced when he came in contact with the tender lump.

"Nonsense. We were all paralyzed by his spell; there was nothing you could have done. Anyway, in this ruckus, you actually did save my life, and got hurt in the process. I'll thank you for that later."

With a contented grin, he fell back, closed his eyes and slipped back into oblivion.

"Don't you need to get back out there?" she asked Silas.

"I'm to guard you."

While he was her front line of defense, she and Dara were Jonathan's.

Briana positioned herself, Nua in hand, between him and Silas. Two Uisneach men joined Silas and made a three-point guard around her and the boy.

"Really, Silas, I can handle this. You ought to be out there with the others."

"We are..."

A cacophony of cawing cut off his reply. Overhead, the sun was temporarily obliterated by a black cloud of whirring wings, hundreds of crows. Briana and Silas followed their trajectory over the field. They began transforming in the midst of landing. With this reinforcement, the Gray Military was now outnumbered, and the skirmish that had been raging for hours ended in minutes. Across the field lay a masterpiece of destruction. There would be no prisoners to worry about.

More disturbing and hard to comprehend was the sudden re-shifting of the crows into their avian form, followed quickly by a carnivorous frenzy. She turned to Silas, wobbling a little. "Are they..."

"They dispose of the carrion," was all he said, turning her away from the grisly scene.

Before she could dwell on that, their own wounded staggered toward them. A few men showed up with cuts and scrapes. After determining that Jonathan was stable, she riffled through an abandoned pack for supplies. Briana tended as best she could to the others, cleaning and applying salve to their wounds. She lost track of time as she worked.

"He's the last," said Silas, helping a young man who wasn't much older than Jonathan toward her. He had a gash across his shoulder.

"It needs stitching," she told him, "but we'll have to make do with a bandage." She did her best to bind the edges together with a clean cloth and sling the arm, adding a dose of healing visualization as she worked.

"Thank ye, milady. That'll do just fine."

"At least until we reach the castle. I do want you to see Cailleach at some point. She can sew it up for you. Any men unaccounted for?" she asked.

"Not as many of ours were killed. Only a handful."

"Good, then. Well done," she said, not knowing what else to say in this situation. One loss of life was too great for her, but he sounded rather pleased with the outcome. "Have a drink and find somewhere to rest until we leave again." He offered her a smile and something akin to a thumbs-up sign, and went off to recover.

He was replaced with a shorter man in a bloodied kilt. "I believe, milady," he said, with a huge smile, "that you are wearing me clothes."

She looked down at her borrowed outfit and back at him, finding her own wide smile. "You must be Malachy O'Braoin."

The small, wiry man bowed so low his head nearly swept the ground. "At your service, and I must say, me clothes look better on you than they do on meself."

She laughed and noted how absurd that sounded on the edge of a battlefield. "Thank you, Mr. O'Braoin, for the clothes. I would've hated to do what I've been doing in a dress."

Epona came through the trees, unharmed, leading Aquila and Banrion. Throwing an arm around Briana, she greeted her with a kiss on the cheek. "I'm so relieved to see you, Briana. What the hell happened?"

"It's a long story, but I'm okay, and happy to see you, as well."

Sigel entered the copse with Orion and Andromeda. He was bloody, his shirt torn, his face lined with fatigue. He tossed the reins to Malachy and put a hand out to stop Briana from going to her mare. "You," he said, roughly, "and you," he said, pointing to Silas, "with me."

"Which part of that sounds like I'm a queen?" she mumbled to Silas under her breath.

He's misunderstood the situation. I think this is where we have to tell him about our gift.

She asked Epona to stay with Jonathan and followed Silas to confront their moment of reckoning.

The lord marshall led them away from the brook. Briana adopted an innocent demeanor.

"I'm glad you're okay, Sigel. You had your hands full out there."

"Aye, and I still do," he grumbled. "Either, or both of you, care to tell me what you've been about? In particular, Silas, I'm curious where you've been since you disappeared from your post."

"I did not 'disappear.' The men knew I was going to help you find Briana."

Sigel's eyes narrowed to slits. "Really? I don't recall giving you that order, nor did I ever see you arrive at our side to 'help.' Instead, the two of you arrive here, alone."

"He saved me, Sigel." Raising an accusatory finger to his face, she went on. "Perhaps you'd care for some facts before you continue making assumptions. Fact one, you saw my abduction. I was taken to Aurum Castle. Fact two…"

"You were in Aurum Castle? With Shamwa?" Panic streaked across his face. "Sweet Maker, what did he do to you?"

"He didn't do anything to me, though he was about to, when I escaped." She paused. "You should probably sit down for this. It's a long story." She sat on a flat boulder and Sigel leaned against one, beside her. Silas sat against a nearby oak. She related the sequence of events, ending with Silas pulling her out of the river and tending to her needs.

Silas finished the story of getting her to Shannon Abbey and all that transpired there. "I'm certain the abbess is up to something wicked."

"It will hurt Cailleach terribly, if she is," Briana said, wondering how she could break the news to the witch.

Sigel was quiet. Cocking his head at Silas, he finally asked, "How did you know where to find Briana?"

Well, a mhuirnin, *here it is. Time to come clean about this.*

Briana nodded.

"It's like this, Sigel. Briana and I are able to talk to each other in our heads." He let that statement sink in for a moment. "She can think something, or say something without words, and I can hear her. It's the same with her when I'm…"

"I get it," Sigel interrupted. "How long?"

"Have we been able to do it? Since Cailleach's. Maybe before, but that's when we realized it."

"And you didn't think you should tell anyone?"

Briana sat straight up. "We considered it, but you know, Sigel, some things really are none of your business. I decided," she said, taking the onus for the decision until Silas gave her a cockeyed look, "*we* decided that should it ever be necessary for you to know, we would tell you. Otherwise, our thoughts and conversations are our own. Today's the day it becomes necessary for you to know."

"Does Cailleach know?"

"No," she replied.

No one said a word. A blue jay screeched overhead, making Briana jump. She and Silas shared a look.

Finally, Sigel stood away from the boulder and turned to Silas. "So you know everything she's thinking and feeling?"

Silas nodded.

"Well, that is going to be damned uncomfortable on her wedding night, isn't it?"

Briana's hand flew to her chest.

With that, Sigel walked away. A minute later, his voice boomed through the forest. "Make camp, men. Tomorrow morning we take the castle and rescue the king."

❧

Cheerful banter rippled among the troops the next morning as they struck camp. Not that there was much to do: they had no tents, just bedrolls to put away, and campfires to douse. Most of their battle gear, other than their personal weapons, was still at the castle, caught by the enchantment – a problem that would be solved today, Sigel said. The crow soldiers continued to guard the perimeter, as they had through the night. *They're perfect guards*, Briana thought, *able to shift in a moment and fly away when necessary, strong and skilled on the battlefield.*

Magic had served them well in this battle. Unlike Lord Shamwa, she was very grateful for it.

Briana tightened the girth on Banrion, watching covertly over the horse's back to where Sigel, looking tired and concerned, was having a conversation with Silas. She couldn't hear their words and couldn't read Silas's mind, but it was evidently a tense discussion, with Sigel doing most of the talking and Silas nodding, while looking mostly at the ground. Then Silas said something that made Sigel look away. When he looked back, he placed a hand on the bard's shoulder. Silas broke contact and walked back toward Briana, joined a moment later by Sigel.

What was that about?

Nothin'. At Briana's disbelieving look, he added, *Just tyin' up a few loose ends.*

His evasion troubled her but Sigel was already giving the order to move out. She sighed, slipped the reins over Banrion's head and mounted.

Silas moved to the front of the line. Sitting tall on Aldebaran, his voice rang out with conviction and pride,

"Rise up, O men, to save your king,

His banner we will fly.

Taranian! Taranian!

Our glad shout shall prevail.

Rise up, O King, and sleep no more,

Your queen is on her way.

A new day dawns, Uisneach restored,

Brave destiny fulfilled.

Will he rise?"

The men of the Uisneach army shouted of one accord, "Yes, he will."

"Will we bow?" Silas demanded.

"We will bow."

"For king and queen, we forward on!"

Epona moved to Briana's side, joined by Jonathan, who was a little wobbly, but otherwise no worse for wear. The swelling was nearly gone. He had a black eye, and what Epona called a "dashing scar," which made him blush and sit up straighter on his horse. Dara pranced around Banrion, who also seemed eager to go. Briana pasted on her best queenly smile and took her place behind Sigel. Silas, his bardic ritual done, fell in behind her, with a line of men forming behind him.

They didn't speak until they found a comfortable rhythm and were assured of safe passage. *Well, we begin a new chapter. I wonder what it will be like for us.*

I've been thinkin' about that. Sigel made a good point about how difficult it will be for us once you and Brath are a… couple.

She shivered in spite of the sun, already warm and promising a hot day.

I think it would be best if we tried to create some kind of wall in our minds to prevent our knowin' what each other is thinkin' once we reach Ard Darach.

Her eyes narrowed. The thought of not having even this little bit of intimacy with her best friend and confidant made her heart pound. But he was right. Sigel was right. She was going to be married, and whatever that meant, she would not have it hurt Silas for anything. It was time to cut the cord. Grief spiraled through her, but she fought against it. She met his searching eyes.

This is what Sigel was talking to you about, isn't it?

Yes. He wondered if we could control the gift.

"Gift?" she said bitterly. "You call this a gift?"

"What are you talking about?" asked Epona.

Sigel also looked back.

"Nothing." Briana shuddered at the misery evident on his own face.

It is a gift, mo chroi, *but one that comes with a cost.*

A very high price. She tightened her grip on the reins when Banrion stumbled over a root. *When do we have to stop? And how?*

I think we can do it the same way you made the wall against Mother Ealga. She sighed. *Briana, I will always be there if you need me. If somethin' happens to either of us, I believe we'll know it, but it won't be fair to anyone if we continue this way. You can't have three people in your marriage.*

She stared at the ground.

He turned silent and she thought for a panicked second that he had already shut her down.

As to the when — let's agree that the minute he takes your hand is when we put the wall up. Fair?

She nodded. Turning forward, she found Sigel once again watching her. She stared back, giving away nothing of her inner turmoil. She was a queen, not a heartsick teenager, and she would conquer the emotions that tightened her throat and brought tears much too close to the surface. *I need is something else to focus on.*

Inspiration was found in the happy faces of the men who marched to their beloved king. Men who had left home and hearth to get her safely to this destination, who were ready to lay down their lives for Uisneach and the Taranians. She couldn't let them down. She couldn't let the faerie kingdom down. She couldn't let Sigel and Cailleach down. But most of all, she couldn't let Silas down. This moment, her support, and a promise to save his kingdom, was all she could give him.

When she was able to meet his eyes once more, they were filled with determination and valor. She smiled at him.

Thank you, a mhuirnin.

It seemed as though they had been on the march for only a short time, though the sun said otherwise. They passed two sparkling blue lakes with green grassy banks. They were close in size, nearly identical.

"Nice place for a picnic," she commented, trying to sound cheerful.

"There have been many such gatherings at Mirror Lakes," Sigel said, wistfully. "I hope there will be again."

When they came to a clearing, Sigel halted them. "Men," he said, then looking at Briana and Epona, added, "and ladies, when we go around that rock," he nodded toward a massive boulder, "we will be at Ard Darach. Maker willing, we will rescue the king!"

His announcement was met with a wave of cheers which came to a sudden halt when they heard whirring overhead. Two fantastically large birds flew just over the tree tops. She recognized the hawk as Merlin, large as a dragon, and gasped when she saw Cailleach stretched out atop him. She looked at the second bird, and then at Silas. "Sir Thomas, I presume."

He grinned and nodded.

The closer she got to the rock, the higher her hackles rose. She stole one last look at Silas.

We knew all along that this was our destiny, he said. *For the sake of this land we both love, we must finish it. Our love will survive whatever happens. Our bodies may be separated by circumstances, but nothin' can touch what lives in our souls. Nothin'.* He wrapped his hand around the warrior's hearts she had given him. *You are, and always will be,* a sonuachar, *my soul spouse, and I am yours. Come,* mo chroi, *let's go together and save Uisneach.*

And so they did. Standing tall, they walked out of the hills toward Ard Darach and King Brath, yielding destiny the victory.

CHAPTER THIRTY-ONE

ARD DARACH

The path wound down out of the hills. Hours later, it opened up to a vast plain at the edge of the sea, giving Briana her first view of Ard Darach. To the north was a knoll, upon which some ruins and an old tower stood. The castle rose impenetrable out of the cliffs, its back protected by the ocean and treacherous cliffs that surged up from the crashing waves. The structure was massive and beautiful, reminiscent of castles she'd seen in Ireland, only newer, its stone gleaming white in the early afternoon light. A tributary of the Long River ran across the front of the castle, forming its moat. A short drawbridge led to the gatehouse. From her high vantage point, she saw three yards: the nearest was the largest; beyond that, a smaller yard in front of the keep; and farthest away, in front of the great hall, a fairly good-sized courtyard. Smaller towers guarded the corners of the castle, and several buildings, including a stable and animal pens, were contained inside its grounds. Behind the castle was a narrow band of what she assumed were the gardens "too long untended," as Sigel had told her. Scraggly vines overran the space, creating a natural barrier between the castle and the ocean just beyond. Outside the thick walls of the fortress nestled a half-dozen cottages, a smithy shed, a mill and a few other buildings for the support of the castle.

All of that held fast under the enchantment, an unnatural clear light that surrounded the castle like some otherworldly fish bowl. Artanin's sorcery.

Competing emotions warred within her as she stared at Ard Darach, the end point of this horrible, wonderful, dangerous and exciting journey.

"Your new home," Silas said.

"Home or prison?" His hurt look prompted a wave of guilt over her bitterness. His blue eyes shone, no doubt partly from the same sorrow she felt, but also because this was his home, filled with happy memories, and after ten long years, he would finally enter its walls and be reunited with a man whom he loved dearly. "I'm sorry, Silas. I'm just…"

"Tired and scared. I understand. I am too, but we'll get through this."

She rubbed her neck and took a deep breath. "Well, are we going down or not?" she asked Sigel, who stared at Ard Darach with a pensive expression.

He shifted in his saddle. "Fan out, men!" The line of troops moved around them and marched down the slope, automatically spreading out to line the perimeter of the field. When only Sigel, Epona, Silas, Jonathan and Briana remained, Sigel gave a nod to Silas. "You three go on down. I want a minute with Briana."

She frowned. *Now what?*

When they were alone, he said, "This has been a hard journey for you, Briana."

"It's about to get harder."

He gave a slight nod. "Which is why I want to know what you're thinking."

"Afraid I'll bolt or embarrass you?"

"No. But you're exhausted, physically and emotionally, and I need to be sure you're up to this. We need your magic. We need you totally focused."

She ground her teeth. The worn-out little girl in her wanted to kick, scream, pout… anything, but give him what he needed. Her inner queen responded with a determined nod.

He took a moment to steady Orion. When the stallion calmed, he continued. "If I thought this wouldn't work out, that you would be miserable as our queen, I would take you back to Wellsland myself. But, Briana, I know you. And I know Brath, and I honestly think you can be happy here. Right now, you're tired and can't see past your loss, but…"

"I will never stop loving Silas," she said, quietly, watching her fingers work the reins.

"I know. But I also believe you'll find something in Brath that's worthy of your respect, and perhaps even affection. This may be more of a gift than you can imagine at the moment. But first, we have to release this damn curse and wake him up."

Raising her eyes, she said, with total conviction, "I will focus and I will do my part to wake him up, but know this, Sigel: I do it for Uisneach and for Evalon, not for a single man."

"Fair enough. I'm happy to let time take care of the rest."

The men down below had grown quiet. Sigel and Briana stood where they were, silent for the moment. The sound of a crow and a hawk echoed in Briana's consciousness. "They're waiting for us," she said, sitting tall and taking a full breath. "We should go. I'm ready."

"Briana, there's one more thing I want to say to you. I realize I've been hard on you. Getting you ready for this moment had to be done fast. But, I want you to know that I…"

Whatever he meant to say ended with a shout and the rattling of swords. Both their heads swung up to see the crow land atop the glassy bubble over Ard Darach, just in front of the castle's drawbridge. Merlin landed on the ground near them. Cailleach slid off Merlin, who then shifted down to his normal size and took his roost on her shoulder.

Sigel and Briana rode down into the field. Sigel waved at Silas to follow him and ordered the men to stay in formation around the castle. Epona and Jonathan stayed back with the Uisneach army. The five druids, Sigel, Briana, Silas, Cailleach, and Sir Thomas, gathered together.

"What do we do next?" Sigel asked.

Cailleach answered. "Sir Thomas and I have concluded that we need to form a circle around the castle, with Sir Thomas at the top of the keep. Then we point our medallions, along with our magic, toward his. We think our combined energy will act like a ley line and break the curse."

Briana pressed her hand to her forehead and sighed.

"What is it, Briana?" Cailleach asked, concerned.

"Nothing. I just somehow thought it would be more complicated, more dramatic. This seems a bit anticlimactic."

Cailleach looked from her to Sigel, confused. "Why would you want it to be harder?"

"She'll be fine," he said, before directing everyone to their places.

Sir Thomas flew back to his perch at the top of the keep. The other four druids moved to the corners, with Sigel on the northeast side of the cliffs and Briana on the northwest corner. Silas took Cailleach to the southern cliff side before moving back to the western tower.

Once everyone was in place, they aimed their medallions at the crow. From the keep came a loud caw. Briana envisioned Brath released from the enchantment. She imagined the light fading and Ard Darach returning to its usual activity. At first, nothing happened. A steady vibration rumbled deep in her body as the meridian lines of their intention connected the medallions. The imprisoning shield wavered, but didn't break. She took another breath and went deeper, assuming the problem was her resistance.

Briana was jerked out of the meditation by a much louder caw, a distinct warning.

"Get down, Briana!"

She leaned low over Banrion's neck as two arrows whizzed over her head toward the hill behind her. The arrows connected with a lone figure at the summit, cloaked in brown, holding out his hands toward the castle as if blessing it. One arrow lodged in his shoulder, but did nothing to stop his prayerful pose. The second hit him in the leg. The druid went down momentarily, but rose again, hands still pointed. Like a comet, Sigel charged across the field toward the hill, both hands on his weapon.

Before Artanin could run or hide, Sigel was on him. The two men battled, one with magic, the other, a sword.

"Stop!" Briana yelled, calling up all the magic she had inside her. She used it to push the men apart. Artanin fell back, even as Sigel fought to break through her barrier.

Spurring Banrion into action, she sprinted toward the hill, with Silas right behind her. "Stop in the name of King Brath of the House of Taranian!" she commanded.

All movement and sound halted. Banrion slid to a stop in front of the two men, who were held apart by her thin conjuring. Briana jumped down and stood between Sigel and Artanin, releasing her focus and the magic.

Realizing the barrier was down, Sigel put his hands on her shoulders, clearly intending to move her out of the way so he could tackle the druid.

"No!" she said. "I am ordering you not to kill him, Sigel. He helped me escape Aurum Castle, and I want to know why."

Nostrils flaring, Sigel stared at Briana, then nodded. "As you command, my lady," he said, "but we will bind him and keep him prisoner."

She agreed, and turned to Artanin. "Can you release the spell?"

"I was trying to do that, but something is blocking it."

Sigel made a disbelieving noise under his breath.

"Then we will release it as we meant to, with the medallions. Have him taken... wherever you take prisoners in Ard Darach, once we remove the fish bowl."

"The fish bowl?" Sigel asked.

"The spell," she clarified.

Sigel turned back to Artanin. "This is what mercy looks like, druid. Count your blessings but do it fast. I'm not convinced we'll yet let you live. Silas, bring me a rope. And call up a handful of soldiers."

When Artanin was secured and removed from the hill by a contingent of Uisneach men, Sigel, Briana and Silas went back down to join Cailleach and Sir Thomas at the castle.

"Let's try this again," Sigel said. "I have no idea what we're going to find inside, so be prepared for anything."

A new and troubling thought occurred to Briana. Everyone inside the castle was in a state of suspended animation. Once freed from the curse, would they grow a decade older in a matter of seconds? What would that do to them?

"No matter what we see or hear, our first priority is to get to the king," said Sigel.

Briana's stomach lurched, but she nodded in agreement.

"Everyone to their corners," Sigel instructed.

As Silas headed off to his post, she turned to him with hopeful eyes. *Last chance to run away with me?*

I would if I could, Briana.

Briana and Sigel took their positions and started the process again. This time, the energy was palpable, and a definite shift began in the wall around the castle. A sharp flash from their medallions raced to the highest point on the keep. Remembering what Cailleach had taught her, Briana used all her might to envision the force field waning, imagined it as a fluid collection of molecules receding from the ground up, replaced by a new vitality in the air around the stronghold. The trees, silent for a decade, took their first resuscitative breaths and stirred in the light breeze. Chickens cackled and sheep blatted inside the walls. She held focus until Sigel called her back.

"We did it, Briana," he said, in a deadpan voice. The others gathered. Sir Thomas transformed into a human. There were no exclamations of victory; too much had been sacrificed to feel triumphant. Silas moved away to brief the men who came forward with Artanin between them.

"What comes next?" she asked, forcing herself to remain calm.

"I need to instruct the men," said Sigel. "Then we go in and introduce you to Brath."

As she waited, Briana wondered what they'd find inside the walls. *Will people be happy? Frightened? Confused? Will we even find anyone alive?*

Sigel had Artanin taken away, to be locked up. Men came out of nowhere, and were given swift orders that made no real sense to Briana. With Dara at her side, she followed Sigel, Cailleach and Sir Thomas through the portcullis, where they were joined by Silas, Epona and Jonathan. Briana couldn't hear anything over the sound of her heart pounding and her breathing echoing off thick stone walls that swallowed her into their shadows. She fought to control the burgeoning hysteria that threatened to overwhelm her. *No turning back*, a voice taunted her, from inside her own head.

Every step she took felt heavy and everything around her seemed to move in slow motion. Two uniformed guards yawned sleepily, then snapped to attention when Sigel passed by. Under an archway, Briana walked into a green yard edged by small cottages. Cutting across the grass, they walked through another gateway into a middle yard where a handful of youths were gaping at each other's grown-up bodies and shouting gleefully. Their voices sounded muted, as though coming from a long distance.

Cailleach glanced at her as they entered another gated postern, into the heart of Ard Darach. Briana's knees wobbled as she passed the great hall. The keep soared into the heavens across the yard.

The rampart, the defensive wall that enclosed the castle, reminded her of a supersized New England stone wall. Its parapet, the notched railing along the walkway on the top of the rampart, offered protection for guards, evenly spaced stone barriers they could duck behind. Squared off at the top with gaps between them, they looked a bit like the teeth people carved into jack-o'-lanterns. These thoughts came and passed in her mind without raising the slightest smile.

She heard Sigel tell a handful of men to spread the word that the curse was broken before returning to meet with the king. Men and women, teenaged boys and girls, wandered around, asking what happened. The rescuers told a few people, who went out to tell the rest.

A cobblestone walkway ringed the space. Sidestepping a cricket, she arrived with her companions at a large wooden door, where a rabbit stood poised as a guard. It said, "Don't be afraid, milady. You're right on time."

Unable to respond or move, Briana just stared until the rabbit hopped aside. Sigel watched her, his scar standing out vividly against his flushed skin. She wondered if she was the only one who saw the animal. Sigel turned back and lifted the latch on the door. She felt Silas' hand warm against her lower back and turned, surprised to find one of his hands on his sword and the other clenched at his side.

It's all right, a mhuirnin. *I've got you.*

She nodded and followed single file behind Cailleach and Sir Thomas up a narrow, winding staircase that opened into a darkened space. Her eyes adjusted as two servants began lighting rushes along the wall, casting shadowy light across an expansive room with vaulted ceiling. Tapestries and banners of the kingdoms of Uisneach hung on the walls and from the curved oak rafters. She swallowed and licked lips that had gone dry. Against one wall stood an ornately carved throne raised two feet from the floor, and on the other side, a second dais, upon which an enormous wood table stretched out. On the floor, ringing the room, were enough tables to seat a hundred people, she guessed. The center was left open. *For dancing?*

A door, presumably to the family's quarters, creaked, and a short, rotund man emerged, blinking and stretching his stubby limbs like a comic ballerina warming up before a dance.

Oh, Maker, you cannot be so cruel. Briana's heart thudded as she considered this might be her future husband. *If this has all been a dream, now would be a very good time to wake up.*

Oh, no, Briana, Silas reassured her. *That is the king's chamberlain, Emmett Ryan.* Her shoulders sank down in relief. A moment later, another man stepped into the room. Sigel let out a sound that was both agonized and overjoyed. He took three large steps and wrapped his arms around him.

The air was supercharged, as it must have been when Dorothy, Toto and the house were whisked away to Oz. For several moments no one spoke. Rumpled hair and dazed expression notwithstanding, King Brath of the House of Taranian was exceedingly regal and incredibly handsome.

"Sigel?" His voice held a slight crackle from years of disuse, but still had a richness to it that wrapped around her like fine whiskey and a peat fire.

"Brath." Sigel said, not bothering to wipe the tears that spilled down his cheeks.

No. Oh, no. Briana sucked in her breath. Dizziness and nausea swept over her. If Silas was her soul, this man was her destiny. Brath was the man from her dream, the one who offered her the crown.

"There's your king, Briana," Silas said, softly.

"I suspect you'd like to know what's going on," Sigel said to Brath.

"That's an understatement."

Sigel explained the events of the past decade, and how this group came to the king's rescue, in fewer words that Briana thought possible. While he talked, Briana studied the man she was to marry. He was not hideous. All those women were right about that. Brath had hair the color of raw cinnamon that swept across his forehead and back from his temples. His dark, hazel eyes reflected a thoughtful intelligence. His angular face, long straight nose and strong cheekbones defined him as a warrior. A full, well-defined mouth and straight teeth would have been inviting to any other woman.

Sigel finished the tale. King Brath ran his hands through his hair. Then the king abruptly turned to Silas, who had been silent, and took him in a huge bear hug before holding him back and giving him a thorough inspection. "Silas, man, damn glad I am to see your pretty face! The ladies of the court will be swooning worse than they were before!" he said, ending the proclamation with a hearty back slap.

She closed her eye, wishing a sinkhole would open up and suck her in. When she opened them again, the King of Uisneach stood watching her with curiosity.

"Are you unwell, my lady?"

Something in the way he said "*my lady*" sent shivers over her body. Blood rushed to her head. Tears formed in her eyes. She couldn't speak. She couldn't control the trembling that had taken her insides hostage. There was no rainbow bridge to help her over this abyss.

You were made for this moment, said Silas. *You are brave enough and strong enough to see this through. You are the Queen of Uisneach.*

"My lady," King Brath said again, taking a step toward her.

She stepped back. "I'm fine," she said weakly. "Fine," she repeated, trying to convince herself, as much as anyone else.

"It's been a long journey, Your Highness," Sigel said. "Milady is perhaps a bit overwhelmed."

"Your Majesty," Cailleach said, stepping forward, her voice strong and indubitable. "May I present, Lady Briana, the Mouse of Prophecy."

Feeling detached from everything around her, she let him study her, the woman he'd just been told would be his wife.

Taking a deep breath, she lifted her eyes and met the king's. She reacted on instinct, stepping forward and meeting his eyes. "It is a privilege to meet you, Your Majesty," she said, offering the deepest, most perfect curtsy of her life.

Brath came forward and smiled as he reached for her hand to raise her up. "The pleasure is certainly mine," he answered, his eyes warm and genuine.

Too late, she realized this touch was the signal she and Silas had chosen to end their telepathy. She tried to pull away but the king's grip was firm. *No! Please, Silas, I'm not ready*. Nothing. His eyes were trained blankly on the couple before him, his face an unreadable mask.

"Lady Briana, I trust these gentlemen took good care of you."

An awkward silence hung over the company. Briana chose her words carefully. "I have never felt safer, Your Majesty. You can be proud of these men of Uisneach."

"Oh, I am proud of them," he said, beaming at his friends. When he turned back to her, his smile softened. "And I look forward to getting to know you, my lady, but unfortunately there are several things that need to be done…"

The door of the hall opened, admitting a man Briana recognized immediately by the color of his eyes: Jameson Stark. From behind her came a garbled noise. Jonathan's face had crumpled.

The older man stared as though at a ghost. "Oh, my Maker. Jonathan? Is it really you?"

"Father," was all the boy could choke out as he flew into his arms. As they hugged, she and Silas shared a tearful smile.

Things happened in rapid-fire succession. People poured into the hall. Brath began issuing orders to get things working again. She appreciated the kind but firm way in which he took control and was impressed with how much the people seemed to love him and want to please him. *Kind, but not weak. A nice balance for a monarch*, she thought, starting to regain a little of her equilibrium.

She and her companions were each assigned a servant and encouraged to rest before an early dinner. Sir Thomas would stay behind with Brath to discuss a few details of Briana's journey and her current needs, and then he and Epona would fly back to Winge Mansion.

"Assuming we have food to prepare for dinner." Brath laughed, the way only a ruler comfortable with having everything he needed all the time could.

Briana considered offering to help, then realized that not only was she exhausted and not fit for service, but she wouldn't have a clue what to do. Instead, she looked to Silas. His expression asked if she was okay.

Hell no, I'm not okay. If he received the message, he didn't let on. All she could do was sigh and try to communicate visually that she loved him and that this was killing her. Their momentary contact was broken by a slightly-built girl who volunteered to take her to her room.

"What shall I do with the hound?" she asked.

"This is Dara, and he stays with me." Briana looked to King Brath, not for permission but to make her position clear. The girl looked at the king also, uncertain of Briana's authority. He nodded and smiled kindly at both women.

"You heard Lady Briana, Gael. Dara stays with her."

Gael led her through a covered walkway to the guest rooms in the keep. Briana was relieved at the distance between her and the king, whose suite was located on a floor above the great hall. Jonathan peeled away toward the cottage he'd share with his father. Everyone was quiet as they walked the short distance to the keep. Sigel and Silas were shown to rooms on the first floor. Briana made a mental note of the location of Silas' room. She and Silas exchanged a weary, sad look before he shut the door behind him. She and Cailleach continued to the second floor. Briana's chamber was right above Silas', not in the least useful, yet comforting.

"Milady, why don't you wash up and take a rest while I go see what I can find for you to wear," said Gael Mulloy, her lady's maid. "You're the same size as Queen Eleanor, the king's mother. I'll come back in time to help you dress."

Here we go again, Briana thought. *Back to being cared for like a helpless baby.* "Gael, before you go, there are a few things we must discuss." She shared her wishes that she not be coddled or hovered over, and that it was perfectly fine for Gael to call her by her given name, at least in private. The girl looked dubious, but nodded. When she left, she said, "Rest well... milady."

Briana sighed, then turned her attention to exploring the room. Not a speck of dust rested on the small writing table. The canopied bed looked freshly made. *That spell certainly kept everything pristine*, she thought.

An armoire stood with the door ajar. Briana peeked in. Empty. Apparently, no one had been staying in this room when Artanin did his nasty deed. A weight of fatigue washed over her. *I came back from the dead. That's got to take something out of you!* After unbuckling Nua and settling Dara, she fell gratefully on top of the feather soft bed and was asleep before tears had time to catch up with her.

෴

Dusky afternoon light shadowed the room when Gael woke her, lighting candles as she spoke her name. Briana dressed in a simple green linen dress that had once belonged to Brath's mother. The floor-length gown was modestly cut, with embroidery on its long, wide sleeves and around the moderately scooped neckline.

Gael also produced soft gold slippers and a light cape. "You might wish it later." After combing out Briana's hair, she pronounced her ready.

A knock at the door set Briana's heart racing. It was only Cailleach, waiting to go down with her. "How are you?"

Briana shrugged.

The witch nodded. "I recommend one step at a time. At the moment, all you have to do is get through dinner."

"Cailleach, we need to talk about your sister."

Cailleach stiffened. "That is a conversation for another time. I'm aware of what happened, but it's nothing we need to deal with now."

True enough. The three women, with Dara plodding behind, made their way down the spiral staircase to the first floor. Sigel came out of his room, clean and refreshed.

Briana edged close to him. "Have you seen Silas? How is he?"

Sigel patted Dara's head absently. "He's quiet, as I would expect, but he understands and will be fine in time. As you will be." He put his hand on her arm. "Briana, there have been losses. A few of the older residents didn't survive the lifting of the curse."

Cailleach said a little prayer. Briana added, "May they rest in peace." She paused for a moment, then asked, "Is there anything I'm supposed to do?" Sigel shrugged. "I'm not sure how the king will handle it. Follow his lead."

They continued out of the keep and across the cobblestoned walkway in silence until they reached the hall. Briana's breath caught in her throat at the transformation that had occurred in the few short hours they'd been napping. When the heavy oak door opened, she was greeted by the sight of the hall bathed in the soft, warm light of a hundred candles, half of them from an ornate wrought-iron candelabra that dangled from the ceiling in the center of the room. The floors had been scrubbed until gleaming. Hulking logs burned in a massive stone fireplace, chasing off any chill attempting to come through the four small windows, one each wall. The smell of roasted meat, herbs and other delicacies wafted up from long tables for the first feast of a freed Ard Darach. Though magical, the hall was subdued, the sad notes of a harpist honoring those who had passed. King Brath stood at the head of the table, striking in his formal attire, his royal-blue trousers tucked into knee-high black leather boots. A long-sleeved tunic of a lighter blue hugged his powerful torso and was mantled with a sleeveless black fur-lined cape. A mighty broadsword hung at his side. The royal medallion of Uisneach, similar to Briana's, but larger, swung from a pendant around his neck. *No crown*, she noted. His luxurious red hair, combed to gleaming, was all the adornment he needed. She recalled, rather sheepishly, her concern that the man she would marry might be hideous. Hideous he was not. Regrettably, Silas, he was also not.

With imperial grace, he walked down the length of the table to greet her. "Lady Briana, would you do me the honor of sitting beside me?"

She sat in the chair he indicated to his left as Sigel sat beside him on the right. To her Next to Briana sat Sir Stark and Jonathan. Cailleach and Silas sat farther down from the king, blessedly far enough away to prevent conversation.

Silas' usual leggings and shirt had been cast off for more courtly attire, blue breeches an embroidered vest and a gold tunic. Handsome, yes, the blue of the cloth complimented his eyes, but she preferred him in his everyday wear, or the kilt.

Dara sat compliantly behind Briana, knowing better than to beg, his soulful gaze reminding her that he had not had supper yet.

"He behaves well," said Brath.

"He does. I wonder, Your Majesty, how I should provide for his food?"

The king leaned in close and smiled conspiratorially. "Beginning tomorrow, maybe he could be fed down in the kitchens before our meals, but for tonight, I suggest slipping a little something his way. He looks like he could use a bite."

As people ate and talked, Briana snuck a few bites of lamb and vegetables to Dara, who sat patiently beside her. The king, seeing the transaction, smiled. She couldn't help but return the gesture.

"What has been done with Artanin?" she asked.

"He's locked in the dungeon. I'll… interview him tomorrow."

"I want to be there."

He shook his head. "That won't be necessary."

"It is to me," she insisted. "He helped me escape and I want to know why."

"He also tried to prevent you from removing the curse."

"I'm not convinced that's what he was doing," she said, taking a sip of wine to wet her dry throat. She'd never argued with a king before, but if she was going to establish the kind of relationship she expected to have with him, she must start now.

He took a sip from his own goblet and studied her with a curious expression. "Very well. I'll take you with me."

Several questions and stories from around the table diverted his attention. She turned to Sir Jameson. "I hope your son told you of his adventure and valuable service to His Majesty?"

"What he says is that he protects the queen, whose beauty he repeatedly tried to describe, though he failed miserably in the attempt."

"You are too kind, Sir Jameson. Seriously, your son has proven his bravery and dedication while traveling with us. I intend to talk to His Majesty about his training as soon as an opportunity presents itself. Is that acceptable?"

"It would be an honor for our family, of course, though I would ask for some time for us to get to know one another before he and I are immersed in training and duty."

"Of course. Take as much time as you need. I'm quite fond of him, Sir Jameson. He's a good boy."

"Unfortunately, I can't take any credit for that. I'm grateful to the Connuckles for looking after him. When things are more settled, I plan to travel to Cedarmara to thank them personally."

"I hope you do," Briana said, touching his arm lightly. "I'm very sorry about your wife's death. It must be a terrible shock to wake up and find her gone."

His eyes clouded. "I loved that woman more than you can imagine. To know I must live the rest of my life without her is beyond my comprehension."

Oh, but I can imagine, and my heart breaks for you, she thought, but only squeezed his arm.

"I must concentrate on the joy of having Jonathan. I could have lost him, too. The last thing I remember before the curse is Lord Shamwa taking the lad from my wife's arms. There was nothing I could do to save him or her."

"That must have been horrible. Well, if you ever want to talk about it, I would love to hear about Lady Stark. Jonathan knew only what the Connuckles knew, and I bet you have some beautiful memories from before the curse."

He looked at her oddly. "Well, thank you, milady. That is most kind of you." She picked at the lamb in front of her.

"Is the food not to your liking," asked Brath, "or are you not hungry?"

"The food is excellent, Your Majesty. I can't believe your staff was able to put this together so quickly, and under such unusual circumstances. I think I'm still a little weary. It's been a long day."

He reached over and took her hand and she jerked back, nearly knocking over her goblet of wine. Startled at her response, he released her hand instantly. "Forgive me, Lady Briana. I didn't mean to…"

"It just took me by surprise. Touchy nerves, I guess. I'm sorry." The interaction between them caught the attention of those sitting closest.

"Don't be. I shouldn't have been so bold." He offered what she thought was meant to be a comforting smile before turning his attention to the other end of the table. "So, Silas, with all that's happened, you must have many stories to tell. Have you anything to share with us this evening?"

The bard's eyes were lined with fatigue. Nevertheless, he rose and moved toward the harpist. "I'd be happy to share a story, Your Majesty, but it's a long one, so fill your tankard and don't hold your breath."

The king chuckled.

"This is the story of a prophecy, a curse and the woman who saved a kingdom."

She groaned inwardly. *Oh, Maker, Silas. Please don't. I'm not up for this.*

He cued the harpist to begin playing a light melody as he recalled the night the King of Uisneach was put to sleep, and then recited the prophecy. Like everyone else, she fell captive to his voice, beautifully pitched for story and song. His performance provided a perfect means for her to watch him and dream about an alternate ending to the story.

She worried at the grief hiding behind the mask of enthusiasm he so valiantly tried to portray. She wanted nothing more than to take him in her arms and sing him to sleep, to offer the type of respite only she could provide.

Out of the corner of her eye, she noticed King Brath watching her intently and wondered how much of what she felt was revealed in her face. She turned to him. "He's a great storyteller. We enjoyed hearing his tales around the camp at night."

He responded with a half-smile. "He's been a gifted bard since his early childhood. That boy could tell a story that would have you falling over laughing, or sing a song that would leave you weeping."

She glanced down at her lap, thinking of their enchanted sea. She raised her eyes, realizing Brath was speaking to her.

"I'm sorry. I didn't hear you."

"I said it must have been difficult spending so much time on the road with two men. I hope you weren't too uncomfortable?"

She met his stare. "Not at all, Your Majesty. I will remember it as the best time of my life."

He leaned closer. "My lady, I pray in time, other memories will replace them as the best times of your life."

Her stomach churned and she looked away.

Clapping and cheers from around the table cued her that Silas was done with the tale. The king went to the bard and clasped his hand in a hearty shake. "Thank you, Silas. It's good to have you home."

"It's good to be home," he replied, equally sincere.

This was his home, after all. She was starting to understand why this prophecy meant so much to him, and why he was so determined that she help fulfill it.

Cailleach appeared at her side. "Ready for bed?"

Yawning on cue, Briana nodded. As she turned to say good night to Brath, he took her hand again and said, "Lady Briana, I would greatly appreciate it if you would join me in my chamber for breakfast tomorrow morning. We need to talk about some things. And I promise to take you with me to talk with Artanin."

"As you wish, Your Majesty."

"Thank you. Gael will bring you." He raised her hand, firmly this time, to his lips, and kissed her fingers. "I look forward to the morning."

She called Dara. The dog's gaze shifted between her and Silas. Ignoring

Briana's repeated command, he deliberately walked over to the bard, who patted him lovingly on the head.

"Go, now, *a leanbh*, your mistress calls you."

Perhaps it was the aged and potent wine or her overwrought emotions, but Briana viewed the scene before her as from afar, with Silas grinning at her and she returning the smile, Sigel staring fixedly at Brath, concern darkening his eyes, and Brath watching the bard and his bride speculatively.

"Good night, Your Highness," she said, calling up a smile, hoping it alleviated whatever troubling thoughts the king might have had.

She and Cailleach were escorted back to their rooms by Sigel. Silas remained behind at the king's request. *Just because you've been sleeping for ten years, doesn't mean the rest of us aren't tired. Let the man go to bed*, Briana thought irritably, as she followed Cailleach out of the great hall.

CHAPTER THIRTY-TWO

GETTING TO KNOW YOU

Briana smoothed the front of a violet day gown borrowed from the previous queen and secured Nua at her side while her new lady's maid knocked on the door to King Brath's chambers above the great hall. The king himself opened the door, dressed casually in brown leather leggings and a linen tunic shirt and vest, loosely laced, tall boots, and a wide leather belt holding a short dagger. He greeted Briana cordially and thanked Gael before dismissing her. Then he led Briana to the breakfast table. An awkward silence prevailed as they assessed each other.

The large open space designed for both work and rest was washed in sunlight from two large windows. Bricks of peat and dried logs stood stacked on either side of two fireplaces, one at each end of the room. Two tables occupied the left side e of the room, a smaller one, where they sat to breakfast, and a larger work table, with maps spread out across it. On the far right of the room, near a smaller window and balcony that let in a cool sea breeze, stood a behemoth of a canopied bed, covered in luxurious red quilts, fur throws, and puffy pillows, surrounded by a red brocade curtain. She shivered involuntarily at the thought that she might be sleeping in that bed with this man in the not-too-distant future. Two polished wardrobes stood side by side near the bed. Gorgeous richly woven tapestries hung from the walls and thick rugs covered the wood floors, making the room warmer than most parts of the fortress.

Brath poured her a cup of tea, and offered cream and sugar. Suddenly shy, polite conversation failed her, so she shook her head.

"Did you sleep well, my lady?"

"I did, thank you, Your Majesty."

"Thank you for agreeing to breakfast with me this morning."

Could she have declined?

"Where's Dara?"

"Gael was kind enough to take him to the kitchen today, but I'll take responsibility for him from here on out."

"We could give his care and feeding to one of the groomsmen, if you like."

"He's not a stable dog. He's my friend and protector. I prefer he stay with me." She picked up the fragile teacup and sipped.

"Of course. He seems fond of Silas, as well," he said.

"We were all a part of his rescue, so he's gotten used to the three of us, but from the start, he's been mine. We're rarely apart. He saved my life and the life of young Mr. Stark a few days ago, during a skirmish with the Gray Military. He's a good dog and dear to me."

"I see."

She wondered what, exactly, his narrowed eyes saw. "I want to talk to you about Jonathan." She graciously accepted the plate of fresh strawberries, peach preserves and a scone.

"I thought you might, and we will, but first I want to discuss a more personal issue."

Already? Her stomach clenched, but she simply inclined her head for him to continue.

"First, and forgive my bluntness, but I need to know, given what I learned yesterday about the expected nature of our relationship, whether you are entering into this arrangement of your own volition."

Speak now or forever hold my peace. A thousand things ran through her mind in a few moments, about Uisneach and the people she loved, who depended on her to do the right thing. The two halves of her heart warred between needing to save Uisneach and wanting to be with Silas, whatever the cost.

Uncertainty wavered in his eyes, as it did in her heart. "I accept the truth of the prophecy, which includes marriage to the King of Uisneach, so yes, I suppose I am entering voluntarily."

"That sounds a bit ambiguous."

"Where I come from, arranged marriages are an ancient idea. I've agreed to it, but I can't say I'm thrilled about the idea of marrying a stranger. No offense. What about you? You also have a choice in this, and you don't know me, either."

He visibly relaxed and studied her thoughtfully before answering her question. "I'm good at reading people, as a rule. It took me only last evening to determine you are an intelligent, brave, kind, moral *and* beautiful woman, everything I would seek in a queen. I find the idea of being married to you appealing, and I hope I won't be a stranger for long."

She took a long breath, any notion of getting out of this union gone with his words. She sipped her tea, hoping she wouldn't choke on it.

His eyebrows drew together at her silence. "Is the idea of marrying me so revolting?"

"Revolting? Hardly. You are all that people said you were. I just think we need to get to know one another before we jump into marriage."

He nodded, looking relieved. "May I suggest we begin by dispensing with referring to each other by titles? Could we just call each other Brath and Briana – at least in private?"

"Never been a fan of the title thing, so yes, I'd prefer that."

"Good. Thank you."

"May I ask you a question?"

"Of course. Please…"

"I've noticed everyone complies with your requests without question. Is it ever acceptable to say no, or to debate with you?"

He burst out laughing. "Excellent observation, Briana, and straight to the point. I won't need to guess what you're thinking."

"You never will, I promise."

"I take it this comes from a woman not good at playing the submissive?"

"Correct." She nibbled a bite of scone that in any other circumstance would've melted in her mouth.

"Now I'm certain Maker is being over-kind to me. Briana, I want our marriage to be a partnership. Hell, I want the relationship between the king and his people to be a partnership. Other than Sigel, seldom does anyone disagree with me or deny me, and truthfully, it can be wearisome at times. Please, you're free to say no, or discuss anything with me that you don't agree with. It will be most refreshing."

"Good, because I'm not too good at obeying orders. In fact, it's only fair you understand what kind of woman you will be marrying."

He leaned back in his chair and crossed his legs. "I'm listening."

"I'm stubborn, argumentative at times and often snippy when things aren't going my way. I can be reckless and manipulative. Oh, and I've kissed many men, though that was before I knew it is forbidden for queens, which I might say I find a ridiculous standard. I..."

"How many?"

"How many what?"

"Men have you kissed?"

She stared at him, cheeks burning. Her answer, when it came, croaked out of her. "Six or seven, I guess."

Moments passed before he said, eyebrows knitting together seriously, "Hmm... pretty promiscuous, my lady. Is that how young women behave in Maine?"

"Well, to be honest, many women my age have gone far beyond kissing."

"And what about you? How far beyond..."

"I beg your pardon?" she interrupted, outraged until she caught the gleam in his eyes. He was messing with her, pure and simple.

"I didn't realize that this morning's conversation would include an interrogation about the status of my virginity."

"Please forgive my poor manners. Is there anything else I should know about you?"

"I guess that's the worst of it."

He nodded solemnly. "Well, you hold quite a low opinion of yourself. Let me assure you, your companions don't share your assessment. Words used to describe you are *brave, loyal, witty, talented* and '*one hell of a warrior.*'"

"Well, Jonathan thinks I hung the moon and Silas..."

"Oh, I haven't spoken with them yet. This is how Sigel described you."

"Really?"

"Yes. He considers you like a daughter and told me, in no uncertain terms, that I had best be very good to you, or I would answer to him."

"Well, I'm shocked about that," she said, though her mouth curved into a satisfied smile.

"I'm confused, though," Brath said.

"About?"

"You just went to a lot of trouble to scare me away from you and yet, you say you believe in the prophecy. Why would you want to talk me out of marrying you?"

"Well, Brath," she said frowning, "I'm a bit confused about that myself." What she didn't say, because she could barely admit it to herself, was that her confusion came from a shocking, traitorous presence deep inside her that hoped she would fail.

They moved on to other topics, such as a commission for Jonathan Stark. Briana was relieved when he agreed to the boy being trained as her squire. He listened attentively as she shared the full story of his arrival at Winge Mansion and smiled when she related how she had interrogated him and how bravely he reacted.

"I believe he, like his father, will be a huge asset to you, Brath."

"To us," Brath corrected.

She dipped her head in wordless acknowledgment and popped a berry into her mouth.

He advised her of his plan to move her, Sigel, Silas and Cailleach into rooms inside the great hall. She told him she and Cailleach had commandeered a seamstress.

He nodded. "I'm glad you felt comfortable making those decisions, Briana. How do you feel about accepting other responsibilities for the household servants? They will be asking questions about your role here soon enough."

She sighed. "Lady Isabella tried to prepare me for this. As soon as I understand your expectations, I'll do what's required."

His eyes narrowed slightly and he gave her a quizzical look. "Hmm... rather subservient for a woman who just told me she didn't take orders well."

"Not at all. I realize there will be things expected of me, and I will rise to the occasion. I didn't say I would like it," she said.

Again he laughed, the warm timbre pleasing enough to bring a half-smile to her face. She flushed as she accepted another serving of eggs.

They talked for a couple of hours about how duties would be divided and when she should consult with him. He provided background history on the staff, people whose names meant nothing to her yet, but for whom she would soon be responsible.

"Well, you're probably overwhelmed with information," said Brath. "Perhaps we should stop here. Unless you'd like a fourth serving of eggs, maybe we could make a visit to Artanin."

Blushing seemed to be a new habit. "I'm sorry, I didn't mean to be such a glutton, but we haven't eaten much in the last few days, and this was so good and…"

"Briana, I'm only teasing you. But we do have an adversary to interrogate, if you still feel the need to be there."

She nodded vigorously, wiping her mouth and setting the napkin beside her empty plate. He was at her side before she could think of getting up and took her hand. A brief knock and the door opened, admitting Sigel, completely outfitted and weaponed, looking fierce and anxious.

"Are the two of you going to sip tea all day or can we get down to business?"

Briana patted his shoulder. "We're ready Sigel."

He led the way out of the hall, where they joined Cailleach, coming from the keep with Silas. Briana and Silas exchanged a smile as Brath invited Cailleach to come with them to the interrogation. When Silas asked if the king wished him there, Brath shook his head.

"Not necessary, Silas. I suspect this is going to be fairly cut-and-dried."

"Very well, Your Majesty," he replied, with a deferential bow. "I'll work on getting things ready for the banquet tonight."

"Thank you, Silas."

Silas should bow to no man, she thought, gritting her teeth, but knew sadly that this was his lot in life. Beside the keep, Sigel opened a door leading down a dark staircase. Lighting two rushes, he handed one to Brath.

"I don't like the fact that she," he looked at Briana, "is staying so close to Artanin."

"She'll be moved today. As will you, Cailleach and Silas."

Both men moved in front of the women and Dara padded behind, the stone steps too narrow to walk side by side. Macabre shadows danced around her. A silken finger grabbed her face and she jumped back, swiping at the cobweb that had attached itself to her hair and down her nose. Only a pinprick of light far below indicated there was an end to the steep stairs. Briana tripped on a rough slab and fell into Brath's back. He turned to help her, and she found herself against his chest. He made a sound she couldn't interpret. They exchanged a glance. She quickly looked away.

"Sorry," she mumbled.

"It's okay."

Bottomless pit? The bowels of hell? The prick of light grew larger until the staircase emptied into a cavernous, musty room. The room was lit with rushes. *At least they aren't keeping him in the dark,* Briana thought. Across the far end was a heavy gate constructed from thick wood stakes. Brath merely nodded at the posted guard who stepped back to let the king confront a disheveled and weary-looking Artanin, who sat curled up behind the bars. To his credit, when Brath entered, he rose immediately to his feet and bowed to his king.

"Your Majesty."

"Artanin. You have some explaining to do," Brath said.

"I do, but first I want to express my gratitude to Lady Briana for not allowing the lord marshall to execute me before hearing the explanation."

Sigel harrumphed and brought his sword to his chest, where Artanin could see it more clearly.

Briana frowned at the lack of food. It didn't seem like a good time to bring up the point.

"Start talking," Brath commanded, his tone neutral.

The man licked his lips. He started to speak but the slapping sound of a dry mouth challenged his efforts.

"Your Majesty," Briana said, quietly, "Maybe he would be better equipped to tell us what's happened if he had some water."

"He's a prisoner, not a guest," Brath responded.

"He's a human being." She held his gaze.

After a short pause, he said, "Very well. Guard, bring a pitcher of water for the prisoner."

Artanin attempted to speak again. "You think I tried to kill you, but the truth is, I saved your life."

"Really? By putting me into a decade-long sleep? That was bloody merciful of you."

"I could've killed you at that banquet. Those were my orders. I chose to disobey them, to allow the Mouse to come and fulfill the prophecy. I..." he stopped, accepting the water from the guard. When the cup was empty, he faced the king.

"I have spent the last ten years trying to convince Lord Shamwa that there was no way to change the spell and hasten your death. I did everything I could to remain loyal to you and still save my own life." Seeing he had the king's attention he continued. "Lord Shamwa believed you were about to legitimize the faeries. He convinced me this was a bad idea. But I never would've been a part of any coup."

"And yet, you were."

"He had an army of Moherians," said Artanin. "I feared that without the Mouse, we wouldn't overcome them. I believed the best thing I could do was play his treacherous game, so I could keep you alive until the prophecy was fulfilled."

"You're a druid, Artanin," Sigel spat out. "You expect us to believe you couldn't use magic to stop him?"

"There is power that is more powerful than magic, my lord," Artanin said.

"How did you know about the prophecy?" asked Briana.

"Likely my sister told him," Cailleach said, her voice bitter. "We were the only ones who knew about the prophecy."

"But why?" asked Briana.

"Probably because magic ruined her life, and she wants to see it destroyed as much as Shamwa does."

"That's right, Cailleach," Artanin confirmed. "She has no love for you and would do whatever Shamwa suggested, if it would hurt you."

"That's not fair," Briana said. "After all..."

"Never mind, Briana," said Cailleach. "It's not important now. Please, Artanin, continue."

He continued to reveal Shamwa's plan, until he came to the abduction of Briana. "That was the moment I feared I'd made a mistake. I had no choice but to carry out his orders. The men he sent on the mission with me would've killed us all if I failed to bring Lady Briana to Aurum Castle. I was afraid he meant to kill her, and was desperately trying to work out a way to prevent that. But you charmed him," Artanin said, looking at Briana, "and he changed his mind and began to improvise. He has a weakness for a pretty face."

Briana stole a glance at Brath, wondering if he knew that Shamwa had been in love with his mother.

"Did you weaken the seal on the balcony door to help me escape?"

He nodded. ""Then I lured Shamwa out of the room by telling him that Uisneach troops were nearby, which was true."

"So how did you get to Ard Darach? What were you really trying to do on the hill?" Sigel asked.

"I came with Shamwa's forces as far as the battle and slipped away, hoping you'd be successful and get here yourselves. I thought I'd be able to release the spell on my own, but it didn't work. Perhaps once Shamwa was alerted to my defection, he had Ealga block me."

"How did he know you defected?" Brath asked.

"There's a tight network of Gray Military that alerts him to every movement within Uisneach. I suggest you make destroying that network your first priority. I would bet he knew I was gone minutes after I left."

"Does he ever leave the castle?" Briana asked.

"No. He has no magic of his own, and feels vulnerable outside of his protected home. He controls others through fear. Your lack of fear, milady, was one of the things that both intrigued and challenged him. However," he said, apparently reading Sigel's expression, "getting to him is not easy. You need powerful magic to break through the barrier that Ealga created for him."

"Let me handle that," said Cailleach.

"In due time, Cailleach," Brath said. "Artanin's right. We need to break up his army first."

Quiet settled over the room. Questioning looks passed between Brath and his team. Words were unnecessary to communicate an accord about Brath's response.

"Well, Artanin. I believe you. However, you'll remain a prisoner here until we kill Lord Shamwa and secure the kingdom."

"Fine with me," the druid said. "I'd be a dead man outside the walls of this castle."

Part of Briana wanted to argue against the killing of Shamwa, but she'd had already questioned whether there was evil that just had to be destroyed. Shamwa might just be a good case in point.

The king and his advisors turned to leave. "Bring food for the druid," Brath ordered.

Briana followed him for a few steps before she remembered something. Turning back, she asked Artanin, "Who was the little person in his salon?"

A wide grin split the druid's face, making him almost handsome. "That, milady, was a faerie. You had more than just me helping you."

Her jaw dropped. "But you said..."

"Aye, he hates faeries. But he's not the only one who has spies. I wish we could've done more, and sooner, but perhaps part of the prophecy is that you learn to do for yourself."

"I'll be damned," she said, earning her a raised eyebrow from Brath.

Cailleach went to her room in the keep and Sigel to the stables, which left Brath to walk her back to the great hall.

"You must have things to do," she said to him, as they approached the door.

"I do, but they can wait until after lunch." He slowed his pace and stopped just short of the door. "Before we go in, there's one thing."

"What?"

He fiddled with the hilt of his sword, looked at the ground and kicked at a clod of dirt. "I, um, you never actually answered the question about your willingness to marry me. Will you? Marry me?" He lifted hopeful eyes.

His vulnerability tugged at newly strung heart strings. Regret and guilt warred with unexpected new emotions, and she felt a tiny crack start in her chest. *Who am I to argue with destiny?* "Yes, Brath, I will marry you." *And that is that. A royal engagement*, fait accompli.

Lunch was a simple affair in the great hall with more reflecting than talking. "I should get busy," Brath said, wiping crumbs from his mouth. "What will you do, Briana?"

"I think I'll go to the stables. I want to check on Banrion."

Emmett Ryan walked in at that moment, accompanied by Jonathan.

"Mr. Stark!" The tense lines that had made his face seem older than his actual years, were gone now. He looked relaxed and happy.

"Milady," he said. "I'm ready to assume my responsibilities as your squire. Thank you, Your Majesty," he addressed the king with natural confidence, "for allowing me the opportunity to serve your wife."

"Well, she's not my wife... yet," he said, his warm expression rousing the horde of butterflies in her belly, "but she will be the queen soon enough, and will need the best protection possible. I hope you are up to the task, sir."

"I am," said Jonathan, standing tall.

"Mr. Stark, you've barely had any time with your father," Briana said.

"We're both anxious to get on with our work. We'll find time to catch up."

"Well, then, you can begin by accompanying me to the stables. Ready?"

He handed Nua to her and nodded. Dara, sensing the opportunity for play, pranced about. Jonathan patted him. "Come on Dara. We've important work to do today." He bowed respectfully.

Brath and Briana smiled at each other. She followed her young squire out of the king's chambers.

The stable was nowhere near as sophisticated as the one at Winge Mansion, but more than adequate to house the horses of Ard Darach. The first stall housed a magnificent bay stallion, his long black mane and tail falling nearly to the ground. He was well over sixteen hands and solid muscle.

"My word, you are a beauty, sir."

His thick neck arched and he snorted in response, but pushed his nose toward her. Slowly, she brought her hand to his muzzle, which he nuzzled without any attempt to nip. "And well-mannered, too. How about that?" She made her way down the aisle, stopping to speak to a little chestnut lady, tossing her head about and snorting prettily. "Yes, milady, you are beautiful as well, anyone can see that." Banrion, hearing her mistress's voice, leaned her head over the rails of her box and whinnied. "Hello, darling. How are you? They treating you well?"

"We treat all the horses here well, milady," a man with a deep voice asserted coolly, from behind her.

Briana stood a little taller and turned toward him. "I'm sure you do, sir. They appear to be exceptionally well cared for. Hello, I'm Lady Briana." She extended her hand to greet the man, and he reluctantly took it. His dark hair was pulled back in a tight knot at the back of his neck, opening a face squarely strong and tough, with hard edges. *There truly is no such thing as a homely man in Uisneach*, she thought. Dark, stormy eyes stared back, assessing her. An intense man who might be easily angered. *Tread carefully*, she advised herself.

"I'm Riordan, Master of the Horse."

She gave him a sweet smile. "I'm pleased to meet you. I came down to see how Banrion was making out in her new home."

"She appears well enough. Nice mare."

"Yes, she is," Briana agreed, caressing the horse's satiny neck.

"From the Winge stable."

It wasn't a question, but she answered, anyway. "Yes, Sir Thomas was generous with the mounts he provided."

Male voices blocked his response.

"Himself will want to move out straight away and go after Shamwa. We need to be ready."

"Naw, he's distracted by the pretty little hen who's to become his wife."

"She's a hen I'd like to…"

Riordan stopped them gruffly. "Enough, men."

His tone stopped the banter of the men who now realized they weren't alone. Five faces stared sheepishly at the woman standing before them.

"My apologies, milady," said the red-haired man who'd been prevented from saying what he'd like to do with the "pretty little hen."

"No worries."

Sir Jameson walked in behind his comrades and broke through them to take her hand. "Lady Briana, a pleasure to see you again. Come down to see your mare?"

She nodded. "She's settled in quite well, thanks to Riordan." She smiled at the Master of Horse, hoping to charm him into a friendly relationship.

"Have you met these fools?" he asked, nodding his head toward the others.

"I believe we were about to be introduced. I'm Lady Briana, but perhaps you already know that." She laughed, and offered them a cocky smile.

They went around with introductions. The redhead was Sir Fergal – no last name, it seemed. He was tall and thin, reminding her of the scarecrow on the *Wizard of Oz*. The man who was bent on going after Shamwa was Sir Niall Harkin. Plain of face, his most remarkable feature was his blonde hair, hanging halfway down his back in a shimmering wave. When Sir Cruahan stepped forward to take her hand, she recalled his near-death experience at the hands of Sir Jameson. He was a large, muscular man with a fierce face, cropped dark hair and a rough beard. Sir Glendon Cavanaugh was the opposite of Cruahan, athletically trim and elegant with strawberry-blonde hair, long but perfectly coiffed. She thought he looked the most knightly of all the men. The last man was the one she was most eager to greet. She took Sir Faolan McPhee's hand and told him she'd met his parents, and how happy they would be to learn he was well.

"Thank you, lady. I plan to go home soon and relieve them of their worry." The short, stocky man had a gentle crofter's face, not unpleasant, with one eye that wandered occasionally, keeping her guessing about the direction of his gaze.

"Maybe we could send someone to Moiria and relay the message sooner rather than later?" she offered, not knowing if this was possible, but hoping it was.

"Most kind of you, milady."

They chatted amiably for a few minutes, recounting what things had been like for them when the curse was lifted. The genial ambiance shifted when King Brath and Sigel walked in. The knights promptly adopted an attitude of respect and servility.

"Hello gentleman. Lady Briana," Brath said, walking through the circle of men to stand next to her. "You found the stables."

The ease she'd found with the horses and men fell away, leaving her once again tense. She forced a smile. "I did. I met Riordan and," she flashed a brilliant smile to the knights, "and these gallant gentleman." Her eyes found Sigel's.

"How's the mare, Briana?" He was the only one, other than Brath, who could get away with not using a more formal title.

"Riordan's taken excellent care of her and she seems quite content."

The exchange was short, as the men turned to doing a full inspection of the stable. Brath took her hand, sending a jolt through her.

Listening to the inventory and assessments gave Briana something to focus on other than the odd feeling of her hand in his. Eventually, he let go, leaving her free to stroke and pet the beautiful animals, a strategy that prevented further disturbing contact. She wanted nothing more than some privacy to sort out the cobweb of thoughts and emotions that were making her a tangled mess.

"Ready to go back? They've moved you to chambers above the great hall. They're moving Cailleach now."

Brath walked her to her room. "I want to make sure everything is just as you would like it, Briana."

Opening the door to her new chamber, she found a spacious, airy room. Lavender and lemon scents danced on the breeze that came in from the open balcony doors. Her bed, a miniature of the king's, swathed in shades of gold and burgundy, stood against one wall, opposite a hand-carved armoire. A writing desk took up the corner.

"Sweet Maker," she said. Thick woven rugs in rich colors were scattered across polished wooden floors. Dara sniffed around, finding a royal pile of blankets that met with his approval, as he did a few turns on them and then lay down, muzzle on paws, for a nap. Green light flashed in Briana's peripheral vision and she turned to find a small table and two chairs atop which stood a stunning green marble *ríocht* board. She walked to it, hand on chest, her mouth forming a silent exclamation, and examined the green marble that glittered when the sun hit it just right.

"Maker, Brath, this is beautiful. It reminds me of the green marble I saw in Ireland."

"It was my mother's. She also loved to play *ríocht*. I thought you might like it. Consider it a welcoming gift."

"I can't take that! It was your mother's."

He smiled. "And now it belongs to the new queen."

She picked up the rook and turned it, watching the colors change as the light struck its different angles. "Thank you. This is much too generous a gift, but I promise to treasure it, as she must have."

"You're welcome. Just promise not to beat me too badly. I understand you're an excellent player."

"Not really," she said, setting the piece down. She walked to the balcony, where she looked out at the overrun garden and the ocean behind it.

"Guards at the door and the cliffs behind. Nothing will ever hurt you here," Brath assured her.

Little did he know that the things that hurt had nothing to do with marauders or evil prime ministers. "I suppose not." He wanted so much to please her, to make her comfortable and secure. She must honor his efforts.

"This is beautiful, Brath. Thank you." She looked around the room. "For everything."

"You don't need to thank me. It is nothing less than the Queen of Uisneach deserves."

She learned this had once been his mother's sitting room, and the furniture pieces were family heirlooms.

"I would love to spend more time with you, but I have a few meetings to attend," said Brath. "There's still a lot to do to get things back in order. I'll see you this evening." A slight bow and kiss to her hand, and he was gone.

Briana heard scraping in the room next door. She walked over to see what was going on in Cailleach's room.

The witch was attempting to rearrange the furniture. Briana rushed to help. When the table was where Cailleach wanted it and level, Briana stood back, eyeing the beautiful, earthy and wise woman before her, wishing her own life could be as uncomplicated and uncluttered as Cailleach's usually was. "I'm so torn," she blurted out. "I'm living in a dream castle, with a dreamy fiancé, wanting for absolutely nothing, and yet I don't want any of it, if it means I live here without Silas."

Cailleach was silent for a moment, studying Briana. "Imagine, for one second, that Silas wasn't part of the equation. What if you had only ever met Brath? Would you feel the same?"

"The problem is, I can't imagine a world without Silas." She scrunched her eyes closed and let out a long breath. "But if I could, then I would consider myself the luckiest woman on the planet. And what the hell do I do about that, because Silas is in my world, and I love him, and I hate the intrusion of these other feelings and responsibilities."

"Try not to overthink things. Just flow with the magic of each day and let nature take its course."

"Easy for you to say," Briana muttered.

"I advise caution. Try to be open to the possibility that your life does not need to be one of complete and dreary martyrdom."

A housemaid knocked at the door and asked Lady Briana to come to the kitchen right away.

"What's wrong?" Briana asked.

Brigit, a cute, well-rounded young lady, wrung her hands. "Mrs. Flannigan says dinner is ruined and there won't be anything to serve tonight."

Turning to Cailleach, Briana forced a smile. "What was it you said about my life being dreary martyrdom? Excuse me while I go solve a domestic crisis. Come along, Dara."

She followed the maid, and her nose, to the kitchen, where the acrid smell of burned flesh assaulted her. She was introduced to Moira Flannigan, a short and wide older woman with a discernible limp, who fluttered around the kitchen, waving her hands hysterically.

"What on earth has happened, Mrs. Flannigan?"

"The meat has all been burned to a crisp! And no time to roast anything else. The king will have no meat for his supper!"

Briana took a second to clarify. "So, there's no meat, but is there anything at all? Vegetables, desserts, bread, anything?"

"Oh, aye, the vegetables are fine, but I cannot serve dinner with no meat!"

"Of course you can. Mrs. Flannigan, we will not all starve without a deer or a goose. Are there eggs and cheese?"

"Yes, of course, for breakfast and baking."

"I am going to teach you how to make a quiche." Moira shook her head, not understanding the word. "An egg pie."

"For dinner?" she asked, flabbergasted.

"Yes, it's wonderful. The king will love it, and I will tell him I asked you to make it special for him from me."

Mrs. Flannigan gazed upon her with adulation and gratitude. Briana went on to explain the making of quiche, and suggested some available side dishes and warm bread to go with the dish.

Patting the cook on the back was her sister, Agnes Flannigan, the head housekeeper. Identical twins in looks, they were otherwise opposites. While Moira was a bit of a mess, Agnes was serious and steady.

Three other women worked in the kitchen: Fionn, a lovely redhead who seemed far too aristocratic to be a domestic; Kenna, a sprightly kitchen maid and Orla, somewhat standoffish, but who Briana hoped would lighten up when they got to know each other better. Pressed and proper Reilly Doherty, the butler, nodded and bowed to her every comment. Underneath his stern exterior, she detected a layer of kindness and knew they would get along well, as long as she executed her queenly duties with equal seriousness.

She was introduced to Mary O'Brien, the senior housemaid and a paragon of efficiency. Dark hair twisted precisely in a bun and a neatly pressed gray dress gave her an austere appearance that bordered on intimidating.

"It is a pleasure to meet you, milady. If there's anything you need or anything you find amiss, please let me know straight away." Like Doherty, her bar for excellence was set quite high. Briana hoped she was up to the challenge.

Brigit, Donal, Lucy and Cavan were housemaids, all friendly enough, but accustomed to standing in the background, so more difficult to evaluate. Not as difficult to notice was the essence of lye, tallow, beeswax and wood smoke that floated like a cloud around them, nor could one miss their black-edged fingernails, identifying them as the staff responsible for getting Ard Darach back in tip-top shape so magically and beautifully.

"I guess you are the ladies who keep this place looking so wonderful."

Four simultaneous curtsies.

"There are no other lady's maids in residence, milady," Gael informed her. "We can call on a few from the village if need be, but for now, I'm it. And I'm all yours," she said brightly, earning a semi-smile from her new employer.

"And Cailleach's," Briana amended.

"Of course, milady. Though she never lets me do much."

Right, and neither shall I, Briana thought, hating the idea of being waited on as much as Cailleach probably did.

⁓

Everyone stood as Briana entered the great hall that evening, dressed in another of Queen Eleanor's gowns, a vibrant red brocade trimmed in black satin, with black velvet slippers. She self-consciously waved them back down. "I'm so sorry," she apologized, as she sat next to the king. With a look to the butler, she indicated the food should be served. "Your Majesty," she said, "I asked Mrs. Flannigan to prepare a special meal for us this evening. It's one of my favorites, called Quiche Lorraine, made with eggs, vegetables and aged cheese. I hope you'll like it."

He took her hand in a kiss, causing her to cringe. "If it is a favorite of yours, my lady, it will surely be a favorite of mine."

She smiled weakly and eased away her hand to grasp her goblet of wine. The meal was served and to Mrs. Flannigan's great surprise and relief, it was indeed a hit. Conversation hummed around the table. Sigel and Cailleach were in deep discussion about something, and Sir Jameson and young Mr. Stark engaged Briana in a chat about Jonathan's training in archery. When she turned to ask Silas a question about it, she saw him chatting with a lovely young woman with cascades of blonde hair and dark, doe-like eyes, who looked at him with adoration. He nodded, smiled and then laughed heartily. There was no denying the pain of seeing him enjoy himself with a woman. *As he should*, she reminded herself, trying to swallow the resentment and disappointment.

The king, in spite of declaring that no celebrations would occur for a week to honor the losses of many of Ard Darach's citizens, laughed at, and even offered a few jokes, and joined in the singing, his rich baritone voice a nice complement to Silas' tenor.

She studied the two men, one dark and the other light. One regal and resolute, the other a carefree heart. Brath took every opportunity to pull her in as his consort. His frequent touching, although gallant and appropriate, made Briana squirm. At one point, he toasted her as the most beautiful queen Uisneach would ever have, and leaning down, kissed her cheek. She nearly fainted and looked anxiously at Silas, who wore a fixed smile on his face as he raised his glass to her.

Her bed, when she finally sank into it, was everything she anticipated. The business and cares of the day disappeared as consciousness gave up its post for the realm of the subconscious.

Chapter Thirty-three

Visions and Contracts

Briana stood, streaked with dirt, her hair draped with dead vines, in the middle of a botanical disaster. Chased by images of two men in her dreams, she'd risen just before the sun and persuaded Arthur, her guard *de nuit*, to accompany her into the garden. He made himself inconspicuous, giving her the illusion of solitude. The sun was now fully up, and she was enjoying the first reward of her efforts, breathing in the scent of the primrose and broom she'd unearthed. Dara, who'd been exploring mole holes and cat trails, shot out of a hole in the brambly, lifeless rose bushes. Swallows swooped and dived overhead, and warblers warbled in the blackthorn tree. Surging waves of a nearly high tide provided a meditative backdrop as she tore through primordial ivy and found a bench beside a paved stone walkway. Uncovering a sundial set in a circle of stones and the remnants of a fountain, she imagined the recovery of this beautiful landscape. Lost in the joy of gardening, she also lost track of time. She was late for her morning ritual of breakfasting with Brath, and wondered why he hadn't sent for her.

Hurrying along the old stone path back to the castle entry, she paused to delight in the mossy swirls and lichen badges that graced the ancient walkway. Her guard reappeared at her side. She found the kitchen, where the cook bustled and sweated over the warming ovens, baking bread.

"Smells wonderful, Mrs. Flannigan."

"Good morning, milady, and please, I'll not ask you again to call me

Moira. I'll bring a loaf out in two shakes and you can have some hot with fresh butter." She reached for the oven even before she completed the sentence.

Briana declined with a smile. "Thank you, but maybe just bring it up to the king's room. I'm late for my morning meeting with him."

The plump cook waved her hand and laughed. "Oh, he's not in his chambers, milady. He came down a while ago and ate in here before going to meet with the knights in the hall. They'll be planning to go after that crooked wretch, Shamwa."

"What?" She was dumbstruck. "Why was I not told of the meeting?"

Mary O'Brien stepped into the kitchen at that moment. "I did ask if he wanted you fetched, milady. He said you were not to be bothered from your gardening."

Her eyes narrowed as she stiffened her back. "Is that so?"

O'Brien nodded crisply.

Briana turned on her heel and headed toward the great hall. With each stride her ire rose, and by the time she reached the door, she was in full warrior mode. A dozen men sat around a long table, Brath at the head, Sigel and Silas on either side of him. Brath was pointing to a spot on one of the maps strewn across the table. At her sudden entry, they looked up, and the room became silent.

"Good morning, gentleman," she said, as she moved in between Sigel and Brath.

"Good morning, Briana. Is something wrong?"

"If I was informed correctly, that this is a meeting to formulate a strategy to capture Shamwa, then my presence seems to have been overlooked. I'm here, reporting for duty."

Brath stood, visibly surprised. "I thought you were going to work on the gardens. You don't need to be a part of this. We'll be the ones going out after Lord Shamwa."

She pulled herself to her full height in front of the king, and looked up into his eyes. "I will not be a stay-behind, baking-cookies-and-weeding-the-garden kind of queen, Brath, while you go after Shamwa."

Something glinted in his eyes. "Oh?" He paused only for a moment. "What kind of queen will you be?"

Slowly, not taking her eyes off his, she drew Nua from her sheath and raised the blade between them. Five knights stood as one, their swords appearing instantly.

"Relax men," Sigel drawled, remaining seated.

"The kind who will have your back," she said, maintaining eye contact. Drawing a sword against her king should've made her knees tremble. It didn't, but the passion she saw in his eyes did.

"Well, my lady," he said, his voice thick and warm as he took the end of her sword and neatly lowered it, "I shall be grateful to have your protection."

Sigel cleared his throat and said, "Brath, perhaps we should leave you and Lady Briana..."

"No need. Lady Briana, the decision to allow you to join us in battle does not solely belong to me. Since every man here would be responsible for your safety, we must be of one accord about this. What say you?" he asked the knights.

They looked tense. No one spoke at first. Silas broke the deadlock. "You're Majesty, I can't speak for the others, but as a man on the winnin' end of Lady Briana's bravery, I would be happy to have her at my side on the battlefield. She's not only a fine healer, which would be beneficial, but she's got a hell of an arm with that sword of hers. I stand by her in this."

Briana turned, hearing an unfamiliar edge to his voice. He looked tired. As the bard, he was required at every gathering, so he could craft the story of his monarchs. As one of the men of Uisneach, he would be included in any military exercises. He would witness nearly every interaction between her and the king. Her heart ached as she saw the toll it was taking on him.

Sigel stood then, as well. "I stand with her, also. She's a courageous warrior, Your Majesty."

The other men had no experience with her, but clearly trusted the leadership of Sigel and Silas, because they stood as one, with expressions of unity.

The king nodded to Briana. "It seems you are to be a part of this team. However, you and I will talk about this later, privately. Let's continue. Sigel, bring her up to speed."

She turned to the table, prepared to work, though not before she and Brath exchanged a curious glance.

They worked through the rest of the morning and past lunch hashing over plans to destroy Shamwa. Agreeing that destroying the army was priority number one, they nevertheless decided to do it en route to Aurum Castle. Brath did not want to wait any longer than it took to pull the troops together. He did approve her suggestion that they assess the damage to the faerie trees along the way. Upon hearing about Briana's personal connection with the faeries, Brath's rejoinder was, "Well, well, another reason for you to join us."

Briana told them about the faerie tree seeds, but it was decided that replanting would not be undertaken until Uisneach was secure.

"I think we have a good plan, men. And lady," Brath said nodding at Briana. He stood and stretched, looking out the window. "Take what is left of the afternoon off. Tomorrow we prepare for battle."

Briana rose, meaning to follow Sigel and Silas.

"Briana, would you please wait a moment."

She sat back down as the men filed out.

"Briana, we need to talk about what happened this morning."

She waited without pretense or guile.

"There are certain expectations of a queen. One of them is that you don't burst into places in an outrage and confront your king. I don't think I need to say you might have found a better way of handling your concern. In future, should you take issue with something I do or say, I would appreciate the courtesy of raising it with me privately, not in front of my men. If we're to be seen as a unified couple, you can't fight with me in front of the whole damn nation."

"Fine. I get it. But, in future, maybe you could talk to me before you go planning things that should include me."

He nodded. "Fair enough. I honestly never considered you would want to be involved in the political or military aspects of things. I assumed you'd be glad not to have to go through that again."

"Well, you know what they say about assume...."

"No, what do they say?"

"Never mind."

He shrugged. "There is one more thing, Briana." He hesitated.

She suddenly felt a boot swinging over her head.

"If you're going on this campaign with me, I would prefer it be as the official queen – and my wife. I know we meant to take some time, but for many reasons, practical and symbolic, I think we should wed sooner, rather than later."

"How soon?"

"I need three weeks to gather the troops and supplies to be battle-ready, and I would like us to have some time to, uh, get used to one another, so I think we should post the banns right away and be married in two weeks. I'll speak to Silas. He'll make the announcement."

Of course, as the royal bard he'd be involved in the preparations and recording of the event. *Oh, Maker, help us.*

Stuck between quicksand and the guillotine. She wandered to the window and stood staring at the landscape. *What would be the point in waiting?* Sigel and Silas walked across the courtyard to the stables. A week or a month, she knew all she needed to know about Brath to marry him. He was the king. She was the Mouse of Prophecy. They had a contract to fulfill. It was that simple.

"Briana?"

She turned, with perfect composure. "Whenever you like, Brath. Talk to Silas."

He nodded. "You can work out the details of the ceremony with Cailleach and Silas. There are certain things that must be done as part of the traditional royal protocol, but I want it to reflect things that are important to you, too."

She nodded. "Thank you. We'll see to the arrangements. Will that be all?"

He frowned, as if there was something more he wanted to say. With a shake of his head, he said, "I need to talk with my chamberlain. See you tonight at dinner?"

She forced a smile. "Of course."

She left him waiting for Master Ryan. Marriage in two weeks! She walked past her own room to Cailleach's to tell her.

Cailleach only nodded at the news. "You seem quite composed about this, Briana."

"What choice do I have? This is why I'm here. I better come to terms with the idea that the time has come for me to fulfill my contract."

Cailleach grimaced. "A harsh way to begin a marriage."

Briana shrugged. "Cailleach, it would be impossible to pretend I enter this out of anything other than duty. I am in love with another man and that will not change – ever. However, I understand that for the sake of the Uisneach, I must do this. And I will."

"Well, you've practiced that little speech. Tell me, please, that you have not said this to the king."

"Well, not all, of course, but we discussed the reasons for our union, and that it is not based on mutual love."

"Has it occurred to you that he might have different feelings toward you than you do for him?"

"He said he finds the idea of being married to me appealing, which I assume means he's attracted to me, but, Cailleach, I will not lead him to believe I feel something I don't."

"In time, your attitude might change." Briana rolled her eyes. Cailleach shook her head. "It might, and you don't want to burn any bridges before you even come to them. There may be some things you should keep to yourself."

"Well, I'm not going to go out of my way to hurt his feelings, if that's what you mean. I'm not stupid."

The witch studied her for a moment and the corners of her mouth lifted in a knowing smile. "No, you're not stupid. You're also not as disinterested as you pretend to be."

᷍

The next three days were busy, filled with the mass funeral for all the poor souls who died when the curse was lifted, and the outfitting and training of the troops.

Briana and Cailleach placed a protection spell around the perimeter of the castle. After that, Brath agreed to allow Briana to be unguarded in the castle, its courtyards, and the stable.

A few local tenants arrived with information and the taxes they could offer. They asked Brath to settle some civil disputes. Briana watched him deal with each person respectfully and kindly. Each left feeling valued and important. She felt valued herself, when he introduced her as their future queen, and included her in their conversations. Since the incident in front of the knights, he'd kept her informed about everything, and frequently asked her opinion. She had to admit, her respect for him was growing.

Brath seemed to be on a personal mission, too. From the personal escort down to dinner, to the frequent attempts to hold her hand, and the chaste peck on her cheek in front of her bedroom door, it seemed he couldn't get close enough to her. By Uisneach standards, this must amount to fast-tracking a relationship.

As they were finishing breakfast, Brath asked, "Briana, why don't we go for a ride today, just the two of us? We'll take a picnic and go down to the beach."

"Sure. When would you like to leave?" she said. "I want to finalize the training schedule with Sigel, and then we can go. A couple of hours?"

After making arrangements for a picnic lunch, she returned to her room, where she found two letters on her desk from Winge Mansion. *Crow mail*, she thought, smiling. It was significantly faster than the equivalent snail mail back home; the crows flew back and forth between the castle and mansion daily. Breaking the official Winge seal, a black crow on red wax, she began to read the note from Lady Isabella.

Dearest Lady Briana,

One hardly knows where to begin, so much has happened in the last week. Sir Thomas reported all that transpired when you arrived at Ard Darach. To say that we're grateful for the part you played, and continue to play, in the rescue of King Brath and the restoration of Uisneach, would be an understatement of unforgivable proportions. Perhaps now Uisneach can come alive in glory once more. Shocking to hear of Artanin's role in events. I hope his story is true, and that he becomes a force for good in the king's army.

I am sensitive to the transition you go through now, and pray you are well and at peace. I believe in my heart that things will eventually turn out for the best and that love will prevail. Love always prevails, sometimes in unexpected ways. This is not meant to be cryptic, dear lady, only to say that one can never predict the unfolding of destiny. Allow yourself to be open to possibility and you may be surprised by what can happen.

I continue to hold you in my heart and look forward to seeing you very soon.

With highest regard,

Lady Isabella

Love always prevails. Briana appreciated every word in the letter, but that line jumped out at her. It was the perfect mantra, but there was a little sliver of doubt in her mind. It was so hard to see how it could. It seemed more likely that duty would win the battle. With a sigh, she opened the second missive, from Epona.

My dearest, best friend,

Oh, I miss you! I never realized how dull things were around here until you came and left. It is quiet and far too sedate at Winge Mansion. No adventure at all! I shall probably die of boredom! But enough of my loneliness. How are you, dear friend? I know what happened at Ard Darach and am of two minds. Of course I'm happy that Uisneach's been saved and the king lives. I'm relieved that Artanin turns out to be not such a bad guy. But another side of me understands the cost, and my heart aches. That is, assuming you haven't come up with some gloriously devious way of getting around 'the issue.' I will never stop hoping that the dashing young man and the beautiful lady live, as you said, happily ever after.

Briana shook her head. Epona went on to ask about Dara and Banrion and to share news from Winge Mansion. Claire was doing well and missed her. Mrs. Jenks and baby Dauphne were getting along splendidly. Epona ended by saying:

And so I expect, with a heavy heart, to receive an invitation shortly. Because you asked I will come, and be of what comfort I can to you and those you love. We will find some way of making the event and the day more bearable for us both. But, oh, that is still weeks away, and a lot can happen between now and then, can't it? Let's neither of us give up hope. Maybe the gods will be good to you and we will celebrate after all.

I miss you madly and love you dearly.

Your sister and friend,

Epona

Briana held both letters to her heart, thankful for the love from Winge Mansion. However, she must find a way to make Epona give up her romantic notions. She must never write them. Briana burned the missives, sadly staring into the flames as the precious words transformed to ash.

There was no reason to wait for Brath to fetch her; she would meet him in the stable. Changing quickly, she went outside. As she and Dara came around the corner of the barn, they were almost trampled by Silas and Lady Seraphina coming out of the barn on their horses. Silas was laughing, and Lady Seraphina, resplendent in red velvet, wore a radiant smile. Briana felt like she'd been kicked in the stomach. And she looked like a hobo in her leggings and tunic, Nua at her side.

The smile disappeared from Silas's face. "Lady Briana."

"Would you care to join us?" asked Lady Seraphina.

"Uh, no, thank you. Brath and I are going riding as well, down by the shore, I think," she finally managed, hoping they weren't all going in the same direction.

"Oh, we're going along the river," the elegant blonde said, in a voice that sounded like a summer morning. Silas was silent.

"Enjoy your ride," Briana said. She hurried into Banrion's stall, glad of the darkness that would give her some privacy to collect herself.

"Are you okay?" Brath's voice startled her from behind.

"I'm fine," she answered overly bright. "Just getting Banrion ready."

"Riordan could have done that."

"So can I."

"You are an incredibly independent woman."

She wondered if that was a compliment or criticism. "I'm not accustomed to being waited on."

"Well, Ruark is saddled, so we can go, as soon as you're ready." While she bridled Banrion, he went for her saddle and helped her finish.

A steep path trailed down beside the cliffs leading away from the rocks to a long, sandy beach. Briana lifted her face to the cool, salty sea breeze. Seagulls soared overhead, screeching with every spiraling dive toward the shore. Dara plodded along behind them, running off occasionally to chase a plover or snuff out a rodent, always returning to his mistress. She looked up at the sun, briefly shading her eyes, and wished she had on a pair of shorts and tank top. Conversation was stilted, punctuated by moments of silence. Brath headed for the harder sand next to the waves, urging Ruark to a canter. Briana could not deny how good he looked on the horse. Not only did his red hair match the bay perfectly, but he sat and moved gracefully, one with the animal, as they ran along the shoreline, water kicking up around Ruark's lower legs. Briana followed behind for a while before giving Banrion her head and passing him. She stopped some distance ahead and turned back to see him grinning at her.

"Well that's a first."

"What is?" she called back.

"No one's ever had the nerve to race past the king. Briana, you delight me."

"This queen follows no man!"

He shook his head, laughing. "Good! Nor should you. Carry on, Your Majesty."

Briana experienced a moment of dizziness as she remembered that in fact, she would be his queen all too soon. The playful urge was lost and she waited for him to catch up. Brath stopped and turned Ruark to face the ocean.

"I don't know much about you, Briana, other than what has happened since you came to Uisneach. I'd like to hear more – where you came from, and about your family. It must have been difficult to leave them."

"I didn't know I was leaving. One minute I was in my yard, and the next, in Wellsland. Once I came through the tree and learned I couldn't go back, I was shocked. I'm not sure I ever had the chance to grieve the loss. I suppose I still believe I will see my mother again, although I don't see how that's possible."

His look urged her to continue, so she launched into the story of her life. He listened attentively, asking pertinent questions about her family and background and expressing fascination with some of the things about her world. At some point, they dismounted and walked along the shore, leading the horses. By the time he was brought up to date, she sensed a shift in the energy between them.

He stopped, dropped the reins of Ruark and removed Banrion's reins from her grip. He held and studied her small hands, nestled reluctantly in his.

She swallowed hard, her heart pounding like a drum. *No, no*, she thought, panicking. *I'm not ready. I can't.*

"Briana, you enchant me. Everything about your story and the woman I am starting to know intrigues and captivates me. We don't know each other well yet, but I would like to kiss you. May I?"

"I've never kissed a king before," she whispered.

"I'm a man, like any other."

She shook her head. "No, Brath, you are not like any man I've ever known."

Before she could decline the kiss, he was taking it. His clean-shaven face carried the scent of pine needles and bergamot. His lips were full and soft, gentle, as he teased hers apart, his searching controlled and considerate, not pushing her past what she was willing to receive.

Her body was confused by this stranger who felt and smelled so different from the one she loved. Yet, he was drawing her in like a hummingbird to nectar. This awareness, and the attraction, stunned her. Her body began to tremble, and as hard as she tried to fight them, tears rolled down her cheeks.

He stepped back and searched her face. "You are an enigma to me,

Briana. You're fearless in most cases. You tell me you've kissed men before and yet you seem so reluctant now…" Confusion turned to sudden awareness. "Oh, Maker. Do you love someone else?"

Revealing the truth serves no useful purpose and might get Silas killed, she thought. Dishonesty settled like a brick in her stomach. *Better indigestion than a hanging.*

"There's no one I'm involved with, Brath."

"Good. I'd hate to have to challenge him to a duel."

"A duel! Sweet Maker, don't even think such a thing."

"I would. To the death." He was teasing, but she shuddered at the image of him fighting and killing Silas. "I'm not sure what to do here," he said. "If we are to be married soon, we've got to find a comfort level with each other."

She nodded. Turning to their mounts, she said, "Why don't we find a spot to have our lunch and talk. Once we know each other better…" It rang lame to her own ears, but she needed a little more time.

They walked their horses in silence until they came upon a sea cave large enough to enter. Making a mental note to explore it someday, she followed Brath beyond the cave to a different path leading up to a grassy knoll with a view of Ard Darach on one side and the ocean on the other. He tied the horses to a nearby branch and sat on the soft grass beside her, facing the castle. Briana brought out fruit, meat and bread and a flagon of wine.

"Bless Mrs. Flannigan," he said. "I can use this right about now."

"Me, too," Briana agreed. Dara returned from one of his jaunts and flopped down beside Briana.

They ate slowly and drank most of the wine as Brath related stories from his childhood. He told her his version of the story of Sigel's accident.

"You'd have thought we would have better sense than to be on that wall with swords, but during the duel, which I'm pretty sure I was winning, I took a stab at Sigel, and he fell off the wall. I cringe every time I look at him, knowing it was my fault he's scarred."

She patted his hand. "You should let go of that guilt, Brath. It was a childish accident and besides, the scar is part of what makes him so attractive to women."

Brath raised an eyebrow. "Is he now? You've heard this from women?"

"I have. Several, in fact."

He glanced sideways at her. "And what about you, do you find him attractive?"

She laughed out loud. "Sigel? I suppose he is good-looking, but I'm certainly not attracted to him. That would be like being attracted to my father."

His look turned thoughtful. She had the distinct impression he was going to ask another question, but changed his mind.

"Brath, do you really think we can take control of the Gray Military and capture Shamwa?"

He took another drink of wine. "Shamwa is a dead man. I trusted him, Briana. He'll pay for what he's done."

"How long do you think it will take?"

He shook his head. "I don't know. I hope this first assault will be a matter of a few weeks, but it's hard to say for sure."

"I want to start getting the faerie trees planted to create that bridge between us and Evalon."

"We need the faeries to be successful," he agreed. "I was thinking about your journey to Evalon and the fact that a faerie was sitting right in Shamwa's parlor. There must be a way to involve them now.

"Excluding Evalon from representation in the governing of Uisneach has gone on far too long. I want to reverse that." Brath's expression changed from wistfulness to determination. "Uisneach cannot flourish without including all members of its society in its administration and decision-making. If we can work together to reestablish the trees, it will go a long way to healing the rift between Uisneach and Evalon. Restoring magic to its former glory would be a great thing for Uisneach."

"You've given this a lot of thought." She was pleased with just how much. "This kingdom means everything to me, Briana. I want to see it grow and thrive. I want villages to spring up, not only in Dromdara, but in all the kingdoms. I want what my parents wanted, a healthy, happy and united Uisneach. If you think you can be the queen to stand by my side and help me make the vision a reality, then I'll do my very best to make sure you don't regret the choice. But if you don't think you can do this, for any reason, please tell me now." His eyes searched hers for an answer.

In seconds, she reviewed her life, the experiences she'd had since coming to Uisneach, and her own heart for the truth of who she was, and whether or not she could abandon her deepest yearning for the greater good of this place she loved.

Releasing a breath she hadn't known she was holding, she said, "Why don't we try that kiss again?"

This time, when he leaned toward her and he took her face in his hands, she opened herself to the possibilities that might come from this marriage. He would never be, could never be, Silas. Silas was her other half, the fulfillment of the deepest part of her soul. She held no deeper longing than for them to be together as one, but Uisneach needed them in different roles now. For the sake of Evalon, the Tollemys, the Winge family, Sigel, Cailleach, and even for Silas' sake, she must commit to this alliance, which would begin with a kiss.

He tasted of wine and bread. His exploration deepened and his hands went to her hair, caressing, as he sighed into her mouth. Her hands found their way around his neck and pulled him closer. They lingered until she gently pulled away. It was done. She'd made the leap and sealed the contract. Though her heart ached, her mind was clear, and for the moment anyway, at peace.

He took her hand and pressed his lips upon it. "Thank you, Briana. I promise I will do my best to make you happy."

They sat silently, looking at Ard Darach and contemplating the future of Uisneach. Finally, Brath stood and reached for her hand. "Are you ready to go home, my lady?"

The word "home" startled her momentarily, but it *was* her home now, not just the house she lived in. She nodded as she rose and allowed him to help her mount Banrion. She didn't need the help, but the symbolic gesture made sense, and she smiled at the man who made it. She considered leaning down to kiss him again, but before she could, he had a foot in the stirrups of his own mount. *Just as well*, she thought. *I need these butterflies to roost for a while.* She was a little saddened by the bridge she'd just crossed.

Grooms received the animals. Brath walked her to her room. Perhaps sensing her ambivalence, he touched his lips to her hand in courtly fashion, and left her with the promise to see her at dinner. She hoped she wouldn't run into Silas on his way down. She hoped she wouldn't see Silas anytime soon. *How could she ever look him in the eye?* She removed Nua from her side, and sat on the bed. Dara jumped up beside her. The dressmaker arrived, and she turned her attention to matters at hand. Chiefly, her wedding gown.

The entire afternoon passed with the dress fitting and readying herself for the evening. With nothing to do but wait, she elected to go down to the great hall on her own. Making a stop at the kitchen for Dara's supper, she was greeted with "ooh's" and "ahh's" over the black and white gown, courtesy of Queen Eleanor. That lasted only seconds before she was bombarded with questions about the coming meals. Turning each query into an opportunity to give the staff confidence in their own decision-making skills, Briana and Dara left the kitchen content with the way things were turning out at Ard Darach.

The great hall was splendid. The fire in the massive fireplace was warm and comforting. It seemed no matter how sunny the day, the nights were always cooler, and peat fires were always kept at least crackling in the hearths. She took time to really examine the main room of her new home. Tapestries and the banners of the five kingdoms led the way to the throne. Evalon's standard featured a faerie tree. On Cedarmara's flag, someone had stitched mountains ceding way to the ocean. Painted across Appleduir's was a brightly colored floral scene. Dromdara's banner featured the insignia of the House of Taranian, a winter-white weasel bearing a crown of gold braids and holly. The last banner, for the kingdom of Tynan Ibor, showed the Uisneach Tree with the dryad's face. *Oh, wise Nionon. I'll never forget your kindness. I hope we meet again, someday.* The tapestries told the glorious story of Uisneach, adding new information to what she'd already learned.

Out of the corner of her eye, she saw a dark shape scurry toward her. The mouse stopped in front of her and looked up, its round black eyes blinking, curious. They stared at each another, aware of a kinship that began the day of her birth.

Good evening, Queen Briana.

I'm not the queen yet.

Don't be coy. Making battle plans, kissing kings and ordering servants about. Of course you are the queen here.

Everything is happening so fast.

So it is. The trick is not to get gobsmacked by it all.

She glared at the rodent. *Easy for you to say.*

Whiskers wiggled as he lifted and balanced himself on delicate back feet. *Oh, you think it's easy being a mouse? Scurrying about, avoiding cats, traps, brooms, feet and any other horrible means of ending my life?*

I see your point. How do you suggest I manage it all?

Be alert but stay calm. Trust your instincts. Focus on Uisneach and avoid traps. Be graceful.

She mulled the words over in her mind. *Do you think... ?*

A squeak preceded a whoosh of air and the yellow straw of a broom sweeping across Briana's line of sight, aiming to crush the wee creature.

"No," she shouted, knocking the broom out of the way, pleased to watch her four-pawed friend scamper away to the safety of a hole near the fireplace. Prim and proper Mary O'Brien simply raised one eyebrow in response.

"Well, now, we can't have every furry creature from hill to glen wandering freely about the castle, now, can we? They'd eat us out of house and home."

"I doubt this one fellow would make much of a dent. Besides, he's a friend of mine."

"You're a lovely woman, milady, but I must say, I think you're a bit daft." Shaking her head, she walked back to wherever it was she had so inopportunely come from. Her words might have been considered inappropriate, but made Briana like her all the more. Near-catastrophe averted, she turned her attention back to the story of Uisneach.

She was standing in front of the throne. Make that two thrones. A second, smaller version of Brath's giant oak armchair had been added. Both were covered with vibrant red canopies, rich brocade cushions and brilliant carvings that were a work of art. Polished to a sheen, each featured an ash tree whose branches reached across to the other throne. Across each backrest was a large, circular carving of the Taranian sigil.

She wobbled, her knees heavy from the weight of the responsibility upon her.

She heard footsteps behind her and made a conscious effort to relax when Brath put his hands on her shoulders and kissed the crown of her head.

"Beautiful, aren't they?"

"Yes," she said. "I thought I knew the story of Uisneach pretty well, but these tapestries, the symbolism of the banners, and the thrones makes it even more real."

"I think something else has made it real for you, Briana. I think today you decided to claim this kingdom and these people as yours."

She didn't argue, but that decision had been made eons ago. It was this man and this home that she may have started to come to terms with today. At least she thought she had.

He turned her around to face him and kissed her again. She closed her eyes and allowed herself to melt into him. Strong arms pulled her close, and her own arms slid around his waist and explored his back. They lingered into the kiss, only stopping when a kittenish purr escaped from her throat. He pulled away with a chuckle and whispered, "You can make that sound anytime."

She opened her eyes to find, with complete dismay, that Silas had come in behind them with his usual catlike quiet and witnessed the moment. She saw the mixture of pain and acceptance on his face and wanted to throw herself into his arms and beg his forgiveness, but she couldn't. The best she could offer was a flushed look of regret and apology.

His smile was fixed. "Good evenin', Your Majesty. Lady Briana."

"Hi Silas," Brath greeted him, sounding a little stilted. "Getting ready for this evening?"

"I wanted to speak with you, but it can wait." Her heart broke to hear his usually bright voice so muted.

I am so sorry, Silas. So, so sorry.

"No, of course not, come in. Briana and I were just reviewing a little of Uisneach's history. What's on your mind?"

He paused, looking at Briana. "It's about the weddin'. I was going to ask you if you had anythin' in particular you wanted for the reception, but really, it can wait."

Briana, sensing an opportunity to speak alone with him, quickly agreed. "Why don't we meet here after breakfast in the morning and talk about it."

"As you wish," he said. "Please pardon my interruption."

"No need to apologize," Brath said, but Silas was already making his way to the back of the room, where his harp stood.

The great hall quickly filled and the sounds of a well prepared meal and sharing of the day's events. When the meal was over, the dishes cleared away and cups refilled with mead or ale, Silas moved to his usual place in the center of the room for storytelling.

"Are you taking requests, Silas?"

"Of course, as Your Majesty wishes."

He turned to Briana and took her hand in his, placing a kiss on her fingers. "I'm in the mood for something romantic."

And so the evening wore on, Brath cheerfully requesting one amorous song or story after another, Silas looking like a water-logged wooden Indian and Briana feeling bilious.

CHAPTER THIRTY-FOUR

MATTERS OF THE HEART

"Briana?"

"Huh... what... Si..." Pine and bergamot – Brath, not Silas. Briana clamped her lips shut.

"Can I come in?" he asked, tentatively.

"What's wrong?"

He cleared his throat. "There's something I'd like to talk about."

"In the middle of the night?"

"Please, Briana. It's important."

"Okay," she said, wrapping herself in her robe. "This can't wait until morning?"

"Please. I've been tossing and turning all night. It's really bothering me."

"What?" she said, sitting up. "What's wrong?"

He lit the candle beside her bed with the flame from the one he carried and sat down on the bed. "We had such a good day, and then during dinner, you seemed distracted. Did I do something to upset you?"

She fiddled with her sleeve, searching for a reasonable response. "You didn't do anything wrong. I just got... confused, and then upset with myself."

"Why?"

She met the question in his eyes, first with silence and then a sigh.

"Things are happening so fast, Brath. I'm having a little trouble sorting through unexpected feelings."

Curling a hand lightly around hers, allowing her the space to move away, he said, "I'd be happy to help you sort things out, but I'm guessing that kissing you into oblivion wouldn't be the way to do it."

She squeezed his hand. "No, it would not, but damned if I don't appreciate the thought." She moved away from him to the table where the *ríocht* set stood, sparkling in the firelight. "But there are other ways for us to get to know each other." She swept a hand toward the green game pieces.

"You want to play *ríocht*? Now?"

She nodded, smiling. "Let's spend some time together as friends. No pressure."

He let out a breath, then nodded. "Yes. I feel so rushed. I hate it. This isn't what I imagined –"

"Then let's just relax and do something fun," she said. "I mean, hey – you're the king. And I'm going to be the queen. Shouldn't we get to make the rules?"

"I like the sound of that." Brath smiled.

Hours later, sunlight filled the room when Briana declared, "Check!"

Brath considered his options. A loud bang on the door was followed by it bursting open to admit a red-faced Sigel and Silas, who went pale at the sight of Briana in her nightgown, leaning on one neatly exposed knee, across the table from an equally disheveled king.

"May I help you, gentlemen?"

"I've been looking all over for you, Brath," Sigel said. "We were supposed to meet with the knights for training."

"Oh, I forgot. Sorry."

"I thought you'd been taken."

"We were supposed to discuss weddin' plans this mornin'," Silas reminded Briana, his face as hard as one of the stones of the dolmen.

"Did it occur to neither of you that I might be with Briana?"

"No, it did not!" Sigel said.

"Yes, it did," Silas said simultaneously, staring at Briana.

"Well, if you all don't mind, I think I'll get dressed," Briana said, wishing the room would empty of men and the hot glut of emotional turbulence they were bringing to the start of her day. "Silas, why don't you meet me in the garden in an hour?"

An hour later, hair and emotions under control, Briana found Silas sitting on the bench, his head in his hands.

He brushed away catkins beside him. "Lovely bench. Care to sit down?"

They sat beside each other. She welcomed the silence of not knowing what to say, was grateful to share the ache in his heart. Two hawks screeched overhead, dipping and diving, circling into and drawing away from one another in an age-old mating ritual.

"I'm sorry, Silas."

"You have nothin' to be sorry for."

She met his eyes. "I've hurt you and I hate myself for it."

"You've only done what you were supposed to do. What I – we, all pushed you to do." He glanced sideways at her. "But, there's the knowin' you belong to him, but then there's the seein' it. Two entirely different things."

She stayed still, waiting.

"You seem to like him well enough."

She heard the edge in his voice and noted the glint of resentment in his eyes.

"He's impossible not to like, Silas; you know that. You knew I would find a kind, caring man and a capable and dedicated king."

"Aye, I only wish you hadn't noticed it quite so soon."

"That's not fair."

He slapped his knees. "No, it isn't, but I'm discoverin' that even the most charitable man isn't made of stone. You do not owe me an apology and I am grateful you won't be locked into a miserable marriage, but don't ask me to apologize for feelin' as I do."

"I'm not asking for an apology. I just don't want to lose us, and I don't know how to manage that and do what I need to do as the queen."

"In this world, there is no 'us,' Briana. In another world, perhaps, but here, you belong to another man. Well and happily, it seems."

Knowing he was taking his pain out on the only person he could, she let his hurtful words pass. "Come with me. I want to show you something."

They walked along the path to three silver birch trees she'd rescued from an overgrowth of gorse bushes. "Birch symbolizes the ability to adapt to changing or difficult situations," she told him. "They can root in shallow soil, in places where other trees would die. They stand strong in the face of adversity."

Sunlight filtered through the delicate leaves, making dewdrops sparkle on a plant in the center of the grove, two enjoined hearts woven from the spiny, tenacious branches of the gorse she'd cleaned away. She watched his chest rise and fall as he understood and accepted the meaning of her display.

He stood and turned toward her, his eyes shining with remorse. "I'm sorry."

"No need to be," she whispered. "It won't be easy, but there will always be an 'us.' I made this our special place, where either of us could come when we need a reminder."

He nodded.

She gave them both a moment before saying softly, "Now, shall we get on with these wedding plans?"

They returned to the bench, where he explained the traditional sections of the ceremony.

"Brath wants me to add something that's meaningful to me." She grimaced. "What would that even look like? Short of bringing my mother here as my matron of honor, or substituting you for him," she paused, "I can't think of a thing."

"I have an idea, but I would keep it from you until the weddin'. Will you trust me?"

"Of course. How will I know what it is?"

"You'll know. Briana?"

"Hmm?" She swiped away a spider, making its way near his leg.

"Thank you. For the talk, for the hearts. It helps. Do what you need to do. Don't worry about me. You can't live worryin' that every move you make with Brath is goin' to hurt me. I want you to be happy, and if he makes you so, then I'll be happy." He offered a half-smile before adding, "Someday."

Footfalls on stone alerted them that they were no longer alone.

"Here you are, my lady," Brath said, admiring what she had

accomplished. "This is remarkable, Briana. It's starting to look like the gardens of my childhood. Do you remember, Silas?"

"I do, sir. Lady Briana is as skilled with growin' things as Queen Eleanor was."

"Yes," he said, putting an arm around Briana, "she has a way of making things bloom."

"You are too kind," she replied. "Did you come for a reason, Brath?"

"Oh, yes. Donla's arrived, bearing gifts."

"Oh! Dresses! I won't need to wear your mother's things anymore!"

The men shook their heads, not grasping the import, but Briana hustled them back to the castle. Before heading upstairs, she turned to Silas. "Did you need anything else, Silas?"

He smiled, honestly and warmly. "No *my* lady, you've given me all I need."

She sucked in her breath at the way he so carefully emphasized the "my" in his address. Heart lifted, she went to examine the dressmaker's efforts.

The day turned unseasonably warm and Briana, pent up and restless, took a notion for a ride to the beach to explore the sea cave. Brath couldn't join her, having been harnessed by his Master of Wardrobe, Darby Duncan, for the fitting of his wedding outfit.

Turning once more to the company of Jonathan, Briana went to the stables, where the head groom insisted on saddling Banrion for her.

"One of the knights should go with you," Riordan said, regarding Jonathan uncertainly. "Where's your father?"

Miffed, Jonathan said simply, but with more authority than he was entitled to, "Busy. I'm the Queen's Protector. I'll accompany her."

"We'll be fine, Riordan."

"Right. As though either of you has enough experience to get out of the rain."

"I beg your pardon…"

"Ah, go on then, but if anything happens to you, I'm not responsible."

"I wouldn't dream of blaming you," she said, taking the reins and swinging up effortlessly on her mare's back. *Point proven*, she thought, but the groom only rolled his eyes.

Jonathan had already discovered the way, and within a quarter of an hour they were racing down the beach, Andromeda doing his best to match Banrion's leggier strides. She slowed the mare to allow the lad some professional dignity, and realized they were near the cave.

"Briana," said Teaguen, waving at her to come in. The faerie was sitting on a boulder just inside the cave. She glowed in her opal-colored sheath. Jonathan did not appear to see her.

"I am invisible to him," Teaguen said.

"Mr. Stark, would you mind waiting here for a minute?"

"I'm not supposed to leave you, Lady Briana."

"I'll be in your sight; I just want a moment alone."

"Okay, I guess, but don't go too far in."

"You know, you're starting to sound a lot like Sigel."

His smirk indicated he took that as a compliment.

She entered the dark, damp cave. Water dripped from the recesses into a small pool. Bats chirred from deeper in.

"It's good to see you, Teaguen."

She grinned. "You too! Amazing getaway from Shamwa. Well done!"

"That was you?"

"None other. It was tricky, inhabiting the crone's body, but I managed, just in case you needed me."

"You could have been a bit speedier getting me out of there."

"I did not do anything. You keep forgetting how much magic you have. You need to practice more with that, Your Highness. Anyway, I am here to talk about your wedding."

Briana stretched her neck toward the roof of the cave. "Everyone wants to talk about the wedding."

"How are the two of you getting along?"

"Fine."

"From the look that just crossed your face, I would say a bit more than fine."

Waves lapping the sandy shore were the only sound for several minutes as Briana tried to come up with the words to express her feelings. "The truth? I really like him. A lot." She buried her face in her hands. "I can't believe I just said that."

"Why not? He is a wonderful man."

"How can I feel this way about him when I love Silas so much?"

"Briana, life rarely orders itself to our expectations. All you can do is open your heart and prepare for the passages. You have, in fact, already walked through a gateway."

"What gateway?"

"A portal. To transformation. Invisible, but a passageway, nonetheless. It is understandable that you might be frightened by the change and new expectations, but you must rise above your fear to accomplish what you have set yourself to achieve, what you are destined to do."

"How do I do that?"

"By letting go of some of your self-limiting thoughts. Remember who you are."

"What does that even mean?" Briana asked, suddenly weary.

"Who did the reflecting pool say you were?"

"A woman guided by love."

"Yes, and you have been given a great many people to love. You are also a faerie, and possess gifts to help you meet this challenge of ruling Uisneach. Let love guide you."

"But love is confusing me. I want more than anything to be with Silas and yet, when Brath kisses me, I just about melt."

Teaguen sighed wistfully. "How nice."

"No, it is not nice," Briana groaned. "It's driving me nuts!"

"Only because you are limiting your understanding of love. Use your magic to expand your vision and your heart, Briana. You love many people here, and they love you and want to help you, but you must first let go of the things that hold you back, that keep you stuck in this place of doubt, guilt and fear."

"Like?"

"Like desiring to love Silas only in the physical sense. Like thinking you cannot love Brath because you love Silas. Like believing you are not enough, as you are, to be a queen." Teaguen hopped down off the rock and scooped up a handful of sand. She held it out in front of her. "Briana, there are more ways to love than there are grains of sand on this shore. You and Silas travel together throughout time. Your souls are inseparable, but you must open up to the other possibilities for your soul's growth, while you let go of the restrictions you have placed on it. You judge that having him as a lover is more valuable than having his friendship, protection, and guidance as you move into your new life. You worry you will miss an opportunity to share an expression of love that goes deeper than any other. This is not true, and learning this is one of your soul's tasks. The other is recognizing that there might be more to this marriage than you can currently conceive of. It is a good thing that you are becoming open to learning what you can from this partnership with Brath."

"I suppose so."

"Well, this isnot the reason I came here. I need to know about any plans regarding Evalon."

Briana summarized Brath's ideas.

"Excellent! We would like to propose a council meeting with the King and Queen of Uisneach shortly after your marriage."

"You'd come to Ard Darach?"

"It requires a dispensation from the actual King of Evalon…"

"He's still alive?"

Teaguen smiled brightly. "We are immortal, Briana. And there's a wonderful king, who can't wait to meet you. Can you arrange the council with King Brath?"

"Of course. Oh my, am I immortal, being part faerie?" she asked, anxious at the thought she would outlive everyone she loved.

"No, my lady, you are not, at least not in the sense you mean. Only pureblood faeries are immortal."

Relief washed over her. "Thank Maker."

"The council?"

"Yes, of course. How will I confirm with you?"

"Keep working in the garden. You'll discover our portal."

"My lady," Jonathan called. "Are you all right?"

"I must go now," said Teaguen. "You are not alone, Briana, and you are stronger than you think. Trust yourself and those who are trying to help you. Even Brath."

"Wait, Teaguen…" But the faerie had already disappeared.

Jonathan's shadow erased the last vestiges of the faerie's glow. "I was worried when you didn't come out for so long."

Teaguen's visit left her a bit dizzy. Briana clung to Banrion as they made their way out into the sunshine. In a moment, she was back to normal. She smiled at her youthful protector and turned back toward the castle. "We should get back, before the king starts to worry." She urged Banrion into a trot.

Riordan stood outside the barn, waiting.

"Better?" he asked, taking her reins.

"Yes," she said, "and I'm home in one piece. Do *you* feel better?"

"I do."

The housemaid, Mary O'Brien, intercepted her as she stepped into the hall. "Milady, a post has come for you." She handed Briana a letter with the Winge family seal on it. Tearing it open and scanning the contents, Briana clapped her hands and did a little jig. Sir Thomas and his family would be here in four days. *I best organize some things to keep Epona busy, or she'll incite a riot.*

CHAPTER THIRTY-FIVE

FALLING

Three days after her meeting with Teaguen, just past dawn, Briana wrestled with a thick tangle of gorse hedge on the southern edge of the garden, digging and tearing away brambles. Her efforts revealed a circular stone entrance framed by smaller curved stones. She whisked moss and debris off the doorway, revealing carved images of Evalon on the lichen-splattered stones.

"I found it!"

"Found what?" asked Lady Seraphina Froud.

Wiggling backward, Briana made her way out of the hedge and bumped her head on a low-hanging tree branch. "Ouch!"

"I beg your pardon! I didn't mean to startle you."

Briana stood, rubbing her head with one hand and pulling twigs and yellow flowers out of her hair with the other.

"Good morning, Lady Briana." In a sea-green day gown, Lady Seraphina looked as elegant and fresh as the rose bush she stood next to.

Briana cringed. *I must start dressing for the part, or I'm going to be the dowdiest, most tomboyish queen in the history of the kingdom.*

"Good morning, Lady Seraphina. You're up early."

"I wanted to catch you alone, and Silas thought I might find you here. What did you find?"

"The portal for the faeries to come from Evalon. I've been searching for days."

"How did you know where to look?"

"I didn't. My gut brought me to this hedge, and I dug and ripped and, well, between Mr. Suleiman and I, we'll open it up in no time, and you'll be able to see it without getting dirty."

"I'm not opposed to getting a little dirty, my lady. Nevertheless, I'll wait. I'm sure you'll want to share this discovery with everyone."

Briana nodded. "So, what can I do for you?"

"Could we sit?" she asked, pointing to the nearby bench.

The two women sat, Briana stiffly, and Lady Seraphina perfectly calm and poised. Dara found his way to the women and, after investigating Lady Seraphina with a cursory sniff, settled down near Briana.

"I'll get to the point. You may have developed the wrong impression of the relationship between Silas and me."

"Your relationship with Silas is none of my affair."

Seraphina smiled. "I know differently, and hope this conversation will bring you some ease. So, if I may continue?"

She knows differently? This can't be good. Briana inclined her head for the woman to go on.

"Silas and I grew up together. We're best friends and absolutely nothing more. The thought of Silas in any romantic way is absurd." At Briana's uplifted eyebrow, she laughed, the sound like the bells on a faerie tree.

Even her laugh is perfect, Briana thought, grudgingly.

"You would find that hard to believe, but only because you love him."

Briana's hand flew to her chest. She breathed in sharply.

Seraphina placed her own hand upon Briana's. "It's okay. I'm a close enough friend that Silas felt comfortable confiding in me. He also feels you could use a woman friend and believes you and I could be that to each other." Lips curved in a charming smile, she added, "I think so, too."

It dawned on Briana that she had no female friends nearby. She nodded carefully.

They chatted and Briana found her kind, intelligent and extremely witty, and knew they would become friends.

"So, you aren't interested in Silas, but I wonder Seraphina, is there someone else you are involved with?"

For the first time since their visit started, Seraphina's smile wavered.

"Well, since I'm credited with your secret, I think it only fair I trust you with mine. There is someone I've loved since I was practically a child. Unfortunately, he's older and was happily married."

"Oh, I see. I'm sorry."

"Don't be. Circumstances are different now. There might be some hope after all."

"I'm all for impossible love becoming possible."

Seraphina laughed. "Indeed, so I shall tell you the man who has held my heart for so long is Sir Jameson Stark."

"Oh, my!" Briana exclaimed, taken aback by this disclosure.

Seraphina nodded. "You understand the difficulty? I am truly sorry for his loss. Lady Stark was a kind and gracious woman. I would never have revealed my feelings to Sir Jameson when she was alive."

"But you will now?"

"When the time is right. He must grieve, of course, but when he is ready to consider his future, I have every intention of making him aware of my affection."

"He's a good man. I bet when he's ready for another lady in his life, he'll be happy to know you care for him."

Briana glanced up to find Ayden Suleiman, Head Gardener, coming their way. "Seraphina, it looks like our privacy's been invaded, so we should probably go, but I look forward to spending more time with you soon. Thank you so much for... well, everything. It's a relief to me, not only to have a friend, but to know Silas has someone he can lean on."

Lady Seraphina nodded and turned brightly to the gardener. "Why, hello, Master Suleiman. It's been ages."

"Greetings to you, Your Ladyships." He bowed. Mr. Suleiman had his mother's compact, gnomish body and his father's high cheekbones, long, thin nose, and small lips, which gave him a thoughtful, mystical appearance. What hair remained was pulled back into a tight ponytail. He moved gracefully and spoke quietly. He'd come to Ard Darach a few years before the curse, and engineered this botanical faerieland Briana was now discovering. On the two occasions she'd spoken to him, she found a kindred spirit and looked forward to more time working with him.

After one last hug, Seraphina took the walkway out of the garden to the cottage where she lived with her aging parents, and Briana apprised the gardener of her discovery in the hedge. The morning unfolded like a list: breakfast meeting with Brath; go over menus for meals during the week of the wedding with Mrs. Flannigan; review final plans for wedding ceremony with Cailleach; fitting for her wedding gown with Donla. All this by noon.

At least I didn't have to check chamber pots, she thought, rubbing her aching temples. Lunch would be served soon and the men weren't back. She grabbed Nua out of habit and headed for the middle ward, where she thought they were training, intending to call them in to eat.

As she walked through the gateway, she heard shouts and laughter. Men stood in a half-circle around Brath, who was stripped to his breeches, his chest gleaming with sweat, his hair falling carelessly across his forehead. He wielded a giant broad sword against Silas. Concentration and the fury of flashing steel sharpened both men's faces as they parried, jabbed, retreated and circled one another. She ran toward them, intending to stop their fighting, but was stopped by Sigel's big hands.

"It's okay, lass, they're only practicing."

"This is not a good idea, Sigel." He shook off her concern.

Heart in throat, she watched as the men dueled. Then, in one weird motion, both swords soared into the air, did a macabre dance under the bright rays of the sun and fell, point down, in front of each man. They stared at the swords and then at Sigel, who was staring with a speculative look at Briana.

She maintained a blank expression. "Guess you're even. Time for lunch." Briana turned to leave.

"Not yet, lass. You need more practice if you're riding with us," Sigel said.

Thinking he was joking, she huffed and started off, but he caught her by the elbow. "Not so fast. I've been neglectful of your training, milady. Face your king."

She stared at Brath, who was breathing heavily and wearing a sly smile. Silas leaned on his sword hilt to watch. A chorus arose, "Rise up, milady! Rise up! Face the king!"

Brath wiggled one finger at her before raising his sword in preparation. "Come to me, my lady."

"No way, I'm not…"

The knights continued heckling. She could walk away to their jeers and be seen as a coward, not worthy to ride with them, or she could face Brath. After a thorough glare at Sigel, she stepped in front of Brath and lifted Nua as high as she could.

"No magic," Sigel ordered her.

Brath took a step closer. His eyes, deep mossy pools, captured hers. "Oh, I think there is plenty of room for magic here."

Butterflies. She swallowed hard but held his gaze. To look anywhere else on his body would break her concentration and give him an advantage she couldn't afford. Hopping into a wide stance, she swung Nua upwards. Brath blocked the arc. She ducked when his blade whipped around sideways and came at her head. Jumping back up, she barely had time to hop over the metal as it made a pass at her feet. Nua found a spot in the center of his abdomen to bury her point in, but the sight of hardened muscle sprinkled with cinnamon hair trailing down to the waist of his breeches distracted Briana long enough for Brath to move behind her and catch her against him, employing his blade as a restraint across her throat. Heat spread across her belly where he held her securely with one hand. She allowed herself only a moment of pleasure before going limp to make him think she was done. The second he relaxed, she dropped down and skittered away, coming back up in full swing at him.

His laugh was rich as he danced away from her. "Nice move, Briana, but you may as well surrender. I'll have you in the end."

The innuendo left her breathless.

He kicked her sword away with his own and she went down on one knee to retrieve it. Motion behind him alerted her to danger and she swung herself behind his back.

"Greeerrrr!" she growled out, using both hands to bring Nua straight up, blocking Sigel's weapon as it came in a downward arc at Brath's back. With that immediate threat removed, she stood panting, sweat forging a river between her breasts and puddling under her arms. Sigel feinted again. Brath cut her no slack and started to raise his weapon.

Are you kidding me? She tightened her grip on Nua's hilt and with both hands, raised the sword to block whatever maneuver Brath had in mind.

Dropping his weapon, he reached up and grabbed her hands, pinning her in mid-air. Despite her readiness, she was caught completely off-guard. Nua fell from her grasp. He deliberately walked her back against the wall. One of his hands slid down her arm and ribcage to rest on her waist. She was helpless, but stood steady.

"Checkmate," he whispered.

His breath felt hot on her cheek. Dizzy from the strenuous workout and the fire in his eyes, she allowed the stone to hold her up. Finally releasing her arms, he moved away, still stabilizing her with one hand around her waist. In a louder voice, he declared, "Guess she really does have my back."

The knights cheered and fell to a knee, honoring the woman who had proven she was a warrior-queen.

"Oh, stop it," she said, still trembling. "Time to eat."

⁓❦

Hours later, she was rested, bathed and deciding on a dress to wear to dinner. Gael held up several that didn't meet with Briana's approval.

"What's the king's favorite color?"

"Oh, so that's how it is," Gael said, grinning. "Green."

Briana pulled out a forest-green gown with gold trim and ruby-red button sleeves.

"Ahh, that would be lovely on you, though the neckline is a wee bit lower than you usually like."

They exchanged sly glances. "It will do." The maid chuckled.

The mirror didn't lie. Wearing the king's favorite color and keeping her hair down, the way he liked it, she couldn't deny she'd dressed for him. Gael put away the combs and pots of makeup. Dara stared up adoringly from his post by the door. Briana dismissed Gael. Then she turned to Cailleach, who sat on the edge of the bed, watching with a pleased smile.

"Why am I doing this?"

"Do I need to answer that?" Cailleach replied.

"Please don't. Thank you, Gael," Briana said. When the door shut behind her, she continued, "This is crazy. I'm in love with one man and wanting to impress another."

"I know you're not looking for an answer, but I am going to give you

402

one," Cailleach said. "You're falling for Brath. He's going to be your husband and I must say, I'm relieved you're attracted to him."

Briana muttered something under her breath.

"What did you say?"

Her cheeks grew rosier. "I am falling for him and..."

Briana was interrupted by a knock at the door. There was Brath, raising the color in her cheeks another shade.

"You look lovely," he said, taking her in, from her slippered feet to perfectly coiffed hair, lingering briefly on the neckline of her dress.

"You look, um, handsome," she said, surprised by how vulnerable her voice sounded.

"May I come in a moment?"

"Of course." She stood back to admit him.

"Oh, hello, Cailleach"

"I was just leaving, Your Majesty. Briana, I'll see you downstairs."

"I have something for you," Brath told Briana. "Actually two somethings." Nestled in his palm were a teardrop garnet necklace and matching earrings.

Briana's eyes widened. "They're beautiful."

"Not nearly enough to do you justice, my lady. But they were my mother's and she would want you to have them. And they match the dress you're wearing. Green. My favorite color."

She met his eyes. "I know."

She saw him take a deep breath before stepping around her, and replacing the necklace she was wearing with the garnet. His fingers finished with the clasp and rested momentarily against the skin on the back of her neck.

Heart beating fast, she willed his fingers to explore further. Slowly they moved down the slope of her shoulder and around its curve to trace a line across her collarbone. His hair tickled her neck as his lips lightly followed behind his fingers.

"We should go down," he said, softly. Sighing, he stepped away.

"As Your Majesty wishes," she said, disappointment mingling with relief.

"Oh, I almost forgot! I have another gift for you."

"Another? Brath, the jewelry is more than generous."

"Darling, the jewelry is something you need, as the queen. I am well aware it doesn't hold any particular value beyond that for you. I heard you say how meaningful Shannon Abbey is to you. What I am giving you is your own little castle in Evalon."

She gasped.

"More like a cottage, really, and one that has stood empty for close to a hundred years. The last time I was there it was livable, but in need of some attention. Obviously, I can't actually give it to you now, but when we can safely get to Evalon, you'll see it. I know it will mean more to you than any necklace would."

She was stunned, unable to find any words adequate to the moment.

"It used to be known as Kailen's Castle..." At her inhale, he smiled, knowing full well the import it had for her. "But you can rename it anything you like."

"I don't know what to say, how to thank you."

"Thanks are unnecessary, Briana, but if you were inclined to kiss me, I wouldn't be opposed." He looked pleased to have done something to make her happy. She willingly went to him.

Throughout the evening they stole glances at each other, laughed at small, private jokes and shared opinions on everything from food to Silas' telling of the prophecy.

Briana could almost believe she was falling in love until Sir Glendon said, loud enough for everyone, including Silas, to hear, "You two are destined to be in love."

She choked on the wine she was drinking and caught the bard's eye. He was as unreadable as he always was these days. She tried again to convey regret, but met with only a passive smile.

"Is it the wine, my lady?" Sir Glendon asked.

"No, the wine is wonderful. What is it, anyway?"

"The Taranians' personal recipe of plum wine, my lady," Brath said. "We make a select few casks of it each year and drink it on special occasions. I'd like to serve this at our wedding feast, so I had Reilly serve it tonight for your approval."

"Excellent choice. I wholeheartedly concur," she said, twirling the goblet for effect.

Later, Briana preceded Brath upstairs to their chambers.

"I'm not tired," Briana said, with a slightly intoxicated giggle.

"I was hoping you'd say that. Neither am I. Would you care to sit out on my balcony for one more cup of wine? It's a clear night and…"

"I'd love to," she interrupted, hoping he wasn't about to deliver a soliloquy about the night, the stars and whatever else he could chatter on about.

He ushered her in. Just before the door closed she heard him say, "Good night Sigel. Silas."

She grimaced, unaware the two men had been behind them. *I'm sorry, Silas*, she thought, then shook her head. *This is impossible. I'm going to be married in a week and he'll see us coming and going through these doors every day. I can't keep feeling guilty about it.*

She went to the balcony, where a small table, two chairs and a decanter of wine awaited them. "Are you trying to be a boy scout?"

"What's that?"

She explained and he shrugged. "I suppose I am, then. I do like to be prepared."

He was right about the night. Stars twinkled and a half moon offered soft light. It was warm enough to forgo a wrap, with a gentle breeze that made it comfortable.

He poured them both wine while she settled in. She picked up the goblet and raised her glass to him. *Surely one more cup won't hurt.*

"I so appreciate nights like this," Brath said. "Did you notice what…"

She lost track of his words, her gaze focused on the red canopied bed behind him. The bed seemed to grow larger and more inviting. *Was the room growing warmer?* She licked dry lips. A feeling like molten lava began to pool in her pelvis. She squeezed her legs together to ease the ache that was becoming beautifully bothersome.

"Briana?"

"Hmm… huh? What did you say?"

"What's wrong? Are you okay?"

"Yeah, I just…" Words were failing her, but her eyes kept going to the bed. He turned and followed the trajectory of her gaze. When he looked back, she noted his pupils had grown larger and darker.

"Briana, what's going on here?"

His voice sounded huskier. *Sexier.* "I was thinking maybe we should get it over with."

"Get what over with?"

She nodded toward the bed. "You know…"

He coughed. "Briana, are you asking me to take you to bed?"

"I think so, yes," she said, lifting the goblet to relieve the dryness of her mouth.

"Sweet Maker," he croaked. Watching her drink from the cup, his expression turned from surprise and excitement to chagrin. "Briana, you've never had plum wine before, have you?"

"I don't think so, but I have to say I love it. It's…"

"An aphrodisiac, according to legend."

"Oh. Well, that explains it."

"Yeah, it does."

"Still…"

He stood and sighed. "No, Briana, that is not how it will be our first time. Come on," he said, reaching out to her. "I'll take you to your room."

She took his hand and tried to draw him closer. "You could at least kiss me."

"No. Not a good idea."

He led her firmly to her room, where Gael had the bed turned down and sat by the hearth, waiting for her mistress's return.

"Glad you're here, Gael. My lady has had a reaction to the wine and could use your help preparing for bed."

He pried Briana's hand out of his, and turned it over to the lady's maid. "Good night, my lady. I'll see you tomorrow." Wheeling around, he left the room.

"Damn," Briana said, staring at the back of the closed door. "I have fallen for him."

CHAPTER THIRTY-SIX

COMINGS AND GOINGS

Bright sunlight on Briana's face made her groan and throw the blanket over her head.

"My lady?"

"Go away. Let me die."

"Cailleach left some medicine for your headache."

"Is that what this is?" she said, from under the bedcovers. "It feels like a 7.9 earthquake in my head."

"Briana?" asked Brath.

"Go away, Brath. You may want to find a new bride because I'm dying."

"Come on, my lady, rise and shine."

"You tried to poison me, didn't you?"

His silence bothered the deep recesses of her mind and she slid the covers down over one eye to look at him. He looked as though he'd eaten thunderbolts for breakfast.

Pulling a chair near the edge of her bed, he sat down in front of her.

"I was only kidding, Brath. I know you didn't try to kill me."

He turned to Gael, hand outstretched. She handed him a cup. "White willow bark that will help with the headache."

Briana eased herself up on one elbow, moaning again when the simple movement created an aftershock in her head. "What time is it?"

"Past breakfast, though I doubt you care about eating at the moment. The Winges arrive today. Soon."

Covering her face with her hands, she sighed. "Okay. I'm up." She slid the covers back and tried to sit on the edge of the bed, but dizziness overwhelmed her and she wobbled forward. Brath caught her by the arms and supported her as she regained her equilibrium.

"I am truly sorry about the wine, Briana. I honestly didn't believe those stories. I've never seen anyone else react like that."

Regret tightened his face. Bracing herself with one hand, she used the other to stroke his cheek. "I'll be fine. Just go away, please, and let me pull myself together."

She watched as he rose from the chair, lips pressed tightly together, shoulders drooping.

"Brath, what's wrong?"

"Nothing. I'll meet you downstairs."

"No, wait, something's bothering you. Please don't worry; I'll be fine."

He paused, looked at Gael and nodded toward the door. The maid left. Brath sat back down, looking at his boots for a long moment. Then he raised his eyes. "Do you remember what happened last night?"

She flushed. "Yes." When he didn't respond, she added, "Brath, I'm sorry. I realize queens are supposed to behave with more..."

"I'm not mad at you, Briana."

"No? Good, because I didn't mean to..."

He nodded. "*That's* what bothering me. You didn't mean to."

She studied him, trying to understand. He cleared his throat and ran the fingers of one hand through his hair which, she noted, was impossibly perfect at this hour of the day. Well-put-together and... *Sexy as hell.* However, she was struck more by the emotional vulnerability she sensed in him. She waited for some sort of explanation.

"I was thrilled when I thought you actually wanted me. When I realized it was only the wine talking, I was deeply disappointed." His hands fell into his lap.

She wanted to remove the hurt that shone in his eyes. Yet to do so would move her a step away from Silas. The image of the crossroad above Ard Darach flashed in her mind. Suddenly, her headache vanished, leaving her clear minded and determined. She took his hands in her own.

"Brath," she said, softly, "I do want you. The wine may have lowered my inhibitions, but the inclination was real enough." She let him search her face, knowing he would find nothing but her desire for him.

Visibly relaxing, he lifted her hand to his lips and kissed the tips of her fingers. "In that case, I'm not sure I can wait another week."

She smiled. "Sorry, Your Majesty. Queens must be pure when they come to the king's bed. Now, if you don't mind, I really need to get dressed and be ready to meet our guests when they arrive."

"Do you want me to have Gael bring food?"

"No. I would like you to give me fifteen minutes to get presentable and then *you* can bring me some food."

"As you wish, my lady." He bent in an exaggerated bow and left.

Briana skipped lunch. She was wondering when the Winges would arrive when she heard the pounding of horses' hooves. Briana raced out of the castle to greet them, Dara barking at her side. Epona flung herself off Aquila and into Briana's arms.

"I've missed you," she said.

"It hasn't been that long, Epona."

"Long enough. I can't wait to hear what's happened since we left."

She went from Briana to Silas, who had just arrived, and gave him a bear hug. Sigel greeted her, as well. When the king arrived, Epona, with perceptibly less cheerfulness, dipped one knee in a quasi-curtsy. "Your Majesty."

"I'm so glad you're here. I know Briana has been looking forward to having you back."

When Brath's arm went around Briana's waist, she responded in kind.

Epona's brows furrowed together, giving Briana a *what-the-hell* look.

Briana returned her stare with a reassuring smile.

"Welcome, Sir Thomas and Lady Isabella," Briana said. "Rooms are ready for you. We hope you'll be comfortable during your time at Ard Darach."

Sir Thomas raised an eyebrow at her formality. "Thank you, Lady Briana. The pleasure is completely ours."

Lady Isabella executed the perfect curtsy and nodded, repeating her husband's words. "And now that we are assured that you are taking on the role of lady of the manor quite satisfactorily, might we dispense with all the stuffiness?"

Briana grinned and hugged them both, realizing for the first time how much she'd missed them. "Oh, I am so happy you're here."

"We've missed you too, Lady Briana. The mansion's been rather dull lately. Now, if you'll excuse me, I must greet our king properly."

Brath greeted his guest with a bow and an affectionate kiss on the cheek. "How wonderful to see you again, Lady Isabella."

"I thought you'd shift and fly here," Briana said to Sir Thomas.

"Where would we pack all the dresses, trinkets and important accouterments for a royal wedding?" He winked at Briana.

"Did you run into any difficulties or see any movement from the Grays?" asked Brath.

"Unfortunately, yes. I hate to be the bearer of bad news at such a..." he glanced at Briana, "happy time, but the Gray Military is on the march toward Dromdara. I suspect Inis Fail is their target."

Brath looked grim. "We must stop them."

"As soon as possible. They've already cut down several more faerie trees and burned out a village."

"Casualties?"

"The people escaped and are headed for Inis Fail. A contingent of crows has been sent to set up a barrier, but we'll need more men, Your Majesty."

Brath nodded, thought for a moment and turned to Briana. "I don't think we can wait a week for the wedding."

She made sure he was the only one who caught the gleam in her eye when she said, "Well, I suppose it can't be helped."

"What happened with Artanin?" Sir Thomas asked.

"He's being kept under close observation," Brath said. He summarized what they discovered during the interrogation. "Briana wants me to bring him up, but I don't trust him. The man put this castle under a decade-long sleep. Ten years of our lives – gone! What's to prevent him from doing so again?"

"Valid point, but I do agree with Lady Briana on this one. He holds critical information about Shamwa and the Gray Military that might help us out on the battlefield. It's hard to predict how the battle will progress and what we might need to know in the moment."

"Having his magic would be helpful, too," Briana said, imploring Brath with her eyes.

"He could just as easily use that magic against us."

Sir Thomas turned to Briana. "Speaking of that, how is your magic coming, my lady?"

She shrugged. "So-so. I've been kind of busy with running the household, practicing for battle and planning a wedding."

Lady Isabella spoke up. "Oh, have you not found someone to run the castle for you?"

Briana saw the hint of amusement in her eye and lifted her chin. "Actually, I enjoy working with our staff. And they are quite self-directed, as I hoped they would be. And I do need to work more on developing my magic skills at some point."

"After the wedding," said Cailleach, as she joined the group.

"Brath, maybe we could release Artanin to the keep under guard," said Briana. "So he doesn't develop pneumonia and die before we learn all we can from him."

"Very well," he said, taking her hand in a gentle squeeze, "but if he does us all in, don't say I didn't warn you. Ask the staff prepare a room in the keep for him. Sigel, arrange for some guards. I'll have another chat with him. Does that satisfy everyone?"

Everyone but Sigel nodded.

The Winge family was taken to their rooms to unpack and rest a few hours before dinner.

"Rest, nothing, I want to hear every single thing that has happened to you," Epona said to Briana, as she passed.

"Take a few minutes to settle in. I'll come to your room later," Briana promised.

Silas and Sigel followed her and Brath into the great hall. "Must be nice to see Epona again," Silas remarked, winking when she turned to look at him.

"Very," she said, smiling. "I'm glad she decided to come."

"Was there some question she wouldn't?" Brath asked, sitting down at the long table.

"Not really," she answered quickly, sitting beside him. "I didn't know if she'd leave the stables."

"Briana, I know you and the staff already planned for this evening's dinner, but now they also need to move up plans for the wedding and preparations for troops. Can you bring them up to speed while you're making the arrangements for the druid's chambers?"

"Of course. I also wonder if I should make a visit to Evalon and alert the faeries. I haven't had a chance to tell you yet," she said, looking at Silas and Sigel, "I uncovered the portal to Evalon in the garden."

"Do you suppose they'd be willing to attend a council meeting the day after we're married?" Brath asked.

"Teaguen said they'd want to meet soon after our wedding. I guess it depends on what the faeries mean by soon. I'll ask."

Underneath the table, his hand found hers and squeezed. "Not much of a honeymoon, I'm afraid. I'll make it up to you, Briana."

She shook her head with a smile. "That's the last thing you should be worrying about."

"You will always be the *first* thing I worry about," he said.

"All right, enough pillow talk," Sigel said. "I'll set up guards for Artanin and advise the troops that we march in four days. Silas, can you be ready for a wedding the day after tomorrow?"

"Everything is in place," he said, not looking at Briana.

The meeting was adjourned. By the time Briana could connect with Epona, she was in the stables. The two horse masters were discussing the advantages of breeding the Winge and Taranian horses when Briana entered the barn. Riordan nodded at Briana and took his leave.

"I thought I would find you here," Briana said.

"Interesting guy!" Epona said, tossing her hair back. "Knows his horses."

"That he does."

They wandered away from the barns. Epona carried on a soliloquy, reiterating how dull things were at Winge Mansion without Briana. "No parties, no adventures, no wondering who's sleeping with who…"

"You're awful, Epona." Briana chuckled.

Epona's dark hair bobbed with the shrug of her shoulders. "No, just lonely and bored."

"Well, you could always come here. I assure you, there is never a dull moment at Ard Darach."

"Seems so," Epona said. "What's up with you and the king?"

"We're getting married."

"Yeah, I get that. But you left Winge Mansion totally in love with Silas and a mere two weeks later, you're arm-in-arm with a man you swore to hate. Quite the change of heart, isn't it?"

Stung by her words, Briana said, "You're being overly dramatic. First of all, you're the one who kept insisting I was in love with Silas. May I remind you that I told you I was going to marry the king? Secondly, I never swore to hate anyone, nor have I had a change of heart. The only difference is that I discovered that Brath is not an ogre, but a kind, intelligent, witty, visionary, and to be honest, really great guy."

Epona put a hand up. "Hey, I'm sorry, Briana. I didn't mean to suggest..."

"That I'm fickle and disloyal?"

"I didn't mean that. I'm just surprised."

"Welcome to my world. I'm more than surprised at the way things are turning out, but I'm trying to make the best of it."

Putting an arm around her friend, Epona said, "I'm not the most sensitive person in the kingdom. Sorry."

Briana shook her head. "Forget it, but please, Epona, don't mention it. We're working very hard to do the right thing."

"Okay, but I'm still confused. Are you pretending to be all about Brath, or do you really feel something for the guy?"

Briana smiled. "Epona, he is absolutely impossible not to like. And," she said, "if you haven't noticed, he's handsome as hell."

"Guess that answers my question." Epona laughed, and hugged her friend. "Okay then, you have my full support. But, what about Silas?"

"He's sad but supportive and says this is all in the best interest of Uisneach."

"So damn self-sacrificing, the lot of you." She sighed. "Well, I'll do what I can to support him, as well."

"I'd be grateful for that. We obviously don't have time before dinner for a ride, but would you like to see the gardens?"

What was left of her afternoon was spent chatting with Epona. Brath came to escort her to dinner.

"As always, you look lovely, Briana." His kiss felt genuine but controlled, leaving Briana somewhat disappointed.

Applause erupted when Brath entered the great hall with Briana at his side. She was wearing a black and burgundy Empire gown of raw silk, with long, loose sleeves. The bold, low-cut neckline showed off the garnet necklace and earrings.

Wine and ale flowed, though Briana only sipped at hers. Laughter bubbled up and around the room.

"You would never guess we are about to go to war," Briana said.

Brath sat beside her, looking elegant in forest-green trousers and a matching surcoat over an almond-colored tunic. A mantle lined with otter fur hung over his back and shoulders. At his waist, a wide burgundy belt secured a small functional sword. For the first time, he was wearing his crown. Tonight, more than any other night, he was their king and she, their soon-to-be queen.

"That's fine with me," he said. "This should be a time of celebration. Even if it only lasts for a couple of days, I'm glad of it. We'll all be in battle mode soon enough."

"Is Artanin settled in?"

"He is. I hope I live to be proven wrong about him."

"You will. Trust me." Dara nudged her hand, wanting his head scratched.

"I do trust you, Briana, with my life."

She wanted to be worthy of the sincerity she saw in his eyes. Dara pushed beyond her hand to lay his head in her lap.

After the meal, Briana danced until her feet ached and smiled until her jaws threatened to lock up. Finding herself in the arms of Sir Thomas, an exquisitely graceful dancer, she thanked him again for coming.

"Travel is dangerous and I appreciate the risk you took. I regret that people from other parts of the kingdom won't be able to join us."

He tilted his head slightly and looked at her. "Feeling celebratory, are we?"

"Yes, I am. I admit I didn't expect to, but nothing here has turned out as I expected."

He smiled. "Splendid. You deserve to be happy. I believe he will make you so."

Her head turned to see Brath watching her, a dreamy smile on his face. "I believe so, too," she said, quietly, wishing she was in his arms.

As though reading her mind, he appeared at her side.

"May I cut in, Sir Thomas?"

"Please do.. I grow too old to sustain lengthy dances."

"Yeah, right," Briana chided him. "There isn't an old bone in your body."

"Nevertheless, I gladly hand you over to the arms of your fiancé."

Brath drew her close and waltzed her around the floor. "Is it too early to call an end to this?"

"Why would you want to do that? Everyone is having such fun."

"Because I want to be alone with you. I desperately want to kiss you."

Heart fluttering, she looked around the room and then back at her partner. "Well, it *is* too early to end the party, but I do believe we could sneak outside for a breath of fresh air. Surely no one would question that."

"Excellent idea, my lady."

He whirled her covertly toward the door of the great hall and the next thing she knew, she was breathing in the cool, apple-scented night air. She shivered.

"Cold?" He put his mantle over her shoulders.

"Thanks."

They stood gazing silently at the burgeoning moon in a clear sky.

"I believe you brought me out here for a reason," she prompted him.

"I did." He turned her to him and studied her face, running a finger along her cheek to her ear, where he cupped her face. "I wanted to do this all day." He lowered his face and took her lips in a kiss, carefully controlled and nowhere near enough for Briana.

Opening to him, she sucked his tongue deeper into her mouth. He groaned and the dam burst. As they had battled with swords in the yard the day before, they now battled with the desire building between them. Arching into him she welcomed the heat of his body imprinting on hers. A noise startled them apart, both breathing heavily and shaking with unsatisfied need.

"Milady?"

The youthful voice from around the corner trembled with concern.

Only her frustration kept her from laughing. "Mr. Stark! What are you doing?"

"I was worried when I couldn't find you."

"Did you not notice I was gone also?" Brath asked, trying to sound casual, but struggling to regain his breath.

"Your Majesty! I didn't know. Oh, Maker, I am so sorry. Forgive me."

"Forgiven," he said. "Now go back inside. My lady is in capable hands."

"Indeed," Briana whispered, into his chest.

"Yes, sir. I'm sorry, sir. Milady." He bolted back inside.

Briana looked up at Brath and wound her arms around his waist. "Where were we?"

He eased her away from his body. "I think we had best go inside, darling."

"What! Now?"

He kissed her forehead. "The lad's interruption might have been an act of providence. I'm not sure I can make myself stop at kissing you."

She took his hand and slid it to her hip. "Did you hear me say anything about wanting you to stop?"

"No, but as you've mentioned on previous occasions, the queen is supposed to be pure when she comes to the king's bed. I think we can manage to wait another two days." He laughed at the throaty noise she made. "I promise to do my best to make it worth the wait."

"As though that statement does anything other than fuel the fire," she said under her breath, earning her another chuckle.

❧

Only Sigel and Cailleach accompanied Briana and Brath to the faerie portal the next morning.

"If this goes the way it did before," said Briana, "I'll just sort of fall down and sleep for a little while."

She took a step toward the stone door.

"Wait!" Brath stopped her.

"What?"

He moved to her side and took her in his arms. She saw the fear in his eyes. "Are you sure you'll return?"

"Promise," she said. "Stop worrying. I'll be fine."

"Just in case," he said, lowering his mouth.

She returned the brief kiss then moved away toward the door and opened it before he had the opportunity to stall any further. The next instant she found herself staring at Teaguen.

"Hello," said the faerie. "You found the portal!"

"I did," Briana said. She hugged the sprite. "Ahh, it's good to be back," she said, drinking in the color of Evalon. She was barefoot once again, shimmering, and dressed in the midnight-blue gown, adorned with a crown and peacock feathers. She cocked her head, just making out the faraway sound of Uilleann pipes and drums. "Is this a party?"

"There is always a party!" Teaguen giggled. "Your arrival gives us an extra special reason. However, I assume there is a purpose to your visit."

Briana nodded. "We need to talk."

Teaguen led the way along the pearly steps down the hill to the lake, where Briana was hailed by the talking swans and an assortment of other magical creatures, all welcoming her like a long-absent family member. Sitting together on the green marble bench, Briana explained the Gray Military's march on Dromdara, the accelerated timeline of her wedding, and Brath's interest in a council.

Teaguen nodded eagerly. "I can speak for Evalon. This is something we have waited a long time for. We will come. With bells on," she said with a wink, but then frowned. "Goodness, you will not even have time to settle into married life."

"I don't mind. We need to stop this maniac, and I'm ready to help Brath do that."

"How are you and the king getting along?"

"Much better than I ever thought possible. Hey, is this where you say, 'I told you so'?"

The tinkling laugh was infectious. "No, I would not say that, but I am glad to hear things are going well, especially since…"

"Since?"

"Briana there is something you need to know."

"I'm listening."

"Do you remember what happens in the prophecy when the king and queen are married?"

Briana scrunched her face. "Something about the wedding breaking the cat." Teaguen nodded. "The queen is surprised, an ancient symbol is taken and two worlds collide. Oh, then a lost treasure… I can't remember what happens with the treasure."

"The cat must find it."

A sick dread uncoiled in Briana's stomach. "I don't understand."

"Yes, you do. Who reminds you most of a cat?"

"Silas." His name thudded between them like a stone. "I always called him my 'great cat.' So Silas is going to find the treasure. What treasure? Where?"

"Where two worlds collide," Teaguen said. "This world, and the world you came from. The treasure is the Evalon Runes."

Briana sunk her head into her hands. When she looked up again, tears flooded her eyes. "Silas is leaving."

Teaguen nodded.

"When?"

"Soon. He does not know it yet, but when it comes up at the council, he will volunteer."

A million thoughts ricocheted through Briana's mind. *He's going to leave me. I'll never see him again. It might be for the best. He won't have to stand by and watch me make a life together with Brath. He might find someone in Ireland and fall in love. He might die getting through the tree. He could meet Mom. He won't be here. He won't be here.*

She held her midsection as though in pain. "Why are you telling me this now?"

"To prevent this very response. We felt you should be ready for this when he announces it publicly. He will need your help."

"Teaguen, sending him into my old world is not a good idea. If he even survives the crossing, what he'll find there could destroy his sanity."

"You will prepare him as best you can and send him to others who will help."

"My mother."

The faerie nodded. "We need the runes to complete the circle and bring magic into Uisneach."

"Why?"

"Four treasures must be present in Uisneach to bring the relationship between humans and faeries full circle and restore magic. The first is the Uisneach Tree. The second is the Sword of Uisneach, which you have in your possession."

"Nua? Nua is a national treasure?"

"Yes, and it is a great responsibility to wield it. It can only belong to a tuathla of Evalon. The third treasure is the Evalon Runes, which were taken to the world you came from, and the fourth is the Flaming Arrow, which will be given to Silas when he returns with the runes."

"So, he will come back?" Briana relaxed a little.

"We hope so. If he does not, then Uisneach and Evalon will continue to be separated and evil will remain a constant threat. However, he could fail in his mission, or he could choose not to return. There are always choices to be made."

"Yeah, tell me about it."

"You have fought a hard battle of the heart."

"One that is far from over," she said, frowning.

The faerie shrugged. "Perhaps not, but even though it may not seem so, you are winning."

Briana didn't feel like a winner. Not because the battle wasn't leaning in her favor, but because people were hurt by her choices and too many secrets still hid under the surface.

"People are waiting for you on the other side, High Lady. Do you think you can go back now?"

She nodded. "Not sure how I'll face Silas."

"Remember, you must not tell him. It must come from him."

"I understand. Thank you, Teaguen for telling me ahead of time."

They walked back up the hill to the tree, Briana with much less enthusiasm than when she arrived. Teaguen hugged her. "Be at peace, my lady. Focus on your wedding and your new husband. Everything will turn out right as the wheel of life continues to turn. Trust in that."

Briana woke in Brath's arms. His face was pale, his eyes, large hazel discs of worry. "Are you okay?" Brath stroked her hair. "You were crying."

"That didn't happen the last time," Sigel said, nervously.

"It was emotional." She sat up and focused all her attention on Brath. "They'll come."

"Good," he said, helping her to stand. He didn't let go until she was steady.

Attending to her guests, submitting to a final gown fitting and checking the staff arrangements kept Briana busy enough throughout the day, but the toll of her time in Evalon, the knowledge she held in secret, and the awareness that her time with Silas was extremely short, forced her to retire to her room. She needed solitude to think.

Back in the great hall, Briana smiled and contributed to the conversation, danced, and did her best to present a queenly persona, but inside she felt ragged. Every time she looked at Silas she wanted to cry. Looking at Brath brought up a plethora of conflicting emotions. Then Silas rose to sing:

"I dive into the watery depths, rise up with a pearl,

Set it on your finger, the promise of a dream.

With every foamy wave that breaks upon the rocky coast,

I hold you close and love you, in our enchanted sea.

Come, my love, and swim with me

In our beautiful, magical sea.

Heart to heart, we dive and dart,

Through the waves of our enchanted sea."

Silas looked at her as he sang. She'd swear the Uilleann pipes were sobbing. It was her undoing.

"I think I'll go up to bed," she said to Brath, rising suddenly. She answered his questioning look by pasting on a smile and patting his arm. "A bride needs her beauty sleep."

"I'll walk you to your room."

Outside her door, he stopped. "Something is bothering you. If going to Evalon does this to you, I don't want you to ever go again."

"I'm okay, Brath. I just have a lot on my mind. I suppose I'm a little nervous about the wedding."

He gave her a steady look and didn't try to kiss her. "Well, good night, then. If you need anything…"

"Good night, Brath. I'll see you tomorrow. Sleep well."

⌘

Wrapped in a heavy, wet mist, Briana held the sword in front of her, ready to defend, or if need be, attack. Who are you? She rose from her hiding place behind the tree. What do you want with me? The auburn-haired man held out a crown. His eyes were kind, and she felt a pull toward him. She dropped her weapon on the ground. She wanted to take the gift, but a flash of blonde hair caught her eye. She turned to find the archer, his eyes filled with longing and pain. In his hands was an arrow wrapped in a garland of ivy and feathers. I'm sorry, she told him. I'm so sorry. He turned and walked into the grayness, out of her vision. The man with the crown waited. She held out her hand, and he placed the crown in it. She felt the weight of it as it settled on her head. The fog dissipated. A magnificent monarch butterfly fluttered out of a sun beam between them.

⌘

Briana woke knowing what she needed to do. Drying her eyes and throwing on a dressing gown, she went to Brath's room.

The king sat at his table, still dressed, with papers, maps and a small painting spread out in front of him. "Briana?"

"I need to talk to you, and when I'm done, you may not want to marry me."

He looked startled, but poured her a cup of wine and sat back to listen.

"I need to tell you about Silas and me." She dropped into the chair.

He never flinched and never made a sound the entire time she told her story, his only reaction a wrinkle across his forehead and a deepening

421

of the green of his eyes. With the weight of the secret lifted, she looked at him, calm and determined to accept his response.

"I know about the feelings you and Silas have for each other."

Her jaw dropped. "How?"

"It's hard to miss. The energy between you is almost palpable. I tried to ignore it, but realized I couldn't marry you, not knowing. So I asked Sigel. He advised that I let you tell me in your own time and way. And so you have."

"How did he know I would tell you? We all agreed it was better not to say anything."

"You're nothing if not honest, Briana. I'm not sure you could marry me holding on to this secret." He took a sip of wine. "I assume what happened today in Evalon has something to do with Silas."

"He's leaving. He doesn't even know it yet, and you can't tell him, but he will be the one to go through the tree, to where I came from, and find the runes. Supposedly, they're on what we call the 'Hill of Uisneach' in Ireland."

"I see. And you don't want him to go?"

"Of course not. The journey is dangerous and he'll be overwhelmed by my world. Nothing here can prepare him for that."

"Just as nothing there could prepare you for coming here."

She shook her head. "You don't understand. Uisneach is a simple kind of dangerous. The world I came from is rife with complication and confusion. The technology alone will throw him into chaos. I can try to prepare him, but it will be shocking and overwhelming.

"I don't exactly know how this tree travel thing works and where he will end up. It would be best if he went to Camden, so my mother could help him acclimate. But he could end up anywhere, alone and lost."

"All we can do is give him as much information as possible to make him successful. After all, he's not the only one making a sacrifice for the sake of Uisneach."

She sat back, unsure of his meaning. An awkward silence separated them until Briana asked, "If you knew about Silas and me, why did you agree to the marriage?"

"Initially, for the same reason you did. I believed we were destined to wed and save Uisneach. I would sacrifice anything to save this kingdom from Shamwa and restore magic. Marrying you didn't seem too high a price to pay. I thought you made your choice for the same reason."

She nodded. "But things have changed for me."

"As they have for me," he replied, reaching out a hand to take hers. "I didn't expect to fall in love with you."

Oh, no, not the L word. I'm not ready for that.

"And because I love you, I am prepared to let you go."

She narrowed her eyes. "What do you mean?"

"I offer you the chance to go with Silas and help him find the runes."

Setting down the goblet that shook in her hand, she stared at him, speechless.

"You did your part in releasing the curse. You could go back to your mother, help Silas find the runes, and then send them back. The two of you could stay there and enjoy a life together."

Back to Mom. Hot showers. Fast food. Her friends. A life with Silas. Blood pounded in her ears as the things she missed ran like a banner through her mind. Then she looked at the man sitting across from her, waiting for her answer. *No Brath. No Uisneach. No Sigel or Cailleach or Jonathan. No Nua or Dara. No Evalon. No saving a kingdom and leaving a legacy of magic.*

"My home is here now," she said. "And I have every intention of marrying you tomorrow." Glancing at the candle, she smiled uncertainly. "Today, I mean. If you'll still have me?"

"I will do everything in my power to see that you never regret this choice, Briana. I promise you."

"Well," she said. "I'm grateful you didn't decide to hang us."

"Hanged! Why on earth would I do that?"

"Sigel said you could, and that if there was a hint of anything between me and Silas, you would."

Brath laughed out loud. "True, the king is allowed to execute traitors, but I find the practice barbaric. I certainly wouldn't do it to someone I cared about. I didn't even hang Artanin. Yet," he amended, grinning.

"Seriously, Brath. Now that you know everything, do you have any reservations about marrying me? I don't want to start our marriage with you worried about Silas."

He studied her. "Whatever your feelings are for the bard, I believe you also care for me. I'm arrogant enough to think I can win your affection and love, given time. I hope that together, we'll restore Uisneach and build a family to carry on what we begin today."

He picked up the picture in front of him. "I was just looking at this painting of my parents when you came in, wondering what they would think of this marriage."

She looked at the couple, smiling and holding toddler Brath between them. "They seem so happy."

"They were, and they would want the same for me. They would love you, Briana, and approve our marriage without reservation, even knowing everything."

"Thank you, Brath."

"For what?"

"For letting me tell you on my own and for being wise enough to not let pride get in the way of what is possible between us."

He stood and took her in his arms. "Thank *you* for being honest. I'm not sure how I would have felt if you hadn't been."

His embrace was reassuring. She believed they would be fine, but hoped Silas would find some solace, as well. Perhaps her thoughts were reflected in her eyes.

"Maybe it's a good thing that Silas is leaving. He's always been like a little brother to me, and though I don't want to see him leave his home, I cannot imagine what it would be like to stand by and watch you build a relationship and a family with another man."

"You need to know he always supported you and urged me to be open to what might happen between us. He's been loyal to you from Day One."

"I have no doubt about that."

She lay her head on his chest. "You're a remarkable king and man."

"I am, aren't I?"

They both laughed.

"Keep that in mind as your heart decides what it feels about me."

"I will."

He eased her away from his body, placing a light kiss on her lips. "My lady, you have only a few hours left to rest before you are dragged out of your bed and to the altar to become my wife. I suggest you try to sleep for a bit."

"There will be no dragging, Brath. I am ready and willing to become the Queen of Uisneach and your wife."

BRIANA – QUEEN OF UISNEACH

A hush fell over the room when the women stood back to behold the bride. The girl who stepped through the tree in Wellsland in a pair of jeans and a ratty tee shirt was now a queen, sublime in her magnificent wedding gown. She'd been bathed in herbs and massaged until her skin gleamed.

Briana and Cailleach stood in front of a full-length mirror. Cailleach, gloriously earthy in a forest-green velvet robe stitched with green and gold leaves, with sleeves that fit snugly at the upper arm and flowed down to drape over her fingers, stared at the woman beside her. "Beautiful," she pronounced, "and a fitting queen to our king."

Elegantly simple, Briana's dress was spun from white silk. Filmy veils attached to satin shoulder caps draped down her arms. The silver embroidered bodice and dropped waist flowed into a full skirt, which pooled around her slippered feet. A gauzy train trailed behind, covering the laces that ran down her spine. A loosely knotted belt hung low on her stomach, reminding her of a more feminine version of a sword belt. Several small braids on the sides of her head joined in a single braid down her back. Color was applied to her eyes, cheeks and lips and scented oil dabbed behind her ears.

"I wish my mother could see me."

"She can," Cailleach said. "Mirrors, like water, are excellent conductors of intuition and magic. Stare with me into the glass, imagining your mother on the other side."

They spent several minutes at the exercise. When it felt right to break the spell, Briana stepped back. "I'll have to trust that she picks up something intuitively."

A knock at the door announced that it was time. Gael admitted Lord Marshall Sigel, who, in a long black and gold tunic over black pants, his boots shined and sword at his side, was head-to-toe the king's man. Cailleach shooed everyone out of the room, instructing them to finish their own preparations quickly and go to the courtyard. She hugged Briana warmly before leaving herself.

"Sweet Maker, Sigel, you *are* handsome," Briana said.

"Should I be offended that you sound shocked?"

"I just meant…"

He laughed. "I know. You, my dear, are stunning. Brath is going to trip all over himself."

"He's more graceful than that," she said. "Have you seen Silas this morning?"

Sigel nodded. "He's fine, Briana. Ready to do his part. How about you? Ready to do your duty?"

"I think we both know I no longer do this strictly out of duty."

"I can see you care for Brath, and I'm glad. For what it's worth, I do believe he'll make you happy."

"A relative term. But, yes, I think we'll be okay. But there is still a part of me that feels sad I won't be walking down the aisle to Silas. Is it possible, Sigel, to love two men?"

"Love is nothing if not complicated, and one of the few things we have no control over. But my advice is to focus on one man today. If you do love Brath, then give him your best today."

She nodded. "I will, but please, Sigel, do something to help Silas. I don't want him to suffer any more than he must to get through this wedding."

"I'll do what I can."

"Oh, and by the way, I did talk to Brath last night about him."

"I know you did, and I'm glad. Keeping secrets is no way to start a marriage."

The sound of pipes and drums cued them. Walking into the hall, they passed an open window, and the music grew louder. A monarch butterfly flew in, landing on Briana's shoulder.

Sigel cleared his throat. "Briana, you have become like a daughter to me, and I wish only your happiness. This is the last time I will ask it. Are you absolutely sure you want to go through with this?"

She put a finger to the butterfly's wings and looked beyond the delicate creature to the gathering outside. Seeing Brath standing beside Cailleach, waiting for her, hope and possibility shining from his eyes, she nodded. "I am."

He hugged her, trying not to muss her gown. "Good. Let's go make you a queen."

The world around her vanished as Sigel escorted her out of the castle and into the courtyard, with Dara a respectful distance behind them. The butterfly fluttered around her. Briana felt embraced by the surrounding stone of Ard Darach. Uilleann pipes and large drums beat out a dirge-like wedding march that sounded less sad and more like the fulfillment of a prophecy, stirring something deep inside her. As if in a trance, she viewed her friends gathered around the arbor in front of the keep. Beautiful wild-flowers, mistletoe and the unmistakable reminder of wedded love, ivy, were woven through the arbor. Cailleach stood framed in the center, focused on the woman coming toward her. Brath stood beside her, waiting to take her from Sigel, his expression intense and a little nervous.

Probably praying I won't bolt at the last minute. She smiled, trying to reassure him, and saw his shoulders relax.

Jonathan stood a few feet away from Brath, leaving a space for Briana.

Her eyes were captured by a movement above Cailleach. Silas, wrapped in the ancient kilt of Uisneach, tall and proud, fully bard and heroically ready for his part, stood on the keep's walkway beside the parapet. Yearning throbbed in her soul. His eyes shone with love and admiration. Her smile faded, and she clutched Sigel's hand tighter.

"Look to Brath," he whispered.

Reluctantly, she turned from her soulmate to her destiny.

Brath was resplendent in black trousers and a russet coat almost exactly the color of his hair, under which a buff-colored linen shirt with black laces peeked out. Black boots cuffed with brown leather completed his outfit. His sword hung at his side.

The butterfly continued to dance around her, almost pushing her forward. Briana passed by Lady Isabella and Sir Thomas, who smiled wistfully. Epona dabbed at her eyes, her mouth in a grim line. Seraphina offered a placid and encouraging smile. Shock struck her momentarily as she noticed Artanin in the crowd, heavily guarded, but present. She glanced with a smile to Brath, who dipped his head in silent acknowledgment. Briana and Sigel stopped in front of Cailleach. Dara sat down beside his mistress, seeming to take the proceedings seriously and with unusual decorum.

Sigel placed Briana's hand into the king's and moved to stand at his other side.

Cailleach began by reciting a short history of Uisneach and the House of Taranian, followed by a reading of selected parts of the prophecy. "Today, we celebrate the ending of a curse and the fulfillment of a prophecy in this marriage between King Brath of the House of Taranian and Lady Briana of Uisneach and Evalon."

"King Brath, please remove your weapon and lay it in front of your lady, a token of your intention to be at peace with her at all times." He did so, laying it crossways between them. She asked Briana to do the same. Briana turned to Jonathan, who offered Nua to her. Briana laid her sword diagonally across Brath's.

"May this house be filled with peace and kindness, mercy and love. May there never be an occasion to raise voice or weapon to one another as long as you live."

Sigel stepped forward with the king's golden crown. The jewels flashed in the sun as the crown was set atop the king's head.

"King Brath of the House of Taranian," Cailleach said, looking from him to Briana. "Is this the woman you choose to be your wife and the queen of Uisneach?"

"She is."

She handed him a second, smaller coronal. Turning to face Briana, he held it out to her, saying, "Lady Briana, I choose you to be my queen and partner in the governing and care of Uisneach. I trust you with the responsibility this bears. Together we will restore Uisneach and defend it from all evil. From today and forever more, you shall be known as Queen Briana of the House of Taranian, in the kingdom of Uisneach."

She knelt before him, accepting the crown he settled on her head, dipping slightly at its literal and symbolic weight.

Cailleach reached into a pocket and produced two wide golden bands carved with the Taranian badge of weasel, crown and holly. She held them up to the sky. "Maker, bless these rings as a symbol of the commitment of this man and this woman to fulfill your purpose for them as a married couple and leaders of this kingdom. Bless them with love and children and under their wise guidance, may harmony spread across the lands of Uisneach."

She offered one of the rings to Brath. "King Brath, this is the lady you have chosen to live your life with, to work with, and to raise children together with, should Maker will it so. Will you love her faithfully, protect and defend her with your life and promise to treat her as your equal in all things?" This last line was Briana's idea. Brath had raised eyebrows but agreed without argument.

"I will," he promised, "and may Maker be my judge if I should fail."

"Briana, this is the man you have chosen to live your life with, to work with, and whose children you shall bear, should Maker will it so. Will you love him faithfully, protect and defend him and his house with your life and promise to treat him as your equal in all things?"

"I will," she affirmed, "and may Maker be my judge if I should fail."

Kneeling in front of her, Brath placed the band on her finger and kissed it. She, in turn, reached for his hand and kissed his sovereign ring. Staring into her face, he pressed his lips to hers, the final seal of the contract between them. They stood, King Brath and Queen Briana of the House of Taranian of Uisneach.

A cheer rose up and reverberated off the walls. On a whim, she initiated a second kiss, to a roar of applause. The butterfly lighted briefly on her head, circled once more around her and Brath, then spiraled up and over the walls.

Brath walked her to the thrones that had been brought out for the celebration. Musicians found their places. Rushes were lit as dusk began to settle around them. Drums sounded and hearts began to stir at the primordial beat. Uilleann pipes evoked a sense of sacredness and sorrow. Above them, Silas walked beside the parapet wall slowly, reverently, and in his lilting voice, began to sing the song he'd written for her.

"Come ye, good people of Uisneach lands.

Hear the tale and celebrate,

the prophecy unfolding, a king and king-
dom saved and new queen crowned.

From deep inside the oak she came,

emerging from between the worlds.

Brave Briana, beautiful healer and warrior at heart.

From Baigsith and the gnomes she left,

across a rainbow bridge to Tynan Ibor,

making friends across the land, in orchards,
forests and village greens.

A map to lead, a crow to guide,

she trusts the knight and bard.

A witch to teach magic and lore, the ancient ways of old.

Devoted hound and mystical sword,

dryad from the Uisneach tree.

Briana and her trusted two, battle evil in
the fort, victorious but scarred.

A journey of the heart and soul,

from Appleduir to Ard Darach.

Discovering her ancient roots and royal history.

Crow's nest a restful place with friends

Gray mare given, friends for life.

Heart wide open, grows in grace, a queen she soon becomes.

Chapter Thirty-seven

Rune stones and warrior bones,

feathers wrapped in ivy.

Beating heart her soul's true home, across the span of time.

All roads lead to Evalon,

faeries dance and heart grows strong.

*Love of Uisneach leading ever forward, guid-
ing her to home and throne.*

The crow and witch, medallions two,

Knight, bard and queen make five!

Their power sent to save the king, Uisneach free once more.

So here we are, a joyful time,

the wedding day is here!

*Let's jubilate this royal pair, King Brath, the
great and Mouse turned queen –*

Briana, brave and true!"

Rune stones and warrior bones, feathers wrapped in ivy! There it was, the meaningful surprise. If he only knew what his reference to the runes really meant. Overwhelmed, she was helpless to stop the tears flowing down her cheeks. Silas walked down the stone stairs and stood in front of her. She saw her own sorrow reflected in his eyes, but could only watch as he kneeled before her.

"To your house and your person as Queen of Uisneach, I, Silas of Cedarmara, pledge my fealty to you. If anyone should threaten or harm you, I will be your protector and avenger. I offer this fealty knowing that should I fail in any way to uphold my oath, my life will be at your mercy. Will you do me the honor, my queen, of accepting this oath from my lips?"

"I will, Silas of Cedarmara, with gratitude." She held out a shaking hand to him and he kissed the ring upon her finger. His lips remained a second longer than necessary.

He moved to the king and repeated the vow.

For the next hour, she accepted the blessings and oaths of her subjects. Her hand was nearly worn out from the kisses, and her heart faint. Darkness fell as the last person went into the great hall to dance, feast and toast the marriage of the king and queen. The monarchs stayed behind for a quiet moment alone.

Brath faced his bride and circled his arms around her, laughing when one of his hands tangled in the train. "Well, my queen, we are married."

"So we are."

"Regrets?"

Looking into his eyes, so hopeful and loving, she answered, "Not one."

"Thank Maker. For a moment this morning, I feared the outcome of this day, but I'm grateful and happy you went through with it."

"And now it's time to celebrate. Shall we join our guests?"

She started to turn, but his hand on her arm stopped her. "One moment, my lady." Lips, warm and promising, claimed hers. She responded with vigor and a promise of her own.

CHAPTER THIRTY-EIGHT

PROMISES AND BLESSINGS

Blessings and well wishes rang out as the king and queen entered the hall and took their seats at a table overflowing with food. Succulent roast pheasant and venison, poached salmon and rabbit stew graced the table beside mountains of vegetables, herb-scented gravy, fruited jellies, delectable pies, tarts and pastries and freshly baked bread.

"Mrs. Flannigan has even prepared us a quiche Lorraine," Briana exclaimed, clapping her hands in delight.

"Is it really your favorite dish?" Brath asked, handing her a slice.

Briana, too nervous to eat most of the day, felt a rumble in her belly. "No, but she thinks it is, and for her to make this especially for us is so sweet."

He grinned. "You are going to be a great queen, my lady."

She cocked her head sideways. "Because I like quiche?"

"Because you helped the cook out of a tight spot and made her think she was doing something remarkable."

Laughter, storytelling and poetry accompanied the music performed by Silas and a host of local musicians who volunteered their skills to celebrate the royal wedding. The songs were beautiful, romantic and joyful, to honor the king and his new queen.

"My lady, I believe it is customary for us to take the first dance." Brath stood from the table and reached for her hand. "Would you do me the honor?" With a curtsy and a bow, they took the floor. A capable dancer, Brath made it easy to follow gracefully as he twirled her around.

"Who taught you to dance?" she asked.

"Sigel."

"What?" She rocked back. She held on to her husband as she tried desperately to control the laugh threatening to erupt from her belly.

"I know. We had a dance instructor once, but she died unexpectedly, and like most things, it went to Sigel to teach me. Beautiful as my mother was, she couldn't dance to save her soul. Two left feet."

"Well, you certainly don't take after her."

"Good. I want to make you proud, my lady."

Cailleach was right; she was not disappointed by Brath's looks or manners. Remarkable in so many ways, he'd make any girl be happy to be his bride. For the most part, she was happy to be that girl. If not for...

While Brath and Briana danced to the music of a local harpist, tables were rearranged and the thrones moved to the head of the room. When the song finished, Brath led her to the throne she would sit on for the first time. Shivering at the import of this moment, she looked at him for reassurance, which he gave with a smile. He held her hand while she stepped up and settled onto the polished wood.

"A perfect fit," he said, inspiring her with confidence.

Silas began the next song. Couples spilled out on the floor in traditional dances and slower tunes meant to allow a closeness between real or would-be lovers. Briana and Brath alternated between dancing and chatting with each other and their guests.

Sir Jameson was guiding Briana across the dance floor when she noticed Sigel whispering in Brath's ear. Anger blazed from Brath's eyes, and he nodded. Sigel immediately left the hall. Briana excused herself when the dance ended.

"What's happened?"

"Nothing, love," Brath replied, an authentic smile in place.

"What did Sigel tell you?"

"Nothing to worry about. He's just being Sigel."

His vague response did nothing to ease her concern, which he must have seen from her expression. "Not tonight, Briana. Nothing is going to trouble us on this night. In fact..."

She watched his eyes change from marble-green to smoky hazel. Butterflies began to rouse.

"I suspect our guests would be happy to see us bring this to a close."

She looked away nervously.

He drew her chin back to face him. "Are you ready to go up to our room?"

Her stomach looped, but she nodded.

Hand in hand, they stood as one. Out of the corner of her eye, she observed Silas leave the room as a harpist continued to play.

"Queen Briana and I would like to thank everyone for sharing in this joyful celebration with us. Too much jubilation, it seems. We find ourselves fatigued..." a twitter rippled around the room at this, "and would bid you good night. Please, stay and dance as long as you like. We'll see you in the morning."

He led Briana down from the dais to the door leading upstairs to their chambers to the discomforting cheers of their friends. Dara traipsed along behind, staying as close to his mistress as her dress would allow.

They didn't speak on the way up. Briana was acutely aware of warmth spreading across her lower back where Brath's hand rested. He opened the door and gave her an encouraging smile as she walked into what would now be their room.

A low fire crackled in the fireplace. A padded bench had been placed in front of the hearth and draped with a rabbit fur coverlet. Fragrant flowers sat on a nearby table, with a flagon of wine and two goblets. The green ríocht board and small table from her room had been moved here.

She smiled. Dara sniffed around and grumbled at his bed, now situated beside Brath's – their – bed. She looked at her new husband.

"Thank you."

"I assumed the hound would be sleeping with us, and the *ríocht* – well, if things don't go well tonight, we can always play a game." Seeing the worried look on her face, he said, "I was joking, Briana. There will be no *ríocht* tonight." He removed his jacket, laying it over a chair before pouring the wine and handing her a glass. She sniffed it.

"It's not plum wine, Briana. I wouldn't do that to you."

"Of course not." She took a large sip and moved toward the balcony.

An unexpected crack and flash of light made her jump. "I guess we're going to have a storm."

"Are you afraid?" At her startled expression, he clarified, "Of storms?"

She shook her head. "Not of storms."

"Are you afraid of anything? Of tonight? Of me?"

"No," she squeaked, surprised by the nervousness she heard in her voice. She cleared her throat and repeated. "No, I'm not afraid."

"No? I am."

She snorted in disbelief. He stretched out his hands, showing the light tremor of his fingers.

"Why? This is not your first time."

"It's the first time I've made love to a queen."

The butterflies lifted.

"And the first time it mattered so much to me to do it perfectly. I want this night to be a blessing to you."

Rain began to fall harder, threatening to wet them.

"Let's go sit in front of the fire," Brath suggested, taking her hand.

They sat next to each other on the bench, sipping wine, watching the fire dance seductively, saying nothing for several minutes.

"Would you mind if I freed your hair from that braid?"

"You don't like what Gael spent hours doing to my hair?"

"It was lovely for the ceremony, but at the moment, I'd rather see it falling down around your shoulders."

Multitudes of butterflies took flight.

Turning enough to allow him space to work, she tried to steady her breath while his fingers worked through the strands of hair, massaging her scalp where the braiding had resulted in tight and sensitive skin. His touch was gentle, warm and relaxing. She leaned back, losing the desire to control anything. Her body turned more liquid than solid as his scent and essence surrounded her like a sheltering cloak.

"Turn around," he said, thickly. He lifted her hair, then released it, letting it cascade down around her. He sat back, looking at her like she was a work of art.

When his stare became uncomfortable, she bent toward him. "Would you mind kissing me or something? I feel like a live version of the Mona Lisa."

"I don't know what the Mona Lisa is, but I'm more than happy to kiss you."

Keeping his eyes open, he pressed his lips to hers. She responded by putting one hand against his cheek and opening her mouth, urging him to do more.

"You're not making this easy, Briana," he whispered against her mouth.

"What?"

"I'm trying to take it slow and make this night last, but if you keep kissing me like that, it will be over before it's begun."

She pulled back. "Oh, well, what's your next move, then?"

He chuckled. "Are we playing *ríocht* now?"

"It kind of feels like it."

"We're not," he assured her. "Tonight there is no strategy, no trying to one-up the other. We both get to win."

Briana stared into the fire, but its rhythmic sway and crackling only made her more conscious of the need growing within her. "I think I'm going to need help with the laces on this dress."

"It would be my pleasure," he said, quietly.

She turned and he pushed aside her hair, pressing a petal-soft kiss to the back of her neck that sent a shiver down her spine. His fingers accomplished the task proficiently, smoothing the cloth away from her back. He ran his fingers lightly down her skin. "So soft," he murmured, lips trailing fingers.

Turning her to face him, he slid the gown off her shoulders and down the slope of her chest until it pooled around her waist, revealing her firm, rose-tipped breasts.

"Beautiful." His hand caressed one soft orb as a thumb grazed its hardened tip. She sighed at the sensation of his palm and fingers on her hyper-sensitized skin.

He groaned and crushed his lips to hers, apparently forgetting that he wanted to take things leisurely. He tasted of mint and mead, making her drunk from his kisses. Her tongue dueled with his, thrust for thrust, until neither could breathe.

She arched into him, moaning, as his hands cradled both breasts, kneading gently, teasing and tormenting her.

The entire kaleidoscope of butterflies took flight.

She reached for the hem of his shirt and lifted it over his head, instantly missing his touch on her skin when he raised his arms. His hands returned to their exploration as she began one of his body. Touching, kissing and nipping aroused them both past a point of wanting to take anything slow. She stood, letting the dress fall to her feet. She stepped out and kicked the material aside.

He closed his eyes, swaying slightly, and she put a hand on his arm to raise him up. When he stood, she reached for the laces on his trousers. Taller than her by several inches, with strong arms and legs and broad shoulders, he had the body of a warrior. The cinnamon hair so becoming on his head looked just as enticing across his chest and down his abdomen. Clothing gone, they explored each other with passionate curiosity. Slippery heat spread between her legs, igniting her. She slid his hand off her breast and slowly down her ribs and belly. Following her cue, he eased the hand lower, finding her silky, swollen bud. She groaned, pushing herself against him.

"Sweet Maker, Briana."

"Could we take it slow some other time," she said, breathless.

He eased aside the canopy curtains to a bed already turned down for them.

He was gentle and her young body yielded, the music of their passion floating around them like a symphony. She clung to him at the moment of penetration and cried out.

"Briana?"

"I'm all right," she said, as the stab of pain lingered briefly then disappeared, leaving her with an impression of being filled and somehow reborn. From the chrysalis of her youth, she emerged, fully woman, fully butterfly.

Brath's lovemaking was thorough and pleasant, his kisses passionate, his hands expert at finding the most sensitive places on her body.

Seeking, stroking and arousing, he repeatedly carried her to the pinnacle of pleasure.

Intuitively touching, stroking and kissing, she did the same for him.

Afterward, he kissed her and gently covered her with the blanket before falling asleep with her in his arms.

She listened to drops of rain beating against the slate tiles on the roof. "I promise to be a good wife to you, Brath," she whispered into the darkness.

∽

They were making love. His hands roamed her body, his mouth devoured hers, and she smelled his muskiness as their bodies interlocked in a timeless dance of ecstasy. She tried to whisper something to him, but he smothered her words with his lips and tongue, turning her words into a hungry moan. Gazing into her lover's eyes, she found, not the green-brown eyes of Brath, but Silas' old-soul eyes that looked so deeply into hers and made her whole. Guiltless, as one can only be in a dream, she welcomed his hunger, his kisses and caresses. Suddenly, his hot body was cruelly ripped away, leaving her cold, heartbroken and lonely.

∽

She awoke in a sweat, her heart pounding, tears sliding down her face. Fortunately, her restlessness hadn't disturbed Brath. She allowed herself time under the cover of night to grieve what had never been and would not ever be.

CHAPTER THIRTY-NINE

E-U SUMMIT

"Bri, wake up."

"Grmmmp…" she mumbled, from under the covers.

"Come on beautiful, time to get up." Brath peeled the blanket away from her face.

The sun was full up, shining through the windows across the bed. She opened one eye to see him kneeling beside their bed, and turned away in disgust. "Must you always look so perfect first thing in the morning?"

"Are you always so grumpy in the morning?"

Slowly the other eye opened, and she stared at this man who had taken her to the moon and back last night. He was ready for the day and regally handsome, but recalling how he'd looked during the night, eyes darkened by passion, hair made wild by her hands and lips reddened by her kisses, she thought she liked him better at night. Heat began to fill the space between her legs along with an unfamiliar ache. "Hey," she said, "you called me Bri."

He pushed a lock of hair behind her ear. "Do you mind?"

"My dad used to call me that," she said, softly.

He pushed her over enough to stretch out beside her. "Maybe I should find another pet name. I don't want you to confuse me with your father."

Waking to a growing desire, she slid a hand across his lap, lightly stroking, and smiled at the result. "Why don't you slide out of those trousers and under these covers and I'll prove I don't have you confused with Dad."

He removed her hand and kissed its palm. "Trust me when I tell you there is nothing on Maker's sweet earth I would rather do, but the faeries will be here soon, and they need their princess dressed and ready to negotiate."

She sighed.

"I'll make it up to you tonight." He kissed her.

"Where's Dara?"

"Fed and out with Jonathan." Reluctantly, he started to rise.

"Not so fast, Your Majesty. Tell me what happened last night between you and Sigel."

"You don't miss a thing, do you?" He sat on the edge of the bed. "The Gray Military attacked Inis Fail yesterday. Most of the village was burned out and there are many dead."

"Damn! You should have told me last night."

"Sigel sent a detachment. We need to hold the faerie council as planned today, and leave tomorrow."

The faerie council. Silas' last day in Uisneach. She threw back the coverlet.

She joined him at the table, already set for breakfast with covered dishes of leftover quiche and oat bread and butter

His eyes grew smoky again. "This is no way to start a marriage. We should be spending time alone together, not racing off to councils and battles. I'm so sorry."

She shook her head. "Brath, you must stop apologizing for everything. We're monarchs in the midst of war. We'll find time later to be newlyweds."

They were interrupted by a knock at the door. Sigel poked his head in. "Everyone decent?"

"And if we aren't?" Briana replied.

"I'm coming in anyway, so you'd better be."

"The king looks happy this morning," Sigel said. He searched Briana's face.

"The king is very happy this morning," he confirmed, winking at his bride. "I'm a lucky man, Sigel."

"Indeed, Your Majesty, you are. All Uisneach is lucky today."

Briana and Brath exchanged a serious look. *Well, not all Uisneach,* she thought. *Inis Fail is toast and Silas is leaving. Other than that, all is well.*

"I hate to disturb all this marital bliss," Sigel said, "but I bring more bad news."

Brath instantly became king. "What?"

"We're pushing the Gray Military back, but in the process, we've suffered a lot of casualties, even among the crows."

"Damn it," Brath swore. "Ready everyone to leave at daybreak tomorrow." He looked meaningfully at Briana.

"Don't say it," she warned him. "We'll be ready, but what will you do with Artanin?"

Sigel gave her a disgruntled look. "Good question. If I'd killed him when I had the chance…"

"We'll bring him along," said Brath. "He might be useful. We can't spare any knights for guard duty, so you best assign a few strong men as his personal guards. It's not a great plan, I know."

Sigel nodded, still frowning.

The castle turned into a beehive of activity. Lady Isabella took charge of overseeing the household staff's arrangements for the summit meeting and the imminent departure of the king, queen and army. Cailleach prepared medicinals and emergency treatments. Epona hustled to the barns to help Riordan with readying the horses. Silas went with Sigel to round up the knights, squires and Jonathan.

Briana and Brath had gone over the agenda for the conclave and now, three hours later, stood waiting at the portal for the faeries. Every person at Ard Darach was also in attendance, except Artanin, creating a wide arc around the gateway to Evalon.

The wind, which had blown stiff much of the day, suddenly went still. The sound of waves crashing against the cliffs became mere background noise, replaced by the haunting music of pipes and drums. Briana closed her eyes and tried to shake off the sense of déjà vu that assailed her. Focus returned as the carved stone door rolled away and music poured forth.

A troupe of faeries paraded out in their finest, adorned with shiny jewels of every color imaginable. Hundreds of them marched out with royal elegance, bowing to the King and Queen of Uisneach as they walked by. Forming a circle within the circle of Uisneachans, they waited for the last of the faeries to emerge, which happened to include the spritely

Teaguen, looking glorious in an opal gown and a diamond tiara, riding a magnificent white horse that was decked out in a fine, jewel-studded bridle and saddle. The last faerie emerged, riding a matching white horse. He was the tallest of all the faeries and as shining as the sun. Briana lost her breath. His hair and beard were the same glimmering gold as his garments, his eyes as green as the fields of Ireland. A golden crown inlaid with rubies, emerald and topaz balanced atop his head. A gold mantle draped over his shoulders and fell down behind him and over his mount. At his side hung a gilded sword and a shield with the symbols of Evalon from the saddle. Briana knew immediately who this was. She curtsied as Brath bowed before Kailen, the faerie king.

"Your Majesty," Briana greeted him. "It gives us the greatest of pleasure to welcome you and the faeries to Ard Darach."

"Thank you, my granddaughter."

Granddaughter? she wondered. Apparently, the faeries didn't distinguish between the generations as humans did. She had a lot to learn about her newly discovered relatives.

He looked at Brath. "A visit long overdue."

"Thank you for coming, King Kailen. I look forward to working with you and the faeries to rid the land of the terrible chaos being inflicted upon Uisneach by Lord Shamwa."

The golden faerie king nodded. "Between us, we should be able to find a way to stop him."

"We're ready to have those discussions, but would first like to invite you to join us for refreshments. Please, follow me, Your Highness." Brath and Kailen led the way to the castle, followed by Briana and Teaguen.

"You didn't tell me he was still alive," Briana chided her faerie friend.

"You knew we were immortal. I supposed you would know he still lived," she twittered back. "Congratulations, my lady. You're married! Is all well?"

"All is as well as it can be, given what I know is going to happen today, but Brath and I are fine."

Following a brief party in the middle courtyard, modeled after the ones Briana saw in Evalon, they moved to the great hall. Brath called the gathering to order.

"King Kailen and esteemed members of Evalon, we regret to inform you that we are actively at war. Last night the village of Inis Fail suffered an attack which took the lives of many of our people. Troops have been sent out and we will join them tomorrow.

"We also deeply regret to inform you that more faerie trees have been destroyed. Uisneach can only be saved by the combined efforts of all members of Uisneach society, including the faerie kingdom. Our purpose in inviting you here today is threefold.

"First, we want to create an advisory team of representatives from all five kingdoms, which would convene on a regular basis to strategize about the war and the ongoing restoration and renewal of Uisneach.

"Second, we seek military aid, both in faerie warriors and supporting magic.

"Third, we need your help in determining the best way to repopulate the faerie trees, with the seeds High Lady Briana was given when she visited Evalon. We hope to begin that process today, planting one of the seeds in the garden of Ard Darach."

King Kailen nodded gravely. "You have prepared well for this historic convention and present a clear vision for the future. The order in which you present your plan is the sequence in which it must be accomplished. There is a fourth item I would add to the list, but I wish first to make a formal gesture to your queen, who happens also to be faerie royalty."

Briana gulped.

Kneeling before her, Kailen pulled something out from a pouch around his neck. She gasped when she saw what lay in his hand, a stunning gold ring dotted with red and white stones, carved with ancient writing.

"It is in Evalonian. It says, 'Queen of Faerie, Mother of Evalon, may the blessings of faerie magic pour from your heart and hands.' As you bless us with your presence in Uisneach and Evalon, so we honor you with the symbol of your nobility."

He slipped the brilliant gemstone on her right hand. "From this day forward, High Lady Briana, Tuathla of Evalon, you represent the interests of Evalon in this world. Any decisions that involve the faeries will require your consent, as well as mine. May Maker, who is the source of all life and magic, bless it so."

Cheers went up and Briana shook her head, unable to take it all in. Royalty in two kingdoms! *This is nuts*, she thought. Seeing the joy in the faces all around her, she realized she must accept gracefully. "I am honored, Your Majesty. I humbly accept with a promise to do my best always for the good of Evalon as well as Uisneach."

The faerie king bowed once more and resumed his place at the table. "Now that the tuathla of Evalon is formally in attendance, let me respond to your items."

Teaguen was appointed to be the faerie emissary for what would henceforth be known as the Evalon–Uisneach Council, or EU Council. Her role as liaison would require her to travel back and forth between the realms with information. Brath and Briana would jointly represent Dromdara. Sir Thomas would speak for Tynan Ibor, and Cailleach for Appleduir. They would need to find a delegate from Cedarmara.

"As to warriors." King Kailen looked around the room. "Everyone skilled with weaponry or magic will be expected to support this effort, as needed. Using Teaguen as liaison, we will help in whatever ways we can. One thousand faerie warriors will await you at Inis Fail, King Brath. If more are needed, we will send them."

"Thank you, Your Highness," Brath responded, pressing his hand over his heart. "My gratitude comes from generations of Taranians who were unable to bring this dream of a united Uisneach to fruition, but who nevertheless hoped for it and instilled the dream in me."

A subcommittee chaired by Gomerein, a faerie Briana had met on her last crossing into Evalon, and Ayden Suleiman of Ard Darach, would work on the seeding and tending of faerie trees. King Kailen approved with a reminder. "We cannot begin this work until the land is secure enough to plant and tend without fear of retaliation by Lord Shamwa."

"There was something else you wanted to discuss, Your Highness," Brath prompted the faerie king.

He looked at Briana, then back to Brath. "These steps will ensure victory over the dark forces of Lord Shamwa and his minions. However, we will not be successful until the four treasures of Uisneach are brought to their rightful home in Uisneach. Two are here, the Tree of Uisneach where the dryad Nionon dwells, and the Sword of Uisneach, which High Lady

Briana has in her possession. The Flaming Arrow is in Nionon's safekeeping. The fourth treasure is the Evalon Runes."

Brath reached under the table to squeeze Briana's hand. She held her breath, dreading to hear the words she knew would come.

"You may have noticed a certain waning of your ability to perform magic over time," he said, looking at Cailleach, who nodded. "When it seemed certain Evalon was at risk of losing all magic, my wife – your great-grandmother, Briana – and I agreed that she should escape through the tree with the runes. She hid them in the Hill of Uisneach, in a place called Ireland.

"The runes must be returned to complete the circle of magic in both the human and faerie worlds of Uisneach, to increase the power of those wielding magic."

Wait a minute, thought Briana. *This story isn't adding up.* "If you were separated from your wife, then how am I part faerie?" As soon as the words left her mouth, Briana blushed and desperately wished she could take them back. *She'd just called the faerie king a cuckold in public!*

King Kailen's eyes hooded over. "Briana, you are my grand-daughter, in blood and name. My wife was pregnant when she left here. Sending Catriona and our unborn child through the tree was the hardest thing I have ever had to do. In addition to protecting the runes, we also believed that we needed to protect our bloodline to ensure the future of Uisneach. With our child not yet born, that meant Catriona had to go to your world. Trust me, if I could have spared her…" He let out a deep sigh. "Travelling through the tree is an uncertain venture. One never knows if they can get through until they do, and then there is no promise of return."

Briana wanted to reach out to him when she saw his eyes water, but with a slight shake of his head, he discouraged the kindness. She bit her lip as more questions rose to the surface. He nodded, seeing them reflected in her eyes.

"Did you ever see her again?"

He shook his head. "She never found a way to come home, though she could send me messages through dreams. Catriona was not immortal. She died long ago."

Her great-grandmother had also abandoned love and home to save a kingdom. Sacrifice was apparently built into her DNA. Briana grimaced, stealing a glance at Silas, who watched the king intently. "I'm so sorry," she whispered, turning back to the king.

She wanted to ask why he hadn't taken another wife and had more children, but figured that she'd used up her get-out-of-jail card already. "Won't you be king forever?"

"I could be, but even immortals get tired after a few thousand years, dear heart." A twinkle in his eyes finally chased away the sorrow. "I might just decide to abdicate my position someday for a new generation of faerie."

"Are there any other descendants in Ireland?" Brath asked

"Surely so, but I don't know who they would be. I only know you because you arrived through the tree when the prophecy was meant to be fulfilled."

Briana's eyes widened. "There are other descendants. My mother's parents live in Tullamore, which I believe is not that far from the Hill of Uisneach. This is just bizarre. I wonder if my grandmother knows where she came from? She must. I think she would be Catriona's daughter. Surely she would know about the runes."

"But not necessarily where they are," King Kailen pointed out.

Cailleach stood. "It's all there in the prophecy: 'From hill to hill an ancient symbol taken. Two worlds collide in time, treasure lost is now to find.' All we need is someone to go back through the tree and find the runes."

"I'll go," Silas volunteered.

A collective gasp circled the room, followed by dead silence. Nausea washed over Briana in waves and when she opened her eyes, Silas was staring at her, looking shocked at his own words.

Finally, King Kailen spoke up. "You make a brave offer, Silas of Cedarmara, to take this uncertain voyage."

"I believe I can get through, and it would be a privilege to play some part in Uisneach's healin'."

"Silas, you can't go," a child called out. "Who will be our bard?"

Silas smiled kindly at the little girl, but turned back to Briana when he answered, "I have to go."

You will break my heart.

He subtly clasped the warrior bone hearts he still wore around his neck. *Bruise it perhaps, but it cannot be broken.*

Several hours and flagons of wine later, King Kailen rose and turned to Brath, who had likewise stood. "On behalf of Evalon, I thank you, King Brath," he said, "and Queen Briana, for your wisdom and courage in creating this council, and for your hospitality. It is time for us to return, but the agreements we've made are an assurance to the entire kingdom that Uisneach is in good hands. We look forward to working with you to destroy Lord Shamwa and restore Uisneach to her former glory."

Turning to the bard, he said, "And to you, Silas of Cedarmara. You go with our blessing and hope that you find the runes. We wish you a safe journey. Peace to you, friend."

Silas bowed to the king.

"King Kailen, there's one final thing," said Brath. "As a sign of unity and commitment between us, Queen Briana would like to plant one of the faerie tree seeds in the garden here at Ard Darach. Would you do us the honor of joining us in this ceremony?"

"It would be an honor to plant a tree with my granddaughter."

Brath led the faeries to a plot Briana had prepared for the occasion, an area protected from the ocean wind by a semi-circle of small junipers that grew against the stone wall of the fortress. Around this were several circular stones that reminded her of Evalon, a large dish-shaped boulder that served as a perfect bird bath, and a longer, rectangular boulder for sitting.

"Briana, you've done wonders with this garden in a remarkably short time," Brath whispered to her. "I'm impressed."

"I had lots of help," she replied, nodding towards the head gardener. Moving that boulder had required him, several men, and a horse. She couldn't guess how many hours he'd spent polishing the stones.

Everyone circled around Briana. She reached into her pocket to pull out the packet of seeds. Brath took a wooden shovel and scooped out a hole.

Briana and Kailen stepped forward. He reached for her hand, the one holding the seed. Clasping it in both his hands, and uttering Gaelic-sounding words she didn't understand, he offered what she assumed was a blessing.

Following the consecration, he explained the meaning of his words. "May this tiny seed grow full and ripe with magic. May it be for all a symbol of peace between the kingdoms of Uisneach. Let it grow taller and stronger with each advancement toward a reign of harmony. Let it be known that when the faerie tree blooms, it is once more safe for magic to flourish in Uisneach."

Stepping back, he nodded for Briana to set the seed. Seeing the purple pod nestled into the moist, dark dirt, Briana silently offered her own prayers for its successful germination and growth. Brath then covered the seed with soil before standing back with the others.

It seemed right to stand by a moment and consider the action they'd just taken, the sound of wind and crashing waves nature's benediction. Briana noticed a gleam in the faerie king's eye. He caught her glance and winked.

The soil above the newly planted seed trembled and cracked. The tiniest sliver of green plant emerged and reached for the sun.

"Oh, my Maker!" Brath exclaimed.

Briana let out her own sound of shock.

"Well, unfortunately, we do not have years to wait for the normal growth process. It needs a little magical encouragement," said King Kailen, with a chuckle.

Within minutes a small sapling stood in front of them, its tiny purple leaves already unfurling. When the process seemed to have stopped, Briana smiled warmly at her grandfather. "You are bloody amazing."

The king shrugged and grinned. "Just a usual day for a faerie king. I'm certain you'll have the same power one day. Now, just tend this young tree as you would any other. I believe it will be fully mature within a few months, though the blooming will not come until Lord Shamwa is deposed and Uisneach is free of his evil."

Brath turned and led the faeries back to the portal. He and Kailen exchanged a few words before the faerie king stepped close to Briana. "You and I will meet again, granddaughter. I could not be more proud to see the beauty of my legacy. There is a light in your eye for the work you do for Uisneach, which I am happy to see, since I know it came at a cost."

"There is no cost too great for Uisneach and Evalon," she replied, with a sincere smile.

The faeries departed to the mournful sounds of the Uilleann pipes and drumming.

Brath turned back to those remaining. "There's much to do before we leave in the morning. You're all excused to finish your preparations. Silas, I would ask you to stay behind."

When only Brath, Briana and Silas remained, the king turned to his bard. "Are you sure you want to do this?"

"I believe this is me quest to complete."

Brath turned to Briana. "Do you agree he should go?"

She blinked back tears. "If Silas is willing to go through the tree for the runes, I would send him..." she swallowed past the lump in her throat, "with all the help he needs and the warm wishes of a grateful king and queen."

"Briana, you need to spend some time providing whatever information you can to help him on the other side. Then we need to figure out who is going to be our bard in his absence. I have things I need to do with the knights, so, I suggest the two of you get busy."

Briana looked at Brath with surprise.

He put an arm around her waist and hugged her. "Your work doesn't involve me. I'll see you both later. Silas, I'm worried for you. I won't pretend otherwise. But it's a vital task, and I deeply appreciate the sacrifice you make."

Silas knelt on one knee before them. "I'm grateful for the opportunity to serve our kingdom. I'll do me best to find the missin' runes and return them to Uisneach."

"I accept your pledge, Silas of Cedarmara," Brath said. He kissed his wife on the cheek before heading for the stables, leaving Briana to walk wordlessly with Silas back to the great hall. O'Brien was busy replacing candles when they entered.

"Please bring us ale, Mary. Better yet, whiskey."

"And tea?" the housemaid asked.

"No. Tea won't quite cut it at the moment."

When O'Brien was out of the room, Silas and Briana stared at each other.

"You weren't surprised."

"No. Teaguen told me it would happen when I went to Evalon this last time."

"Why didn't you tell me?"

"You needed to choose to go on your own. And quite frankly, I hoped you wouldn't."

"You know I have to go, Briana."

She stared at her hands and nodded, wiping away a solitary tear. "I'm so sorry, Silas. Now our choices have put you in danger. I'm not sure it's worth it."

"I know now I can't spend the rest of me life watchin' the two of you fall in love. And you can't be worried every second that I'm goin' to see somethin' that hurts me."

She didn't respond.

"So, tell me everythin' I need to know," he said, clapping his hands to his knees.

Voice failing her, she switched to telepathy. *Find my mother. She'll help. She'll get you to my grandparents in Ireland and they might also help. Tell her I love her, I miss her terribly and...* She paused, studying every inch of Silas' face, wanting to commit every laugh line and every blue pixel in his eyes to memory. *Tell her she's looking at the man who holds my heart in his hands.*

His eyes welled up. *I'll tell her you're well, happy and a wonderful queen. And I'll tell her I love you more than all the ale in Uisneach.*

She laughed, then they smiled at each other and got down to the business of preparing him for life in the world she came from.

Over the weeks of their journey, she'd told him many things about her world. Now she focused on things to make his transition easier. She told him about money and the basics of good manners. Mundane details about taking a shower, taking out the trash, operating a microwave and the toilet seemed odd, but they were little things that would help him. At one point she went quiet.

"What's wrong?"

Sadness sprung up like a fountain in her chest. "If you find someone you care about…" she had to pause and choke back the mental picture, "and you decide to become intimate with her and aren't ready to have children…" After several attempts, she explained birth control.

His eyes practically bugged out. "Really? That's bloody amazin', but," he said, *not likely to happen. My heart's already taken.*

Well, I don't want you to be lonely. Part of me hopes you do find someone to love.

And the other part?

Would rip her face off.

"I believe you would." He asked, "What about the tree, Briana? Is there anythin' I need to know?"

"I've told you what happened to me, but I have no idea if you can even get in, much less what your experience would be."

They hadn't realized how much time had passed until Brath entered the room, lit a candle and sat down beside her, across from Silas. "Did you come up with an idea for a temporary bard?"

"Based on what Briana's said, Ripparivendar is the obvious person, but gettin' him here will be tricky," Silas said.

"There's no one to train him," Briana pointed out.

"Yes, there is," Silas said, smiling at her. "You."

"Me? Are you crazy? I can't train him to be a bard."

"The fact is, milady, you are all Ard Darach has until he is trained. If singin' and storytellin' is what's needed, you're the only one I know in residence who has any gift for it. Teach him the basics. When I come home, I'll work with him."

"So you do plan on coming back?"

"I hope to. I need to bring the runes back, aye?"

Servants began to arrive with food. Soon the room filled with hungry men and women. Discomforting quiet filled the hall as people ate, trying not to think of the coming changes.

Silas broke the pall with a cheerful offer. "How about a song for the road?"

He received mixed responses, but continued as he did every other night, moving to the center of the room and said, "Tomorrow, men and ladies, we leave for Inis Fail. You'd do well to remember what and who you battle for." Banging out a few licks on the drum, he began Uisneach's fighting song.

"Across the veil a sign appears,

A hero's call to arms.

A crown to save and nation free,

Release from evil charms.

Will you come?"

"Yes, we will!" they shouted, of one accord.

Come, a mhuirnin, *sing with me this last time.*

She hesitated only a moment then decided if she was going to step into the role of bard, if only temporarily, they might as well get used to it. She rose and moved to stand beside him, putting on her warrior-queen persona.

"Crossroads coming, make a choice,

Remain and die, or fight.

Your hearth to leave, the future calls,

Hide no more – your battle cry.

Between the tree and standing stones,

Your destiny awaits you.

To save the ways of older days,

For Uisneach's sake, we'll try or die!"

Voices rang out, ready for the campaign. For a few moments, most of them forgot that their beloved bard would be going on a different journey. Briana and Silas did not forget, but did their best to keep everyone's spirit up, including their own.

The evening ended on a high note. Back in their room, Briana and

Brath sat in silence, listening to the crackle of the fire, until Briana said, almost to herself, "Mother never told me there would be days like this."

"My mother did," he reflected back. "I didn't believe her."

"Brath…"

"Briana…" he said, at the same time, and smiled.

"You first," he said.

"Thank you for giving Silas and me the time to say good bye."

"I can't pretend to be so gracious. You needed to prepare him and to say your good byes, but I won't say I wasn't anxious about it the entire afternoon."

"Why?"

He walked over to the table and poured two glasses of whiskey. He handed a glass to her, then sat down. "I worried that you'd rethink your decision and go with him."

Sipping the fiery liquid gave her a moment to consider her response.

"I won't lie to you. I care deeply for him, but he and I have always known our feelings for one another were one fiber of a much bigger tapestry."

"I suppose I'm another fiber, and the tapestry is Uisneach." At her nod he continued. "I'm a patient man, Bri, but I'm not sure I can live forever knowing you love another man."

"Brath, we came into this relationship with no love for each other. I'd say we've come some distance from that point. Can't you allow that we are a work-in-progress and let our shared vision and affection guide us forward?"

He sipped his drink and studied her. Setting the drink down, he put a hand to her cheek. "I love you, Briana. If time is what you need to let your love for me grow, I'll give you that."

She leaned into his palm. "Thank you. And now, Your Majesty, it's been a long day, with a big day ahead of us. Do you think we might go to bed?"

They settled behind the canopy curtains, keeping a hair's breadth between them, neither saying anything. Briana turned to her husband. "You probably don't feel much like making love after today, but would you be willing to just hold me? I need to be close to you."

He pulled into his arms and laid one hand on her belly, making little circles with his fingers. "I have no reservations about loving you, Briana. I thought you might be too tired or sore. If you want…"

Putting her lips to his effectively moved them from thinking to feeling. While one part of her heart was breaking, another had opened and was hopeful that the dream of Uisneach would come true.

Loving came gently, and when they spiraled up together in ecstasy, she called out his name. He brought her back to earth with feather-light caresses. Calm and certainty stole over her.

She leaned up on one elbow and put a hand on his face. "My timing may be off, but I want you to know something."

"What's that?"

"I'm beginning to understand why you were in my dreams. I didn't expect to, but every day, every moment, I find one more reason to fall in love with you."

"Your timing is perfect, Bri." When he pulled her against him, she let her head rest against his strong and steady heartbeat, finding a new place of comfort and peace.

CHAPTER FORTY

FAREWELLS

orses snorted, men shouted, dogs barked, children ran about yelling with excitement, and women cried softly as husbands left with quiet reassurances that they would return.

But we might not, Briana thought, anxiously. Wearing her warrior tunic and breeches with Nua strapped on, and with her baldric and shield hooked to the saddle, she sat astride a calm and ready Banrion. Jonathan sat beside her on Andromeda, his eyes wide with anticipation for his first official assignment as Protector of the Queen. Pride dripped from every inch of his boyish frame. Dara stood quiet and alert beside them. She looked around at the group. Cailleach looked odd sitting on a horse, unnatural in breeches and tunic, though both were more practical for her journey with Silas back to Appleduir and the magical oak tree. After Silas volunteered, she'd convinced the king that Briana was healer enough to serve the troops, and she'd do more good by using her magic to help Silas get through the tree.

Sir Thomas, Lady Isabella and Epona were returning to Winge Mansion, though Sir Thomas promised to join the troops later if needed. Sigel trotted up and down the line of men, checking and double-checking everything.

Brath gave final orders before mounting Ruark, whose pre-battle energy was the exact opposite of Banrion's. Men took formation and Briana sought Silas once more, hoping against hope he would change his mind.

He stared at her with a strange, faraway look in his eyes.

What is it? Her heart skipped a beat.

Nothin'.

"Bri— are you ready?" Brath moved Ruark up beside her, every line in his face taut.

"Are you nervous?" she asked, suddenly realizing they had barely talked of what was to come.

"Only about taking you with me. I wish you'd stay."

She shook her head. "Not happening."

"I know."

Sigel cleared his throat. "Shall we get on with it?"

"Ready, men?" Brath asked, facing his army. A roar rose up in response. "Silas of Cedarmara, present yourself!"

Silas, seated on Aldebaran, his shield and bow secured to his back, moved to the front, and the drums began to boom. Silas, and the king moved forward as Uilleann pipes joined the tattoo. The bard's voice rang out:

"Voices are calling.

Drums are beating.

Pipers are playing.

The time is now, the time is here.

Come men of Uisneach,

King and Queen,

Noble steeds and hounds.

We ride today and raise the fear.

We ride as one, we ride for you.

Shamwa, beware our mighty force,

Our battle cry, your deathly declaration."

He continued with a few more stanzas about their mission, the king and queen and the brave men of Uisneach, to which Briana and Epona shouted, "And brave women!"

Silas smiled and repeated, "And a brave woman, the beloved Mouse of Prophecy and Queen of Uisneach!"

As the men proclaimed their loyalty, Silas moved to the back of the line.

The Taranian army walked under the portcullis, across the drawbridge and toward the ridge that surrounded Ard Darach. Briana's heart pounded as they neared the crossroads that would take Silas in one direction, possibly forever, and her in another, at the side of the king.

She nearly ran into Ruark when Brath stopped at the boulder and dismounted. Silas, Cailleach and the Winges followed suite.

"I've said my good byes," Sigel grunted, and led the company ahead.

Briana slid off Banrion onto shaky legs. Sir Thomas and Lady Isabella both hugged her.

"When things settle down, you must come for a visit."

"We will," she replied. "If things ever settle down."

"I don't think I can do this," Epona said, misty-eyed, as she squeezed her friend tightly. "Take care."

Cailleach embraced Brath, then wrapped Briana in her arms.

"Make sure he gets through safely," Briana whispered in the witch's ear.

"I'll do what I can. It's mostly up to the tree, aye?"

Cailleach mounted her horse and turned in behind the Winges.

Brath reached out a hand to the bard. "Thank you, Silas of Cedarmara. You go with our prayers. We look forward to the day your sunny smile brightens Ard Darach once more."

Briana knew he was sincere. They were like brothers, and she regretted being a wedge between them. It took every ounce of strength in her body not to weep.

Taking her hand, Silas kissed her ring. "I will not fail you or Uisneach. The runes will be returned."

The peculiar turn of phrase jolted her. *You're not coming back, are you?*

After a moment's hesitation, he said, *I hope to, Your Majesty.*

With the grace of a mountain lion, he swung up on Aldebaran, turned the reins, and headed south behind the Winges and Cailleach.

Briana stared after him, feeling her heart shatter with every step he took into the forest.

Briana?

Her mind filled with words promising a love that could not be broken in a single lifetime.

Unbroken, one soul, given forever. I'll always love you, a mhuirnin. *Always.*

Then he was gone. She took in a ragged breath, remounted Banrion and turned to face Brath. She refused to hide, and he didn't turn away from her pain. He offered his hand. She rode up next to him and grasped it, as though for her life.

"Let's go fight for Uisneach," he said.

Setting her chin and eyes forward, she urged Banrion beside him and side by side, they rode to Inis Fail.

EPILOGUE

atrina stared at the cards in disbelief. She laid out a seven-card spread and for the third time in a week, drew exactly the same cards. In exactly the same positions. The initial card, Briana's card, always came up Deer, the card for gentleness. *That makes sense. Briana is nothing if not gentle.* When she laid an opposing male card in hope of getting some sense of where the "romance" was, she pulled the Archer. A second card fell from the deck on top of it – the King of Bows. This had happened all three times, in one way or another. She wondered at the significance of a card having to do with leadership and dominance. Two male cards together. *Another relationship?* The card she pulled for the present, the Wanderer, and the next card for challenges, Journey, indicated a change about to occur, which likely included the death of something, or the change from one state of being to another. *Is Briana coming home? Oh, how she wished that were the case.* The fifth position she called influences, and for the third time, it came up Lovers, only in reverse. Katrina's eyebrows knitted together. *Some kind of problem with her lover?* The next card – Six of Bows. *She seems to have a lot of men in her life,* she mused. Travel. Transition. Cycles. Eight of vessels was the last card pulled. Rebirth, healing and new possibilities. She tried to center and focus her mind on Briana. *Was her daughter sending a message?* All she knew for certain was that something huge was about to happen. And all she could do was wait patiently.

The End

GLOSSARY

a ghrá (uh hraw): my love

a leanbh (uh lyah-noo): child or baby lyah-noo

a mhuirnin (uh war neen): sweetheart

a sonuachar (uh sun uh khar): my true spouse or soulmate

art: mountain

a stor (uh store): my treasure

Banrion (ban-reen): queen

bodhran (bow rahn): a handheld Irish drum

Cailleach (kyle-yock): witch

cath: fort

Leanach (lee a nock): plains in Uisneach

mo chroi (ma kree): my love

Nuada Airgetlam (Noo-a-da/tha AR-gid-lawv): first king of the Tuatha DéDanann, known as "Silver Hand"

ríocht (rot): kingdoms, realms; an Uisneachan form of chess

smooring: banking a fire in a hearth

Teaguen (Tee gin): faerie of Evalon

Tir fo Thuinn (Cheer fo hin): the land under the sea

Tuatha DéDanann (too-ah-day-don-an): children or people of the goddess Danu

Tuathla (Too uh la): princess of the People (the faeries)

Tynan Ibor (Tinin i bor): kingdom in the center of Uisneach

Uilleann pipes (ill-in or ill ee un): Irish bagpipes

Uisneach (oosh-nay): mythical place and geographical center of Ireland

Some terms or names in this book are fictitious or based loosely on Irish words, using pronunciations consistent with Ulster. Elsewhere in Ireland, pronunciations would differ.

ABOUT THE AUTHOR

There are worse things than living in a world of kings, queens, warriors, bards, and all manner of magical beings. After a life spent burying myself in the imagination of others and lamenting my inability to create such a story myself, I was challenged by my husband and a friend to bust down the barriers to my own creativity and just do it! I did, and the Kingdom of Uisneach series is the result.

I have been blessed by careers as a Registered Nurse, an interfaith minister and a hospice chaplain, but ever-flowing beneath the surface was my passion for books and writing. Whether I was writing care plans, weddings or journaling my own personal odyssey, I crafted words in ways that others found… interesting.

The Kingdom of Uisneach series taps into the core of my Irish heritage, evoking the spirit of ancient myth and legend. I hope you enjoy this story and would love to hear from you.

Website: kingdomofuisneach.com

Facebook: Heidi Hanley Author Page:
https://www.facebook.com/heidihanleyauthor/

Blog: Kingdom Musings, https://kingdomofuisneach.blogspot.com/

If you enjoyed this story, I invite you to review it on Amazon.

Made in the USA
San Bernardino, CA
29 June 2020

73890182R00266